Until We Meet Again

Until We Meet Again

Rosemary Goodacre

hera

First published in the United Kingdom in 2019 by Hera

This edition published in 2020 by

Hera Books
28b Cricketfield Road
London, E5 8NS
United Kingdom

A CIP catalogue record for this book is available from the British Library.

Print ISBN 978 1 80032 159 5
Ebook ISBN 978 1 912973 32 3

Printed and bound in Great Britain by Clays Ltd, Elcograf S.p.A.

2

To my husband Ian, adjusting to having a writer in the family.

Also to Elaine Everest, tutor at The Write Place Creative Writing School at Hextable, and to my group of writing buddies there. They have given me so much help and encouragement, and together we have enjoyed often hilarious social events.

Chapter One

Larchbury, Sussex, June 1914

The afternoon sun blazed on the band of young women marching down Larchbury High Street carrying banners proclaiming *Votes for Women*! Amy Fletcher joined in their cries of 'Our views matter!'

As they passed the horse trough a few folk glanced curiously in their direction, then looked away again in disdain.

'Where is everyone this afternoon?' Lavinia Westholme complained. Beneath her wide-brimmed hat, her dark hair contrasted with the cream of her lawn dress. Across her chest she wore the violet, green and white colours of the Suffragette movement, though as yet she was the only one of them to have obtained a sash.

'Sitting in their gardens,' Amy suggested.

'We need to shake them out of their complacency.' There was a dangerous gleam in her dark eyes.

'Let's not do anything silly,' begged Florence Clifford.

They had discussed plans for their demonstration a week earlier. There was an eager group of Suffragettes in the nearby town of Wealdham, and they had joined them for a meeting, determined to set up a branch in their own corner of Sussex. Some members there were proudly wearing the Suffragette sash, signifying white for purity, green for hope and violet for dignity. Lavinia and other hotheads had reminded them of their sisters in London chaining themselves to railings, or breaking windows. They had even set fire to pillar boxes.

'It'll only antagonise everyone,' Florence had said.

'How else can we make our cause known when they choose to ignore us?' Lavinia had asked. She had proposed a focus for their activity, targeting a particularly male institution.

'The team's playing away this week, isn't it?' she checked now. 'Let's do what I suggested.'

'You mean, like in Tunbridge Wells?' Amy asked. 'You're not planning to burn it down, are you?'

Even Lavinia agreed their Kentish sisters had gone too far.

Amy followed her anxiously as they turned down the lane to the village green. There was often a cricket match there on summer Sundays, but not this week. A few children were improvising a rough game approximating to cricket. Otherwise the green was deserted apart from an elderly couple sitting on a bench and a woman walking her dog.

The young women followed Lavinia in an uneven group as she hurried towards the pavilion. From her bag she produced a small pot of green paint and a brush. Levering open the tin she advanced on the white painted pavilion and wrote *Votes for Women!* in bold brush strokes. Amy and Florence cheered while some others watched in awe.

Amy felt inside her handbag for the stick of chalk. Would she dare take action?

Lavinia turned, grinning feverishly as though drunk with her own bravado. 'Let's get inside!' she cried.

The others stared, nonplussed. Then Lavinia stooped beside the nearby flowerbed and pulled out a large, sharp-edged stone. They watched, disbelieving, as she aimed it hard at the glass panel in the door, which shattered with a loud crash. She felt inside and fiddled with the handle.

'Watch out for the broken glass!' cried Florence.

Triumphantly, Lavinia pulled the door open. 'Let's leave our mark here!' she urged them.

Amy and two of the others followed her into the dark interior with its smell of old socks. Lavinia found another stretch of light wood where she painted their slogan once more.

Amy produced her stick of red chalk. She added the slogan to other places on the wall, half alarmed at her action.

'Take care!' Florence called from outside. 'Someone's gone for a policeman.'

Then they heard a distant whistle. Even Lavinia looked nervous now. She abandoned her paint pot and led the stampede for the door. They began to run off in the opposite direction to the whistles, along with their other supporters. From here they could return to the High Street by a narrow alley between gardens.

'Are you all right?' Amy asked Lavinia. 'Your arm's bleeding!'

'It's only a scratch.'

There was an ugly streak of green paint down her pale dress as well.

'We'd better disperse,' Lavinia told them, hastily pulling off her sash and cramming it into her bag. Some ran faster than others and when they reached the High Street they set off in different directions. Lavinia disappeared down a lane leading to the brook.

'Your bag's open,' Florence warned Amy and she fastened it. Then they saw the unwelcome sight of Constable Swift, one of the village policemen, on his bicycle. He was staring at them suspiciously.

3

Florence tucked her arm through Amy's. 'Excellent sermon this morning, wasn't it?' she said loudly, as they passed a familiar terrace of Georgian houses.

'I thought it was one of Uncle's best ones,' she replied a little breathlessly. At nineteen years old how could she have broken the law? She was the demure young niece of the vicar, wasn't she?

They tried to saunter calmly along the street and were rewarded by seeing the policeman cycling on.

Amy continued to her corner and said goodbye to Florence, then turned and walked to her home in Sebastopol Terrace. She let herself in to the little brick house and checked her appearance in the hall mirror. Had she any tell-tale signs of irregular behaviour, like Lavinia? Of course, there were red chalk marks on her fingers. She hurried to wash her hands. Then she took off her hat and combed the long trailing curls of her fair hair.

She walked through to the back garden where her parents were sitting in deck chairs. Behind them dahlias were flowering, in shades of vivid gold and deep red. Further down the garden, the young runner beans were beginning to scale their canes in Father's vegetable plot.

'Hello, darling – had a nice walk?' her father asked her, his faced relaxed. Whatever would they say if they knew what she had been about?

'Yes, thanks.' She fetched another chair and joined them. There was the hum of insects and sound of chatter from a neighbour's garden.

She leant back and closed her eyes. She could not help enjoying a feeling of pride that she had taken action for the cause. Even so, she worried about the damage Lavinia had wilfully caused. She was half anxious, half defiant, wondering

4

when the deed would be widely known about. Would anyone have recognised them?

The shadows were lengthening now. When Mother got up to prepare tea, Amy went and joined her as she usually did, handling the familiar items – the plate with the freshly made Dundee cake, the cut-glass pot of jam and the milk jug with its muslin cover weighed down with glass beads. Soon they were all arranged in their usual positions on the back room table with its white cloth with the lace edging. Mother made the tea and Amy took the pot, with its cosy, and placed it carefully on its stand.

Father took his place at the table. He was wearing his Sunday best suit, and was smart as usual, as befitted a school teacher. His hair was grey now but his lively eyes showed his interest in all about him.

'I hope Bertie won't be much longer,' Mother said, as she brought in a plate of ham sandwiches. Her fair hair was fading now, and she wore it piled up on her head. Bertie, whose real name was Albert, was Amy's brother. A moment later there was the sound of the front door and he came running into the room. He was fair-haired, like she was, but a few inches taller, with grey eyes like his father. In common with most young men, he had grown a moustache. He was only a year and a half older than Amy and beginning to grow bored with his work as a junior accountant. He longed for weekends and on summer Sundays he welcomed the chance to join his old school friends in their favourite pursuit: he would have spent the afternoon down by the brook fishing.

'Have you heard?' he cried. 'Some women have broken into the cricket pavilion and caused havoc!'

Her mother stood still in astonishment and her father's mouth dropped open.

Bertie was not good enough at cricket to be selected for the team and did not generally travel to support them in away matches. He must have heard what had happened on his way home.

A little belatedly, Amy tried to look startled by the news.

'What kind of havoc?' Mother asked.

'Well, you know, broken glass, slogans painted and chalked on the walls – it's been done by the Suffragettes, they say.'

'What? Those silly strident women?' her father demanded.

'You think they're rather fine, don't you, Amy?' Bertie asked her.

She had said as much in the past. Now she struggled to find a reply that was less than incriminating. 'Well, they've got a point. Why shouldn't we have the vote?'

'But really, causing damage!' Mother said. 'You don't know anything about this, do you, Amy?' She turned her blue eyes on her, probing.

She tried to look unconcerned. 'I hear there's an active group in Wealdham,' she said carefully.

'Well, whatever next! Anyway, Bertie, you'd better sit down and start your meal before the tea gets cold.'

Why am I being such a coward? Amy thought. *Well, for one thing, what Lavinia did was criminal damage and I don't want to get her into serious trouble.*

'I hope you won't get involved with women like that,' Mother told Amy as she poured their tea. 'Don't consider taking part in anything political. You should find yourself a nice young man and settle down.'

Amy smiled. Mother had said the same thing more than once, as though that should be her only aim in life. She had met Bertie's friends and a few other young men but none had made much impression. Occasionally an image floated into her mind of an attractive, charming young man, intelligent and interested in everyone he met. She seemed to visualise him as dark-haired, with a broad smile. Was it possible she had once met someone like that? If so, she could not think who it was.

They had nearly finished their tea when there was a knock on the door. Her mother went to answer it and Amy hoped she hid her stab of fear as Constable Swift walked into their dining room.

'Excuse me barging in like this,' he began. 'I just need to ask Miss Amy a few questions.'

'How can I help you?' she asked.

'Where were you this afternoon, around four o'clock?' The constable stood respectfully near the doorway but fastened his light blue eyes on her resolutely. He had ginger hair and a freckled face.

'I went walking along the High Street with my friend Florence.' She knew he had seen them there.

'Did you notice anything unusual?'

'I believe there were some women with a placard, something about votes for women.'

'And you aren't involved with any such group?' The constable was probably only around her age, for she seemed to remember him starting school about the same time, but he looked keen to fulfil his duties.

'I gather there's a group in Wealdham.'

She felt herself perspiring. What would happen if she was found out? She might lose her job, and she would upset her parents greatly.

'A few people on the village green saw the group there, though only in the distance, and they say one of them was wearing a straw hat with a blue ribbon on it.'

Her mother looked towards her and away again. The constable would have seen her straw hat in the hall as he came in.

'I can't help you, Constable. My brother tells me they did some damage in the pavilion.'

'They broke in and wrote slogans on the wall. They left broken glass on the floor and spilt green paint.'

'Disgraceful behaviour,' said Father.

'Colonel Fairlawn has just got back from the away match,' the constable said. 'We won, I'm happy to say. But when he saw what's happened to the pavilion he was beside himself. He's determined to get to the bottom of it and have those responsible severely punished.'

'It's such unladylike behaviour – who would do such a thing?' Bertie said in a way she did not take entirely at face value.

'So you can't help us at all, Miss?'

'Sorry.' What would Father think, and Uncle Arthur, if they knew how deceitful she was being?

He seemed to accept her ignorance of what had taken place, for at last he apologised for disturbing them and left.

Amy was barely aware of the sweet, spicy taste as she ate the rest of her slice of cake. Her parents were shocked at what had happened. As the others finished their tea, she tried to put aside the impression that they were all looking at her.

It was vital to act as though nothing was wrong. She helped Mother clear the table and wash up, then sat with the others in the parlour at the front of the house. Mother still looked thoughtful but after a while she went to the piano and raised the lid. Her hands were soon flying over the keys in familiar tunes from *The Pirates of Penzance*, as though the afternoon's drama was left behind. It was a relief when dusk finally fell and Amy could take her leave.

She went upstairs and realised that Bertie was following her.

'I hope Lavinia is careful,' he said to her on the landing. 'She had a noticeable stain of green paint on her skirt.' He winked at her.

She was grateful for his support. At last she was able to go to her room and reflect quietly on the afternoon's events. If only her parents understood her feelings about the Suffragettes and could see the merit of their aims. In spite of everything, she felt a burst of pride for having made a stand.

Chapter Two

Sussex, June and July 1914

'Did the police call at your house?' Amy asked Lavinia on the train to Wealdham the next day. Lavinia had boarded at Alderbank, the next station up the line from Larchbury, and Amy had waited till the other woman occupant of their small second-class carriage had alighted at a little country halt before talking freely.

'They did,' Lavinia said with a grin, 'but Mother swore I'd been at home all afternoon.'

Amy sometimes wished she had an unconventional, artistic mother like her friend. Lavinia's father was a surgeon and both her parents sympathised with the movement for universal suffrage.

'Did you get that paint out of your skirt?'

'I had to throw the dress away, unfortunately.' Lavinia stood up to pull down the window of the compartment, which was already growing stuffy. She sat down again on the upholstered seat below the little pictures of seaside scenes. Coils of her long dark hair hung down below her felt hat.

Amy travelled to Wealdham each weekday. After leaving school she had taken a course to learn to use a typewriter. She had found work in an insurance office in the town. At first she had loved the independence of working there, but now she was tiring of the monotonous clatter of the keys as she and another typist prepared similar letters most days.

Lavinia was over a year older than Amy and they had met at the small typing college. Before long Lavinia had decided to leave, to develop her artistic skills. She travelled to Wealdham each day to her lessons at art college. Florence was Amy's closest friend from her childhood, but Lavinia fascinated her with her determination to challenge old-fashioned attitudes.

'Have you heard that Colonel Fairlawn is determined to find who's responsible and punish them?' Amy asked as the train steamed along between high banks of birch trees.

For a moment a frown formed on Lavinia's large-featured face. Colonel Fairlawn was respected and feared, thanks to his position in society and distinguished military career. With him exerting pressure, the local police would not shirk in seeking the culprits.

A moment later Lavinia's expression had changed to a grin. 'I told you we needed to hit the male population in their favourite haunts,' she said. 'I wish I'd been there to see his face when he went into the pavilion.'

Amy could not help admiring her friend's bravado. 'I'm not cut out for this kind of action,' she admitted.

Curiosity had made Amy and Florence attend a Suffragette rally in Wealdham. They had found Lavinia giving out leaflets and explaining the aims of the organisation. Recently they had attended a meeting held at the large house in Alderbank where Lavinia lived with her parents, to plan future events and the possibility of starting a branch in Larchbury, or staging a protest there.

'Do you think there'll be another peaceful march like that great one you joined in London last year?' Amy asked.

'I certainly hope so,' Lavinia said. 'Thousands of women from all classes came to the rally in Hyde Park – it was amazing. They came from all over the country and some of them had walked miles to be there.'

'I'd prefer to do that, rather than carry out more civil disobedience.'

'It's not as easy as you might suppose. There was a lot of hostility towards the march. I heard of some women even being stoned or beaten up. There were men throwing dead rats and ringing hand bells to drown out the speeches.'

Amy winced at the injustice of it.

The train was slowing down as it rattled over the bridge on the outskirts of Wealdham. To the east of the town they could see the industrial area with its smoking chimneys. The train would continue north to join the main line to London, nearly forty miles from Larchbury. They got up ready to alight.

–

One weekend Amy travelled with her mother to Hove to visit her Aunt Louisa, who lived there with her husband, Uncle Harold, a few years older than she was. The weather was fine and they spent the afternoons on the beach, though Uncle Harold, who had a heart condition, remained at home.

Along the shore there was a line of bathing machines, available for swimmers to change their clothes inside as the horses drew them down into the shallow water.

'I simply must go for a swim,' Amy said, picking up her beach outfit.

'We might go for a cup of tea,' said Aunt Louisa, who was like a shorter, slightly plumper version of Mother. 'We won't be away for long.'

Amy found that all the bathing machines were taken, except the last one. She hurried towards it and was just about to claim it when a young man stepped forward to seize it.

'Oh!' she gasped in disappointment. She had thought she was there first.

'I'm so sorry, Miss,' he said, raising his straw boater. 'I thought I was first. But allow me to offer it to you.'

He was charming, after all, with an appealing smile. She had the feeling she might have seen him somewhere before.

'Thank you,' she said. 'I hope you don't have long to wait.'

She went up its wooden steps and inside, and began changing into the short dress and breeches which would protect her modesty to some extent in the water. The horse drew her vehicle down to the water's edge and she stepped out into the cold tide. How refreshing it was, after the hot beach! She walked out across the soft sand until the water came almost up to her shoulders. The sun shone down, seagulls wheeled overhead and little waves lapped around her. It was a delicious feeling, swimming cautiously in the sea.

Before long, she saw her rival for the machine, his arms cleaving the water as he swam vigorously. He nodded to her courteously but did not approach her closely. Where had she seen him before?

Soon it was time to return to the beach, frantically drying herself and putting on her clothes in the machine. She was conscious of her long fair hair drooping round her shoulders, still dripping as she struggled to dry it. It was time to relinquish her vehicle for the next bather.

She picked up all her belongings and stepped out on to the beach. She looked round briefly for the young man and thought she could see his dark head still bobbing in the water.

She looked for her family and at first saw only empty deckchairs. Then she noticed Mother and Aunt Louisa approaching along the beach. She went and joined them, then sat down towelling her hair. The hot sun helped dry it as she combed it to try to tame her tangles. She noticed the young man returning from his bathe a short distance along the beach.

'Let me help, dear.' Mother combed her hair and Amy tried not to cry out when she accidentally pulled it. At last it was restored to something approaching its normal state. People often complimented her on her natural curls.

'Might I join you?'

She looked up to see the young man again, raising his boater. He was tall with dark hair, still spiky from his swim, and clear blue eyes. Unlike most young men, he was clean-shaven.

'I believe we've met before,' he said, addressing her mother as well as her. 'Aren't you the Fletchers from Larchbury?'

'Yes…'

She still could not quite place him.

'You must be young Mr Edmond Derwent,' her mother said. 'I've seen you in the village and at events at The Beeches, though I'm not sure we've spoken since you were a boy.'

Of course, the Derwents – how could she not know Edmond? They were a prominent local family, though the boys had been sent away to boarding school and for years they had only appeared in the holidays.

Her own father was a teacher, who had a good position in the school at Larchbury. When the Derwent boys had been small their home tutor had died suddenly, leaving them without lessons. Amy's father had gone to work at their large house, The Beeches, though returning each evening to his family. For a while, when she was small, their lives had been strongly linked with the Derwent family, though they had been conscious of their different position in society. She remembered wearing clothes passed on from Miss Beatrice, Edmond's sister.

Then the boys had been sent away to boarding school – first Peter, the elder son, then Edmond – and her father had returned to being a normal school teacher. For a while they had been invited to the occasional informal party at The Beeches, but gradually the invitations had become less frequent, so that now they might only go there once a year, for the fête held at the end of summer.

'Of course, I remember you now, Edmond,' she said. She would probably have placed him at once if she had met him in Larchbury. She had always liked Edmond, and was pleased to meet him again. 'I don't seem to have seen you for a while, though, or your brother.'

She sometimes saw his parents in the village, in the stylish motor car which had replaced their carriage. Sometimes Beatrice accompanied them, a scarf anchoring her smart hat. If Amy met them in a shop, Mrs Derwent and Beatrice would nod in her direction and wish her 'Good day' before hurrying on. Edmond seemed far more friendly.

'My brother's working out in India,' he told her. 'He has a good position there in the Civil Service. And I've been at Cambridge University for a year now.'

'I believe my husband mentioned you were going there,' Mother said.

'How's Mr Fletcher keeping? He was one of my best tutors.'

'He's fine. He's well respected at the school. Are you enjoying university?'

'Very much. It's the summer vacation now, of course,' he told them. 'We're staying in a hotel here for a few days. This afternoon Pa has driven Ma and Beatrice into Brighton. They'll probably spend most of the afternoon shopping. I decided to come to the beach instead.'

'It's lovely here today,' Mother approved his choice.

'Might I treat you ladies to ice creams, or some other refreshment?' he asked them. 'There's a pleasant café on the promenade nearby.'

'How very kind,' said Mother. 'We just recently had a cup of tea there while Amy was bathing. Would you like an ice or something, Amy?'

'That would be lovely,' she said, thankful that he was in no hurry to rush off and she had the chance to spend time with him alone.

'Don't be too long, dear,' her mother said. 'We've got to catch the train back.'

She followed Edmond's tall figure up the beach, sand sinking into her shoes. He looked round for her and supported her arm gently as they went up the steps to the promenade.

They sat at a small table outside the café, overlooking the beach, and he asked what she would like and ordered ice creams.

'I didn't spend much time in Larchbury last summer,' he went on. 'I was very fortunate, for my aunt and uncle took me on a Grand Tour of the continent. We went to France and Italy and Greece, and visited some of the important cultural sites.'

'How wonderful,' Amy said wistfully. She looked across at her companion, with his slightly tanned face. He had grown into a good-looking young man. 'What are you studying at Cambridge?'

'I'm taking science,' he said. 'My parents would have preferred me to read classics, but I wanted to learn about some of the new scientific advances, engineering and so on.'

A waiter brought dainty glass dishes of ice cream. She took tiny spoonfuls of her ice, enjoying its subtle strawberry flavour.

'Do you have an occupation?' he asked her. He must know that a young woman in her position would need to do some kind of work, rather than expecting her family to support her. She was fortunate that she need not go into service in a wealthy family like his, for such work was poorly paid and usually involved working almost from dawn till bedtime.

She told him about her typewriting course and work in Wealdham.

'That sounds interesting,' he said. His face was broad across the cheek bones and his smile was wide too. 'I somehow imagined you'd have an occupation that's up to date. What does your brother do?'

She told him about Bertie's work as an accountant, without mentioning his restlessness.

'I'd like to stay in touch now we've met up again,' Edmond said, fixing his eyes on hers.

'Yes, let's!' She felt herself blush. She recalled their meetings as children. She remembered seeing him on his horse in the village once. He had stopped to greet her, as though there was no social difference between them, and let her pat the animal. It seemed delightful that they might go on meeting but she had a feeling his family would not approve.

'Of course I'll be away at college a lot but we can meet in the holidays. You know, I've actually forgotten where you live in the village. May I write down your address?'

'Certainly.'

He produced a diary from his pocket and a fountain pen. She told him the address and he began to write it down, but the pen was not flowing properly. 'I'm running out of ink,' he told her. 'Have you got a pen?'

She looked in her handbag for her fountain pen. She pushed aside her comb and handkerchief, struggling to find it. She had discarded the remains of the red chalk in a bin in Wealdham.

'That's strange,' she said, 'I seem to have lost my pen.' It bothered her, for it was a smart one, overlaid with nickel with her name engraved on it. Uncle Arthur, her father's brother, had given it to her on her last birthday.

At that moment, Mother and Aunt Louisa appeared in the café. 'Time we were going, Amy,' her mother said. 'We need to pick up our luggage from Louisa's house and get the train.'

'Have you got a pen, Mrs Fletcher?' Edmond asked. 'May I borrow it?'

He wrote down her address.

'Allow me to accompany you to the station,' he said.

They stopped at Aunt Louisa's house briefly and said goodbye to Uncle Harold. They collected their small overnight cases, which Edmond insisted on carrying as they walked through the sunny streets. At the station they found they were, after all, early, for Mother liked to allow plenty of time.

Outside the booking hall was a news placard with the caption '*Threat of War.*' For a moment, Amy was alarmed.

'Could we really go to war, do you think, Edmond?' Mother asked.

There had been intermittent statements like that in the papers since the Austrian heir had been shot at that place with the name no one was quite sure how to pronounce.

'It's hardly likely,' he said as he accompanied them on to the platform.

There was a puff of steam as the train approached. 'I've enjoyed meeting you again,' he told them, with his charming smile. 'Give my regards to Mr Fletcher.'

'It's been a perfectly lovely afternoon,' Amy replied as the train came noisily into the station.

Aunt Louisa kissed them goodbye and Edmond helped them on board and shook their hands. They all waved as the train set off.

Chapter Three

Larchbury, July to August 1914

'Edmond is a nice young man,' her mother said on the way home. 'Shame we're not of his class.'

'He spoke to me as though I were his equal,' Amy said.

'Don't imagine the rest of the family would treat you that way if he chose to court you,' Mother said.

Amy suspected she was right. 'Don't men ever court or marry women below their station?'

'The courtships usually end badly for the women.' Her mother looked regretful but firm. 'They rarely wed them.'

All the same, her encounter with Edmond and his warmth towards her filled much of her thoughts. Of the few young men she had met none had appealed like Edmond.

–

The following Sunday he called at their house, renewed his acquaintance with her father, and invited her for a walk beside the brook. The weather was turning cloudy as they dawdled along its banks. Through the clear waters there were glimpses of watercress and tiny fishes dashing hither and thither. She would like to have paddled, were it not for the difficulty of shedding her stockings and holding up her skirt. Edmond was casually dressed in plus fours.

'I love coming here and trying to catch the fish,' he said. There was a suggestion of his public school education in his accent. They came to an area where the water was slightly deeper, lined by trailing willows. Some young men, including Bertie and one of his friends from school, were paddling in the brook as they fished. Amy remembered that Bertie had mentioned Edmond joining them there occasionally the previous summer.

'Caught anything?' Edmond asked them. Bertie displayed a few minnows in a jam jar.

'Just look at that stickleback!' Edmond pointed into the translucent water. 'See its zigzag courtship dance?' He caught Amy's hand and led her carefully to the edge of the bank so she could enjoy the little fish's progress along the stream margin. She was gladdened to find him friendly with local village boys.

He wished the others good luck with their fishing and he and Amy continued further along the bank. 'Mind that patch of mud,' he warned her. They skirted a clump of kingcups as a golden dragonfly flitted through them and ducks squabbled in the nearby water. She had often enjoyed an afternoon walk here, but now, as his warm fingers gently held her hand, she was thrilled to have him beside her.

Towards teatime they returned along the lane back into the High Street, picking handfuls of pale blue scabious as they went. As they returned to her house, Amy noticed Miss Miller's curtain twitching next door. She seemed to remember that their neighbour had once given singing lessons to Beatrice, Edmond's sister. Larchbury was just a large village, and people like Miss Miller wanted to know everyone's business. Sooner or later Edmond's family would almost certainly intervene and point out that she was not of his class and he should not court her.

When they reached her house, Edmond presented her with his share of the flowers before he left for home. Dreamily, she joined her family for their meal.

–

'He's a good chap, Edmond,' Bertie approved next morning over breakfast. 'He's not afraid of getting his feet wet if he sees us fishing. He's not stuck up like some of the other chaps from better-off families.'

'He always struck me as good-natured when he was a boy,' Father said. 'And he worked hard in their schoolroom, more so than his older brother.'

Mother, neat in her large white apron, poured them cups of tea. 'People are bound to gossip about seeing Amy with him,' she said, apprehensively. 'They'll imagine she's a social climber, eager to marry into a wealthy and prominent family.'

'It's not like that!' Amy cried.

Her fortuitous reunion with Edmond had seemed like a gift from fate and since then she had been unable to contemplate not seeing him.

'Well, that's what they'll think.' Mother went out to the kitchen to cook their bacon. Father had finished his breakfast and followed her to clean his shoes.

'Don't take any notice of Mother!' Bertie said, grinning at her. 'Walk out with whoever you choose.'

She felt a little relieved at his approval.

Bertie worked in an office in Wealdham, but his firm began work half an hour earlier and so he would take a train before hers. He glanced at his watch. 'What a waste of a fine day, adding figures in ledgers,' he complained. 'What else can I do, though?' Father would have liked him to attend a university but he had failed to win a scholarship. 'Perhaps when I pass my exams there'll be a better choice of jobs.'

'My work's not much better,' she said. 'I suppose I could look for a different position when I've improved my typing speed.'

'We both need fulfilling work,' he said, determination in his grey eyes.

She was pleased, for people still questioned that a woman might want to find a career.

They fell quiet as Mother came in briefly with plates of egg and bacon.

When she had left, Bertie went on. 'I won't stay long in employment I don't care for, even if I have to disappoint Mother and Father,' he told her.

'They don't deserve rebellious children like us,' she said ruefully. Their parents were conventional but loving and she would hate to hurt them.

'You mean leaving your mark in the cricket pavilion? I'm afraid there's still interest in what happened there,' he told her with a smirk. She knew that the broken window had been replaced, her chalk slogans removed and the building hurriedly cleared in time for the next match. As yet the green paint remained. 'One of the team told me they're talking of making a more thorough search, in case there's any evidence of who did it,' he said.

Anxiety seized her momentarily. 'I'm pretty sure we didn't leave any clues,' she said.

'You don't look like a criminal,' he said, winking, as he got up to leave for his train.

Amy gathered up their dishes and took them out to the kitchen. She had time to help Mother with the washing up before she left.

On Bank Holiday Monday Edmond asked her out for a walk once more. It was a warm, sunny afternoon, as they walked along the brook in the opposite direction to before, towards the little waterfalls, where there were generally fewer strollers. Edmond seemed quieter, absorbed in his own thoughts. She wanted to ask him how soon he would be leaving for Cambridge, but hesitated to express an interest in his future, or hint at a time when it would be hard for them to meet. The future soon impinged, however.

'I'm anxious there will be war,' he told her suddenly. 'I had thought Parliament would do everything to avoid it, but now there seems a real chance it will happen. Tonight they'll decide.'

'The very thought is horrible.'

'Unfortunately some young men seem to regard the prospect as a great opportunity for adventure.'

'That's not what Uncle said in his sermon yesterday.' She had seen Edmond there with his family in their pew, listening to the sermon about the futility of a European war. Peacemakers were blessed, Uncle had said.

'The politicians think differently.' Edmond sounded reluctant to accept war but his eyes were bright with interest at the new situation. 'The Germans are threatening Belgium's neutrality and we have a treaty with them. People say there could be a brief, decisive campaign.'

She struggled to comprehend how they had got into such a position.

'Our military are very confident we can defeat the Kaiser and his men,' Edmond went on. 'Colonel Fairlawn came to dinner last week and he reminded us of our supremacy. We were always being taught at school about the Boer war and the great triumphs in Victorian times.'

The mention of Colonel Fairlawn made her flinch, and for a moment she was even distracted from the prospect of war. So Edmond's family were on friendly terms with him. Whatever would they think, and what would Edmond think, if they knew she had been involved in the damage to the cricket pavilion? She could not find a way to ask if there were any developments without arousing his curiosity at her interest.

She knew there were plans to erase the slogans in green paint inside and outside, but for the moment they remained, and she had to suppress a smile at their constant reminder of the Suffrage movement.

They rounded a gentle bend in the brook to an area where the foliage was thick. Edmond stopped and put his arm about her. 'You're so lovely, Amy,' he said. no one else was in sight. Gently he tipped her face towards him. 'May I kiss you?'

She smiled in anticipation. Then his soft, warm lips brushed hers. The kiss was sweet, gentle and gallant. A warm glow swept over her.

He took her hand in his larger one and led her further along the brook.

'One day I'd like to take you for a walk on the high land near our forest,' he told her. 'There's a splendid view.'

'Father took us up there a few times, though of course we kept to the path, outside your land. I remember looking right across the village.' The Derwents owned the forest and made their money from the timber. She recalled seeing horses pulling wagons of tree trunks. 'It must be lovely up there in autumn, when the trees round the village are changing colour.'

But he'd be back at university by then, she realised at once. Probably he would lose interest in her. It would be easier if she could care for one of the other young men she knew, but now she had met Edmond, no one could compare with him. It was not just his wealthy, privileged background that appealed, as Mother expected people to suppose. He was intelligent, and a merry companion. He was handsome, too, and his kiss had thrilled her, and surely she was not deluding herself when she imagined he returned her affection.

Already they were turning back towards her house. She slowed her pace, wanting the magic to go on for as long as possible. If only she could live in this afternoon for ever.

–

The next day it was official: Britain had joined the European war. The existing army was mobilised and young men were encouraged to join up. Outwardly their lives carried on as normal and at first it felt as if they could ignore the new development, as though it was unreal. But soon the village was buzzing with accounts of two young men who had rushed to join up.

The fête held by Edmond's family each year at The Beeches was going ahead as usual but would now include fundraising for the war effort.

Amy went along to the event with her family. Edmond would be there, of course, and she wondered if he would acknowledge her as a friend, in front of his family.

She put on her best summer dress of white lawn with a delicate pattern of pink flowers. She was thankful for her new straw hat with the artificial flowers, anxious to avoid being seen in the one she had been wearing when they had damaged the pavilion.

As they joined other villagers walking up the avenue of beech trees towards the great house, she could hear the hubbub of voices and ragtime music from the bandstand. When they reached the wide lawn there were clusters of people around booths supporting various charitable causes, and, she soon realised, the war effort.

'Look! They've set up a recruiting station!' Bertie exclaimed, hurrying over in that direction.

'Oh, no, Bertie!' Mother protested as they all rushed after him.

She too felt alarmed. Then, as they approached the booth, gaudily festooned in Union Jacks, she flinched at the sight of Colonel Fairlawn, imposing in his uniform. Young army officers were standing with him.

'Hello, John,' Bertie greeted a friend from school who was already in the khaki uniform. Amy remembered that John Spencer had joined the army in peace time, when he left school.

'Hello, Bertie. It's very exciting – we expect to be sent to Flanders soon. You planning to join up?'

Amy noticed a private, who was handing pen and paper to any young men who could be persuaded to enlist.

The colonel was red-faced with a bristling moustache. 'Young man?' he accosted Bertie. 'I daresay you're ready to serve your country.'

Bertie looked as though he was considering the opportunity.

'See here, this is my son Wilfrid.' The colonel indicated the very tall young man who stood rigidly with a cane beneath his arm. 'The army's his life.'

'I'm longing for the adventure of war,' Wilfrid told them. 'I can't wait for my unit to be mobilised.'

Bertie shuffled from one foot to the other.

'What's your occupation?' the colonel asked Bertie.

'Junior accountant, Sir.'

'And where did you go to school?'

Bertie mentioned the high school.

'Possible officer material,' approved the colonel.

Amy noticed Wilfrid staring at her in a manner which was less than gallant. She looked in the opposite direction.

Other young men were crowding round the booth now.

'I'll think it over,' Bertie managed.

'Don't leave it too long to take the King's shilling,' the colonel said. 'It could all be over by the end of the year. There's a recruiting office opening in Wealdham.'

'Hey, Colonel,' came the voice of an older man. 'Have you found who defaced the pavilion yet?'

'Not yet,' he replied, to Amy's relief. 'But I'm not going to let that go unpunished, believe me.'

Bertie was drifting away from the booth now.

'Really, Bertie, have more sense than to join up!' Mother said, smart in her summer suit and flowered hat. 'There'll be horrible casualties. Miss Miller next door lost her fiancé in the South African conflict. You've got an important career to follow.'

'Don't do it, Bertie,' Amy begged.

'But shouldn't I serve my country? It seems the decent thing to do.' His face was animated as he considered the possibility.

'Don't rush into it, Son,' Father said, as they made for the next group of stalls.

Amy caught sight of Wilfrid, the colonel's son, striding across the grass towards them. She had an uneasy feeling that he might try to engage her in conversation and clung to her mother's side.

Then suddenly Edmond appeared, raising his boater. 'Amy! Mr and Mrs Fletcher! Let me find you some refreshments. And you, Bertie.'

Amy let him take her hand and the others followed them across the lawn. This large lower lawn was given over to the fête, but beyond she could see the upper lawn, flower beds, a greenhouse and in the distance, what looked like a kitchen garden, around the substantial stone house.

'Most of our gardens are here, in front of the house, facing south,' Edmond told her. Mature beech trees lined the drive, but beyond the house she could see the land rising towards the forest, consisting mainly of conifers.

Amy was aware of neighbours watching as they passed the tables of refreshments provided for villagers attending the fête. Miss Miller was there in a rather plain summer costume, her greying hair swept up beneath her floral hat, staring as Edmond led them towards the area occupied by the Derwent family and close friends. Ahead were his parents and sister.

'Ma, Pa – you remember Mr Fletcher, don't you? He's here with his family.'

Mr Derwent, Edmond's father, raised his hat courteously to the ladies and shook hands with Amy's father. His wife, dressed in a summer suit trimmed with lace and an elaborate hat, nodded distantly and stared at Amy, whose hand was still in Edmond's. Beatrice was elegantly dressed and one of the loveliest girls Amy knew, with curls of chestnut hair showing below her hat. Her face was as dainty as that of a china doll, though unsmiling.

'How is Peter liking India?' Amy's father asked Mr Derwent.

Edmond's father was tall and self-possessed, with a pleasant smile. 'He still enjoys it and intends to make his career there,' he replied, 'though we all miss him.'

The men continued talking for a while, for Mr Derwent still seemed to value her father's contribution to the boys' education. Soon Edmond led Amy and Bertie further away from the fête.

A man with grey hair, who Amy took to be the butler, hovered beside the steps to the upper lawn as Edmond led them up to an area with some tables and wicker chairs, near a bank of pink hydrangeas. Edmond called to a maid and ordered them some tea and cakes. As they all sat down he chatted to them comfortably.

In the distance Amy could still see the other members of Edmond's family. Wilfrid Fairlawn swaggered towards the group and began talking to Beatrice. She seemed content with the attentions of the colonel's son.

'Have you seen the recruiting station?' Amy asked Edmond as the tea arrived and the maid poured cups for them all. 'They were trying to persuade Bertie to join up.'

'And will you do so?' Edmond asked him.

'I haven't decided yet.' Bertie reached for a slice of Battenberg cake.

Amy drank down her tea thirstily. 'Try to keep out of their clutches, Edmond,' she said a little playfully.

'I've already seen them,' he said. 'I've joined up.'

She set down her cup with a clatter, feeling the blood drain from her face.

'It seemed the right thing to do,' he told her. 'I'm prepared to march into war for a just cause.'

'It makes me think of King Arthur and his knights, defending the oppressed,' said Bertie.

She was dismayed by their views. They continued with some more small talk, but the afternoon was ruined.

'Come and take a look at our south garden,' Edmond invited her. 'The roses on the pergola are very fine this year.'

She got up and followed him. He took her hand again.

'Why did you do it, Edmond?' she demanded. 'Why do you have to go and fight?' Apprehension had not engulfed her this way when Bertie had talked of joining up.

'I see it as my duty. We've got an enemy.' He turned to her with a serious expression in his blue eyes. 'They've invaded Belgium. Have you heard about all the refugees arriving here?'

'Yes, but – other men can fight. You've got your place at university – you should take advantage of the opportunity to study.'

'I believe I can defer my place and continue at university next year when the war is over,' he told her.

Only the sweet perfume drew her attention to the roses when they reached the south garden. Other select visitors were admiring the flourishing blooms but Amy's mind was elsewhere.

'When will you have to leave?'

'I'm going to start officer training very shortly. It'll be a few months before they send me to Flanders.'

A few months, she thought. Please God, the war might be over by then.

The usual captivating smile returned to his face. 'It'll be all right, Amy. I promise I'll write to you.'

Chapter Four

'So you see, Amy, we'll have to suspend the struggle while the war lasts,' Lavinia told her on the train one morning.

'I suppose so,' she said, unwilling to admit her relief. She hoped the war might distract Colonel Fairlawn from his urgent search for the perpetrators of the damage to the pavilion. She was anxious to avoid any similar activity for the foreseeable future.

Two young men in privates' uniform sat opposite them, presumably on their way to a training centre, or to London to join a troop train. Raindrops were running down the outside of the windows.

'It seems unpatriotic now to challenge the government,' Lavinia explained. 'The Suffragists, our sisters who oppose any kind of civil disobedience, are involved in helping the Belgian refugees. Have you heard Florence is helping with the project in Wealdham?'

'Yes.' Amy was impressed with her friend's commitment. She must find it tiring, helping there as well as training to be a teacher.

'Some of the Belgians are practically destitute when they arrive. Our women are knitting socks and gloves for them, and collecting second-hand clothes in good condition. Now

32

the weather's turning colder Florence wants us to set up soup kitchens.'

'I'm sure I can help with that,' she said, resolving to play her part.

'And we can look out for any meaningful activity we can do to support the war effort. It gives us the chance to prove we're more than fluffy-headed creatures who can't be trusted to make responsible decisions.'

'That makes sense.' Now that Edmond had signed up, it was important that she found some role too.

'They're planning to enrol young women into nursing organisations, like the Voluntary Aid Detachment. They may even be sent to casualty clearing stations abroad, near the fighting. I plan to find out about it. I might enrol.' There was a sparkle of excitement in her dark eyes.

It was bound to interest Lavinia, Amy thought, since her father was a surgeon.

'Nursing! That would be so worthwhile.' Already, shockingly, there were reports of young men being killed or injured in Flanders. 'Do you imagine it'd be difficult? I know nothing about medicine.'

'I suppose I'll find out if I enrol. They won't let anyone near wounded soldiers who doesn't have some aptitude for the work. You might consider it, but office work is important too, now young men are leaving for the Front.'

'Let me know if you find out any more about it.' As they approached their station she got up and buttoned her coat.

'We must play what part we can in the war. When it's all over we can go back to promoting our cause again.'

'Yes – we must do that.' Now Edmond was involved, Amy felt that ultimately the cause was worthy and she should make some contribution.

They got out at Wealdham. Advancing along the street towards them was a column of soldiers, marching briskly through the drizzle. There was a pride about them, a sense of destiny. She watched them march past, keeping in time, arms swinging jauntily, towards the station, and could not help feeling admiration.

–

Edmond's training was taking place some twenty miles away and before long she received a letter from him. *The discipline is hard,* he wrote, *really it's like being back at school again. We have parades and training in the use of arms.* There was a paragraph at the end when he reminded her of their recent meetings with a tenderness which touched her. *I'm longing to see you again,* he said.

Before long he had weekend leave. On the Sunday he called at her house, smart in his khaki officer's uniform, and bearing a bunch of pink roses for her. Bertie began to bombard him with questions about his training.

'You soon find comrades there,' Edmond said. 'I knew some of the others at school.'

She put the sweet-smelling flowers in water, then set off with him for a walk. 'Let's go uphill towards the forest,' he said. As they went along the High Street passers-by turned to admire him in his uniform, and she attracted some glances too. They walked to the edge of his family's land and took the path along the perimeter. To begin with, it was muddy and he held on to her arm so she should not slip over. The path became steeper as they skirted The Beeches. The leaves were turning golden on the birch trees which grew along there, but ahead the commercial plantation remained green as the trees were mostly conifers.

She listened to his account of his new life, trying to gauge how soon his unit might be sent abroad, but it seemed there was no imminent danger of that as he needed to complete his training first. When she thought of the casualties, she could not help hoping the war would come to an end before he could be sent abroad. She read Father's newspaper most days to follow the progress of the war, and had learnt of the rival armies forming an extended front across much of Belgium and northern France. Sometimes there was talk of a breakthrough, but on other days it seemed the British were barely holding their position.

'A lot of the men want to be part of the cavalry,' Edmond was telling her. 'It's enjoyable, exercising and parading on the horses, but I'm not sure they're appropriate for modern day warfare.'

They reached the steepest part of the path and paused as she became a little breathless. There were few people to see them together up there. He took her in his arms and kissed her. His kisses were more lingering now.

'You're such a sweet girl,' he said. 'I'm so thankful I met you again. I hope the war doesn't part us for too long.'

She leant her head against his shoulder. *That's what he wants*, she thought, *a sweet young girl. It's what he needs, as a soldier planning to fight for his country. Should I try to live up to his illusion of a totally sweet young woman or confront him with who I really am? There's still the chance that my role in the attack on the pavilion might come to light.*

She was tempted to try to keep her secret, but as they continued uphill, he seemed concerned about her.

'You're quiet today,' he said. 'Is everything all right?'

She concluded it was best to tell him straight away.

'I'm not always sweet,' she said, pulling away a little. 'I have a few ideas of my own, sometimes ones some people regard as shocking.'

His eyebrows rose and he grinned. 'Go on, shock me.' They dawdled at the top of the slope, just below the forest. Further down she could see the greyish roof of The Beeches to one side, with the centre of Larchbury beyond, with its remaining clumps of yellowing larch trees on the outskirts.

'What do you think of the Suffragettes?' she asked him.

'I've a lot of sympathy for their cause. I'm disturbed when they go on hunger strike and need to be force-fed… So, you're a supporter?'

At least he did not condemn them or dismiss them as foolish. 'Yes,' she told him. 'But what about their acts of civil disobedience?' she pursued.

He shrugged. 'There's an unfortunate attitude that they're wild, blue-stocking types, lacking in femininity. It must be hard to have their views held in contempt. I can see how frustrating that must be. I suppose that's why they feel an urge to take action.'

'I need to tell you something. Please don't give me away. There are other women involved besides me.'

They came to a bench facing south towards the view, and he spread his tunic on it as it was damp. 'Are you actually part of a Suffragette group, Amy?' he asked as they sat down.

'Yes.'

The expression in his eyes was soft and sympathetic. 'In a way, I'd rather you had some views than being an empty-headed creature like Beatrice, my sister. She's pretty and charming but thinks of little except gowns and hats. She spends her days shopping or at the dressmaker's and her evenings at parties and balls whenever possible, or playing cards.'

The leaves on a nearby birch were wafting away in the breeze.

'I was involved in something illegal,' she admitted.

He searched her face, intrigued. 'I promise not to tell.'

She confessed her part in the break-in at the pavilion. Whatever would he think of her now? He would have every reason to end their friendship, or even report her to the authorities.

'Oh, Amy! What a naughty girl you've been!' He was laughing. 'I'm sorry, I know it's not funny really and you'd be in trouble if you were found out. But I can't help laughing when I think of Colonel Fairlawn seeing the slogans scrawled in his precious pavilion.'

'The painted ones are still there, so far as I know. Aren't you shocked at what I did?'

'A little surprised, maybe. But it's not a significant crime. The colonel is so overbearing I like to think of him shaken by the incident. His son Wilfrid was at my school and he was a terrible bully when he was a prefect.'

There was still an uneasy feeling in the pit of her stomach. 'What would your family say if they knew what I'd done?'

'I don't suppose they'd approve. But times are changing gradually.'

'Thank you for being so understanding.'

'I'm actually quite proud of you, darling.' He kissed her again.

'The Suffragettes mean to suspend their activities during the war.' Florence, who had come with her and Lavinia to the cricket pavilion, though she had not gone inside, was relieved that no further events of that kind were planned. She had turned her attention to helping the refugees.

'It's probably as well. It could be seen as unpatriotic. I'd rather you don't do anything else risky, at least for a while.'

He actually accepted her stand and almost excused her actions. It drew them even closer.

They got up and began to dawdle back. The sun went in and light rain began but her euphoria lasted during their return journey, until she reached home.

Mother offered Edmond a cup of tea before he returned to The Beeches. Soon he was sitting with them all in their parlour.

'It's been good to see you again, Edmond,' Bertie said. 'I've come to a decision. I'm going to sign up. I hope to become an officer, like you.'

There was a gasp from Mother and Amy saw tears welling into her eyes. She herself was alarmed at the news.

Edmond got up and shook Bertie's hand. Then he became aware of the atmosphere. 'I'd better leave for home.' He thanked them for the tea and Amy showed him out. In the hall, he took her into his arms for a final kiss.

'Isn't it bad enough that *you* want to fight?' Amy cried when he released her from his embrace. Her feelings were in turmoil.

'Your brother wants to do his duty,' he replied gently. He left more abruptly than usual, seeming to sense the family's impatience to discuss Bertie's news.

Amy went back into the parlour. In those few steps she realised that she hated the idea of Bertie fighting. *He always understands how I feel about women's rights and supports me*, she thought. *If only we agreed about the war.*

'No, Bertie, promise me you won't join up!' Mother was saying, dabbing her eyes with her handkerchief.

'I must play my part,' he said. As Amy sat down she had seldom seen him so solemn. 'Most of my class at school are joining up. And Edmond signed up almost straight away.'

Amy's eyes were filling with tears now, chiefly from the reminder of the perils Edmond would soon face.

'What about your career in accountancy?' Mother asked Bertie, catching hold of his arm. 'You'll fall behind.'

He won't care much about that, Amy thought, for he still grumbled to her about enduring boring days in his office. If only he had more inspiring work, to make him unwilling to leave.

'Tell him he mustn't do it!' Mother begged Father.

He had said nothing up to now, but his face sagged. 'Don't join up just because it seems like an exciting adventure,' he told Bertie now. 'Give it some serious thought.'

'I already have. I'm going to the recruiting office tomorrow.'

'It's your decision, Son,' Father said slowly. 'I won't stand in your way if you're determined to do your duty.'

Mother was still crying as she went to prepare tea, and Amy hurried after her to help.

—

'The refugees have been found temporary homes in a big house left empty when an old lady died,' Florence explained to Amy as they set out by train to Wealdham. Amy had decided it was high time she joined her friends, and the women, often Suffragists, who were helping the unfortunate Belgians. It was a Sunday when Edmond did not have leave.

'I joined in last weekend when we collected clothing,' Florence went on. 'We've been laundering the garments and sorting them, and now we need to take them to the families. It would be lovely if you could help.' Her light brown hair was tucked beneath her felt hat.

From Wealdham station they walked to a nearby church. In the hall there were baskets of clothing, sorted into bundles with labels indicating whether they were intended for men, women or children, and the size. Two boy scouts helped load several basketsful on to their trek cart and began pushing it through the streets towards the home of the refugees.

'Be careful!' Florence told the boys as she picked up stray bundles which had fallen off.

'The place is just here,' she said soon, indicating a three-storey house in grey stone and directing the scouts into its drive. 'You speak some French, don't you, Amy?'

'Only what I remember from school.'

When they rang the bell, a stout woman in a dark dress opened the door and beamed at them. 'You are from the relief people? Please to come in. I am Madame Rousseau. You may unload the clothing parcels and bring them into our common room, if you would be so kind.' Her English was accented and Amy could barely understand her words.

As they stepped inside there was a hubbub, suggesting several families were crammed into the limited accommodation. The aroma of soup and cabbage came from nearby rooms. Amy and Florence helped the scouts unload the parcels and carry them through to a large front room. Along the hallway, doors were opening and men and women hovering expectantly. Some curious children squeezed to the front, while more timid ones peeped from behind their mothers. Now more families were appearing, craning over the banisters from upstairs.

'*Attendez!*' Madame Rousseau told the others. She seemed to be telling them she would call them when they were ready.

Amy had not known what to expect and it was only now she began to imagine what it might be like to have to flee one's country. They arranged the bundles according to clothing size on a large table. When they were ready, Madame Rousseau supervised the distribution, using her influence to keep the flow of anxious men and women to a steady trickle.

'*Bonjour Monsieur – bonjour, Madame.*' Florence was greeting them warmly from the end of the table, prepared to talk a little if they hovered and asked for news of the war.

Amy began to do the same. Sometimes it was possible for her to maintain a short dialogue in simple French and occasionally someone could speak English.

'My husband is in the local hospital,' a grey-haired woman told her. 'He was injured in the fighting before we managed to get away. They have set aside a ward in Wealdham hospital for Belgians.'

'I hope he is making good progress,' she replied.

Another woman accosted her in a guttural language which was not French. 'Ah, the English women will not understand you!' cried her friend, and began translating what was being said. 'Some of our people speak only Flemish,' she explained. 'My friend is trying to tell you how they had to wait at the port for over twenty-four hours before a ship brought them across the Channel.'

Madame Rousseau was trying to keep the column of refugees moving through the room as they claimed their bundles. As the last families reached the common room there were only just enough parcels remaining. Some of the Belgians continued to recount their experiences.

'Ah, the Boches!' complained one man, his features distorted in indignation. 'Destroying out cities, plundering our crops, violating our young women! When will we have our own land back?'

Amy exchanged glances with Florence, moved by what she had heard. Why had the world suddenly gone mad like this?

'It's true, what he says,' Madame Rousseau told them. 'When our people tried to stop the Germans invading our land they took hostages and shot them.'

Amy shivered. What would happen if the Germans invaded Britain? But that was impossible, surely – they would never succeed in crossing the Channel?

'We will form our own regiments here and return to liberate Belgium,' said the man.

'Some of our young men managed to escape,' Madame Rousseau went on. 'If they could not reach the coast they sometimes headed for the Dutch border. There was talk of brave people taking risks to help them, including nuns and nurses.'

It was hard for Amy and Florence to concentrate on giving out the parcels, but at last their task was nearly complete. Madame Rousseau beckoned forward a dark-haired girl of about fourteen. 'Here, Yolande, see if this skirt looks the right size for you.' She selected a few clothes for her daughter and herself.

'Thank you so much,' she said finally. 'You have been like angels to us.'

'We're trying to collect furniture,' Florence told her. 'I hope that will be ready soon.'

'I hope you'll soon feel more at home here,' Amy said as Madame Rousseau accompanied them to the front door. It had been a moving experience, meeting these vulnerable people, and she was determined to continue helping them.

They stepped out into the autumn dusk.

Chapter Five

'I'd really appreciate it if you'd invite Amy Fletcher to the Christmas dance,' Edmond told his mother. 'And her family.' He knew that his parents' social circle was wide and the Fletcher family were not generally included in smart events.

'I really couldn't say if that's possible,' his mother said, stately in her dark blue woollen dress with lace at the collar and cuffs. She was sitting at a small bureau in their drawing room, preparing a guest list. 'We have so many people we should invite... It's getting dark in here.'

Dusk was falling so he got up and turned on another lamp to illuminate the large, comfortable room with its traditional sofa and easy chairs.

'Oh, do let's make it a great occasion this year,' Beatrice begged, looking up from a fashion magazine. 'So many young men have joined up. They may get Christmas leave, but who knows how soon they'll be sent abroad? Remember when they said this silly war would all be over by Christmas? Not much sign of it, is there?'

'I've been walking out with Amy Fletcher when I'm on weekend leave,' Edmond persisted.

'So you told us before. You've been seen together and it's causing comment.' A frown formed across Ma's pale forehead.

43

'She's a decent young girl but you could do so much better. I hope you're not becoming attached to her.'

'Yes, I am.' He could not dodge the issue any longer. 'None of the other girls I know compares with her.'

'What's so special about Amy Fletcher?' demanded Beatrice. 'She's pretty enough, I suppose, and well-spoken, but she doesn't mix with girls of our class. She works in an office, I hear.'

He was captivated by her. It was only partly her beautiful fair hair and trim waist, and the sprightly way she walked. 'It's not just her appearance. I feel our ideas are in tune too.'

He did not want to anger Beatrice by telling her that Amy's work in a modern office brought her into contact with a variety of people, so that her conversation was often far more stimulating than that of Beatrice and her sheltered friends.

'Please don't become too involved with her,' implored Ma. 'You're bound to meet someone more suitable with the right kind of background.'

'With respect, Ma, I must make my own decisions about who I choose to walk out with.'

She pursed her lips. 'It's fair to say Mr Fletcher was a good tutor to you, and managed to bring Peter on with his Latin. I suppose we might fit them in at the dance. I'll invite the parents along with Amy and – what's the brother called?'

'Bertie – Albert. Thanks, Ma.' He knew she was inviting the whole family to make his interest in Amy less obvious.

–

'Your ballroom looks splendid,' Amy's mother told Mrs Derwent when she greeted them upon their arrival.

Their hostess seemed to be looking Amy over more closely than usual.

44

Around them there were vases laden with sprigs of holly, pine garlands festooned across the walls, and the great pine tree, decorated with glass ornaments. At one end of the room a large fire stacked with logs threw out heat so that Amy scarcely needed her shawl over her pale blue silky gown. She caught sight of Florence, pretty in an ivory dress, standing with her family, and smiled at her. Her friend's father was the local solicitor.

'It seemed important to make a special effort this year,' Mrs Derwent said, 'and of course we always choose a magnificent pine from the forest as our Christmas tree. We wanted as much foliage as possible to provide a festive effect, but it wasn't easy, as some of our forest workers have enlisted. And George, our gardener, joined up at the same time as his school friends.'

'I daresay it's difficult to replace him now so many men are training to fight,' Amy's mother said.

'George's brother Henry has taken his place. He's too young to fight. But he's not so skilled in the garden.'

Edmond was suddenly at Amy's side, handsome in evening dress, smiling at her in his irresistible fashion. She was proud and nervous all at once, seeing the groups of giggling young girls around the room. Beatrice, gorgeous in a lemon-coloured gown that became her curly chestnut hair, was gossiping with them. Their dresses looked like the latest styles, not like her one, bought two years earlier. *I can't compete with them in elegance,* she realised. *Edmond will need to decide whether he can accept me how I am.*

From the invitation, and what Edmond had told her, she knew that the evening would include a buffet meal, followed by dancing. She hoped it would not be too obvious that she did not often attend such a smart event.

Mrs Derwent was shaking hands with Amy's father and Bertie. 'So you've joined up now?' she asked him.

'Yes, Mrs Derwent. I'm training to be an officer. I was fortunate to be given Christmas leave, like Edmond.'

Mr Derwent was eager to greet them too. 'I understand you work as a typist, Miss Fletcher?' he asked her.

'Yes, I go to an office in Wealdham each working day.' Was Edmond's father making the point that she needed to earn a living? Probably not, for he looked kindly.

'I believe you know the Westholme family,' Amy said. 'They live nearby at Alderbank. I'm good friends with Lavinia.'

'Ah, yes, the father's a surgeon, isn't he?' Edmond's father said.

'Beatrice was at school with Lavinia,' his mother said. Amy had noticed that the young women had similar refined accents. 'But they had little in common,' she went on. 'Lavinia has a very fine singing voice, hasn't she? Beatrice doesn't quite reach her standard. But Lavinia's tall, not an elegant height like Beatrice, but nearly as tall as Edmond, and she seems to rush everywhere, besides being rather opinionated, I find, like her mother.'

'Come and meet some of my comrades,' Edmond said, addressing Bertie but placing his hand lightly on Amy's arm. He guided his young friends towards a group of men around their age.

The butler was circulating with a tray of drinks. In one corner, a quartet of musicians were launching into a melody.

One towering figure was dominating the area where they were headed. Amy shivered a little as Colonel Fairlawn addressed the young men, applauding their determination to join the war effort. 'My son Wilfrid is a captain now,' he was telling them. 'Sadly he wasn't allowed leave, so he can't be here this evening. I myself could not be spared from the War Office for long.'

One of the young men asked him about the latest progress at the Front.

'It's all going famously,' he told them.

Edmond seemed to sense Amy's disquiet and he drew her a little further from the colonel. The latter was greeted by a middle-aged friend and Amy breathed a little more easily as he left their group.

Edmond introduced her and Bertie to some of the other young men, most of whom had joined up. They generally spoke with the same kind of public school accent as Edmond and were courteous to her. Even so, when they began talking of hunting and weekend shooting parties on someone's country estate she felt like an outsider, and doubtless Bertie did too. He had told her that most of the others on his officer training course had attended a public school, and that some disdained his humbler background. 'If I try to join their conversation they're liable to ignore anything I say,' he had complained. She knew what he meant. If she happened to meet Beatrice in a local shop the older girl barely returned her greeting, looking beyond her as though she were invisible.

One of Edmond's friends, Charles Shenwood, was tall and confident-looking with black curly hair. He was describing Paris, with its sights, and prominence in art and ballet, having visited the city earlier that year. Amy had never had the opportunity to travel abroad, but descriptions of his experiences made her long to go to France.

'You've been abroad, haven't you, Edmond?' she said. 'Did you visit Paris?'

'Only briefly, I'm afraid, en route to Italy.'

'When we get sent abroad I'm hoping I can wangle some leave there,' Charles told them. 'It's well south of the Front, of course.'

Soon the butler announced that the buffet dinner was served. Edmond steered Amy into a large reception room at the side of the house, which had a long dining table, lit by dozens of candles. Beyond, there was a way through to a leafy area at the front of the house, which looked like a conservatory.

The table was stacked high with platters of ham and turkey, salmon and pies. Two maids were cutting portions and serving the guests. 'Try some of the game pie,' Edmond advised her, pointing out the dish. 'It's Cook's speciality.'

Amy nibbled, scarcely hungry, a little overcome by the occasion and the way Edmond had singled her out for attention. She was thankful to have an ally in Florence. Which other families were here who she knew well and visited socially? Her uncle, the vicar, was often invited to The Beeches, but she knew that tonight he and his family had already accepted an invitation elsewhere when they had been asked somewhat belatedly to the Derwents' party.

'I haven't seen John Spencer here,' she remarked to Edmond. 'Do you think he's been sent to the Front?'

'I daresay he has by now. It's odd, though, his family don't seem to be here either.' John's father was the owner of the local hotel.

On the other side of the table she could see the jovial-looking mayor, and Mr Brownlee, who was an auctioneer at the local livestock market. Edmond's family was one of the most prominent in Larchbury and they had invited some of the local landowners, businessmen who worked in Wealdham or other nearby towns, and some of the leading local shopkeepers and craftsmen, like Mr Mead the cobbler and Mr Grainger, who made fine clocks and sold them in his high street shop.

Beatrice came over and caught Edmond by the arm. 'When are you going to introduce me to your fellow officers?' she demanded.

A girl of around fourteen had followed Beatrice across the room. She had ribbons in her long auburn hair.

'Will you introduce me, too?' she asked breathlessly.

'Don't be silly, Vicky,' Beatrice told her. 'You're too young to stay up dancing. After the meal Ma will send you to bed.'

The girl looked desperately disappointed. 'Vicky is our cousin,' Edmond explained.

'Come on, Edmond,' Beatrice persisted.

'Right away,' he agreed. He led her towards some of his friends.

Young Vicky hovered awkwardly. Amy smiled at her. 'Are your parents the ones who took Edmond round Europe?' she asked.

'No, those are his other uncle and aunt, on his father's side.'

Amy suggested she tried the game pie.

'Do you think they'll let me stay and watch, for the first few dances, at least?' Vicky said, her light blue eyes wide and appealing.

'It's worth asking.' Amy could remember her own longing at that age to join in social events.

Before long, Amy noticed Beatrice chatting eagerly to Charles.

Edmond returned to her side. 'Now my sister will have plenty of dancing partners,' he told Amy.

Somehow she did not feel tongue-tied with him, as she did with most of his well-off friends. 'I gather your brother is still in India?' she asked.

49

'Yes, Peter has become settled there, making a career. His accounts of the country are always fascinating when he writes.'

Amy could not even imagine that far country. She knew that Peter, older than Edmond, had been there for a few years.

'Of course, he may decide to return now,' Edmond went on. 'Britain is crying out for men to join the army. Apparently the younger men in India are considering whether to return to take their part.'

The sound of dance music came from the ballroom next door, and people began heading in that direction. Edmond offered Amy his arm again and led her into the ballroom. Others were hovering around the dance floor, waiting for the dance to begin officially.

As she stood beside Edmond, she noticed questioning glances from Mrs Derwent and Beatrice. *They know I don't fit in here,* she thought. *What would it be like, living in a house like this, being waited on by servants?* She could hardly imagine such a future, but if Edmond could see her by his side, anything would be possible.

'Please, Aunt!' she heard Vicky's voice. 'Let me stay and watch – just for a little while. Mother's been sending me to dancing classes, but it would be so much more fun to stay and watch an actual ball.'

'Very well – just for half an hour.' Mrs Derwent led Vicky to a seat beside a plump matronly figure.

The musical quartet were beginning to play a popular waltz. Mr Derwent led his wife to the floor to open the ball. They swept stylishly around the room to a buzz of excitement. Then suddenly Edmond was leading Amy to join them. She was instantly nervous, anxious about how his interest in her would be perceived by the other guests. It was as much as she could do to follow him to the floor, trying to appear at ease and thankful she had taken a few dancing lessons. Then he held her in his arms and began leading her confidently around the room. Happiness swept over her and she no longer felt the slightest bit awkward. They swirled enthusiastically around the ballroom. A few other couples were joining them now. Amy was scarcely aware of anyone else until the dance ended. She noticed Beatrice hanging onto Charles's arm.

Then the music began again and Edmond led her back to the floor. This time it was a lively polka and she needed all her concentration to keep up with the steps.

'Enjoying it, dearest?' he asked as the music finished.

'It's simply wonderful.' She noticed that Bertie had been dancing with Florence. They made a good couple, she reflected.

'I need to ask a few other girls to dance. It's expected of me.'

'Of course.'

She sat as serenely as she could on one of the little chairs. Her parents were dancing contentedly together.

Edmond was dancing with one of Beatrice's friends now, a classy girl with an elaborate hair style. Her smart gown and pretty amethyst necklace marked her out as one of the young women from a better-off family. Then there was a tinkle of laughter as Beatrice swept by with another of her dancing partners. She was wearing a little feathery ornament in her chestnut hair.

When the next dance began Edmond chose another acquaintance as his partner while Amy continued to sit alone. She watched young Vicky being led from the room by her aunt.

Amy's mother and father were talking to Florence and her family. She was proud of the way her parents could fit in at a smart event without appearing overawed. Soon they came and sat beside her.

'Are you enjoying it, darling?' Mother asked. 'Of course, Edmond has a wide circle of friends. You mustn't be too disappointed if he can't dance much with you.'

'Might I have the pleasure?' said a voice, and she found Charles Shenwood by her side. Happily she joined him for a waltz.

'I hear you've been helping the Belgian refugees,' he remarked, steering her eagerly round the room.

'How did you know that?'

'I just enjoyed a waltz with Florence, and she told me.'

'It must be so upsetting for them to be away from their homeland and relatives,' she told him. 'Florence and I helped at the party they arranged for them in a church hall.'

Before long, Edmond asked her to join him in a polka again. He seemed anxious she should enjoy herself, but had to dance with some of the young women who were regular visitors at his home.

Florence joined her when she was without a partner. 'How devoted Edmond is becoming to you!' she said, smiling.

Amy smiled back. It would be presumptuous to suggest that her dreams could come true.

The evening began to fly past and all too soon the last dance was announced. Edmond led her to the floor again. She seemed to melt into his arms, and tried not to care if his family were less than pleased that he was partnering her again.

When the melody came to an end the quartet played 'God Save the King' and all the guests stood respectfully. The war effort was making them increasingly patriotic.

Edmond took her hand and led her into the dining room, where the buffet table had been cleared. Her neighbour, Miss Miller, stared at her and Edmond as she got up from the small card table where she had been playing with some of the older visitors. As the last card players left, Edmond drew Amy towards him and kissed her passionately.

'Darling, I'm falling in love with you,' he murmured.

'I feel the same.' She could scarcely stop thinking about him, whether they were together or apart.

The butler came into the room, excused himself and left.

'I really must be going,' Amy said. 'My parents will be growing impatient.'

'Might I order the chauffeur to drive you all home?'

'There's no need, Edmond. Thank you, but it's not a long walk.'

He accompanied her to the entrance hall where her family were waiting. A maid helped her change into her boots and Edmond held out her coat, easing it over her shoulders. He waved as they left.

It was a frosty night but she felt warm, radiant even, as her mind dwelt on Edmond's embrace. She fancied she could still feel the pressure of his lips on hers. Then, as they set out, she realised suddenly that the others were unusually silent. She looked at Bertie and was shocked at his serious expression.

'Is something wrong?' she asked.

'It's John Spencer. He's been killed in Flanders – someone just told me.'

Her glow of happiness trickled swiftly away.

'His parents received the telegram today. That's why they didn't come.'

The icy night seemed to penetrate her coat suddenly, chilling her heart with foreboding.

Chapter Six

Larchbury, February to June 1915

'I begin training as a VAD next week,' Lavinia told Amy one morning on the train.

'Oh – well done. It sounds very worthwhile.' Once again she was intrigued that young women were being encouraged to learn nursing skills and join the Voluntary Aid Detachment to help the wounded. 'Will they send you to Flanders?'

'Not at first. There are injured men being sent back here for treatment. I'm beginning my training at a hospital in Surrey.'

Amy had heard of casualties arriving on trains from the Channel ports. 'You must tell me how you get on. I might consider becoming a VAD myself.'

'You could – so could Florence.'

'She's training to be a school teacher. She'll already have an important job.'

Amy buttoned her coat as they alighted in Wealdham and went off in different directions. It was her duty to help the war effort, she supposed, but if she was sent away to train it might be harder to meet Edmond when he came home on leave. If he was actually sent abroad it would be a different matter. There seemed no sign of a quick victory.

There was snow in February and Edmond could not make it home one weekend when he was due for leave. He wrote regularly, asking for her news and telling her how he was longing to see her again. She told him that Bertie was away training now, though he had not been able to join the same regiment as Edmond. Then there was the latest news of her refugee work. Some of the Belgians were beginning to find jobs and their own homes, becoming more settled.

At last, Edmond had weekend leave again. Normally he stayed with his family on the Saturday and called on her on the Sunday, so she was pleasantly surprised when he arrived at her house one Saturday afternoon.

'Amy! It seems so long. I couldn't wait till tomorrow to see you.'

'Come in out of the cold.'

His face was chilled as he embraced and kissed her swiftly in the hallway. Then he followed her into the cosy back room where her mother was sitting knitting and Father was reading the newspaper.

'Edmond! How delightful to see you,' Mother said. 'Let me fetch you some tea and cake. And you'll stay for dinner, won't you?'

'That's very kind, Mrs Fletcher.'

'If we'd known you were coming we'd have made up a fire in the front parlour,' Mother said awkwardly. They normally entertained guests there, with the smarter furniture, the piano and the flourishing aspidistra in its china bowl, but in winter it was cold there if they had not lit the fire in good time.

'It looks very comfortable here,' he said.

Mother went to fetch some tea, Edmond sat down, looking as though he was hovering, waiting to snatch another kiss but wondering how her father would react. He held on to her hand in his still cool one, and she enjoyed the delicious feeling of belonging.

Her father built up the fire. Mother brought in a tray and distributed tea and cake. There was a comfortable atmosphere, for her father had always liked Edmond when he tutored him and her mother too was growing close to him as the months passed.

He asked after Bertie and they told him he was enjoying army life. They discussed the war with him briefly. 'Any news of you being sent abroad?' Father asked.

It was the question Amy had dreaded asking.

'In the summer, maybe.'

The delight of seeing him began to dissipate with dread for the future. *I must try to keep brave for him,* she thought. *But he may go to Flanders, so may Bertie – how can I bear it?* As the weeks passed it seemed less likely that the war would end quickly, and the loss of John Spencer had brought home the grim possibilities ahead.

Before long, Mother got up to prepare their evening meal. Father went outside to fetch some more logs for the fire. Amy was glad they trusted Edmond enough to leave the pair of them together alone for a while.

'Darling, I can't wait any longer,' he said suddenly, squeezing her hand. 'Tell me you'll marry me!'

'Edmond!' She was almost speechless. Within her chest, her heart seemed to flutter wildly. 'Yes, oh yes, I want so much to be your wife. But what will your parents say?'

'They'll have to respect my wishes. And they recognise that you're a decent young woman. They'll grow to love you.'

It was not quite the assurance she longed for, that they would unreservedly welcome her into the family. They would prefer someone from their own circle.

'Suppose they don't give consent?' she faltered. 'You're only twenty.'

'I'll wait for you if I have to,' he said forcibly, 'but I don't think they'll make difficulties.'

'Oh, darling – being your wife – it's my dream.'

When her father came back into the room they were kissing tenderly and could scarcely break apart. Her parents barely needed to be told their news.

—

The Derwents were in church next morning and, apart from Edmond, merely nodded to them. Before the service began he rushed over and told them they were all invited to lunch at The Beeches. After church, Amy's family returned home briefly before walking the short distance to the large house in good time for lunch. Amy could not remember feeling so nervous.

The butler admitted them and Edmond hurried to greet them. Soon they were shaking hands with his parents and Beatrice, who seemed less than enchanted to see them. They were served sherry, which Amy barely sipped.

'Edmond has told us of his plans to marry,' Mr Derwent said, smiling. 'Naturally we are pleased to welcome Amy as his bride.'

The words were sufficient: he was not opposing the wedding. All the same, she would have preferred him to sound more enthusiastic. She sensed reserve from Edmond's mother, too.

She followed the others into the dining room with its sparkling cutlery and fine china. It was smaller than the reception room they had used for the meal at the Christmas party. Soon a maid was serving them leek soup.

'Edmond hopes we can arrange the wedding for early June,' his father went on. His hair and moustache were greying but his eyes were clear blue, like Edmond's.

'It will be a proud day for us,' Amy's mother said.

'If only there was time for a little more reflection,' Edmond's mother said, fingering her amethyst necklace. 'They're both still very young.' Her light blue eyes focussed on Amy, regarding her critically, as though she was a disappointment.

'I'm liable to be sent to the Front in the summer!' Edmond reminded them. 'We deserve some time together first. And if I'm old enough to serve my country I'm surely old enough to choose my bride and wed her.' He spoke without hesitation. How resolute he could be. She supposed this was how he had presented the news to his parents.

'It's the way young people come together now,' Mr Derwent said. 'It's harder to accept a long engagement.'

'But Edmond's still a student!' his mother reminded them.

'It's not ideal,' Edmond admitted. 'I'd have preferred to have taken up a profession before marrying. But who knows how long that will take now? We want to be together.'

His father seemed prepared to accept his wishes with few reservations. More plans were made as they progressed from the soup to the roast beef, served with horseradish sauce and an array of vegetables. Edmond's parents offered the use of their house for the reception. Beatrice graciously accepted the invitation to be bridesmaid, providing the dressmaker was called in at an early stage to make her a suitable gown.

'Perhaps Amy has a friend or two she would like as brides-maids?' Edmond said.

'I should like to ask Florence,' she said, 'though of course I'm delighted Beatrice will be bridesmaid as well.'

Her future sister-in-law looked put out that she would need to share the distinction. Amy would have liked to invite Lavinia to be bridesmaid as well, but she was away training with the VAD and Amy could not be sure she would be able to get leave.

Edmond was at her side, asking her if she would like more vegetables but she could barely eat what was on her plate. The dining room was lined with wooden panels, making it gloomy. Were it not for having him beside her she would have preferred to be at home, eating a less lavish meal in a more relaxed atmosphere.

'In time we'll find a home of our own,' he was promising her. 'It will probably be quite small, at least at first. But while I'm serving in the army we'll stay here. Ma and Pa have agreed I can have a larger room and we'll have everything ready for the summer.'

To live with him in a little house of their own – what more could she wish for in life? But it would not be possible, for a while at least.

At last dessert was eaten and they went through to the dining room to be served coffee. Beyond the window, the grounds stretched damply between the bare trees. The afternoon was not sufficiently fine to make a walk an attractive prospect.

'Amy, may I show you our conservatory?' Edmond said.

'I'd love to see it,' she replied.

The others seemed content for him to lead her through to the glazed indoor area at the front of the house, with its orange trees and miniature palms.

He took her in his arms and kissed her tenderly, then brought a tiny box from his pocket. 'I bought you this,' he told her. 'I hope you like it. We can have it adjusted if it isn't quite the right size.'

He took out a ring with garnets and tiny diamonds. She was speechless with delight. He reached for her left hand and eased it gently on to her finger.

'It's beautiful,' she told him breathlessly. It fitted well. 'Darling, it's a perfect choice.'

As they rejoined the others she kept looking at the dainty ring sparkling on her finger. How fortunate she was that he was as eager as she to marry. Edmond went to speak to his father and her parents about wedding arrangements. Amy wandered towards Beatrice and Mrs Derwent; she should make an effort to become closer to them.

'I suppose we'll have to accept Edmond's decision,' Amy overheard Beatrice say.

'Let's hope Peter finds a more suitable bride,' their mother said. Then they noticed Amy and fell silent.

She faltered at their words, feeling paralysed by dismay. Did Mr Derwent feel the same, she wondered. *It's as well Edmond has an older brother,* she thought. *His parents might have actually refused consent if he was the heir.*

She summoned all her resources to approach her future in-laws.

Mrs Derwent turned to her. 'Do you play the piano at all?' she managed. 'We have a good instrument here, for Beatrice is very talented.'

'I've had lessons and play a little,' she said. 'I shall love hearing Beatrice play.' *I must try to win their affection,* she thought, *for Edmond's sake.*

'Of course you will give up work before you're married,' Mrs Derwent said.

'I plan to continue in some kind of useful occupation,' Amy replied, for she was thinking of applying to join the VAD.

'We can't have you working!' exclaimed her future mother-in-law, her eyebrows rising towards her hairline. 'Women in this family don't work!'

Edmond came to Amy's side, to her great relief. 'It's all right, Ma,' he told her. 'Women are expected to work whenever possible now, to allow men to serve in the army. Haven't you read the papers?'

She referred the question to her husband, who agreed with Edmond, and that difficult issue was resolved.

As they left, Mr Derwent embraced her for a moment and the womenfolk exchanged a brief kiss on the cheek with her.

–

On Easter Sunday Amy and her family, including Bertie, who was on leave from his training, went to lunch at the vicarage. Uncle Arthur was vicar of St Stephen's, Larchbury's church. It was an old stone building, in which the better-off families, like the Derwents, had their own pews. Uncle kept a pony and trap to help him visit his more distant parishioners.

They joined Aunt Sophie and their son James in the dining room. The vicarage had large rooms with high ceilings and as usual it was chilly there. A vase of daffodils adorned the table. Aunt Sophie had light brown hair plainly arranged upon her head. She was quiet by nature but kind, and had taken an interest in Amy's aid to the Belgian refugees. She sliced the roast pork and served it.

Amy helped pass the gravy and vegetables.

'What a lovely ring!' Aunt Sophie exclaimed, seeing it sparkling on Amy's finger.

Soon after giving her the ring Edmond had explained he had used part of his legacy from his grandfather to buy it. 'I'm only a student and it wouldn't have seemed right to ask Pa to contribute,' he had told her. 'But one day I hope to be in a position to buy you some more valuable jewellery.'

She had assured him she was perfectly content with the lovely ring.

'I'm sorry Edmond couldn't get leave this weekend,' Uncle Arthur said now. He was shorter and stouter than Father and had an air of serenity suited to his calling. 'I shall be proud to officiate at the wedding.'

'We'd like James to be an usher, along with Bertie,' Amy said. James was her cousin, a plumpish lad of sixteen, who was sitting next to Bertie.

'I'd be honoured,' he said a little shyly.

'I gather you entertained the Derwents to lunch last weekend,' Amy's uncle said.

'It was rather a trial,' Mother admitted. 'We haven't got a cook like they have.'

'Your lunch was fine,' Amy assured her. 'Edmond loved your apple pie, didn't he?' He had had leave that weekend.

'He has perfect manners, your young man.'

Mr and Mrs Derwent had been polite but less effusive, and Beatrice had stayed away, apparently having a prior engagement. After the meal they had gone into the parlour, where a fire was blazing, but Edmond's parents had not stayed much longer.

'They have several servants at The Beeches, I gather,' said Aunt Sophie.

'Yes – I don't even know their names yet,' Amy said.

'It'll seem strange,' Mother said. 'We make do with Mrs Johnson.' She called in twice a week to help with the washing and cleaning.

Amy got on well with Mrs Johnson, giving her errands occasionally. Dealing with the half dozen or so servants the

Derwents kept might not be as straightforward. She needed to discover who was responsible for which task, and suspected there were approved ways of addressing them. Somehow she must manage to fit in with Edmond's family when she lived with them.

'And how are preparations going for the wedding?' her aunt asked next.

'Admirably,' Mother said. 'I'm making Amy's gown myself.' She had always been skilled with the needle, and the ivory silk was being transformed into a gorgeous dress. Mrs Derwent had belatedly enquired what Amy was to wear, offering the services of her dressmaker, if required. She had also insisted on having Florence's bridesmaid's dress made to match the one being worn by Beatrice, who had chosen a subtle pale green shade, a foil for her chestnut hair.

'Now, who'd like more meat and vegetables?' Aunt Sophie pressed second helpings on them. 'Bertie, I'm sure you can eat some more.'

He accepted gladly.

After lunch they went into the parlour, with its dark, old-fashioned furniture. Uncle Arthur began enquiring about Bertie's training. James was listening curiously as he mentioned their manoeuvres.

'I hope there's no more talk of general call-up,' James said. He had grey eyes like Bertie's and their fathers'. 'I, for one, would try to avoid fighting.'

'Not go and fight for your country if you were called on to do so?' Bertie asked in amazement. All the others were looking at James now.

'No, I don't believe I could bear to set out to kill men. There must be some way to find a peaceful solution.'

There was distaste now in Bertie's stare.

'You would place yourself in a very difficult position, if there was conscription,' Amy's father said sternly.

'I would have to make the stand.'

Amy felt sympathetic towards him. He wanted to oppose the warlike spirit which was taking over the country. He had principles, rather like the ones she had about universal suffrage.

'It would be a difficult situation,' Uncle Arthur said, an unfamiliar frown forming. 'The warmongering and hostility to our enemies is so much at odds with Christian principles. I was troubled when I needed to speak at the memorial service for John Spencer and it concerns me when I compose my sermons.'

Amy had been in his study once and knew it was well stocked with serious-looking books, many of them leather-bound, mostly on religious topics.

'You were very inspiring today,' Father told his brother.

'Well, yes, it's Easter, and the sermon was a timeless one of resurrection and new life.'

'As for the memorial, you have to honour a man who has given his life for his country.'

'Certainly. But I feel that we blundered into this war, scarcely aware of what lay ahead. I could not persuade any man to serve who was not determined to do so.'

The atmosphere had become sombre suddenly. 'I don't suppose it will come to conscription,' Amy's father said.

–

Edmond came on weekend leave in May and called for Amy on the Saturday afternoon. It was fine and they set out towards the brook. It was some time since she had seen him, though they wrote to each other regularly. She had sent him a cutting from the local paper, mentioning the spring picnic she and Florence had helped to run for the Belgian refugees.

'Only three weeks now to our wedding!' She could scarcely contain her excitement. 'They'll read the banns tomorrow morning.'

He looked at her seriously. 'Listen, dearest, I've been given my date for going to Flanders. It's the Monday after our wedding day.'

'Oh, darling.' She clung to his arm, devastated. 'That would give us so little time together before you leave – there must be something you can do. Ask them to give you an extra week's leave.'

'No, the whole unit has to travel together.'

Her delightful anticipation was blighted. 'I thought there'd be weeks of seeing each other regularly before you had to go abroad.' It seemed a vain hope now that the war might come to a quick conclusion.

'I'll have several days of leave before we set off. I thought we could ask your uncle if we can bring forward the wedding date to earlier in the week.'

'Yes, we must do that,' she said, a little relieved.

'Let's go round to the vicarage right away and see if he's at home,' Edmond said. 'Mother's on the brink of sending out the invitations.'

They headed along the High Street towards the church. A familiar shiny motor car was being driven fast along the street and she recognised Colonel Fairlawn at the wheel. He generally chose to drive himself rather than call upon his chauffeur.

'You would think that man has more to do at the War Office,' she said. 'This is the second weekend running I've seen him in the village.'

'He's trying to find players for the cricket team,' Edmond told her. 'It's awkward this year, with so many young men joining up.'

'I suppose so.'

'Listen, darling, if your uncle can change the wedding date I'll change the hotel booking too.' He had booked them into a hotel in London, and they had plans to visit the theatre, besides exploring the parks in the daytime.

'The important thing is to be with you for the little time we have,' she told him.

–

A few days before the wedding Edmond arrived home on leave and soon called on her. After a blissful embrace he encouraged her to pack some clothes and other belongings. The family chauffeur was waiting to take her luggage to The Beeches.

'You can arrange your things in my new room – our room, that is – ready for you after our honeymoon.'

'Yes, I must do that,' she said. It was an important stage in becoming his wife, even if she had reservations about living at The Beeches while he was serving abroad.

'Remember I told you I'd like to be a VAD? I've signed up!' she told him excitedly as the chauffeur drove them to her future home. There was still some resistance to allowing married women to work, so at the interview she had not worn her ring or mentioned her imminent wedding. She hoped to have made herself useful by the time they found out her status, so that they would do everything possible to keep her on.

'A VAD? If that's what you want, darling.' His smile had faded.

'They were surprised at work when I gave my notice, but on the whole they approved… You don't look happy about it.' She was suddenly concerned.

'I understand that you want to contribute to the war effort,' he said. 'I just hope we can manage to get leave on the same dates.'

'Once you've gone abroad it seems an appropriate thing for me to do, nursing the injured.'

'I suppose you're right.'

She did not like to tell him that her resolve to serve her country was increased by the possibility that nursing might involve living away from The Beeches. Her office job would have kept her out of his family home for most weekdays, but as she did not feel entirely welcome there, the chance of living elsewhere was appealing.

He still looked anxious. 'I don't imagine nursing is an easy life,' he said. 'I know you're not afraid of hard work, but you'd see some disturbing sights, tending men sent home from the Front.'

'I realise that.' *Am I really prepared to face soldiers with war wounds?* she asked herself. *Someone has to help them recover*, she thought, as they turned into the drive at The Beeches. *If Edmond has to fight, I can adapt to difficult circumstances too.*

Soon they were unpacking her belongings in Edmond's new room which, he told her, was considerably larger than his previous one. He had installed a gramophone on a table by the window.

'This room is lovely,' she said, admiring the view over the azaleas at one side of the garden.

A maid had come to help her unpack, *and perhaps also act as chaperone,* she thought, blushing at the sight of the double bed. Edmond opened the wardrobes – handsome pieces of furniture in walnut wood. His uniform and other clothes were hanging in the smaller one and he invited her to hang her clothes in the larger one. There was ample space.

The room was also furnished with a smart dressing table, with a fine set of china ornaments in a tray, including candle-sticks and dishes for trinkets. It was only when she began unpacking her books that she found anything lacking.

'There aren't enough shelves to take your books as well as mine,' Edmond said, moving out some of his from an alcove to accommodate hers. His books remained stacked on the table. 'We need some more shelves. Where are your gramophone records?'

'Oh, goodness, I haven't sorted through them yet.'

'Perhaps when you bring them we can put them with our ones downstairs,' he said. 'If only there was more time.'

'I don't want to waste much of your leave packing.'

He caught hold of her and kissed her, regardless of the maid. 'They plan to send VADs to Flanders, don't they?' he said, brightening.

'I believe you have to complete a year of service before they send you abroad,' she said. She still hoped the war would be over before then, but if not, there would be the prospect of travelling to Flanders to be near him.

Chapter Seven

Amy's wedding was now arranged for the Thursday of that week.

'Is Lavinia coming?' Florence asked when she reached Amy's house in good time that morning.

'No, she couldn't get leave.' In spite of that one disappointment, Amy was tingling with anticipation. She led Florence up to her bedroom, her comfortable little domain, with its chintz bedspread and curtains. Somehow she preferred it to the new room with velour curtains and damask bedspread at The Beeches.

The bridal gown and bridesmaids' dresses were hanging in her room, and the girls stripped down to their underwear. Soon Beatrice arrived, with a maid. She had been driven there by the family chauffeur, who would now return to the house to transport Edmond and his parents to the church, along with Charles Shenwood, who was best man.

'Did Bertie manage to get leave?' Florence asked.

'Yes.' He and her mother would set out to walk to the church, before the Derwent motor car returned for Amy, her father and her attendants.

Beatrice paraded in front of the mirror in her pale green gown. She had an excellent figure and was taller than the others.

She allowed the maid to put the finishing touches to her hair and its flowery ornament. Then the young woman offered to help Florence and arrange the bride's veil.

When the maid had finished, Amy looked in the long mirror. She could scarcely recognise herself in the ivory gown with its lace trimming.

'You look beautiful,' Florence told her.

Beatrice nodded and smiled.

Mother squeezed into the bedroom. 'Now don't forget to make the most of the opportunity to meet Edmond's other relatives,' she said.

'Yes, of course.' Amy knew that was important, but she felt as if she were in a dream, scarcely able to think of anything but Edmond. *I hope he likes my dress,* she thought. *I feel sure he will.*

'I'm so happy for you, darling!' Mother said, embracing and kissing Amy. They had been disappointed that Uncle Harold's health was deteriorating and so Aunt Louisa could not come to see Amy wed.

Mother carefully put on her new flowery hat and went down to set off with Bertie.

Florence was looking through the window. 'The car's back!'

They went downstairs and picked up their dainty bouquets of creamy roses. Amy's father, smart in his new suit, held her arms as he gazed at her, then bent to kiss her. 'You're every bit as lovely as your mother was on her wedding day.'

As they went outside, Amy's dress looked dazzling in the bright sun. Beatrice's maid accompanied them to the car and helped the young women in.

'I'm worried our gowns will be crushed,' Beatrice said, as the three of them settled in the back.

'But you're all slim, Miss Beatrice, and it's only a short distance.'

Father stepped into the front and the chauffeur drove off towards the church.

'My parents have arranged for a photographer to come to The Beeches to take a picture of the wedding group later,' Beatrice babbled.

In a few minutes the service will begin, Amy thought breathlessly. *The organist will play the anthem and Edmond will look round to see me.* She had moved her engagement ring to the other hand to make it easier for him when the time came to place the simple gold wedding band on her finger.

The car stopped outside the church and they alighted. In the porch, Bertie and James were acting as ushers, greeting guests. As she placed her arm in that of her father, she was aware of people approaching. Through her wispy veil she noticed a policeman heading towards her. Still elated, she smiled at him, though curious why he might be there.

'Miss Fletcher, I believe I have something of yours,' Constable Swift said, showing her a small item.

Peering through her veil she saw her fountain pen, the one with her name engraved on it, that she had lost some time before.

'Goodness, it's finally turned up! Thank you so much. Do you know where it was found?' She reached out to take it but the constable held on to it.

'In the cricket pavilion. In a crack in the wooden flooring.' He spoke as though its discovery had some special significance.

For a moment its reappearance seemed irrelevant, a minor incident on her wedding day. Then her heart seemed to flutter as the implications became clear. She noticed someone else approaching. The towering figure of Colonel Fairlawn loomed ahead.

'Do you have any explanation for how your pen might be in the cricket pavilion?' his voice boomed.

She felt herself swaying, and Florence catching her arm.

'What's all this fuss?' Father demanded angrily. 'My daughter is about to get married. Can we continue these enquiries afterwards?'

'It's not as simple as that, Sir,' said the constable. 'Unless Miss Fletcher can give some innocent account of being in the cricket pavilion, we will have to assume she was with the Suffragettes who broke in last summer.'

Father gasped. 'Why were you in the pavilion, Amy?'

She could not provide an innocent reason.

'If you have no explanation you will have to face the charges of breaking and entering and criminal damage, Miss.'

She felt her face flush with guilt and embarrassment 'Very well,' she said, trembling and anxious for the ceremony to begin. 'When and where should I report? I give you my word I will attend.'

'The court is in session this morning. You are to come before the magistrate straight away.' It was then that she noticed the police vehicle waiting at the side of the road, next to the car in which she had just arrived.

'But – I can't! I'm getting married. My future husband is in the church, waiting.'

'We can't make any exceptions,' snarled Colonel Fairlawn. 'It's especially important, now we're at war, that this kind of appalling behaviour is punished. We have to make a firm stand.'

'This is completely unacceptable,' her father tried to protest.

'Will you come quietly, please, Miss?' the constable urged. 'I don't want to have to restrain you.' She thought she saw a flicker of sympathy on his freckled face.

'Let me come too,' Father said. 'I'm sure there's an innocent explanation.'

'That's not possible, I'm afraid, Sir. We'll be at the courtroom. It's only just down the road.'

Tears began running down Amy's face. She handed her bouquet to Florence, pulled off her veil and handed her that as well, then allowed the constable to lead her to the police vehicle. Scarcely believing what was happening she got in, smoothing out the skirt of her bridal gown. The constable got in beside her. As the driver set off she caught sight of Beatrice standing in her fine dress and staring at her, eyes wide with horror.

Edmond's waiting for me, she thought frantically. *I'm supposed to be in church.*

It took only a few minutes to reach the courtroom, which was further down the High Street. The old wooden-beamed building had been used for a century or more as a magistrates' court for Larchbury and the surrounding smaller villages. Constable Swift led her into a small office. 'Just sit down here, Miss.'

A young man explained that he was clerk to the court. 'There's another case on at the moment but we don't expect it to last long,' he said, before leaving the room.

The constable sat on a nearby chair. Amy tried to stop crying. What was she to do?

It's Colonel Fairlawn, she thought. *With his superior position in society he thinks he can orchestrate this. He's an alderman, and with his blustering manner he can bully the police to do his bidding. He sometimes serves as a magistrate, too. How dreadful if he's my judge! He wants to humiliate me. Very probably he's one of those men who believe Suffragettes to be unfeminine.*

The clerk came back. 'Your father would like the case postponed so you can consult a solicitor,' he said. 'Would you like me to ask for an adjournment, or to go ahead and have the matter settled quickly?'

Should they consult Florence's father, the local solicitor? She could hardly deny she had been part of the incident.

'I'd like it settled quickly.' She must plead guilty, accept the fine she imagined they would impose, and trust there was still time for the wedding to go ahead that day.

But how awful all this is for Edmond, she thought. *Thank goodness I told him what I did, and he didn't seem to mind. But Mother and Father will be upset, and whatever will the Derwent family think?*

She was aware of a buzz of conversation outside and then the clerk asked her to go through to the courtroom. The constable led her into the dock. She heard a gasp from the few spectators in the public gallery, and shrank at the sight of the three magistrates gazing at her from the bench, though at least Colonel Fairlawn was not one of them. What a sight she must look, standing there in her wedding gown.

Now more people were filing into the public gallery. There was her beloved Edmond, smart in his uniform but white-faced. He nodded to her, looking concerned but not angry. Father and Mother and Bertie followed him, then Florence, still clutching two bouquets, then came Uncle Arthur, Aunt Sophie and James. Mr Derwent and Charles Shenwood followed them in. There could seldom have been a better-dressed group witnessing a court case, even though there was no sign of Mrs Derwent or her daughter.

Colonel Fairlawn came into the court and sat down to one side of the bench, apparently there in some kind of official capacity.

The chairman of the bench was a sober elderly man who was an alderman, and ran a business locally. She thought he had attended the ball at The Beeches. Mr Brownlee, the auctioneer, was also on the bench, along with a younger man she did not recognise.

The chairman read out the charges. She was accused of breaking into the cricket pavilion and criminal damage. The clerk passed her a copy of the Bible and made her take the oath to tell *the truth, the whole truth and nothing but the truth.*

I can hardly lie now, she thought, *even if I could think of a convincing falsehood.*

'Amy Maud Fletcher, do you plead guilty or not guilty?'

She found herself clenching her fists, still enclosed in their lacy gloves. 'I – well, I personally did not break into the pavilion, but I accompanied other women into the building.'

'Guilty,' said the chairman.

There was a gasp from the gallery. It sounded like her mother.

'I wrote some slogans in chalk but I did not use paint.'

'Guilty.'

She turned her head briefly to glance towards the gallery. Her mother was dabbing her eyes with a handkerchief and her father looked shocked, but Edmond was smiling at her as though to encourage her. Florence looked pale and seemed to be trying not to cry.

Now Colonel Fairlawn was called to the witness box. He elaborated on the damage, and the cost of replacing the glass in the door and removing the painted slogans. At last he finished.

'So if you did not break into the pavilion yourself, who did?' asked the chairman of the bench sternly.

She drew a breath. She simply must not implicate Lavinia. 'I am not prepared to say, Sir.'

There was a kind of snort from the colonel.

'And then you assisted in defacing the pavilion?'

'Yes, Sir.'

'You think this is an appropriate way to behave while our country is at war?'

She was trembling as she sought the right words. 'With respect, Sir, this took place last summer, before war was declared. The Suffragette movement has suspended acts of civil disobedience now.'

'Hummph! Have my colleagues any questions to ask?'

'Are you in sympathy generally with the views of the Suffragettes?' asked Mr Brownlee.

She paused. Would she dare uphold her views in these circumstances? 'I believe women should have the vote,' she replied as steadily as she could. 'But I very much regret my foolish actions on the day in question. I am planning to help the war effort. I have been accepted to become a VAD.'

She thought he looked more sympathetic than the chairman.

'I believe we have a character witness for the accused,' said the chairman.

She breathed a little more easily as her uncle came forward, climbed into the witness box and took the oath.

'Well, Reverend Fletcher?'

'My niece is of previous good character,' he said. His voice was clear and authoritative, the way he sounded when he led a service. 'As she pointed out, the offence took place before the outbreak of war. She is planning to be a VAD and has also been helping the Belgian refugees. There was an article in the local paper recently about a picnic she helped to arrange for them.'

'Thank you, Vicar. The bench will now consider the case.'

Amy was led out of the courtroom back into the office. The clerk brought her a glass of water. She felt exhausted. How could the prank from last summer have rebounded into her life at the worst possible moment? Would they still be able to hold the wedding today or would they need to try to rearrange it for tomorrow or even Saturday? *How dreadful it will be if the reception has to be postponed,* she thought – *will the Derwents ever forgive me? And all the guests will know what I did…*

Within a few minutes she was called back into court. The colonel was sitting in his same position as the magistrates returned.

The chairman remained standing. 'We have formed the opinion that we must take a firm stand on this case,' he said. 'While acknowledging the culprit's expression of regret and determination to serve her country, we must make it clear that this kind of criminal activity is completely unacceptable. Calling it civil disobedience does not excuse it.'

How Amy hated the colonel's gloating expression.

'This court imposes a fine of twenty-five pounds and sentences Amy Fletcher to serve a week in jail.'

There was a gasp, and she heard Edmond shout, 'No!'

Amy gripped the edge of the dock, the sentence ringing in her ears, though it seemed beyond belief. She thought the other members of the bench looked less resolute than their chairman.

'Please!' she said. 'Please allow me to serve the sentence in a week or two, so I may be married! My fiancé is to set off for Flanders on Monday.'

'The sentence is to be carried out right away,' the chairman said.

She swayed and Constable Swift caught her arm. He led her down the steps from the dock to the cell beneath.

The room was dark and stuffy and she felt faint.

'Bear up, Miss! It's only for a week.'

'But I'll miss my wedding!'

He unlocked the door at the other side of the cell. 'Come along, Miss.' He led her through the yard to the street and back into the police car. Passers-by began to stare. The sun was still shining from a perfect blue sky as though nothing was amiss.

'Where are you taking me?'

'Holloway.'

'But – at least let me change out of this dress.'

'They'll give you a prison gown when you get there.'

Then she saw Edmond running into the street. 'Darling, I love you!' he was crying as they drew away.

Tears were coursing down her cheeks as though they would never stop.

Chapter Eight

London, June 1915

The police car took her to London, to a dingy suburb where they drove to the forbidding gates of the high-walled prison. The gates opened to admit them and she was led across a courtyard and inside the building.

'Blimey – were you on your way to a ball or something?' A harsh-faced woman in uniform inspected her.

Constable Swift handed over her papers. 'Suffragette,' he remarked.

'Oh – well at least she probably won't have lice.' She led Amy away into a grim room with little daylight and took some garments from a shelf. 'Just get into these.' She folded her arms and waited.

Amy realised she was meant to change her clothes in front of her. She remembered hearing that Suffragettes were systematically humiliated in jail.

It was impossible to change into the coarse prison clothes without letting her bridal dress trail onto the floor. Afterwards, she folded it as tidily as possible and handed it to the warder, who looked at it curiously before cramming it unceremoniously into a bag and attaching a label with her name on. A fresh tear ran down Amy's face.

'I'd better look after that ring for you.' Reluctantly, Amy handed over her garnet and diamond engagement ring to be locked in a box.

The warder led her along a foul-smelling gangway. At length she was let into a cell and the door slammed behind her. The key grated in the lock.

The cell was dim and hot. It had two metal beds, though there was no other occupant. Amy collapsed on to the lumpy mattress of the nearest bed, emotionally drained.

No other punishment could be so dreadful, she thought. *I've missed my wedding and it's all my own fault. Edmond will go to the Front and Heaven knows when I'll see him again. He could even be killed.*

What if I'd told them it was Lavinia who broke in and used the green paint? Would they have been less harsh — would I have avoided jail? But it didn't seem right, betraying another member of the movement, one of my friends.

The fine's not so bad. I can just afford to pay it from what I've saved from my earnings, though it's taken me over a year to amass that much. I meant to use the money to help set up home with Edmond.

And what of my parents? What will they think of me now?

What will Edmond's family think? They thought I wasn't good enough for him before this happened. They were dressed in their fine clothes, waiting to admit me to their family. They weren't expecting a jailbird. They'd prepared a banquet and invited dozens of guests. Everyone will hear about my disgrace.

Edmond, my beloved, I'd do anything to turn back the clock. I should never have joined the Suffragettes.

Her head ached as she reviewed her principles and the options she had faced.

But we deserve to have the vote, she thought. *I was right to be part of the campaign. But I should have left the protest when Lavinia suggested that provocative action, that's what I should have done. I can't bear having ruined our wedding day.*

—

By evening the cell was brighter as the sun now faced it, shining between the iron bars. She turned round at the sound of the hatch in the door opening. A plate with bread and a scrap of cheese was passed through, with a tin mug of tea. She had not eaten since breakfast but could only manage a little of the stale bread.

At last the sun was sinking lower. She took off her top clothes, crawled between the straw mattress and rough sheet, and tried to sleep.

Eventually she must have dozed off. She awoke in darkness, aching from the uncomfortable bed, and remembered where she was. There were voices outside her door.

She was suddenly alert. *Have they come to release me?* she wondered. *Have they decided the sentence was unjust?* The key sounded in the lock and a shaft of light was visible.

There were angry protests as another woman was pushed inside. Goodness, Amy had scarcely ever heard such language, especially from a woman. As the door was locked again the hatch opened and there was light again momentarily.

'Try to get into your bed without disturbing the other prisoner,' came the voice of the warder.

Obscenities rang round the cell and Amy saw the vague shape of her new companion, lurching on to the other bed. She had the impression the woman was not much older than herself. The hatch was closed and the room was dark again.

'For Chrissakes!' her cellmate ranted. 'Do they think I ain't tried to get an honest job? Once they know you ain't respectable no one will take you on and you're back on the streets again.'

Amy noticed the smell of alcohol now. 'It's the men what cause all the bother,' her companion went on. 'It's all Stan's fault – he put me on the street in the first place when we couldn't pay the rent, and he makes me stay there. He gets all the money and I get roughed up by the men and belted by Stan if I ain't earned enough.'

Amy tried to close her ears as the woman mentioned Stan again and another man and said what she would like to do to them.

If only she'd stop I might get some sleep again, she thought.

After a while the woman fell silent. *She's one of those lost women who walks the streets,* Amy thought. She had heard stories about their lives of degradation, and occasionally she and her close friends had speculated on what life must be like for such a person. Usually they had moved on swiftly to a more wholesome topic of conversation, for it was barely respectable even to contemplate such subjects.

Now the woman was starting up again, rambling incoherently about the evil men she knew. Amy pulled the thin pillow over her ears, reducing the volume and making the words less distinct. At last she made out snores from the other bed. It was not how she had imagined spending her wedding night.

–

The remaining hours of darkness were soon over and there were noises outside. Amy's cellmate was still snoring. Amy felt stiff and her mind would not stop reviewing the events of the previous day. She clenched her fists, still furious with herself for causing her own downfall.

Bread and tea arrived and her companion woke up and grabbed her breakfast. She sat at the small table while Amy perched on her bed, scared to approach her cellmate.

'Here, you,' the woman said, 'was I loud when I came in last night? I'd had a skinful, but trust me, I needed it.' She was plump, with lank light brown hair, and smelled as though she had not washed recently. 'What are you in here for?' she went on curiously.

'I'm a Suffragette,' Amy said.

'Oh, my gawd. Do you and your mates think you can do any good? Mind you, we could do with someone standing up for women. Don't suppose you'll ever make things right for people like me, though.'

Something with a lot of legs scuttled across the stone floor.

'I know there's lots of injustice in the world,' Amy said, thinking of the unreasonable power wielded by Colonel Fairlawn. 'What's your name?'

'Polly.'

'I'm Amy.' She was appalled by her cellmate's way of life but curious just the same. She listened compulsively as Polly gave a rambling account of her daily life.

'It was that first fellow what got me into trouble that began it all,' she said. 'I had me little boy and the man scarpered. Me and me kid and me mum, we can't afford to live if I don't do the job.'

A jug of cold water was delivered and Amy washed as best she could. Polly splashed her face absentmindedly.

Amy's day stretched ahead mercilessly – and not just one day, but a whole week.

Before long, there were footsteps outside and another warder unlocked the door. 'Polly Carter, we've got a different cell for you.'

'Oh, for Chrissakes.' Polly lurched to her feet and shuffled to the door.

'Sorry you were made to share with this coarse woman,' the warder said to Amy.

'Goodbye, Polly,' she said, not wanting to appear unkind, though relieved she would not have to spend more time with her. Would she have another companion, with a similar background? If only she could be placed with another Suffragette, but they had given up civil disobedience now, so it would only happen if another unfortunate was belatedly caught for a crime from a year or so earlier.

The cell was quiet now, but her thoughts were oppressive. Then the warder came back and moved her to a cell where she could be in solitary confinement. 'You won't have to share with a street woman,' she said, apparently having taken pity on Amy.

The new cell was darker and even smaller than the first, with only one bed.

'Is it possible to have something to read?' she asked, desperate for diversion.

'What do you think this is, a public library? Tell you what, I'll see if there's an old newspaper one of the staff has finished with.'

When the warder brought a plate of thin stew for her lunch there was also a two-day old newspaper. The stew was fatty and unappetising. When she had eaten what she could, Amy turned her attention to the war news with more than usual interest.

–

The weekend seemed interminable. Amy found herself compulsively counting the bricks on the wall.

Edmond will be preparing to leave, she thought desperately. *If only he'd write to me. Do people get mail in here?*

84

What about visitors? I feel sure he'll have tried to get to see me – perhaps it's hard to visit at short notice?

Sometimes her thoughts turned to Polly. She was forced now to think of the hideous lives some other women lived. The woman had made mistakes, but the abuse she had suffered upset Amy. Her lack of means to extricate herself from her problems made it all the worse.

She had read almost every page of the newspaper, except the casualty list. On the entertainment page she had found a favourable review of the play being performed at the London theatre she and Edmond had planned to visit, compounding her frustration.

–

By Monday morning she heard the sound of rain dripping outside and the air was fresher. *Edmond will be setting off with his comrades*, she thought, *off to Flanders*. Her tears flowed freely. *I've only got three more days here now,* she realised, *but when they let me out it'll be too late.*

She had stared at the wall ahead for so long that she could visualise the rows of bricks with her eyes closed.

A warder she had not seen before arrived next morning with some letters for her. 'One of these arrived on Friday,' she admitted. 'We lost track of which cell you were in.'

She was angry as she snatched the envelopes, though it was true she had been moved. She recognised Edmond's handwriting on two of them and ripped open the one with the earlier postmark.

My darling Amy, she read.

It's terrible the way they treated you. I hate Colonel Fairlawn for making an example of you. As you know, I understand what you did.

85

I admire you for refusing to give them the names of other women who were there.

I am worried about how they are treating you in jail.

I can't describe how wretched I am that our wedding was prevented and we will not see each other before I leave for Flanders.

As soon as possible I'll get leave so we can be married.

Yours forever, Edmond

She clutched his letter, feeling brighter just from reading his tender words. She turned to the other letter. It was a brief note of farewell.

I'm off to Flanders tomorrow, darling. If only they'd let me wait for your release. I must make the best of the situation and try to serve my country bravely.

I promise to write regularly. Please write to tell me all your news.

Please God it isn't long till we're together again.

Now her spirits were failing anew. She remembered how long the list of casualties had been in the newspaper she had been reading.

The other letter was from her father. He wished her sentence had not been so harsh. He had been anxious about how she would get home when she was released, for he could not take a day off work. However, Uncle Arthur had now offered to come to London and escort her home.

Father doesn't actually condemn what I did, she thought, *but I can tell he was hurt at discovering my guilt. Edmond doesn't say what his family think either. They're bound to be horrified.*

I must write to the Derwents, and say how sorry I am for all the trouble I've caused. I'm not sure they'll ever forgive me but they deserve an apology. Will they give me pen and paper to write a letter here in jail? Even if they do, I don't trust the warders to post it. I'd better leave it till I'm released.

There was nothing for it but to leave jail in her wedding dress, to the hilarity of those of the staff she passed on the way out. As they opened the gate for her what a relief it was to see Uncle Arthur's solid figure waiting nearby.

He rushed to embrace her. 'My poor Amy! Are you all right?'

'Yes, Uncle. I suppose Edmond left as planned?'

'Yes, there was nothing he could do to delay his departure. Your parents went to see him off at Larchbury station. They said he looked very smart.'

She wiped away the tears which insisted on falling. Somehow she had hoped for a miracle, some way they could still be wed before he left.

'Your mother's sent you some clothes to change into,' he told her, passing her a Gladstone bag as they headed for the nearest underground station.

'Thank goodness! Do you think there'll be a convenience at the underground station where I can change?'

'I don't know, dear. There'll be one when we get to the mainline station.'

The Ladies' at important mainline stations were well maintained, she had found in her limited visits to London. In any case, who was she to worry, now she had experienced the squalor of a prison cell? How she longed to take a bath and wash her hair. She contented herself with taking a jacket from the bag and putting it on over her dress.

'Thank you for speaking up for me in court, Uncle.'

'You didn't deserve to be treated so severely.' His voice was gentle. 'I so wish I could have persuaded them not to send you to jail.'

'Is everyone very angry with me?' she asked him as their underground train clattered through the tunnel.

'Your parents were shocked and disappointed at first. Edmond and Bertie were quite effective at talking them round, though, and James understands how you feel.'

'The Derwents – I dread facing them.' She fiddled with her engagement ring, newly restored to her.

'They've taken it badly, I'm afraid, though Edmond is determined they will still accept you. Your father told me that while they were seeing him off they could sense something of an atmosphere. Mr Derwent said "Good day" to them but his wife and daughter shunned them.'

Poor, dear Edmond. The effect on him was what upset her most.

Chapter Nine

Larchbury, Summer 1915

When Uncle accompanied her back from the station, Amy attracted curious glances from some of the neighbours. *What a disgrace I've become*, she thought.

She walked into her home, where Mother greeted her, neat as ever in a blue cotton dress. She was anxious to hear that Amy was well, though her manner seemed distant. Her uncle soon went on his way.

'There's a letter for you.' Mother passed the envelope, which had come from France. Amy ripped it open to read Edmond's news. He and his comrades were settling into their camp, a few miles from the Front. *He's so far away now*, she thought.

Mother was unusually tongue-tied as she served Amy a large portion of steak and kidney pudding, which she fell on gratefully.

After her first greedy mouthfuls, she felt awkward. 'I don't smell, do I?' she asked.

'No. But you've only yourself to blame for getting in such a predicament,' Mother said sharply.

Bleakly, Amy continued eating. If only her parents would at least try to understand. As for Bertie, he was away, training.

Mother brought her a cup of tea. 'We did consider visiting you,' she said, milder now. 'It seemed difficult to arrange in the short time.'

She was thankful Mother had not witnessed her degradation in the prison. 'I didn't expect you to come,' she said. 'I was only there for a week… May I have some hot water for a bath?'

'Yes, I'll see to it.'

As soon as she could, Amy washed her hair and enjoyed scrubbing herself clean.

Later in the afternoon a knock came at the door and there was Florence. The two girls hugged. 'What you've been through!' her friend said, her soft hazel eyes fixing on Amy.

Mother offered them some tea, and the girls went into the garden, which allowed them to talk privately. They settled in deckchairs, though a wind had sprung up and the sky was darkening, threatening a storm.

'I felt so guilty,' Florence said. 'I was at the demonstration too – I ought to have owned up.'

'You didn't come inside the pavilion or write any slogans,' Amy said.

'You were meant to be Mrs Derwent by now,' Florence said as Mother came out and poured them some tea. 'You should be living at The Beeches.'

Mother went back indoors.

'There's no question of going there now. What must they think of me? I've caused them so much embarrassment and trouble, however unintentionally, with the way the wedding had to be cancelled.'

'At least Edmond will stick by you, and Bertie, of course.'

'On Monday week I'm to report at Wealdham hospital to begin my VAD training. I'm impatient to start now.'

'Was it very horrid in jail?'

'I wouldn't recommend it.' She was trying to decide whether to tell Florence about Polly when it started to rain and they went back indoors and Mother joined them in the parlour. Amy sank into an easy chair: never before had she so appreciated her comfortable home.

Florence asked them for the latest news of Edmond.

Amy passed on what he had said in his letter; they could hear the great guns now. They were becoming accustomed to life in their camp, but as yet had not been involved in any action.

'Bertie said he might be sent to Flanders soon,' Florence said. 'Have you heard any more, Mrs Fletcher?'

'No – he's impatient to go, of course.' Amy's mother looked more careworn than she could remember.

When Florence had left, Amy wrote to Edmond. Besides the limited news of his movements he had assured her how much he was missing her. Now she thanked him for the letter and the ones she had received in jail. She told him how much she longed to see him again, but words seemed inadequate.

If only I hadn't missed the chance to be fully yours before you left, she wrote.

Soon Father was home and it was time for their evening meal. 'Can you forgive me for the trouble I've caused you?' she asked her parents.

'I never expected to have a daughter who went to jail,' Mother said reproachfully.

Shame swept over her. 'If only I hadn't taken part in that stupid prank!' she said. 'Did anyone say anything about it at the school, Father?'

'Some of the other teachers were shocked,' he told her. Mainly the older ones, she guessed. 'A few support the movement for universal suffrage, but there's little sympathy for women who take direct action.'

'So long as I haven't made life difficult for you,' she said. She supposed his years of respected teaching would save him from any harsh reaction.

She put down her knife and fork. 'I still support the cause,' she told them, hoping that one day they would recognise its importance.

'Bertie stood up for you,' Father told her, though he still sounded unconvinced.

If only she had stayed outside the pavilion and simply written a slogan or two in chalk, she thought. She could have expressed her views but there would have been far less chance of arrest.

'Mrs Derwent was very put out,' Mother told her. 'Imagine how she felt, calling off the wedding because the bride was in custody! She remained dignified as she told the guests the ceremony could not take place, but I could tell she was seething.'

Tears filled her eyes. Edmond's family had disliked her from the start: how must they feel now? She got up and left the room.

Once in her bedroom she gave way to sobs. How could she have compromised her future like that? But of course the incident had taken place just before she got to know Edmond.

How can I ever face the Derwents again? she thought. *I should simply accept that I'm not worthy of them, or of Edmond, give him back his ring and try to make some kind of life without him.*

For a moment it seemed the only way ahead, but remembering their tender moments, the prospect of losing him made her feel as though a shaft was piercing her heart.

Gradually she became calmer. *He doesn't want me to give him up*, she reassured herself. *He's been supportive. All his letters say he's determined to still marry me as soon as he can obtain leave.*

She wiped her eyes, reached for her writing paper and wrote a simple letter to Mr and Mrs Derwent. In it, she expressed her

92

heartfelt regret at what had taken place on what should have been her wedding day. She hoped they and Beatrice would in time be prepared to forgive her for all the trouble she had caused.

She wondered whether to deliver the letter by hand to The Beeches, but fearing a hostile reception, she dropped it into the pillar box, along with the letter to Edmond.

On Sunday she went to church with her family, noticing stares from Miss Miller and other acquaintances. Just before the service began, the Derwents walked past to their pew near the front, without glancing in her direction. Had they received her letter, she wondered, as beams of light streamed through the narrow windows, tinted red and gold from the stained glass. *Just over a week ago I should have been here getting married,* she thought. *It ought to have been the happiest day of my life. How different my situation is now!*

She was scarcely aware of Uncle's sermon. After the service, Edmond's family were among the first to leave. Would they greet her as they passed her pew or linger outside to speak to her? Beatrice walked past, pausing only to fling her a poisonous look. Mrs Derwent, wearing a large hat decorated with an abundance of artificial flowers, swept past without acknowledging her. Only Mr Derwent looked towards her and nodded politely. By the time Amy left church, their motor car was drawing away.

That afternoon Amy retreated to her room. Never had she felt so desperate. Edmond had been supportive in his letters, but was he simply acting out of loyalty? Now his family were disgusted with her and most of their friends and relatives had learnt what had happened.

She picked up her pen, the fatal pen bearing her name, now returned from the police, and began writing to Edmond.

I don't expect you to stick by me after what happened, she wrote. *You're close to your family, and enjoy a comfortable life with them. I don't want to ruin your life. You'll be better off without me.* She broke off and laid down her pen.

Wait, how could I be so foolish? she thought. *He says he still loves me and wants to marry me. Yes, but when he's had time to reflect on what's happened he'll change his mind. I should let him go, without any fuss.*

She went back to her letter.

So just forget about me, she wrote, *and find yourself a decent girl of your own class, who won't give you any trouble.*

She dabbed at the tear that had fallen on her letter.

I'll always love you. I remember our times together, respect you and wish you every happiness.

Yours, Amy

She folded the paper and reached for an envelope, but on the brink of inserting it, she hesitated.

He says he still loves me, she reminded herself. *How will he feel receiving this letter when he's facing danger in Flanders?*

She gripped the paper and screwed it into a ball. *I simply can't send that,* she decided.

She began a fresh letter.

Darling, she wrote, *you say you love me and still want to marry me, but are you certain, after all that's happened? I can't hold you to your promise. If you've any doubts I'll release you from the engagement.*

She continued much as before, urging him not to stick with her if it would ruin his life, and completed the letter wishing him future happiness.

He loves me, she told herself desperately. *He'll write back quickly, assuring me that we are to be married. But if he has any doubts – even though I'll be miserable for the rest of my days, I'll release him.*

94

She put the letter in its envelope, slipped out to the pillar box and posted it.

She did not tell anyone what she had done, waiting for his reply. Would he reaffirm his love in spite of everything? she wondered. She convinced herself that he must still care for her.

If she received a letter from him quickly it would have been written before he received hers. Monday and Tuesday passed with no letter. Her spirits sank as more days passed without any word. He could be deciding how to reply, or simply ending their relationship without comment, relieved that she was releasing him from an unwelcome commitment. Then it occurred to her that he could even be injured or dead. Saturday began and she went for a long walk by the brook, trying to conceal her wretchedness from her family.

The week had passed without any contact from the Derwents. *But if Edmond was injured or dead they would have informed me,* she thought. *I'm sure Mr Derwent at least is decent enough to do that.*

In church on Sunday Edmond's family made their usual appearance, shunning her except for Mr Derwent's polite nod. Nothing untoward had happened to him, she decided; if it had it would be common knowledge by now. Her spirits lifted at this discovery: he was alive, that was all that mattered now.

–

The next day Amy reported for duty at the hospital, forcing herself to concentrate on making a fresh beginning. She was provided with a blue dress and a white apron and cap to wear. 'Matron wishes to speak to you,' she was told.

She knocked on the office door and waited outside in the corridor, which smelt of carbolic. Soon the door opened and an unsmiling, grey-haired woman in a rigidly starched cap asked her to step inside.

'Miss Fletcher?'

'Yes, Matron.' She had had the impression that married women were less welcome as VADs. She had enrolled in her maiden name, meaning to delay mentioning her marriage until she was well established. Now at least she had no need to explain what had gone amiss.

'Sit down.' She sank onto a hard chair as Matron settled on one at the other side of a large desk, tidily piled with textbooks and paperwork, along with a newspaper.

'Are you the Miss Fletcher who was in the papers recently, admitting to criminal damage to a cricket pavilion?' Matron asked gravely.

Amy felt the blood drain from her face. Was she about to be dismissed from the VAD unit before she had even had the chance to begin work?

'I'm afraid that was me,' she said. 'The incident took place last summer, before war broke out, and I now bitterly regret my actions.'

The woman turned a penetrating gaze on her. 'There's no place for disobedience in the VAD service.'

'I understand that, Matron. I'm anxious to serve my country now and try to make amends.'

The woman consulted the newspaper. 'You spent a week in prison?'

'Yes, Matron, in Holloway.'

'Hmm.' The woman looked her up and down, apparently without finding anything out of place. 'I suppose one could say you've paid your debt to society. But we need to be very careful whom we employ.'

'I promise I'll obey all the rules.'

'I sincerely hope so, Miss Fletcher.' Her expression softened a little. 'I have a younger sister who has sympathies for the Suffrage movement… Well, I suppose we must give you a chance.'

'Thank you very much.'

'Make sure you do not give us any trouble. Don't make me regret my decision, or I will have to dismiss you.'

-

The first week there Amy worked harder than she could ever remember. Washing floors and making beds were tedious tasks and emptying bedpans was distasteful but she dared not complain, knowing that she was already under scrutiny. Occasionally she was shown how to do a more responsible task, like taking someone's temperature. Some patients were convalescing from war wounds, but it was not one of the main Army hospitals. She would need to complete her initial training and gain certificates in First Aid and Home Nursing before being sent to one of the major wartime hospitals.

Most evenings she reached home so tired that she did not stay up chatting to her parents. She fell asleep quickly and when she awoke it was time to get up again. There was only the dull pain of despair at losing Edmond, for it seemed increasingly likely that he had chosen to end all contact with her. Once Mother enquired if she had heard from him.

'Not lately,' she replied as calmly as possible.

'People are saying there's been hardly any mail from Flanders recently,' Mother said.

On Friday evening she alighted wearily from the train at Larchbury station and saw Mr Derwent stepping down from a first-class carriage. For a moment they exchanged glances, then he raised his bowler hat to her. She stood on the platform, wondering if he would speak to her. He carried on towards her, looking her up and down, seeming to approve of her VAD uniform.

'Good evening, Amy,' he said, stooping a little to speak to her.

'Good evening, Mr Derwent. Have you heard from Edmond lately?' she asked him desperately.

'Not for days, but a letter came this morning. He's still fine, in the reserve trenches.'

'Thank heavens — it's nearly two weeks since I heard.'

'Lots of families are without mail from Flanders,' he said as they continued along the platform. 'Did you hear about that ship that was sunk in the Channel?'

'Yes.' Even in her miserable state she had been shocked at the number of casualties.

'They say it was carrying a considerable amount of mail, especially as other transport delays had led to an accumulation at the port.'

'Oh! So there's a reason why I haven't heard.' She had to stop herself embracing him.

They reached the exit. 'Might I offer you a lift home, Amy?' he said unexpectedly. 'You look tired.' The chauffeur was waiting with the motor car.

She hesitated momentarily, then accepted. The chauffeur held the door open for her. She stepped in and settled on the comfortable leather seat as Mr Derwent sat down beside her.

'I had to spend the day in London on business,' he told her. 'There's considerable demand for timber in wartime.' The car drove off. 'Are you settling down to your training?'

'Yes, thank you.' Her tasks until now had been so basic that she could not claim to have learnt much, but she supposed she was completing the work more quickly than she had at first.

He was thoughtful. 'It was a bad business, that court case,' he said. 'Thank you for your letter.'

The familiar feeling of regret and shame at the interruption of her wedding resurfaced. 'I can't deny those foolish actions,' she told him, almost relieved that he was prepared to discuss it with her. 'I never dreamt it could disrupt the wedding. It's the biggest regret of my life.'

'It's the general opinion that you were dealt with somewhat harshly,' he admitted. 'But, as you can imagine, the sudden cancellation of the wedding caused a good deal of embarrassment and scandal. My wife was extremely angry after all the time and trouble she had spent organising the banquet.'

'I'm dreadfully sorry for spoiling it all, when you'd been so generous and she had made all the preparations.'

'Unfortunately Beatrice was also very put out. As bridesmaid she felt particularly mortified to see you arrested.'

She expressed her regret once again. She understood that she had subjected them to a series of humiliating events.

'You have some good friends, Amy. Did you see last week's local paper? A Mrs Rousser or some such name wrote a letter praising you for your efforts for the Belgians.'

'Oh – I haven't seen it.'

They stopped outside her house.

'It may take some time, but I'll work on the others,' he said. The chauffeur opened the door for her.

When she went inside there was at last a letter for her from France.

How could you write me such a foolish letter? Edmond wrote. *Of course I still love you. I don't hold it against you that the court made an example of you and sent you to jail. In time my family will accept what happened.*

Trust me, we'll be married as soon as I can get home leave. Nothing and no one will keep us apart.

–

A week later she was standing outside her home, not long after returning from the hospital, when she saw Bertie walking down the road with his kitbag. She ran to embrace him, home on leave for the weekend.

'What on earth's going on?' he asked, for the Derwents' car was parked outside their house. He stared as the chauffeur and Janet the maid unloaded luggage from the vehicle.

'It's my clothes and other belongings I had at The Beeches,' she said. Back in June she had taken them there ready for her wedding, and she had been wondering since how to reclaim them. She had had only a few of her older garments left at her parents' house. It mattered less about her top clothes now she was wearing uniform most days, but she still needed her better clothes and other possessions back.

'I spoke briefly to Mr Derwent after church on Sunday and he arranged for Janet to pack my things and bring them back.'

The front door was open as Bertie went in, and deposited his kitbag. There was the sound of an exuberant reunion with his parents. He came back to Amy just as Janet briskly unloaded the suitcase with the clothes she had packed for her honeymoon.

'That's all now, Madam,' the maid told her. Her expression was sympathetic.

'Thank you so much for returning everything,' she said.

The car set off.

'So, what about your wedding?' Bertie asked when he had helped carry her belongings inside.

'Edmond hopes to get leave in the autumn, so we can get married, by special licence if necessary.'

Bertie hugged her. 'Give me as much notice as you can, so I can try to be here.'

—

There was a knock at the door one Sunday afternoon. Mother answered it and Lavinia walked in.

'I hope you don't mind me calling,' she said. 'I'm on weekend leave from the VAD and I came over on the train. Is Amy here? I'm hoping to speak to her.' She was wearing a floral dress, rather than her uniform.

'We could sit in the garden,' Amy said. Her relations with her parents were almost back to normal now, but she would prefer to chat to Lavinia without them there. It was late July and the weather was warm.

'I'll bring you out some tea and shortbread,' Mother said.

Lavinia followed Amy out to the garden, where deck chairs were already placed on the lawn, facing the lofty pink hollyhocks.

'Are your family in mourning for someone?' Lavinia asked, for both Amy and her mother were wearing dresses in a subdued shade of mauve.

'My Uncle Harold has died,' she said. 'It wasn't a great shock as he's had poor health for years.' Her parents had attended the funeral and said Aunt Louisa was talking of moving away from Hove, perhaps to be near an old friend in London.

Amy shifted her chair as the sun had moved round. 'I'm in the VAD too now, have you heard?' she told her friend. 'I'm able to train at Wealdham now. But I'm not assigned to one of the major hospitals yet.' They were allowing her to change dressings now, under supervision.

'Amy, I had to see you,' Lavinia burst out. 'Florence told me what happened, how you were arrested for what we did last summer – and how your wedding was prevented.' She fastened her dark eyes on Amy in a look of sincere contrition. 'I've scarcely stopped thinking about it since. I blame myself for what happened. It was so brave of you not to give me away for my part in the break-in.'

'There's no point in both of us being punished.' She fell silent as Mother brought out the refreshments and set them on the small garden table.

When Mother had poured the tea and returned indoors Lavinia wanted to hear all the details of her ordeal in jail. Amy told her about Polly, for up to now she had not mentioned her cellmate to anyone. Mother would have been shocked to hear an account of the woman's life, and Florence might have been too.

'It's as I thought,' Lavinia said, putting down her teacup. 'There are poor women who lead dreadful lives as a consequence of one mistake.'

'You can imagine how pleased I was to be released, but I can't quite forget Polly.' Amy passed Lavinia the shortbread and took a piece herself.

'I can't forgive myself for being the cause of you missing your wedding,' Lavinia told her. 'Who'd have thought it would come to light on that particular day?'

'Don't blame yourself. no one could possibly have foreseen it.' Amy still awoke full of regrets each morning at how her happiness had been snatched away.

'Before the war started there was a tradition of welcoming fellow Suffragettes when they were released from jail,' Lavinia told her. 'They would take the woman to breakfast at the Savoy to celebrate her stand for the cause and generate publicity. I joined them one time and it was a great occasion.'

'I believe I did hear of that once.'

'I suppose everyone is too busy with war work to do that now.'

'I wouldn't have wanted it,' Amy assured her. 'I've caused so much embarrassment. The last thing I want is to draw attention to my spell in jail.' She told her friend how hostile Edmond's womenfolk had become.

'They'll forgive you soon, won't they?' Lavinia's flowery summer hat was perched over the loops of her glossy dark hair, which hung down a little further one side than the other.

'I hope so.'

'Let's hope you needn't wait too long.'

'Bertie may be sent abroad in a month or two. I'll have two men to worry about then. Did you know, when he's come home on leave recently he's been walking out with Florence.'

'She told me she'd been seeing him.'

'The two of them seem well-suited.' They had been for walks to some of local beauty spots she and Edmond had used to visit. Once when Amy was walking back from the station she had seen the couple dawdling towards her, holding hands and laughing. If their courtship continued she could not wish for a sweeter sister-in-law. All the same, Bertie seemed boyish still and she could not quite imagine him contemplating marriage.

'Tell me about the place where you're working now,' she asked Lavinia presently.

Her friend had been sent to an Army hospital in London. 'We receive wounded, sent back in ambulance trains,' she said. 'The work's gruelling: you can't allow yourself to be squeamish about what you see there.'

Amy listened, half alarmed, at her account. 'Make sure you stay in touch,' she urged Lavinia when they parted.

—

It was a day in late September when Bertie had to set off on the first stage of his journey to Flanders.

They all accompanied him to the station; Amy, her parents and Florence, wearing her best suit and dabbing her eyes with her handkerchief. They stood on the sunlit platform, waiting for the first distant wisp of steam to announce the approach of the train which would take him to London. Once there, he would go on to join other soldiers in his battalion boarding the train to the Channel coast. He had spent half the morning brushing his uniform and polishing his shoes.

Further down the platform another officer nodded politely to them before turning back to comfort the woman who was seeing him off. His uniform was more worn and faded than Bertie's. Probably he had already seen active service and was returning from leave.

I should have been here to see Edmond off, Amy thought, distressed once more at what had taken place.

There was a distant whistle and they caught sight of the train. Now Mother was beginning to cry.

As the engine pounded noisily into the station, Bertie and Florence enjoyed a brief embrace. Then it was Amy's turn. 'Promise you'll write regularly!' she begged.

His parents wished him well as the train drew to a halt. *How fearless he looks,* Amy thought, as he strode the last few yards to the carriage. He opened the door and Father helped him heave his kitbag aboard. He stepped up into the second-class carriage and slammed the door. He leaned a little way out of the window for a final farewell. Then the stationmaster blew his whistle and the train began to chug out of the station. He waved, then withdrew inside the carriage. They stood watching as the train gathered speed, until they could see it no longer.

'I'm so proud of him,' Father said.

Amy accompanied Florence back to her house. How subdued she was, Amy thought. It was clear how much she cared for Bertie. Amy was not sure how involved he was. She remembered he was a year older than Edmond, but he somehow lacked the same maturity.

'Bertie asked me for my photograph to take with him,' Florence confided. 'I found one for him and made him give me one. It's a recent picture of him in uniform.'

Before long, Amy returned home. One of the new photographs of Bertie, smartly dressed as an officer, stood on their mantelpiece. He was smiling at them confidently.

Chapter Ten

Flanders and Larchbury, Autumn 1915

Dusk fell earlier now and the trench was bitterly cold. After the evening meal, Edmond made his last patrol of the day; the night sky to the east was lit up with a yellow glow and intermittent flashes. He thought he would never grow accustomed to the stagnant smell of mud, much worse now the weather was wet. He had to make his way as best he could along the trench on duckboards.

As last he reached his dugout, the cramped subterranean area carved into the mud, framed with wooden planks and sheets of corrugated iron, which he shared with a fellow officer. He sat on his camp bed, rereading the latest letter from Amy.

'Everything well with your young lady?' asked Frank Bentley, his comrade, lighting his pipe. He was a red-haired, vigorous young man, interested in football and amateur boxing.

'Yes.' She seemed content with her training to be a VAD, though she told him repeatedly how she missed him and longed to see him again. And her brother Bertie was in Flanders now, she had written.

'Difficult to know what to tell them when you write, isn't it?' said Frank.

That was the challenge: to write home giving some flavour of their life without revealing exactly what it was like on active service. Once you had described the food, which was dull but adequate, the church parades and occasional trips to a local town or village, there was little left to say that would not alarm your relatives.

You could just about describe the mist, the sodden fields and barbed wire. You could tell your womenfolk of the songs they sang on long, tiring marches, and the gramophones and card games which helped them pass their time off duty.

You had better not mention the cold and stench in the cramped trenches, and the bouts of sickness. Soldiers tried to hide homesickness, which affected some more than others. Horror and dread overcame them when a comrade was lost or badly injured.

You could not convey the suspense and terror of climbing out of the trench to face the enemy around Loos. It was as much as he could do to rally his men and launch himself towards the Germans, trying to maintain an air of confidence. At the end of most encounters there were casualties, men with fairly light wounds, men badly injured or dying, men who were beyond care. Sometimes there were hideous cries from men lying injured in No Man's Land.

Edmond would steel himself to stay with the injured, applying field dressings and administering water and cigarettes, sometimes even morphia, until the medical orderlies could take over. Some nights it was his task to write a letter to the next of kin. They would receive a telegram, telling them that their son or husband would not return, but it was his job to send a more personal letter. He would express his appreciation of the man's contribution and assure the relatives that he had died quickly and without much pain. He did his best, even when his account of a peaceful death was far from true.

Before Edmond had left for France, Bertie had told him that his cousin James was determined not to fight when he was old enough. He had been shocked at the time, but now, on days when there had been a high toll of casualties, he too began inwardly to rebel against the relentless mutilation and loss of life.

There was a loud boom from the artillery, then further ones. The noise came from some distance away, further up the line, and they were in no immediate danger, but the racket would put an end to conversation and keep them awake.

How much longer would it be till they allowed him home leave? They had said they hoped he could take at least a week soon, but they had still to give him an official date.

He took out Amy's photo from its place in his breast pocket. Proudly, he had shown Frank her picture. His comrade had admired her lovely hair and clear eyes, but for Edmond it was her smile and warm expression that chiefly raised his spirits. When he turned out the light he could still see her face in his mind's eye, as he remembered the softness of her lips. How exasperating it had been when their wedding was interrupted; sometimes he had to remind himself that he had not dreamt that courtroom appearance. By now she should have been his.

There had been that desperate letter from her in the summer, when she had offered to end the engagement, and he had had to assure her of his continuing love. What agony of spirit had possessed her to suggest ending their relationship? He would not be satisfied until they were officially united.

The guns went on booming. From time to time their unit made some progress, gaining ground across the muddy fields. Once, they had needed to fall back into trenches they had occupied in the summer. They were told that soon they would begin to drive back the Huns and march on to victory, but was it true? Occasionally he was struck by the thought that if he did not marry Amy soon it could be too late.

—

It was November before he reached Larchbury once more. He had had sufficient notice of his leave to set in motion arrangements for their marriage by special licence.

It was early evening and he went straight to Amy's house, hoping to find her at home. Mr Fletcher let him in eagerly and he deposited his kitbag and ran through to the back room, where she looked up from her knitting and a rapturous expression appeared on her face. She flung down the needles and they rushed into each other's arms.

'Oh, darling, at last!' she cried.

Her parents left them alone for a while. His pulse raced at the feel of her soft body and the faint perfume of her skin and hair.

'Every minute you've been away I've worried about you,' she said.

'You shouldn't.' He was afraid his face might reveal the tension of those weeks at the Front. Lately there had been more concern in her letters.

'I know you're too brave to tell me everything that goes on in Flanders but I read the papers.'

'While I'm home I want to forget and be just the way you knew me before.'

Her mother brought him a bowl of soup and he fell on it eagerly.

'Let me get you a meal,' she begged.

'Thank you so much but the family are expecting me,' he said.

They were asking him about his journey and wearily he began to describe the choppy Channel crossing. He asked after Bertie, who seemed to have settled in with his unit.

'Friday morning,' he told Amy triumphantly when there was a pause. 'That's when we're getting married.'

'In three days' time! Oh, how wonderful!'

'You will be able to get leave from your VAD work?' How smart she looked in her uniform.

'Yes – I told them we were planning to marry when you arrived on leave, and Matron has been understanding.'

A dreamy expression came on her face and it was as much as he could do to tear himself away and head for his home.

–

'So, Peter has decided to come back from India!' The family were eager to give Edmond the news as soon as he reached home. 'He'll be on his way by now. He intends to join up.'

'He'll feel he must do his duty,' Edmond said as he sat down and began eating dinner. They had made Cook wait for his arrival before serving it. 'I only wish he'd be here in time to see me married. I don't know when I'll next be on leave and whether I'll get the chance to spend time with him.' It was years since he had seen his brother.

'Are you absolutely sure you want to go ahead with this marriage?' his mother asked, infuriatingly. 'After all, Amy has a criminal record. It was extremely embarrassing when her offence came to light. I even caught the servants talking about it.'

There was something about Ma's trim, elegant, pastel-coloured dress and impeccably coiled hair which antagonised him. It was as though her opinions had fossilised in Victorian times and she could not accommodate any new ideas.

'You've found out about her past,' she went on. 'There's no need to honour your promises to her in the circumstances.' She passed him the gravy boat as though administering food was the ultimate sign of her love. The polished table with its lacy cloth, the vase of yellow chrysanthemums and the array of dishes all seemed irrelevant after his recent life at the Front. He needed her to welcome and love his chosen wife.

Beatrice was nodding her head and only Pa looked angry.

'You know very well I'm determined to marry Amy!' Edmond screamed at the women.

He had made it perfectly clear before he left and in his letters home. Thank goodness he was twenty-one now and there was no way they could legally prevent him from marrying her.

'You could postpone it – wait till the end of the war and see if you still feel the same,' his mother said.

'Absolutely not!'

Beatrice fidgeted and looked cross.

'Edmond has chosen Amy as his wife,' Pa said firmly. 'I regard her as a decent young woman, even if she has made one bad mistake. We will all welcome her here when they are married.'

Thank goodness he supports me, Edmond thought.

'Well, don't expect me to provide a lavish wedding feast,' Ma said, shrugging her shoulders. 'I went to endless trouble last time, and look how it ended.'

'There's no time to prepare anything elaborate,' Pa said. 'We'll invite our closest family and friends, provided we can contact them in time. Weddings tend to be less lavish now we're at war.'

'If you insist on marrying that creature I won't be there!' Beatrice declared, setting down her glass of wine. 'I was prepared to be bridesmaid last time and it ended in the most humiliating fashion.'

Edmond remembered waiting impatiently in the church with Charles that day, imagining that at any moment the organist would play a chord and his beloved Amy would proceed up the aisle on her father's arm. He recalled the sudden hubbub outside, and Bertie rushing into the church to explain what was happening. After almost collapsing from shock, he had pulled himself together enough to rush out to the magistrates' court. There he could at least smile encouragingly at her in moral support. He admired her for the way she had behaved in court, expressing remorse for the damage but upholding her principles. Then he had had to accept the barely credible fact that she would not be released to become his bride.

His parents had told him later of the astonishment of the congregation as they left the church without the wedding taking place. He had eventually arrived home to find his mother and sister watching angrily as the vast table was cleared of the banquet intended for fifty guests. There had been recriminations which had lasted almost until they went to see him off for Flanders.

'Don't be like that, Bea!' Edmond confronted his sister now. 'You'll come to love Amy.'

'She's brought disgrace to our family,' she said. 'Her arrest could hardly have been more public.' Beatrice's bridesmaid's dress had remained at The Beeches and his mother had had to intervene once when she wanted to throw it away, persuading her that it was a becoming gown.

'Amy's a VAD now,' Pa reminded them. 'She's serving her country. She's making amends.'

Edmond would have liked to shake Beatrice and ask her what she was doing for the war effort. He struggled to control his anger.

'This wedding is going ahead,' he shouted at her, just as the maid came to clear the dishes. She withdrew.

'Kindly don't shout like that in front of the servants,' Ma said. 'Come in, Janet,' she called loudly to the maid.

'I hope very much you'll be at my wedding, Bea,' Edmond told her firmly though more quietly.

'You'd better be bridesmaid, like before,' Ma urged her, 'otherwise it might encourage unpleasant gossip.'

Beatrice was unwilling to commit herself.

'If you refuse,' Edmond told her, 'the ceremony will take place just the same and Amy will still become your sister-in-law.'

—

Amy could hardly believe the long delay was almost over.

'There isn't any other incident of civil disobedience you haven't told us about?' Father asked, half joking.

'No! Believe me, my behaviour before and since has been exemplary.'

Bertie had asked her the same question flippantly before he left for Flanders.

Mother was cutting out fabric on the dining table. The days were cold now and she had barely time to prepare capes for the bridal party. There was enough ivory velvet for Amy and the bridesmaids.

'I couldn't match the green of their dresses,' she said, 'but the ivory colour will look fine. There's plenty for Florence and Beatrice.'

'Edmond isn't sure Beatrice wants to be my bridesmaid this time,' Amy said.

'Nonsense! She's bound to relent.'

'What a shame Bertie couldn't get leave. I believe Charles Shenwood will be best man, though, as planned… What about my dress, Mother? Is it really clean again?' The trip to prison had sullied its purity.

'Yes. It was a struggle to remove all the dust and dirt, but Mrs Johnson helped me and it looks as good as new.'

Amy was seeing Edmond for as much of each day as they could manage. She looked forward to every minute they spent together but there was no denying he had changed. He was still merry with her but sometimes fell quiet now, as though unable to shake off memories of his experiences at the Front. His face looked leaner, less boyish than she remembered.

Once they were married they could have only two more days together before his return. It seemed unreal that she would be living at The Beeches when not on duty at the hospital. 'Are you sure your family have forgiven me?' she asked Edmond. 'Will they all be happy with me living with them?'

'Of course they will!'

She packed up her belongings again, including winter clothes this time, and took them back there. The minutes and hours dawdled towards Friday, when she could at last be Edmond's entirely.

Chapter Eleven

Larchbury and London, November 1915

Edmond's uniform had been cleaned and pressed to the best of the servants' abilities. He was determined to look smart.

Charles had managed to get leave briefly from his unit, and had arrived the night before the wedding, handsome as ever in his uniform, ready to be his best man. At the dinner table Beatrice, beautiful in her newest gown of creamy silk, had eagerly engaged him in conversation.

'It's so heroic what you men do in the war,' she had told him, fixing her greenish eyes on him. Her lustrous chestnut hair was piled in curls upon her head and his gaze barely left her.

'We all do our best,' he said.

'I'm determined to contribute,' she told him. 'I'm going to join the women's working group, preparing comforts for the troops, bandages and socks and so on.'

Would she really join the group? Edmond wondered.

On the morning of the wedding she asked to be driven to a friend's house, saying she had been invited to stay there for the day. It was fortunate that Charles had left the breakfast table and missed hearing the row when Edmond begged her to attend the wedding and Pa refused to instruct the chauffeur to drive her elsewhere. In the end she got up stiffly and left the table.

Shortly afterwards he thought he heard her in the hall on the telephone to someone. Then a car arrived bringing Vicky, eyes bright with excitement at the prospect of the wedding. Edmond went upstairs to change into his uniform. As he started downstairs with Charles close behind him there was a ring at the doorbell and they were in time to see Beatrice's back view as she hurried out of the house, without her bridesmaid's dress. Edmond ran after her but she was already being driven off in her friend's family's car.

'Won't Beatrice be at the wedding?' Charles asked Edmond as he came back into the hall.

'She's refused to take part, because of what happened last time,' he said, almost spitting out the words, not sure he could ever forgive her for this.

Charles' eyebrows rose. 'That's a bit extreme. Of course, it was disturbing – it's not often a wedding is called off like that. Amy's a spirited young girl but decent enough, anyone can see that. She seemed sincerely sorry for that prank in the pavilion. I'm sure Beatrice will come round soon.'

Edmond consulted his watch. 'Another half hour and we should set out for the church.'

He looked out of the hall window at the pale sunshine. A young man in a peaked cap was cycling up their drive.

'Looks like there's a telegram,' Charles said. 'Must be someone sending congratulations,' he added nervously.

These days most telegrams brought bad news. 'I imagine so,' Edmond said.

He stepped outside to collect the wire, which was addressed to him. He ripped it open, read it quickly and gasped. *They can't really mean that,* he thought, and read it again. He began walking back mechanically towards the house. He screwed up the telegram and stuffed it into a pocket.

'Nothing serious, I hope,' said Charles.

'Nothing important,' he replied.

–

Amy and Florence were dressing for the wedding. They were glad that Lavinia had been able to get leave this time.

'How long will you have for the honeymoon in London?' Florence asked.

'Only two full days, then Edmond has to set off back.' If only they could have more time together.

Florence had arranged her light brown wavy hair in curls at the front and a coil at the nape of her neck. 'If Beatrice is coming, she's leaving it till the last minute,' she said.

'No – look – there she is,' Amy said with relief as the Derwents' motor car drove up. But the figure getting out was not Beatrice, though she was followed by the Derwents' maid.

Amy's mother brought up the new arrival. 'There's been a last-minute change to the arrangements,' she said nervously.

In walked Vicky, Edmond's cousin. Her auburn hair still hung long and loose but she seemed to have grown up a little since Amy had first met her at the party nearly a year before.

'Is it all right for me to take Beatrice's place?' she asked. 'Edmond asked me, and I'd be thrilled to be your bridesmaid.'

'Of course you can!' Amy hugged her.

'Only I haven't got a bridesmaid's dress. Beatrice's one wouldn't fit at all, even if I tried to wear a fearsomely tight corset like she does. There's just this pale yellow dress I brought with me.' She held up a delicate silk gown in front of her.

'It'll be perfect,' Amy assured her, and the maid helped her dress.

–

Edmond waited breathlessly next to Charles in the chill stone church as the organist played a piece from an everyday repertoire. He hardly dared look at his watch. Suddenly the music was interrupted with a dramatic chord and the man began to play Widor's Toccata. He turned to see his bride entering the church on her father's arm. How beautiful she was, and with a wide smile which seemed just for him. Overcome, he gazed at her as she advanced up the aisle to join him.

There was an almost audible sound of relief from the congregation. Amy's Uncle Arthur stepped forward and the service began. Was it Edmond's imagination or was he hurrying through the service a little faster than was usual, anxious some catastrophe might occur to interrupt it?

But of course nothing went wrong. At last Edmond was able to place the golden wedding ring on Amy's dainty finger, gently lift her gauzy veil and kiss her sweet face. Then they went to the vestry to sign the documents. His parents joined them to witness their signatures. Pa was gracious but Ma subdued, exchanging the briefest of kisses with her daughter-in-law. Young Vicky was beaming.

The organist played another anthem as they walked back down the aisle, past the smiling congregation. Besides the guests they had invited there were many local people. Miss Miller, who had once given Beatrice singing lessons, looked curiously at Amy. Was she expecting some kind of disruption, having heard what happened last time? She was bound to notice that his sister was absent.

He sat beside Amy in the car, his arm round her shoulders, breathing her floral fragrance. Soon they were arriving at his home for the reception. Only half as many people had been invited this time and the banquet was more modest, but the ones coming were those he loved. As he helped Amy out of the car she smiled at him, seeming to brighten the autumn day.

'I've never been so happy,' she whispered.

–

Amy greeted Aunt Louisa, who was slowly adjusting to widowhood and had managed to come to the wedding this time.

'I knew Edmond was the right one for you, when I met him that time last year before the war started,' she said.

Amy smiled at the memory of that momentous day at the seaside. She hurried on to hug Lavinia, tall in a well-tailored light brown autumn suit. 'Was it hard for you to get leave?' she asked.

'Fairly, but I was determined to be here!' Lavinia clasped Edmond's hand warmly. 'At last the two of you are together,' she said, beaming.

Then Amy clung to her husband's arm as she was introduced to some of his friends and relations she had not met before, and who greeted her warmly. The only embarrassment came when guests enquired after Beatrice. *If only she had grown to like me,* Amy thought. Edmond and his family moved the conversation on as smoothly as they could. Amy had the impression a few of his relatives were gossiping, and whispering to late arrivals not to enquire about his sister's absence.

She resolved not to dwell on the awkwardness. With her hand in Edmond's she felt enveloped in a joyful glow, so that the reception passed in a blur. She noticed Charles talking to Lavinia. The two of them had met occasionally at social events, she gathered.

When luncheon was served, Amy was aware of an impressive array of dishes but could scarcely eat or drink. When the speeches began she hardly noticed what was said, except when

Edmond spoke of his bliss at finding the girl to share his life. Then he gave a start, for some reason, as Father produced a telegram to read. It was from Bertie, disappointed he was unable to attend and wishing them joy.

At last Florence accompanied her upstairs to change out of her wedding dress. She took off her veil and her friend brushed her hair.

'I didn't know Lavinia was friends with Charles Shenwood,' Florence said.

Amy had been vaguely aware of Charles being sociable as ever, attentive to Florence as well as Lavinia. 'They're both part of the same social set in Alderbank, I gather,' she replied as she put on her best blue winter skirt.

'I've been longing for the hours to pass so we can leave,' she told Florence, 'yet I can hardly remember how I've passed them.' She slipped into the matching jacket. 'I hope one day you're as happy as I am,' she told her friend. She was thinking of Bertie, but it seemed premature to suggest what a fine couple they would make. She picked up her bouquet and presented it to Florence. Her friend looked overcome with delight as she breathed in the heady fragrance of the roses, then set them down and made sure Amy's hat was straight.

When they returned downstairs, Edmond seemed as impatient as his bride and hurried her past their relatives, crying out their goodbyes and thanks and waving to those furthest away. The chauffeur helped her into the family car.

They embraced in the back as they passed dim fields and copses. Flocks of birds swooped round against the reddening sky. Edmond's lips claimed hers.

At last the chauffeur was driving them through the outskirts of London as night fell and then on to their hotel in a square in Kensington. Once there, they were shown to their room, beautifully furnished with dark red brocade curtains and bedspread. A vase of giant white chrysanthemums adorned the walnut writing desk.

'Do I need to change for dinner?' she asked, for she had packed her blue silk gown.

'Only if you want to,' he said. 'People observe fewer formalities now we're at war.'

'Maybe I'll wear it tomorrow.'

He led her down to the dining room. 'I don't think I can manage much to eat,' she told him. He ordered them a light dish of poultry and some wine. She was aware of the draped curtains and high ceiling of the smart restaurant, and the buzz of conversation around them. There were other young men there in uniform. She ate a little of her meal, her eyes resting repeatedly on Edmond's handsome, smiling face, barely able to believe that at last he was her husband.

Soon they were heading, hand in hand, into the lift. He held her and rested his face against hers during the brief flight between floors. As he unlocked their room he turned and gazed at her with an intense expression which made her tingle with excitement.

He turned off the lights except one lamp to shed a soft glow, then took her in his arms. 'Dearest, I've longed for this moment,' he said as he led her to the bed. As he gently helped her ease off her clothes he fondled her fair skin, whispering words of love.

—

Amy awoke as it grew light, which was not especially early at that time of year. There was the sound of traffic outside. She yawned and stretched luxuriously. All the waiting was over: she was finally Mrs Derwent. But there were only two days until

Edmond left. As he slept, she admired his straight nose and well-spaced features.

He stirred, then sat up and consulted his watch, which lay on the bedside table. 'It's gone seven!' he exclaimed. Then he caught her in his arms and kissed her tenderly. The stubble on his unshaven face was a little rough against her skin. 'Last night was perfect,' he told her.

The next minute he was on his feet, gathering together his clothes. She admired the strong arms and broad chest she had first noticed when he was swimming in the sea at Hove that time: he was a fine, healthy-looking young man. 'We'd better get up and make sure we don't miss breakfast,' he told her.

What's the rush? she thought. She wanted to get the most from the day, go for a walk in nearby Kensington Gardens if the weather was fine, perhaps go to a show in the evening. But she had imagined a leisurely start to the day. When he seemed determined to get ready quickly she too began her preparations.

Before long they were sitting in the breakfast room, giving their order to the waiter, who would fetch their meal from the array of hot serving dishes.

'There isn't any particular hurry, is there, Edmond?' she asked him.

His cheerful manner dissolved into a look of concern. 'Yes, I'm afraid there is. I shouldn't really be here.'

'What?'

'I was due to take a train back yesterday. They sent me a telegram. They need urgent reinforcements at the Front, apparently.'

'But you're on leave till the day after tomorrow!'

'It seems the war takes precedence.' He pulled the crumpled telegram from his pocket. 'I should have taken a train at five pm yesterday. We could still have got married but we'd have enjoyed scarcely any time together afterwards. I was determined we'd at least have one night together.'

'So you ignored the order?' Her heart fluttered with alarm.

'Yes. And I don't regret it.' He seized her hand across the table and fixed his blue eyes on hers. 'Nothing was to keep us apart this time.'

'Oh, darling!' How could she question his disobedience in these circumstances? 'Will you be in terrible trouble?'

'I'd better go to the station before they come to arrest me,' he said. 'I need to make it clear I'm not flunking my duties.'

'I can at least come to the station with you and see you off.' How could she bear to part with him so soon?

'I should see you on to a train home and then go to my station,' he said.

'It's all right, I can get an omnibus or an underground train and then the mainline train home. I can manage.'

'You must take a cab. It'll be wonderful if you can see me off. There might be a hoo-ha, though, because I was meant to travel on a certain train yesterday and now I've missed it they'll need to find a place for me on another one.'

The morning was spoilt as they rushed their breakfast. He went to the foyer to phone his father to explain why Amy was returning earlier than expected.

'Someone's already phoned them to enquire about my whereabouts,' he told her with a rueful smile.

They returned quickly to their room to collect their outdoor clothes and luggage. As they went to the foyer, two stern-looking senior officers came in.

Now Edmond looked pale, but the newcomers wandered to the reception desk and seemed to be calmly booking rooms.

'We'd better go before they really do come to arrest me,' he said, hurrying her through the large glass doors into the chilly street outside. Thin sunlight shone on the very last golden leaves on the trees in the square as he hailed a cab. As their vehicle wound its way between motor cars, buses and horses and carts in the teeming streets her stomach churned with shock that he was leaving her so soon.

They reached the station, crowded with soldiers. An incoming train was offloading casualties on stretchers and one of the men was groaning with the movement.

'Which is your train?' she asked, surveying the busy platforms and hoping she would not start crying.

'The one which left yesterday afternoon,' he shrugged. 'Now I've got to ask someone in command how best to get back.'

He strode through the crowds, still carrying her suitcase as well as his kit, and she hurried to keep up. He made for an officer who was checking typed sheets and gave an account of his predicament.

'You missed your train? You're in a lot of trouble,' she heard the officer tell him. 'You'll probably find yourself on a charge.'

'I'm eager to rejoin my unit on the first available transport,' he said.

'Going Absent Without Leave is a very serious offence,' the officer barked at him, shuffling his papers. 'And now it's not just a case of finding you a place on a train to the coast. Your transport all the way back to your unit was planned for yesterday. Have you any idea how much disruption you're causing?'

'Very sorry, Sir.'

The officer ran his finger down a sheet of paper. 'You'd better board that train on platform two. I'll put you in the charge of Captain Purbright who'll find you a ship and ongoing transport back to your unit.'

'Platform two, darling,' Edmond told her.

'Look lively, man! It leaves in five minutes.'

They hurried to the platform and the officer handed him over to Captain Purbright.

Edmond gave Amy her suitcase and money for a cab.

'Get on board!' The captain made no concession to her presence.

Edmond gave her a quick embrace. 'I'm most desperately sorry, darling,' he cried, then climbed on board and blew her a kiss. 'I'll write. Let's hope it's not too long before we're together again.'

The whistle blew and she watched in dismay as the train began to move off.

She broke into a run. 'I love you so much, darling! Stay safe for me.'

—

Amy got off the train at Larchbury and walked along the street with her small suitcase. The previous day had been momentous but how swiftly and disturbingly their honeymoon had ended! How could the army seize Edmond back so soon after they were wed? Were they fated to never have more than a few snatched hours together?

He was heading back into danger at this very minute, to say nothing of probable sanctions for disobeying an order. Her steps slowed as she headed for The Beeches, wishing she might have gone home to her parents' house in Sebastopol Terrace.

It was past midday as she walked up the driveway between the beech trees, almost bare at this time of year. The family would be taking luncheon.

The butler let her in. 'Good day, Miss – excuse me, Mrs Derwent.'

She set down her case and outdoor clothes. She would have liked to slip quickly up to her room, but it seemed rude.

She walked into the dining room. They all looked up and Mr Derwent stood up. 'Sit down, Amy, I'll get Cook to bring you some luncheon.'

'Thank you, though I'm not very hungry.'

His wife looked put out and Beatrice downright hostile.

'The authorities were on the phone, first thing this morning, enquiring about Edmond,' Mrs Derwent said, her cool blue eyes probing Amy's face. 'It was very embarrassing. We had no idea he was due to set off back yesterday afternoon.'

'I saw him off on a train soon after ten,' she said.

His father rang the bell to summon Cook. She arrived, a little flustered, and happily agreed to bring Amy some lunch.

'It's a serious matter, going AWOL,' Mr Derwent said.

'I expect Amy put him up to it,' Beatrice said. 'She's got no respect for the law. We were a decent family before he got to know her.'

'That'll do, Beatrice,' said her father.

'I didn't know he was supposed to go back yesterday,' Amy said miserably. 'I didn't find out about it till this morning.'

Would they believe her, she wondered as she consumed her soup.

Cook brought her a plate of meat and dumplings. How far had Edmond travelled by now? she speculated. Perhaps he was crossing the Channel. What kind of disciplinary action might he face when he returned late to his unit?

Beatrice fidgeted as Amy picked at her main course.

'Please begin your dessert,' she said. 'There's no need to wait for me.'

'Take your time, Amy,' Mr Derwent insisted.

Beatrice continued to watch her sullenly. Amy was relieved Edmond had not revealed sooner that he was disobeying an order. She doubted if she could have found the resolution to persuade him to rush to the station immediately after their wedding ceremony.

But she was part of the Derwent family now and must do her best to get along with them.

Chapter Twelve

Flanders and Larchbury, November to December 1915

Edmond found himself in a carriage with two other men, both privates, who were late back, and Captain Purbright, a broad-shouldered man who was anxious to make them aware of their disgrace.

'I'm very sorry for missing my train, Sir,' he told the captain. 'I got married yesterday.'

'You needed to wed her in a hurry, did you?' sniggered one of the men.

'This is no laughing matter,' snapped the captain.

'No!' Edmond cried indignantly. 'It wasn't that kind of wedding. But we deserved a brief honeymoon before I set off back to war.'

He thought he caught a sympathetic glance from the other man.

'You can't just please yourself when you return,' retorted the captain. 'Aren't you ashamed to set these privates such a bad example?'

'Sorry, Sir.'

'It'll be the devil's own job, finding you all transport back to your units, when you're not arriving at the planned time.' When put like that, he could see his action had been irresponsible.

He sat up straight, anxious to conceal his embarrassment as the train travelled through the suburbs, and then through fields and woodland. He closed his eyes and thought of Amy. It had been agonising to have to break the news that his leave had been curtailed, and tear himself away. As soon as possible he must write and tell her again how he regretted having to interrupt their honeymoon, though he knew she was thankful he had contrived to spend one blissful night with her.

The sea crossing took much longer than last time, for there was talk of fresh minefields and they had to make an extended journey with a pilot on board to guide them through the most dangerous areas. Then he and the other miscreants were left in a room at the harbour station while Captain Purbright tried to find trains to convey them in the right directions. Dusk was falling. An orderly brought them tea and some lopsided sandwiches.

At last he and one of the others were marched along the platform and on to a grimy local train, where they were placed in the charge of a superior officer. It chugged off slowly through the night, calling at minor stops on the way.

It was still dark when they alighted at a small station. He huddled into his greatcoat and sat down on an uncomfortable bench near some milk churns while further transport was arranged. When daylight came, they left the station. Outside, a horse and cart were waiting to take them on the next stage of their irregular journey. He stared curiously at the small stone houses of the town, and its impressive bell tower. They crossed a canal with a barge approaching slowly in the distance. Then the fields of Flanders began to look familiar.

By the time they had marched the last few miles along an uneven road he was ravenously hungry and another short day was drawing to its end. By now he must be well over twenty-four hours late.

He hurried along the trench, the rank smell of mud greeting his nostrils, and back to the dugout he had last inhabited a week earlier.

'What kept you?'

'Wouldn't she let you go?'

There were cries of derision and ribaldry from the men drinking their tea. Frank Bentley greeted him calmly, clearly trying not to draw attention to his late arrival.

Something was different. Their quarters were stripped down to the essentials, and some of their equipment was packed in crates.

'Are we moving on?'

'Yes – we're advancing further east.'

He supposed it was good news. Someone brought him a bowl of steaming stew and a mug of watery tea.

'Just as well you weren't any later,' Frank said as they withdrew to their officers' quarters. 'We're moving on tomorrow. There's another offensive planned, if the weather holds out.'

Edmond slumped wearily on to his bed.

'And Major Saunders said that if you made it back today he wants to see you first thing tomorrow morning.' Frank looked at him ruefully. 'You're in a lot of trouble.'

'All I wanted was to spend the night with my new wife!'

Frank smiled momentarily and then turned serious again. 'Better not tell the major why the marriage didn't take place last time. It might make a bad impression.' Few men in the military had sympathy for Suffragettes.

Edmond stood to attention in front of the makeshift desk. Major Saunders did not take kindly to insubordination.

'I should have you put on a charge,' he said, glowering at him. He had large features and streaks of grey in his hair and moustache. He sounded as though he was suffering from a cold, likely enough now they were spending winter in the trenches. 'If I thought you were a coward I would have you court-martialled. What have you to say for yourself? Don't tell me your connecting train ran late. We're not accepting that as an excuse – it's your responsibility to allow sufficient time to reach the London terminus.'

There was no point in pretending he had not received the telegram. 'I was getting married, Sir.'

For a moment there was a faint flicker of understanding, but the stern look soon returned.

'You can't allow your private life to interfere with your duty. I've been considering having you reduced to the ranks.'

Edmond gasped in horror at the prospect. What would Amy think? And how could his parents bear the disgrace?

He struggled to justify his actions in any way possible. 'With respect, Sir, I set out for the station first thing in the morning, the day after we were married.'

'I'm relieved to hear it, Derwent. But you can't simply decide for yourself when you're going to return.'

'No, Sir. I very much regret the difficulties I've caused. I give you my word it won't happen again.'

'You're damn right it won't.' The major rose to his feet. 'Up till now you've been a valuable member of the unit, Derwent, good at keeping the men motivated. I wouldn't want to lose you. I'm stopping all your leave for the next three months. And it'll be another month before you get weekend leave. Don't expect any home leave before next summer.'

With difficulty he suppressed his urge to protest at such severe punishment. 'Very good, Sir.' He saluted.

As he returned along the line of trenches to his quarters, his spirits sank at the injustice of it all. How could they expect him to rush off and leave his bride within a few hours of the ceremony? But now the punishment seemed even worse. Once more he was faced with not seeing Amy for months. How could he bear it?

—

Amy was sitting with her in-laws in the drawing room after dinner, with the deep blue velvet curtains drawn to shut out the chilly night. Beatrice was arranging sprigs of holly in several vases.

Amy had new nursing skills now, like preparing dressings and cleaning small wounds, and she had been taught a good deal about preventing infection. She was tired from her day's work at the hospital but supposed she should offer to help Beatrice. She moved across to the table and began arranging shorter sprigs of holly in a smaller vase. She struggled to trim the ends. When she tried to position a sprig it was apt to fall in a different direction from the way she had planned.

She glanced across at her sister-in-law's work. There in her vase was an elegant arrangement of holly, the red berries beautifully spaced. Beatrice paused thoughtfully and then positioned a slightly longer sprig right in the centre. Amy gasped. Beatrice's arrangement was almost completely symmetrical.

'How artistic you are!' she cried. She herself had occasionally picked some of Mother's marigolds or dahlias and arranged them in a vase, but without Beatrice's skill.

'I love to display them just so,' she replied. 'If you can trim any which have particularly long stalks, I'll do the actual arranging. ...Ouch!' she said as she pricked her finger. She sucked it for a minute and then carried on.

For a moment Amy worked alongside her sister-in-law.

'Remind me which day you've chosen for the party,' Mr Derwent asked his wife from his armchair by the fireside.

'I'm inviting guests for the thirtieth of December,' she said. 'Peter will be back from India by then.'

'It'll be wonderful to have him home,' Beatrice said. 'Too bad Edmond won't be here.' Her good humour dispelled and she glared at Amy, as though she still blamed her for his late return to the Front.

'I miss him dreadfully,' Amy told her. She had expected they would punish him for his late return, but the extended loss of leave was harsh. The idea of him spending Christmas away in some distant trench made her wretched. 'Even if they hadn't stopped his leave it's unlikely he'd have been allowed another week so soon,' she said.

He had told her they had been fighting again, but the Front was relatively quiet now as the weather was poor. His reminders of their wedding night were tantalising. When would they ever find the chance to be together for more than a few hours?

He wrote regularly and she was adding to the pile of loving letters she had collected ever since he had joined up. She kept them wrapped in red ribbon in a drawer in their bedroom. His photograph smiled out at her from the top of the dressing table.

'The party will be a quieter affair than last year,' Mrs Derwent said. 'For one thing, so many young men are away. For another, I'm struggling to manage without Mary.'

Their kitchen maid had given notice and left to work as a waitress at the inn. Mrs Derwent had immediately advertised for a replacement but it seemed other maids were leaving to fill vacancies once occupied by young men, and there was a shortage.

'Janet tells me your room is cluttered,' Mrs Derwent told Amy. 'It's difficult for her to clean.'

Janet had to help in the kitchen now as well as performing her usual duties, and Amy supposed it would be a disaster if she left too.

'Edmond encouraged me to bring my belongings here,' she explained. 'Might I bring down some more of my gramophone records to place with your collection?' So far she had only added the ones she thought might suit their tastes. 'And the books on the table are Edmond's, because he took them out of the shelves to make room for mine. May we have a bookcase, or more shelves, for them?' Up till now she had not ventured to ask.

'Why didn't you tell us?' Mr Derwent asked. 'This is your home now.'

'Of course you may have more shelves,' his wife said, milder now she recognised her difficulties. 'Bring down your records and I'll see what can be done about the books.'

—

When the guests began to arrive for the party, Beatrice was sitting at the piano, playing '*If You Were the Only Girl in the World*', singing the words charmingly. Her fingers moved lightly across the keys as she performed the romantic tune. She was a gifted pianist and could play classical pieces creditably. Her soprano voice was fine, too. Amy sometimes regarded her as indolent but she was coming to realise that Beatrice had ladylike accomplishments.

Peter had arrived a few days earlier. It was years since Amy had seen him. He was in his mid-twenties, tall and good-humoured. His face was narrower than Edmond's and his hair a lighter brown, though it may have been bleached to some extent by the hot Indian sun. He had greeted her warmly, regretting that he had missed the wedding.

'But I've brought a present for you and Edmond,' he told her.

She had exclaimed with delight at the intricately carved wooden cabinet that he had brought back on the ship. 'It's perfect,' she said. 'We're short of storage space, and this is so exotic and unusual.'

He had also brought his family a small table with a circular brass top, which they had placed in the drawing room.

Now, for the evening of the party, he stood with his parents greeting their guests. Amy went to stand with her in-laws, trying to blend in with the family, hesitant without Edmond there to boost her confidence.

'And how is Edmond?' asked Mr Leadbetter. He was around thirty, the new headmaster at the school where Amy's father taught.

'Fine, thank you. I understand the Front is still quiet.'

'Did his late return cause problems for him?' The question came from Mrs Leadbetter, a thin woman with her dark hair in a severe bun.

'Only minor ones,' she said, concerned the news of his disobedience had spread. Having his leave restricted was far from minor: it was disastrous for them. She had to force herself to be as discreet as possible about his being disciplined. Somehow Miss Miller or one of the other gossips had heard about it. Many local families now had a relative at the Front. Might such news might slip past the censor if a soldier mentioned it in a letter home? How many of the guests here had heard about it?

Then Amy's parents arrived, with Bertie, who was on leave. She rushed forward to greet them. Whoever had related Edmond's questionable behaviour, she could trust her brother's loyalty.

'How lovely you look in that gown,' Mother said.

'I remembered just in time that I was short of smart clothes and the dressmaker made me a new one.'

'That dusky pink colour suits you.'

She loved the flattering dress in crêpe de chine; if only her husband was there to see it.

'I got a letter from Edmond today,' she told her family. 'He wrote it on Christmas Day. He and some of his comrades had received food parcels from home and they boiled up the Christmas puddings in German helmets.' Being apart was made just a little more bearable by learning that he had enjoyed some jollity on the day.

She had spent the day after Christmas with her parents, glad to see Bertie again. His unit was not especially near Edmond's one and they had not seen each other. Bertie had been less talkative than usual and unwilling to describe his experiences at the Front, sometimes staring ahead as though recalling disturbing events. He seemed more appreciative than usual of his home, though he had soon gone out to visit the Clifford family.

'Is Florence here?' he asked Amy now.

'Not yet, but she and her family are definitely coming.'

She stuck by Bertie's side, determined to make the most of his leave. The butler, whose name was Chambers, she had discovered, brought round drinks.

Her father and brother were anxious to renew their acquaintance with Peter. 'I suppose you'll train as an officer,' Father asked. Amy knew he had liked Peter when he had been his tutor, though he had found him less hardworking than Edmond.

'Yes, I begin in the new year. Then I might take up an administrative post at the War Office,' Peter said. 'My work in India has prepared me for that kind of position.' He was immaculately dressed, his hair and moustache finely trimmed.

'If I were a few years younger I might think of joining up myself,' said Mr Derwent, 'but I suppose my work running the forestry business is valuable in its way.'

'Certainly,' her father agreed.

Amy knew that Mr Derwent hoped that in the future one of his sons might work with him managing their forest, to take over when he retired, but neither showed any inclination at present.

'It's too bad I missed attending Edmond's wedding,' Peter began telling Amy's parents. 'I was on my way in November. It seems strange, my younger brother having a wife already, but I'm sure Amy will fill the role very well.' He smiled at her. He had admired the wedding photos, expressing surprise that Beatrice was not there. He had previously heard only the vaguest account of their wedding not taking place as planned in June. To explain why Vicky had stood in for Beatrice in November she had had to reveal all the details of the disaster on her first intended wedding day, though he did not seem to hold what happened against her.

'This time last year we weren't even engaged,' she said, remembering the delight of their courtship.

Charles Shenwood joined Peter and the two of them were soon discussing the recent hunt on Boxing Day, the Monday, as Christmas Day had been a Saturday.

Beatrice joined them. 'How fortunate you were granted Christmas leave,' she told Charles, for it was not long since he had been Edmond's best man. 'How many more days do you have?'

'I need to set off back the day after tomorrow,' he told her.

Uncle Arthur and Aunt Sophie arrived with James and they renewed their acquaintance with Peter.

Then Florence arrived with her family. She was pretty in a fashionable gown with a lacy bodice that extended below her sash and over the top of her skirt. Bertie rushed to greet her and her face dimpled with delight. When they moved into the next room for the buffet Amy was relieved Colonel Fairlawn and his son had not arrived. She stood with her mother, who was congratulating her hostess on the meal.

'It's been a trial managing this year,' Mrs Derwent confided, her deep blue gown set off with a dainty platinum necklace. 'I'm short of a maid.' The Derwents were generally courteous to her parents, if a little reserved.

'I wonder if I can help?' Amy's mother said. 'My Mrs Johnson comes twice a week, but I don't really need her so much now Amy has left and Bertie is away such a lot. I could spare her on one of her days if she might be useful to you. Her daughter Elsie is fourteen now and she's looking for a place too.'

'I suppose I might see if they can be of service,' Mrs Derwent said.

'Mrs Johnson is very capable.'

'Thank you for recommending her.' Edmond's mother seemed reluctant to give work to their maid, probably doubting she would be suitable for a smarter household, but in her present plight she would consider her.

After the meal the dancing began and Bertie was soon enthusiastically partnering Florence. Sometimes talking or laughing, sometimes quiet, they seemed wrapped up in each other.

Vicky was there and had persuaded her aunt to let her enjoy the first hour of the ball.

'I don't remember ever meeting your parents,' Amy said.

'Mother has poor health,' Vicky told her. 'Father doesn't much enjoy social events, so I'm very grateful when Auntie invites me here. The chauffeur drives me over.'

James invited the young girl to be his partner for a waltz. He was an awkward dancer but she seemed thrilled simply to be taking part.

Between dances, Bertie looked at James anxiously. 'There'll be conscription soon,' he told Amy.

'He's still determined not to fight, isn't he?' she said. James would be eighteen in the summer. He looked very like Bertie around the eyes, but his face was broader, with a turned up nose. He seemed reluctant to talk to the fighting men present.

Bertie frowned with distaste. 'I've tried to persuade him it's his duty to join up,' he said. 'If he doesn't, people will think he's a coward, and he could even get sent to prison. I dread to think what your in-laws will make of that.'

Her skin prickled with anxiety. She had a good deal of sympathy for her cousin but she imagined there would be recriminations, especially from Beatrice. The menfolk would question his reluctance to serve his country. Even Edmond might be critical.

'Amy,' Peter broke into her reverie. 'Would you join me for a waltz?'

She tried to set aside her concerns, enjoy the evening and establish her position in the family, for Edmond's sake. She found Peter was a good dancer.

'You've been abroad so long, I suppose you haven't got a young lady in England?' she asked, hoping her question was not too intrusive.

'No – to be honest, there's a young British woman out in India who I care for.' She was intrigued.

'Does she return your affection?' she asked, for he had not mentioned her before.

He dropped his voice. 'She does, but I'd rather you didn't mention it to my parents. There are so many difficulties. Her father has a high rank out there and I hesitate to ask for her hand.'

'But now you're joining the war effort,' she said, her hand lightly on his arm as they swirled around to the music. 'I suppose it may be a considerable time before you can be reunited with your young lady.'

'Yes, it's a dreadful wrench, but I felt I should enlist,' Peter said. 'I plan to go back to India afterwards, though Pa would prefer me to stay here and join him in the forestry business.'

She sympathised with him for all the complications in his life. 'Does Edmond know about your young lady in India?' she asked.

'Yes, I told him about Patricia in a letter, and he understands. To be honest, one of my motivations for serving in the war is to improve my prospects. Promotion to a good rank would help me win my sweetheart.'

She noticed Bertie was partnering Florence again. The pair had spent most of the evening together.

Vicky bade them goodnight. Later, Charles claimed a dance with Amy. He led her confidently and was as charming as ever. 'Has Beatrice forgiven you yet for that business about the interrupted wedding?' he asked suddenly. He had become aware of the situation when he was best man.

'Oh – yes, she accepts me now,' Amy said quickly. It would have been hard to describe the reserve her sister-in-law sometimes showed, or mention her occasional hostile comment. Beatrice was clearly attracted to Charles, and Amy felt it would be mean to criticise her.

'I'm so glad,' Charles said.

Later, James waltzed with Amy. 'You're quiet tonight,' she remarked.

'I'm torn,' he said. 'I'd like to express my views on the war, but your in-laws might prefer me not to be controversial. I don't wish to upset my host and hostess.'

'A disagreement would be liable to spoil the festive atmosphere,' she agreed. 'It's hard for you, I can see that.'

Later Bertie spared her a dance.

'You've not lacked partners,' he remarked.

'The ball makes an agreeable diversion but no one can fill the gap left by Edmond,' she assured him. 'If only he was here! Make the most of your time with Florence.'

'I intend to do so,' he assured her.

A year ago Amy and Edmond had been totally swept up in their blossoming love. Did Bertie and Florence feel the same? Last year they had been optimistic, she recalled, still hoping that the war would end soon.

Amy and Florence found time between dances to sit together. 'Bertie's changed,' Florence said. 'He's become more serious. It's the war, isn't it?'

'Edmond changed once he'd seen active service. I'm afraid they see distressing sights,' Amy said. 'It's bound to affect them.' Occasionally Amy would get a glimpse of Bertie's familiar carefree expression, but then his face would cloud, as though he could not forget his imminent return to Flanders.

Towards the end of the evening, she found herself standing in a group with Florence, Bertie, Charles, Peter and Beatrice.

Peter raised his glass. 'Here's to 1916. May it bring peace!'

James belatedly joined their group.

'Let's drive the Huns back where they belong!' Bertie seconded.

'May we advance boldly and destroy the enemy divisions!' cried Charles.

Beatrice smiled and clapped her hands.

James could not hide his dismay at these sentiments. 'They're young men, little different from us,' he protested.

'To peace!' Amy cried. 'An end to the fighting!'

Chapter Thirteen

London and Larchbury, Winter to Spring 1916

Amy had gained the necessary certificates now, and early in the new year she was sent to work in west London at St Luke's hospital. It was controlled by the War Office, and received severe casualties sent home from the Front. Lavinia, who wrote to her from time to time, had warned her that army hospitals were meant only to take women over twenty-three. *But they took me at twenty-two*, she had written. *They don't always enquire too closely, because they need more nurses.* Amy had kept quiet about being twenty-one. There were rumours of eager young men lying about their age to sign up for the army when they were little more than boys. There was a shortage of competent soldiers and of nurses too. She had informed the authorities that she had got married, and had not been asked to leave on that account.

She had to stay in a hostel now, sleeping on an iron bed in a room with Katherine, another nurse, who was plump, with curly dark hair.

Edmond's photo was soon installed on top of her tiny chest of drawers. 'So he's your husband?' Katherine asked, catching sight of her wedding band. She had left her garnet and diamond engagement ring at The Beeches.

'Yes.' She confided that they had enjoyed little married life together so far.

'He looks a fine young man,' Katherine said.

Amy would look at his photo last thing at night, before they extinguished the lamp, and first thing each morning. She yearned for the feel of his warm body close beside her, like on their wedding night. How soon would he be with her again? She read and reread his letters, trying to imagine what his life must be like, and spent much of her limited free time composing replies.

Each morning she and Katherine would put on hats and coats over their VAD uniform and set off through the chilly streets to the nearby hospital, a substantial building of dark brickwork. The wards had not been full to start with but now the fighting had begun again and fresh casualties were arriving. Compared with her last hospital, the senior nurses were less obsessed with keeping the blankets perfectly straight and more concerned with the patients, brave young men injured while serving their country. Amy was working in a ward where most of the men were making good progress and were cheerful and appreciative. Here, besides the tedious bed-making, they took round tea and Bovril for the patients, and were allowed to perform a few more responsible tasks. They prepared dressing trays, and occasionally changed dressings, usually for patients who were almost fully recovered. The hours were long, and their break some time in the middle of the day might be curtailed if they were especially busy. She could seldom get weekend leave now.

'I'm exhausted,' Katherine said as they returned to the nursing home one evening. She looked in dismay at the gristly meat they were served for their evening meal. 'I never thought

I'd sleep on an iron bedstead and eat food like this. Have you ever known anything like it?'

Only in jail, Amy thought, recalling for a moment the smell of overcooked cabbage which had frequently heralded a prison meal. She made a vague reply to spare her new friend this information.

'I should take a bath and wash my hair,' Katherine said, 'but I don't believe I can find the energy.'

'There might not be any hot water,' Amy said. There was seldom enough to go round.

The next day, large numbers of ambulances arrived with new patients. Amy was forced to accept that there was no sign of a breakthrough in the war. Edmond and Bertie were over there, perhaps in the thick of it. One of the other nurses had received a letter from home recently, with news of her cousin's death. The sight of a young man bearing a telegram struck fear into the heart of anyone with a relative at the Front.

Bertie was a poor correspondent. He hardly ever wrote to her and seldom to her parents, so she had to resign herself to receiving limited news of him.

Edmond wrote regularly but his letters could take anything up to five days to arrive.

I keep a photo of you next to my bed, he wrote, *and one in the pocket of my tunic. Thinking of you helps me to bear the difficult days. They tell us we are fighting for the future of Britain, so I like to imagine I'm fighting for you. I long to be eligible for six days' leave, so I can be with you once more.*

News from him would brighten her day.

Nurses were succumbing to colds and flu, so Amy and Katherine were sent to help out on another ward. It was pandemonium as they made up beds and new arrivals filled them immediately. Some of them were groaning, though she sensed that most were trying to be brave. Doctors were moving among them, deciding if any should be rushed to the operating theatre.

On this ward the wounds generally needed urgent attention. They got their first views of gangrenous limbs, slimy and green, sometimes with the bone exposed. She tried to suppress her shudder at the smell of putrefaction. As VAD recruits they helped support limbs while the fully trained nurses tended them. Her first sight of an amputated leg had been horrifying, but she had managed to stand there resolutely helping. The trained nurses were calm and efficient, setting them an example. As the day passed, she faced more such wounds. She longed for the gramophone music and cheerful atmosphere of their old ward. Here there were cries from delirious patients, coming round after operations. She forced herself to behave in a matter-of-fact way, helping as best she could, determined she would not shirk her duty.

'Do you think we'll be back on our usual ward tomorrow?' Katherine asked her when they had returned to the hostel. 'I don't know if I can go on seeing such mutilations. I felt faint more than once.'

'Yes, but just think, we've helped some of the men begin their recovery,' she said as they made for the canteen. 'You should be proud of that. We must do what we can. Have you got anyone at the Front, Katherine?'

'Only a distant cousin. My young man is at university, though he might consider enlisting when he completes his course next summer, if the war lasts that long.'

They sat down and Amy poured them some water from the jug. 'I suppose it's different for me. I keep thinking that my challenges are very limited, compared with what the men face in the trenches.'

'I never would have imagined a year ago that I'd be living like this,' Katherine said. She had just reached twenty-three and came from a small town in west Kent. 'An old friend from school became a VAD and gave me the idea. I'd never even made my own bed before I came here. I suppose I've led a sheltered life.'

It was easy to tell which young women were not used to brushing their clothes, cleaning shoes or sewing on buttons, and the domestic work came as a shock to many. At first Katherine had had dainty white hands like Beatrice, but now they were becoming red and rough, for here it was impossible to avoid cleaning tasks. Such work had come as a shock for her friend, but Amy suspected many girls from the lower classes experienced worse conditions in their homes.

'You don't have to go on,' she told Katherine. 'We're on a month's probation, so you could decide to leave.' She would be sorry to see her friend give up.

'I feel I should make the effort,' Katherine said. 'I'll keep going and hope I can grow accustomed to it.'

When Amy tried to sleep that night, the memory of those appalling wounds haunted her. She tried never to think of Edmond being wounded, but lately the number of casualties horrified her. He too was facing the danger of death or mutilation. She tossed feverishly through the night.

–

Amy went home for a weekend in May, trudging into The Beeches in the early afternoon. She had changed out of her uniform when she came off duty but had not found time to bath or wash her hair. It was only now that she realised how drab she must look, her shoes dusty from the walk from the station and her hat growing shabby. Lately, she hardly considered clothes.

Chambers, the butler, opened the door to her with a cheerful greeting. He suggested she joined Edmond's family in the drawing room. They welcomed her politely and Mrs Derwent rang the bell for Cook and asked her to provide a meal for Amy. Beatrice, elegant in a dress of pale green and white, looked at her critically. She supposed it must be inconvenient for them when she arrived well after a mealtime. *But I've been working long hours serving my country*, she thought, indignantly, *while Beatrice lives idly at home*.

'Peter's managed to secure a position at the War Office,' Mr Derwent told her.

'I begin next week,' he said proudly as she congratulated him.

She wondered whether to wash her hair before lunch, but that would only emphasize her lateness. Before long, Mr Derwent led her into the dining room, followed by Peter. Then Mrs Derwent came in, and Cook arrived with a plate of ham and salad. She was a plump middle-aged woman who had a nephew in Flanders and was well disposed towards Amy, gladly preparing meals for her even when she arrived at some unexpected hour due to wartime contingencies.

'It's good news about Peter,' Amy said.

Mrs Derwent looked jubilant. 'Having both sons in France would be simply unbearable,' she said.

Mr Derwent sat down with Amy as she began her lunch. His wife and Peter went to leave, then Peter looked embarrassed and joined them at the table, as though anxious she should feel welcome.

'Do you get Zeppelin raids in your area of London?' he asked.

'Not many. They mainly plague East London, round the docks.' Sometimes they caught sight of one of the sinister

German airships in the distance. 'There was one about three weeks ago and next morning we had to dodge round the broken glass in the street as we walked to the hospital.'

After the meal they joined the family on the terrace, at the sunny end where they could look down towards the town. Beatrice was merry as she and Peter were invited to a party that evening, held by a local family whose son was on leave. Such occasions were rare now.

Peter went to the stables and reappeared riding a chestnut horse. He paused by the terrace. 'Edmond and I used to ride Wanderer when we were younger,' he told Amy, 'though perhaps now we should learn to drive the motor car.' He smiled at her. 'Do you ride at all?' he asked.

'I'm afraid I never have,' she said. 'Are you planning to go far?' It was a mild, breezy afternoon.

He patted the animal's flank. 'Perhaps to the forestry plantation and back,' he said. 'Wanderer is older now. Henry, the gardener, takes him out for a trot sometimes, and Pa does too, but most of the time he just grazes in the paddock. Gee up, old friend.' The horse trotted off towards the side of the house.

As the shadows began to lengthen, Beatrice retired to her room so Janet, the maid, could arrange her hair.

Amy tried to pay attention to her mother-in-law's complaints about her shortage of servants. After her own experiences nursing injured soldiers, domestic concerns at The Beeches seemed trivial.

Just then there were noises and raised voices from a distance, round the corner of the house. Mr Derwent got up to investigate while his wife and Amy exchanged anxious glances.

Soon he was back with Peter, who was walking a little awkwardly and holding his arm, below his torn sleeve.

Mrs Derwent stood up. 'Whatever's happened?'

149

'I fell off Wanderer. It wasn't his fault – a swarm of bees flew in front of us suddenly and startled him so he reared up.'

'Come and sit down,' his father said.

'Thank heavens you're not hurt any worse,' Mrs Derwent said. 'Dear me, where are my smelling salts?' She went looking for them.

'Let me look at your arm,' Amy told him. She took hold of it gently. It was badly grazed and bleeding, grimy with earth and what looked like lichen.

'This needs cleaning up and dressing,' she said. 'Are you uninjured apart from your arm?'

'I'm a bit shaken, and I'll have bruises. I managed to break my fall by reaching for a tree,' he told her. He was grinning and making light of the accident. 'Actually, I could do with a cigarette.'

His father produced his case and lit him one. 'I hope the horse will be all right,' he said.

'Wanderer galloped off, away from the bees. Henry's gone after him.'

At that moment the young gardener came round the corner of the house, leading Wanderer, who looked only slightly agitated.

'I think he's none the worse for the incident,' Henry said. 'The bees seem to have all flown away now.'

Mrs Derwent came back and there was a pungent aroma as she sniffed from her small bottle of salts.

'The wound probably isn't serious,' Amy said to Peter, 'though it'll hurt for a while. But it's important to disinfect it. Let's go through to the kitchen and see if Cook has any iodine.' At the hospital the fully trained nurses generally tended the most severely injured patients, but Amy was becoming confident at dealing with lesser wounds.

In the kitchen, Cook was fetching down pans for the evening meal and Janet was washing cabbage leaves. Mrs Derwent followed Amy and Peter and watched as Cook examined a cupboard for first aid items.

'Do you think you'll be all right to go to the party?' Mrs Derwent asked. 'You need to set off soon if you're to get there on time.'

'I'm sure I'm fit enough to go,' he said. Janet found him an ashtray and he put out his cigarette.

Cook produced a bottle of iodine and some cotton wool and Amy rolled up Peter's sleeve. 'Sit down while I deal with it,' she told him. She shook some salt into warm water and began by sluicing out the wound. When she had washed away the dirt she saw it was worse than she had thought. 'It's quite deep in the middle,' she said.

Peter winced as she probed the wound lightly with her finger. 'A twig caught it,' he said.

Amy sluiced it some more, feeling around gently for any splinters but not finding any.

Just then Beatrice burst in, wearing a cream-coloured lacy gown Amy had not seen before. 'Pa told me you've hurt your arm,' she said. 'You won't be long, will you? We need to set out soon.' She peered at his arm. 'It's nothing serious, is it?'

'It should heal well,' Amy told her, 'but I need to clean it thoroughly.'

'It's quite superficial,' Peter said.

'Not really – the gash is quite deep in the middle.' Amy became aware of them all looking at her. 'It could do with stitching.' That would mean he had to go to the hospital in Wealdham.

Beatrice looked perturbed.

'It'll be all right without that,' Peter protested.

'Believe me, I've seen enough wounds to know how vital it is to treat them properly to prevent infection,' Amy said firmly. She considered the situation. It was borderline, as to whether or not it needed to be stitched. 'It should be enough for me to disinfect it with iodine and bandage it well,' she said.

'Let's hope it won't take too long,' Beatrice said. Between her other duties, Janet had arranged her chestnut hair so there were little curls round her face.

Amy dried off Peter's wound and then tipped some iodine onto cotton wool. 'I'm afraid this will sting badly,' she told him. He winced as she applied it to his arm. Then she began carefully bandaging his injured limb.

Beatrice was pacing up and down, trying to persuade her mother it would be acceptable for her to attend the party without Peter.

Amy paid little attention as she completed the bandaging to her satisfaction.

Peter smiled at her. 'Thank you so much,' he said. 'It's wonderful having someone with medical knowledge in the family.'

'If you feel at all unwell, feverish for example, you must ask your host to call a doctor,' she told him firmly.

'Will you be long getting ready?' Beatrice asked.

'No – and my bandage will hardly show,' he assured her.

When Amy had helped the staff put away their first aid items, she left the kitchen. In the hall, Mr Derwent was returning from checking on Wanderer. 'He's not too shaken now,' he told her. 'Have you seen to Peter's arm?'

She told him what she had done. 'I'm very thankful you were here to give it expert attention,' he said.

Before long, Peter came downstairs in evening dress and Beatrice put on her Indian shawl. Amy watched as the chauffeur set off, taking the brother and sister to their evening engagement.

–

Next morning Peter was there at breakfast, with his parents. 'The arm still stings from the iodine,' he told Amy, 'but it hasn't given me any trouble.'

Cook came to serve Amy a kipper. 'After breakfast I'll take the dressing off and check it's healing well,' she said.

'Doctor Stanhope was at the party,' Peter told her. 'He's recently retired. When I told him what happened he said Amy did absolutely the right thing by disinfecting the wound. He said it's essential to prevent infection.'

'There! We've cause to be grateful to Amy for dealing with it thoroughly,' said Mr Derwent, beaming at her. 'I knew your skills would be an asset to the family.'

His wife looked in her direction, appreciation showing in her face.

Beatrice came in, looking half asleep.

'How was the party, darling?' her mother asked her.

'It made a pleasant change to go out. It's not the same, though, with so many young men away in Flanders.'

Amy checked Peter's arm after breakfast and found it showed no sign of infection. She joined the family setting off to church. Peter went on foot so there was plenty of space in the car for the rest of them. Amy had arranged to join her own family for lunch. She walked back with them after church.

'You look tired, dear,' Father said as they arrived at Sebastopol Terrace.

'We work long hours in the hospital,' she admitted, not prepared to discuss the distressing sights they sometimes witnessed.

'Did you come back from London all by yourself?' Mother asked.

'Yes – I'm used to it now,' she said. Mother would probably be shocked at the times she had walked back from the hospital to the hostel after dark on her own, on days when her hours were different from those of her friends. The demands of the war were easing the restrictions on women's movements, and generally she welcomed it.

'Listen, Mother, have you got any spare ribbon? My hat needs smartening up,' she said.

'Yes, of course, dear, I'll see what I can find.'

Soon Amy was attaching a new length of rose pink satin ribbon to her hat.

'I've invited Florence to lunch,' her mother said.

'Oh, thanks – it'll be lovely to see her.'

'She and Bertie seem very close. When he was on leave a couple of weeks ago he was invited to join her family for an outing in their motor car. They took a picnic hamper and seem to have enjoyed a splendid day out. He was quite elated when he arrived back.'

Before Amy could explore this news any further, Florence arrived. She seemed in a merry mood as the girls exchanged greetings.

'I hear Bertie joined you and your family on a picnic,' Amy said.

'Yes – we only went as far as the Ashdown Forest, as I'm afraid I'm prone to feel a little sick on long car journeys. But we had a wonderful time.' Her face dimpled with a smile. She paused, as though wondering whether to say more, but changed the subject. 'When will Edmond manage to get home leave?' she asked.

'In summer they said – I hope they'll let him come soon.'

A bowl of lilac blooms graced the table as her mother served the simple roast meal.

'Has anyone heard from Bertie since he went back?' Amy asked.

'No, it's high time he wrote,' Father said.

'I heard from him the day before yesterday!' Florence's eyes were bright as she told them of his assurance that his part of the Front was relatively quiet.

'I hope I can see him next time he comes home,' Amy said.

'Bertie and me...' Once again, Florence seemed to be considering how much to tell them. 'We've reached an under-standing,' she said, smiling shyly.

A glow of happiness engulfed Amy. 'You mean – you're engaged?' she exclaimed. Florence was sitting next to her and she looked in vain for a ring on her dainty hand.

'We only talked of it the day before he had to go back,' she said.

'Bertie's still quite young,' Father said, 'and I believe he's surprised at his sudden feelings and urge to marry. But you'll make him a fine wife.'

It was true, Amy thought, for though Bertie was a year older than Edmond, he had always been easy-going and playful.

'Won't it be wonderful, being sisters-in-law, you and I?' Florence said, reaching out to embrace Amy.

'Perfect!' She wondered if the couple would plan a wedding to take place when Bertie next came on leave.

The day was drizzly and after lunch they went to sit in the parlour.

Florence was still working with the Belgian refugees, and told her they were settling well now. 'I started some more war work,' she told Amy. 'I've joined the group in the village hall, helping roll bandages and knit and so on. I only have time in my holidays, of course.' She was completing her training to teach and hoped to begin at a local school in the autumn.

Soon the doorbell rang and James was there.

'Not watching the cricket, then?' Amy's father asked him as he joined them in the parlour, knowing he was a keen spectator. Amy winced at the mention of cricket, still sensitive about what had happened at the pavilion.

'There isn't any this summer,' he told them. 'Most of the able-bodied young men are away fighting, and Colonel Fairlawn is in France. Mr Leadbetter is talking of trying to start junior matches.'

'Have you any plans for the future?' Amy asked him nervously, knowing he was due to be conscripted, against his will, when he reached eighteen.

'I've resolved to volunteer to be a medical orderly,' he told them. 'That way I can serve my country without actually fighting.'

'I'm so glad!' Amy rushed to hug him.

'My parents approve of my decision.' He was taller and looking more grown-up now, she thought.

Amy's father was less impressed. Now there was conscription, choosing a non-combatant role might seem motivated by cowardice. Florence did not comment, as though she felt it was a poor contribution to the war effort, compared with the active service of Bertie and Edmond.

'It's valuable work,' Amy assured the others. 'I've seen the casualties arriving from France. Orderlies help, getting the injured to the casualty clearing stations, escorting them on the trains and supporting the qualified medical staff.'

By late afternoon, the rain had stopped. 'I'd better get back to The Beeches,' Amy said reluctantly. Florence was leaving too.

'Is it official about you and Bertie?' Amy asked her as they left. 'Can I tell everyone?'

'Perhaps not yet. We barely had time to discuss the details,' Florence said.

Amy smiled at the memory of that precious time when she and Edmond had been falling in love, but their feelings had seemed too fragile to share.

'Let me know as soon as he's given you a ring!' she told her friend. Of course, her parents would be sure to tell her when there was a wedding date.

She set off back to the Derwents' house. High tea would be served there shortly, with due ceremony in a formal atmosphere.

–

Edmond had been counting the weeks till he was eligible for home leave. As soon as his restriction was lifted, he applied to his senior officer.

'I'll let you know when we can spare you,' Major Saunders said.

The battalion had been moved on, further south, beyond the Flanders area, but he still shared quarters with Frank. 'I can't bear it,' Edmond told him as they settled in their dugout that evening. Back in the autumn his early return from his honeymoon had been for a fresh offensive, but it had barely begun when the winter weather set in. The punishment for his late arrival meant he had not seen his wife since.

'You can get weekend leave, I suppose.'

'Yes, I'm taking some at the end of next week,' Edmond said without enthusiasm, lounging on his camp bed.

'You can go into one of the nearby towns.' Frank passed him a steaming mug of cocoa. 'Some of the bars are lively.'

'They're more like brothels, from what I hear.'

'They're not all like that.'

In the end, he spent his free time wandering the countryside. Certain areas had been scarred by the artillery now and some of the farmhouses reduced to rubble but he found a stretch by a river which was still unspoilt. He sat beside the tranquil water, as ducks swam past and dragonflies flitted through the reeds. For a moment, he could forget there was a war. Then the artillery opened up again in the distance.

Two weeks later, brilliant poppies were beginning to flower in fields nearby. The trenches were still muddy as the early summer had been very wet. He reminded Major Saunders of his request. 'Prospects for leave don't look good at present,' his superior officer said.

Edmond absorbed this information. 'You mean, the new offensive will begin soon?'

'Yes. We're not to discuss it with the ranks, of course.'

There had been rumours all through spring that a major offensive was planned.

'We won't know the exact date until the last minute,' the Major continued. 'Troop movements will take place at night, where possible, to maintain secrecy.'

Edmond stood there glumly.

'Come on, lieutenant! You know how important it is to make a breakthrough. This war has gone on quite long enough. We need to send the Huns packing.'

–

Back at the hospital, Amy received a letter from Peter. She had checked his arm and put on fresh iodine on the Monday morning, before setting off back to work. Now he was confirming that it was healing well and repeating his gratitude.

Two weeks later, there was a letter from Lavinia and Amy found she had contrived to be posted to nurse in France.

'I'd like to be sent there,' Amy told Katherine as they put on their white aprons ready to begin work. 'I might not be able to spend time with Edmond – we'd probably be stationed at different stretches of the Front – but I'd like to be nearer him. I've really very little idea what it's like over there.'

'You'd be receiving casualties straight from the Front,' Katherine said.

'Yes – would you consider working there?'

'I'd far rather stay here. My young man is still at Oxford university, remember.'

'Yes, of course. It's different for you.'

She was glad that Katherine no longer talked of leaving nursing. She had summoned up some inner strength, forcing herself to come to terms with the mutilations she might see on the ward and to accept their working conditions. As July approached they were completing their probationary period at the army hospital and planning to sign on for a further six months.

Edmond had still been unable to obtain leave for long enough to come home. One day towards the end of June Amy saw a form pinned to a noticeboard asking for volunteers to serve abroad and immediately added her name to those on the list.

The following day, they found that lots of convalescent men were being sent home.

'They've practically emptied the ward,' Katherine said. They gazed at the rows of vacant beds.

Then they were told to make them all up ready in case there were new patients. Amy had an ache in the pit of her stomach.

She had heard rumours that a great offensive was in the offing. She guessed it would begin soon.

Chapter Fourteen

At daybreak on the first of July Edmond was awoken by the great bombardment. Though it was aimed at the enemy, the ground all around was shaking, and dust flew around their dugout. They looked anxiously at its flimsy supports, worried the structure might cave in and entomb them, as had occasionally happened to other men.

He and his platoon were in the reserve trenches, some way back from the Front Line. When the bombardment ended, he and Frank exchanged glances. By now, the men in the Front Line would be surging over the top of their trenches to begin their advance. The preliminary bombardment had been meant to incapacitate the enemy but almost at once they could hear the German artillery beginning to pound.

As the sun rose higher, they waited tensely. For miles, men should be advancing now. The pandemonium coming from the direction of the Front Line suggested the advance was not progressing as smoothly as had been hoped.

Soon afterwards, the first wounded were being brought back, some carried through their trenches on the way to the casualty clearing station. There were groaning soldiers with bleeding wounds, hastily bandaged – they had witnessed this kind of pitiful scene before, but today the casualties kept passing through for most of the long day. Their men fell quiet, demoralised.

—

Over the following days, they heard reports of ground gained ahead and elsewhere along the Somme. The bombardment often started soon after the early midsummer dawn.

Then they moved into the forward trenches. One day soon after, orders came that the following morning Edmond and Frank had to lead their platoon into battle as part of the major attack near Pozières. The men had few illusions now that the advance would be as straightforward as the plans predicted.

Edmond lay awake. They got up before it was light, dressed and waited by the step ladders. He was shivering though it was not particularly cold. As usual, he had Amy's photograph in the breast pocket of his tunic. Would he live to see her sweet face again? Dawn came and soon they were propelling themselves out of the trench and towards No Man's Land. Shells whistled past them as they surged forwards, trying to keep going under the enemy onslaught, dodging round 'crump-holes' left by the explosions. The bombardment paused momentarily. His unit were among the leaders of the British advance, yet the pounding from the enemy had not sounded so heavy as on other days. As it began again, rather sporadically, he started to believe that his comrades actually had made some impression at this part of the line.

He shouted out words of encouragement to his men as they continued towards the German lines, raising his voice to its limit when the bombardment became noisy again. He ordered the men to fire if the enemy appeared. Starting to become breathless, he hurried on. He seemed to have been running for several minutes, but maybe it had not been that long. They must be approaching firing distance now. There was a sudden movement ahead and a bullet whistled past. Edmond fired back in the direction of the movement. For a few moments there was a volley of shots on both sides, and he was aware of a cry behind him. He looked round to see one of his men falling, injured.

'Clark's been hit, Sir!' As Edmond hovered, trying to decide whether or not to continue, the enemy fire dwindled and stopped.

Sam Clark was a popular private who often led the singing of saucy songs in the trenches. Now he was pale but conscious, shot in the leg, but without the serious bleeding there would be if a major blood vessel had been damaged. They propped him up in a shell hole and Edmond detailed one of his comrades to apply a field dressing from the basic first aid equipment he carried. He must stay there with the casualty until Edmond could send a stretcher party.

There was a good chance now that they might secure the trenches ahead. As they ran forwards towards the enemy position there were explosions from shells and occasional shots. Edmond ran on, breathless, until suddenly an explosion threw him off his feet and nearly deafened him.

Is this it? he thought. He had landed heavily on his arm and his right wrist was agony. His whole body was jarred from the fall, but he realised gradually that only his arm was injured.

'You all right, Derwent?' Frank helped him shakily to his feet. There was no enemy fire now, and the artillery had fallen silent.

'It's my wrist.'

'I think the enemy are retreating back up their line,' Frank said. 'Let's have a look at your arm.'

'It feels as though my wrist is broken.'

'Keep supporting it like that with your other hand while I prepare a sling. We'll have the medics look at it as soon as they've dealt with the serious cases.'

Deftly, he applied the sling to Edmond's arm. 'Sit down and take it easy,' he said, handing him his water bottle.

—

Once they were certain the enemy were in retreat, Frank Bentley prepared to lead their men on towards the German trenches. He begged Edmond to seek medical help, so he accompanied the orderlies carrying Sam Clark on a stretcher. They had given the man morphia and splinted and bandaged his leg as best they could. Retracing their steps across the churned up area of No Man's Land was particularly challenging.

The clearing station was a basic one under canvas. As they arrived, they found the wounded waiting outside on their stretchers, for there had been a rush of casualties earlier in the day. Edmond sat on the warm grass next to Sam and passed him a cigarette. Before long, a doctor came out to examine the fresh arrivals.

He instructed the orderlies to move Sam inside. 'We'll dress his wound better and prepare him to travel,' he said. They were positioned next to the railway and the wounded would be sent on by train to the nearest military hospital.

Eventually, they looked at Edmond's wrist.

'It's broken,' the doctor said. 'I'll send you on the ambulance train too. You might even get the damage examined properly with one of those X-ray machines. There's a woman scientist who drives round with a machine in her ambulance. The injury will probably take a few weeks to mend.'

So he would be out of the fray for a while. Relief surged through him, followed by guilt at his reaction.

'Sounds as though your battalion advanced well today,' the doctor remarked.

'Yes.' His men were taking over trenches recently occupied by the enemy.

–

News of Edmond's injury reached Amy two days later. There was an official notification from a nursing sister that he had a minor injury, and a note to her in unfamiliar handwriting that he had dictated to an orderly, being unable to write himself for the moment.

Our advance went well, it said. *My wrist is broken and in plaster but otherwise I'm unhurt. I shan't be able to fight for a while. Still struggling to get leave.*

'It's such a relief to know he isn't fighting for now,' she told Katherine.

Their wards were full of men who had returned from the great offensive with 'Blighty wounds,' injuries severe enough to require them to be sent back to Britain. The operating theatre was in practically constant use. The gangrenous wounds were particularly distressing, because the limbs needed to be amputated. If the surgeons were not drastic enough, the gangrene might return, requiring further amputation. She and Katherine were not senior enough to be required to help in the theatre, but they followed the progress of their patients, behaving professionally but unable to avoid agonising about the plight of the worst injured.

'Have you heard from your brother?' Katherine asked.

Amy wrote to him regularly with her own trivial items of news, in the hope that he would write back, but he seldom did. 'My friend Florence heard earlier this week,' she said. 'He's been in action too. He doesn't tell us much in his letters.'

If only there could be some end in sight.

–

Edmond was staying in the convalescent ward of the French hospital. Until the plaster was removed he could not rejoin his unit, and, impatient for his return, his superior officer would not let him go on leave either. He asked recent arrivals in his ward for news of the offensive. Accounts varied, according to the part of the line where they were positioned. Early claims of a great advance seemed exaggerated.

One day he saw a face which looked familiar. It took him a while to recognise the tall, thick-set figure as George, their former gardener. He must have been around twenty but looked older now, with shadows under his eyes. His shoulder was heavily bandaged.

Edmond told him how much his work was missed at The Beeches. In the background 'It's a Long Way to Tipperary' was playing on someone's gramophone.

'You making good progress?' he enquired.

'Yes, Sir. They'll send me back to my unit soon.'

'You joined up with your school friends, I remember.'

His once cheerful face clouded. 'They're dead now, Sir. It won't be the same without my comrades.'

'Dead – what – both of them?' They were village lads who Edmond had known.

'We all went over the top together, and the artillery got the three of us, only I got off lightly.'

Edmond gave him a cigarette and took one himself. He could just about light them with his stiff wrist. As they smoked, George told him of the friend who had died instantly of his wounds, and the one who had had severe abdominal injuries.

'They got him on a stretcher and tried to ease his pain with morphia. I was walking with him as they carried him off towards the ambulance, but he died before they reached it.'

'I'm very sorry to hear that, George.' Edmond tried to control his dismay. It was sometimes a relief for soldiers to talk of the horrors they had witnessed.

He remembered the merry group who had set off from Larchbury. They were young men from poor families, and at home some of them had had to share a bedroom with a brother or two. Life in the trenches, and the unappetising food, had not struck them as much of a hardship. The opportunity for them to leave their village and travel to France had seemed a once in a lifetime opportunity.

George grabbed his arm, his eyes wide. 'You won't tell his family how he died, will you?'

'No, of course not.'

–

The stream of casualties reaching London scarcely diminished as July and August passed, and the VADs were allowed little leave. One weekend in September Amy was granted twenty-four hours away. She reached The Beeches on Friday evening, managing to arrive in time to change for dinner.

Her in-laws were anxious about Edmond. It seemed they had received a similar letter to her own earlier in the week, reassuring them of his progress.

'Someone else had to write it for him,' Mr Derwent said.

'Mine too,' Amy told them, 'but he wrote a couple of lines at the end. His writing was very poor, but I could tell it was his own hand.'

Peter was still busy at the War Office in London, so he was relatively safe.

'Have you heard about George, our gardener, and his friends?' Mr Derwent asked.

'No,' she said warily.

'Must you talk constantly of the bad news from the Front?' his wife complained, as Janet served them blancmange. Beatrice excused herself from the table.

'Amy will hear soon enough – the whole town is talking of the casualties,' he said. 'George has been injured, though he should recover, I understand. His friends from school have been killed, both of them.'

Amy set down her spoon, sick at heart.

'At least you're working to save our wounded,' he tried to comfort her.

Next morning, she walked over to Sebastopol Terrace to see her parents.

'We've time for a cup of tea before I get lunch,' Mother said, and went on to complain about the price of sugar and tea now that there were shortages.

'James is away training,' Father said as they settled in the parlour. 'They say he'll be sent to France in a few weeks.'

'Good. As an orderly he'll be doing vital work but he won't be actually fighting.'

Mother came in with their tea things on a tray. 'You don't need to serve me in the parlour,' Amy said, for they treated her as though their back room was not smart enough now she was a Derwent.

'It's sunnier in here in the morning.' Mother poured her a cup of tea.

Just then, a boy came riding along the street on a bicycle and stopped outside their house. She watched as he opened their gate and came up the path and suddenly she felt the blood drain from her face. He was one of the young men who delivered telegrams.

Her father was on his feet before the man knocked at the door. Mother gasped as she too realised the significance of the visitor. She and Amy followed Father into the hall.

Father snatched the telegram and tore it open. 'No reply,' he said bleakly. He turned and faced the others, his face drooping. 'Bertie,' he said. 'It's Bertie…' He shook his head.

Amy seized the sheet of paper. *Regret to inform you second lieutenant Albert Fletcher killed in action*, she read.

Her mother, who had read it over her shoulder, let out an unearthly cry. Amy turned to catch her arm and steadied her. She led her back into the front room and helped her into a chair. Now Amy felt dizzy herself. She could keep steady while seeing grim sights on the wards but was still unprepared for family tragedy. She grabbed the nearest chair and lowered herself into it.

Mother began to sob while Amy and her father sat, unable to find words for their loss. Amy was so frightened of losing Edmond that she had been less aware of Bertie's part in the fighting. Now she suddenly realised how much he had meant to her. For several minutes none of them could speak coherently. In one moment all their lives were changed.

From the mantelpiece Bertie's photograph smiled out at them, reminding Amy of his cheeky good humour. When she had been involved in the incident at the cricket pavilion he had understood and kept quiet for her. How was it possible that she would not see him again?

'Florence has to be told,' she said desperately, placing her teacup back on the tray. She went and drew the curtains.

'Will it be their lunchtime?' Father asked.

All thought of lunch had left her mind. 'I don't think they'll be eating yet. I'll change into my mauve frock.' A few dresses remained in her old room and mauve was an acceptable colour for mourning.

She set out through the sunshine which seemed to mock her mood. At the end of the High Street, she turned off onto the drive leading to Florence's family's substantial house. Mr Clifford, her father, opened the door to her and must have been able to tell from her face that there was bad news.

Florence was summoned, in her dainty floral dress, not unlike the one Amy had been wearing.

She looked at Amy's face and her usual composure faded. 'Just tell me,' she said, trembling.

Amy told her and her friend crumpled into her arms. As Florence's tears began to flow Amy too began sobbing.

After a few minutes, Florence's parents brought them glasses of sherry, as though that might revive them, but they sat in complete dejection.

'Tell me if there is anything I can do,' Mr Clifford begged.

'Might I use your telephone?' Amy asked. 'I want to phone Matron and ask to extend my leave.'

Matron took some time to come to the phone. She was sympathetic but reminded Amy that she was not the only one to have been bereaved. She might stay for an extra day before returning to work, and of course she would be allowed time off to attend the memorial service.

'I suppose I'd better go home to be with my parents,' Amy said, hugging Florence.

When she reached home, Father set out for the vicarage to tell Uncle Arthur the news.

–

Next day they endured the Sunday service as best they could. There were other families in mourning now and nothing Uncle Arthur said in his sermon seemed to make sense. Afterwards, he invited Amy and Florence back to the vicarage.

They refused the offer of sherry and Aunt Sophie brought them cups of tea.

Florence was pale and her hair tousled. 'I wrote to Bertie early last week,' she told them. 'Do you think he got my letter before he was killed?'

'Probably,' Amy said.

'It's as though God hates us,' Florence cried out suddenly. 'Our young men are so brave and yet they're getting killed or mutilated. What's the purpose of it all?'

Amy had never known her friend so outspoken, yet her words chimed with her own thoughts.

'It wasn't God who started the war,' Uncle Arthur pointed out.

'Why doesn't He listen to our prayers?' Amy asked. Never had her faith been so challenged.

'I can't explain it,' Uncle Arthur said, his usual smile missing, 'but we must keep our trust in Him.'

-

The memorial service for Bertie took place just over two weeks later. The church was packed. Amy stood, disconsolate, beside Florence. She had hoped Edmond might manage to get leave to attend but it had not been granted. His letter to her had been full of regret and commiseration.

News had arrived eventually from Bertie's unit that he and some of his comrades had been killed by enemy shelling while taking part in a major offensive. The notification gave Morval as the nearest town to where he had been buried in a temporary grave. There was also an official document signed by the king in gratitude for the officer's sacrifice. A letter came from Bertie's superior officer, saying how much his contribution had been valued and commending his bravery. His wounds had been severe, and he had died almost immediately, they were told. Amy hoped that part was true.

Since first hearing of his death she had woken each morning with a feeling of dread at the back of her mind before recalling what had happened. She tried to spare herself the torture of imagining what his last moments might have been like but could not always banish this concern from her thoughts.

As the service began, the music and words which were supposed to bring consolation swirled around her. She remembered the wicked twinkle in Bertie's eyes as he had encouraged her in childhood mischief. This was not what was supposed to happen to him, snuffed out before his twenty-third birthday.

The Derwents attended the service. Peter had managed to get leave from the War Office. Father's eulogy, recalling their bright, merry son and brother who had set out bravely to fight for his country, brought tears to Amy's eyes and those of others close to him.

Afterwards, Mrs Derwent and Beatrice went home but Edmond's father and brother came back to Sebastopol Terrace with them and expressed their regrets.

Florence sat there, a slight figure dressed in black. She had kept asking Amy if there were any details about how Bertie had died, so Amy had shown her the correspondence.

'He was so proud to be in the army and serve his country,' she said, as though still pondering his sacrifice.

James was there too, on leave from his training to be a medical orderly. 'I'll miss Bertie so much,' he told Amy. 'He was like a brother to me.'

Florence stared at him, as though questioning his courage, critical of his decision to be an orderly rather than fight. Amy was sorry to see her friend so disapproving, but today was not the day to challenge her views.

By late afternoon, Amy had to set out for the station to return to the hospital. She hugged Florence and promised to write between visits.

It's worse for me, she thought as the train steamed off noisily. *My husband is still in France. I could lose him too: other people have lost two or more close relatives. We've been married for ten months but we've only spent a day and a night together and I don't know when I'll see him again.*

She scarcely slept that night. When she got up at first light and looked outside the London street was shrouded in mist. Trees were ghostly shapes and the traffic barely visible.

My life's like that now, she thought. *I can't see the way ahead. I know what I want – a life with Edmond. But there's no signpost telling me what lies ahead. I have to grope my way forward, through the thick mist, longing for the time we can be together.*

When she eventually reached the hospital, Matron wanted to see her. It seemed Amy would shortly be sent to work at a hospital in France.

Chapter Fifteen

France, Autumn 1916

After the Channel crossing, Amy stood waiting with a group of VADs for transport to the hospital. She was not being sent to the Somme region, where Edmond was stationed, but further north near Arras. The harbour area was teeming with a variety of forms of transport. Trains were often used now to bring casualties for evacuation, but there were also motor ambulances and old-fashioned horse-drawn wagons.

An officer approached her. She had passed him on the ship and seen him staring at her. The tall, florid captain looked familiar. 'You're from Larchbury, aren't you?' he asked.

'Yes.' Oh, heavens, it was Wilfrid Fairlawn, the colonel's son. She remembered him from the recruiting station at the fête at The Beeches, two years earlier.

'Might I drive you to your hospital? I have a motor car here.'

'No, thank you. We have transport arranged for us.' She took a step towards the nearest VAD, whom she had only just met.

At that moment, an ancient omnibus drove up nearby and she picked up her luggage and headed for it. By the time she had discovered it was not the right one for her hospital the captain had gone on his way.

Soon her bus arrived and she set off with some other young women through the flat countryside as dusk fell. They travelled a little way beyond the Flanders area. It was late by the time they reached the hospital but they could hear artillery in the distance. They were served a supper of cold meat and potatoes, then she was shown to her small Alwyn hut, made of wood and canvas, which she was to share with another VAD, called Emily. She was small and slightly built. Amy discovered she was one of the older daughters from a large family.

'I must write to my parents tomorrow,' Amy said. 'They didn't want me to come to France.' As they had seen her off on the train, Mother had been crying. Father had told her he was proud of her, but his smile was a shade unconvincing.

'There's no need for them to worry!' Emily told her. 'They're bound to take good care of nurses over here.'

'That's what I told them.' Mother had wiped her eyes, but Amy wished she was not leaving them at this particular time. 'My brother was killed on the Somme earlier this month, you see,' she explained. 'They could do with my support.'

'Oh, how dreadful!' Emily said. 'I'm very sorry about your brother. But the injured men at the Front need our help urgently.'

The September evening was mild as she and Emily settled into their beds. What were the chances that Edmond would manage to visit her here, Amy wondered. How frustrating it would be if they still remained apart.

Next morning they walked up a drive to the hospital, which was a substantial building with rows of windows on three storeys and a turret at each end.

'Is this what you call a chateau?' Emily asked, not pronouncing it quite correctly.

'It might be. I suppose a wealthy family used to live here.' They continued across the lawn, bounded by cypress trees. They went through the main entrance and into Matron's office.

She was a middle-aged woman, preoccupied-looking, who passed them over to Sister Reed. The latter had curly dark hair, glasses and a serious expression. She addressed the new arrivals before they started work.

'You should know we have some German casualties here,' she told them. 'We treat them the same as we treat our own men. We hope any of our wounded men who are captured behind German lines will receive similarly decent treatment.'

As they followed the sister to their ward, Emily exchanged glances with Amy. They would meet real Germans. 'My father is a schoolteacher…' she began to say.

'So is mine!'

'Mine actually teaches German,' Emily whispered, 'though it's much less popular now. He studied in Germany for a short while, many years ago. He finds it hard to believe the Germans are as bad as people say.' Her Belgian friends had told Amy some horrifying incidents relating to the invasion of their country and newspapers were still suggesting they were ogres.

It turned out the Germans had been assigned a ward of their own, and for now Amy and Emily would not be working there.

The artillery was louder and they could feel the vibrations from the direction of the Somme as they began work in one of the surgical wards. Some of the men were mumbling incoherently as they came round from operations. There were still fresh casualties arriving. Though Emily was tiny, she seemed to have boundless energy as they rushed around making up beds and administering saline solution to the new arrivals to stabilise them.

At lunchtime, Amy joined some of the other staff who took their break at midday. As soon as she walked into the canteen she heard a familiar voice nearby. Lavinia was just about to leave with a colleague, her starched cap perched a little crookedly on her abundant dark hair. 'Amy!' her old friend called out as they came face to face and hugged, delighted to see each other. For a few moments they caught up with each other's news.

Lavinia frowned. 'I'm very sorry about your brother,' she said.

'I don't suppose I'll ever come to terms with losing him,' Amy said. Tears came into her eyes as she remembered him. Lavinia put her arm round her.

'Has Edmond recovered now?' she asked after a few moments.

'Yes, he's back with his unit. I'm hoping there'll be some chance of meeting him, though he's further south, in the Somme area.' She had posted a quick letter to him first thing that morning, confirming her arrival.

'My father's in France now,' Lavinia said. Amy remembered he was a distinguished surgeon. 'He works here and at other hospitals. They call on him for some of the more difficult cases.' She looked at her watch. 'I must go back to the ward. We're supposed to have three hours' break in the middle of the day, but we seldom get the chance when we're busy.'

For Amy too there was a rushed lunch and a tiring afternoon in the stuffy ward. As she finally left, a woman she recognised as one of Lavinia's colleagues came up to her.

'Are you Amy Fletcher?'

'I used to be. I'm Amy Derwent now.'

'There's an officer at the gate asking for you.'

Could it possibly be Edmond? Would he have received her letter by now? But surely he would not have called her by her old surname. She hurried down the drive between the areas of parched grass towards the gate. There was only one officer waiting there and it was Wilfrid Fairlawn, standing beside a shiny motor car.

'Good evening, Amy,' he said with an ingratiating grin. 'I was wondering if you'd care for a little jaunt into Arras.'

She struggled to remain polite. 'No, thank you, Captain Fairlawn. Perhaps you haven't heard, I'm married now.'

'I daresay – but your husband isn't here, is he? I could show you around.'

'That would not be appropriate. Excuse me, I have to get on.' She hurried away without turning back. As she walked towards her hut, she noticed Sister Reed and Lavinia watching her.

The sister stepped forward. 'I must make it clear, Nurse, that we don't allow fraternising with officers or male medical staff. All relationships must be professional.'

'Of course, Sister. In any case, I am married. That officer is an acquaintance and I have just declined his offer of an outing with him.'

The sister seemed satisfied with her explanation.

'Oh, dear, Captain Fairlawn,' Lavinia said when Sister had gone. 'He's got a reputation for unwanted advances to VADs and nurses.'

'I assure you I won't be going anywhere with him.'

–

The next morning, a convoy arrived with fresh casualties and some of them were German. Emily and Amy were now sent to their ward to help. The young men seemed little different from their own troops and just as vulnerable. There were perhaps more with fair hair, but many of them were indistinguishable from British Tommies; only the uniforms were different. It was impossible for Amy to understand most of what they were saying to each other but they behaved in a respectful manner.

She found Emily understood enough German to translate some key phrases.

'Did you notice that inscription on their belts?' Emily asked. ' "*Gott Mit Uns*" – that means "God with us." '

Amy gasped at the idea of British and German soldiers praying to the same God for victory.

At lunchtime, she emerged from the ward to receive a message from an orderly. 'Amy Derwent? There's an officer waiting for you at the gate.'

As she hurried down the drive a few of the staff were enjoying the sunshine on nearby benches. *Please don't let it be Wilfrid again*, she thought. But long before she reached the gate she made out Edmond's beloved figure. She broke into a run and he hurried through the gate and caught her in his arms. For a moment she was aware of nothing but blissful kisses.

'Nurse Derwent!' she turned to see an outraged Sister Reed.

She detached herself from his embrace. 'Sister, may I present my husband, Lieutenant Derwent?'

Edmond smiled charmingly as he shook the sister's hand. 'Excuse my exuberance, Sister. It's been nearly a year since I've seen my wife.'

The woman unbent a little. 'Try not to exceed the boundaries of propriety, please.'

'We'll do our best,' Edmond said as the sister returned towards one of the benches.

At last he was here, beside her! 'You can't imagine how I've missed you!' she cried. 'How long did it take you to get here?' If only his visits would be frequent.

Edmond took her hand and led her through the gate. He pointed to a modest-looking motorbike. 'That's my transport,' he told her. 'It took me two hours to get here on these awful roads, but I had to see you.'

There was something different about him which she had been very aware of when he kissed her. 'You've grown a moustache!'

'Yes – I've resisted having one for so long but it makes preparations a shade faster each morning. You don't mind, do you?'

'I'll get used to it.'

He went over to his machine and opened up a panier attached to it. He brought out a bunch of creamy roses and thrust them into her hands. They were fragrant and their petals silky, like the ones she had had in her wedding bouquet – both times.

'They're wilting in the heat,' he said.

'I'll put them in water as soon as I can and they'll revive.'

'I've only got eight hours' leave,' he told her, 'and I've spent over two hours of that waiting for you to come off duty. We haven't much time.'

'That's just not fair – I haven't seen you for nearly a year! When will we have the chance to spend longer together?'

He led her to the grassy bank beside the road and they sat down in the midday sun, still warm though it was the end of September. 'I promise I'll try to do better next time. I'll get twenty-four hours, a weekend – as much as they'll give me.'

She tried to be satisfied with this assurance. He was the same Edmond with the loving blue eyes. His face was tanned from the hot summer.

'I was horrified to hear about Bertie,' he told her. 'He's such a loss for you and your parents. I'll miss him too.'

'Sometimes I can't believe I'll never see him again.' In her last week at the London hospital she had received a pitiful letter from Florence. 'He's buried somewhere near a town called

Morval,' Amy told Edmond. 'Can you take me there to see whereabouts he was killed?'

'We can't take visitors there – it's too near the Front Line. I'm sorry, darling. On days when it's quieter, nurses sometimes go to nearby graves and lay flowers there. After the war there'll be proper cemeteries.'

After the war? Whenever would that be? For a few moments they were both quiet.

'Is there still a lot of fighting round Amiens?' she asked. Once more there was the sound of artillery in the distance.

'It's lively. You know I can't tell you any details.'

'Let me see your wrist. Is it better now?'

'Good as new.'

She examined it and it seemed to have mended well, allowing him full movement of the joint. It had at least kept him from fighting for a few weeks, she thought, as she sat there with his arm round her, basking in the delight of his presence.

There was a faint drone from above. He looked up and pointed to a small brownish biplane travelling across the blue sky. 'It's one of ours.'

'Oh – I haven't seen one before. What must it be like to fly over the fields like that?'

'They mostly use the planes for reconnaissance. We occasionally meet some of the pilots in a bar.'

All too soon, he rose to his feet. 'I simply can't afford to be late back,' he said.

She wanted to protest, to prevent him from rushing away, but could not risk him being punished again and losing more leave.

They enjoyed a lingering kiss, though it could not satisfy their need of each other, and she watched him climb onto his vehicle and speed off noisily in the direction of the Somme.

She picked up the delicate roses. She must find a glass and some water, then see if there was any time left for lunch.

—

They wrote to each other regularly and within three weeks Edmond had the promise of twenty-four hours' leave. Amy spoke to Sister and was granted leave for the same time. *At last we can be properly together,* she thought. *We must make each hour count.*

They would spend the day in Arras. That morning, she was already waiting outside the gate in the drizzle when he arrived on his motorbike. She had changed out of her uniform into the autumn suit she had brought with her, a darker, more robust outfit than the best one she had worn on their brief honeymoon.

He took her small bundle of belongings and placed them in the panier on his bike. 'I'm sorry you've got to travel like this,' he said. 'Only one officer I know well has a motor car and he wouldn't let me borrow it.'

'I don't mind,' she said.

'Is your hat anchored well?'

'Yes.' She climbed on the back of his vehicle and tucked up her skirt as best she could so it did not catch in the wheels. She clung on tightly as he roared off along the bumpy road. She hoped no one would see her, for it was almost certain to be deemed inappropriate behaviour for a VAD, even one travelling with her husband.

The wind rushed around her head and the few locks of hair which were loose whipped her face. Edmond smelt of oil from the machine and mud, for it had rained for the last week. His trenches must be becoming waterlogged again.

After a few uncomfortable miles they rode into Arras. Lavinia had told her it was the main town of Artois, just south of the Flanders area. Some of the buildings here were badly damaged, but her dismay gave way to joyful anticipation as Edmond stopped outside a small hotel.

'Is your skirt all right?' he asked, helping her clamber off.

'It'll be fine,' she said, though the hem was damp and muddy.

He stood looking across the street towards a pile of rubble. 'Shame this is the nearest town,' he said. 'It's seen a lot of punishment. The Germans occupied it in 1914. They were sent packing by the French, but only after heavy fighting.'

A middle-aged couple with sabots on their feet trudged along the opposite side of the street. What must it be like to see your home town become a battleground, Amy wondered.

Edmond turned back resolutely towards the hotel. 'I'm told this place is comfortable,' he said, then hesitated, suddenly solemn.

'What's the matter?'

'I'm afraid they've cut short my leave. I have to be back by midnight.'

'What!' She could hardly believe their time together was to be curtailed again.

'They're planning to move us on somewhere any day now.' He held her in his arms. 'I daren't risk disobeying them again.'

'No.' Their day was diminished.

'We're going to take a room, no matter what. They'll understand if we spend part of the day there.'

She put her arm through his as he led her into the hotel and booked a room. They were shown to a simple upstairs room, clean and light, where they could leave their limited luggage. She looked at the double bed and they exchanged glances.

'Dearest, how would you like to spend our day?' he asked.

183

There was something not quite respectable about making use of the bed at midday.

'How about a short walk, and lunch before we come back here?' he asked.

'Yes, I'd like that.'

He took her hand and they went back out. The rain was still falling fitfully and browning leaves were blowing off the trees. They passed houses with crumbling stonework and soon arrived at a market square, where a few traders were packing up their stalls. One was loading his remaining produce onto a dog cart. Across the square was a massive amorphous pile of rubble, apparently the debris from a large building. The only Frenchmen they saw were elderly ones, and the women looked sombre.

'One of our officers told me the baroque city hall was burnt down in 1914 and the belfry was demolished,' Edmond said. 'Last year the cathedral was destroyed. It's dreadfully sad.'

'People are being killed, remember.'

'I know; one shouldn't mind so much about buildings, but it's as though the Germans are trying to wipe out their culture.'

Amy hoped desperately that one day normality would return.

At the end of the square were a couple of bars and a small restaurant that Edmond had been recommended. As they approached, they saw some off-duty soldiers emerging from one bar, somewhat drunk. The other bar was frequented by officers, Edmond told her. A captain was leaving this bar with a young woman on his arm who was murmuring a few words in poor English. From her tight dress and elaborate hairstyle, Amy suspected she might be a prostitute. Edmond hurried them into the restaurant.

Amy suddenly remembered Polly, the woman she had met in jail. Her French equivalent had not looked so downtrodden, and Amy wondered if there was less of a stigma here to that way of life. Perhaps one day she would tell Edmond about Polly, but not now when they had so little time together.

The waiter brought him a menu and spoke to him in heavily accented French. 'There are shortages here now,' Edmond told Amy. 'They can offer us trout from a river nearby, or omelettes.'

'Trout would be lovely.'

He ordered their meal and they heard the waiter talking to the kitchen staff in an incomprehensible patois.

They sat holding hands still, happy simply to be together. They were the only customers as the clock in the corner struck one. When their meal arrived, Amy found it was tasty and well cooked, more refined than the food at her hospital.

All the same, she set it aside without finishing it. 'Let's go back to the hotel,' she whispered, feeling herself blush.

Edmond took a fresh folded handkerchief from his pocket and wrapped the slices of bread that were in the basket on their table. He thrust them into his pocket.

The day was cloudy and dim but there were still a few hours before it would grow dark. They went back through the town and into their hotel and climbed the stairs to their room. Edmond pulled the curtains across to shut out some of the daylight. Joy swept over Amy as he took her in his arms.

'Dearest, I've waited so long for this moment,' he told her. He began gently undoing her clothes. Lovingly they embraced each other and sank down on to the bed.

-

When he awoke it was only just light enough to make out Amy's blonde hair strewn across the pillow. He could detect the faint aroma of her flowery perfume.

A bell was ringing, probably from a nearby convent. He peered at his watch and found it was six o'clock. He stroked the soft, warm flesh of Amy's arm, then shook her gently.

'Dearest, I need to leave soon.' He dared not put off starting their return journey till the last minute. He lit the oil lamp. How sweet and innocent she looked in its soft light as she reached for her clothes.

He tried to be patient while she arranged her hair, passing her the pins. Then they shared the bread he had brought from their lunch table before going back to his motorbike. The street was nearly dark now and he needed the light on his machine. They set off out of the quiet town and back to the road towards her hospital. Though it was the main road in that direction, it was scarcely wide enough for two cars or carts to pass. The half moon appeared and disappeared as clouds flitted across the sky. Before they had gone very far they saw a convoy of army wagons ahead, filling the full width of the road, dawdling at the steady pace of the horses that pulled them.

Edmond sounded his horn. There was no response from the carter ahead. In any case, to allow him to pass, the wagon would need to veer dangerously near the ditch. He followed impatiently behind until the road widened a little, then hooted again. At last the wagon drew to the side and he was able to squeeze past, only to find himself stuck behind the next vehicle.

'Edmond – what are you going to do?' Amy said, valiantly hanging on behind him.

He tried not to panic as their slow progress continued. Occasionally he was allowed to overtake, but he could still see more wagons ahead. Then they reached a narrow lane to the right and he turned off thankfully.

The lane wound between the fields. 'Do you know the way?' Amy asked him, sounding anxious.

'We marched along here once in the summer, when the main road was clogged with vehicles.' But it had been light then, and he had simply followed others who knew the way. Here and there the lane forked and he had to peer at a signpost, if one existed.

We're going downhill, he thought. *That's right, because we should cross the river soon. Besides, the sound of the artillery is still more or less ahead.*

The road was uneven. 'Hang on tightly,' he implored Amy.

Should it really take this long, he wondered. He had forgotten what a roundabout route this was. At last the lane swooped down to the river, and the bridge ahead looked familiar. They crossed and continued on a slightly uphill course. It was almost pitch black now either side of the beam of his light and he was only vaguely aware of fields and trees.

He came to another fork in the road and this time the signpost was reassuring. He turned left. Then at last they reached the main road again at a familiar village. The convoy must be behind them now. He stopped momentarily.

'Are you all right, Amy? It's only a couple of miles now to your hospital.'

'Yes.' She sounded a little dubious.

'Don't worry, this is a narrow road, but it's the only one round here that amounts to more than a lane.'

At last the dimly lit hospital loomed up just ahead. He pulled up outside and helped her down.

'If only you didn't have to get back,' she said as they embraced.

He took her luggage out of his panier. 'Till the next time, darling,' he said, kissing her again, reluctant to let her go.

'Will you get back in time?' she said.

'Yes – I'll make it in spite of the detour.' He tore himself away and stood by his bike waiting to see her pass safely through the gate. Then he waved and set off.

In theory I've still got time to get back, he told himself. *It's just a question of whether my petrol lasts out till then, after all those extra miles.*

Desperately he rode on towards the Somme. He tried not to drive faster than he needed, for he suspected that would consume more petrol each mile.

The road was deserted now. He tried to recall which village could supply petrol, but in any case the place would not be open at this time of night. He made good progress to the point where he had to turn off the main road for the nearest village to his unit's position. His petrol must be almost exhausted by now but he could not tell exactly when it might run out.

With two miles to go, the bike spluttered to a standstill. He got off and dragged it into a bush behind a prominent tree. His eyes had become used to the darkness, and the moon had emerged again, so he was able to take stock of a farm entrance nearby. He would have to acquire some petrol and return for the bike whenever he could.

Meanwhile, he had under half an hour to reach his unit. He set off running along the lane, slowing to a walk as he became tired. He panted into his trench with ten minutes to spare.

Chapter Sixteen

France and Larchbury, November and December 1916

'The roads seemed a little better this time,' Amy said as they walked through the chilly streets of Arras at nightfall. It was towards the end of November and they had finally managed to get leave again.

'Sometimes they manage to get German prisoners of war to repair them,' he said.

It had not seemed such an ordeal on the motorbike this time. 'At least they've allowed us the whole weekend,' she said as they went into the restaurant. They would have a blissful uninterrupted two days.

They were the only customers and the waiter, probably in his fifties, brought them a brief menu. Perch from the river seemed the best option.

The room was warm, with its blazing logs. *I've been waiting so long to see him again*, Amy thought, suddenly tongue-tied. The busy wards occupied her days but gave her little to tell him, for she could not bring herself to describe the injuries she witnessed there. Physically he looked well, if less buoyant than he used to be, before he became battle-weary. She knew that although it was late in the year, there was fighting around Thiepval.

'Are you keeping warm in the trenches?' she asked him.

'Mostly,' he smiled. 'We've been receiving parcels of socks and mittens. And the YMCA have arrived. They're running a stall behind the lines where we can get hot drinks.'

She was a little comforted. The waiter brought their meals and Edmond looked disappointed for a moment at the frugal portions of fish, before beginning his dinner without complaint.

'Are they treating you well at the hospital?' he asked presently. 'Some of the men can be coarse but I imagine they generally behave themselves in front of young women.'

'They're usually very grateful for what we can do for them. You mustn't worry about me.'

She remembered the times she had walked into a ward to hear the men hastily suppressing a questionable song or saucy joke. Usually they were polite and appreciative. Occasionally one was wild or offensive, but usually that was because he was out of his mind with pain or misery, and the nurses tried not to be judgemental.

He set aside his empty plate. 'Mind if I smoke?'

'No – go ahead.'

He lit a cigarette from his case. 'You haven't started smoking, have you?' He let out a curl of smoke.

'No, though a few of the nurses do when they're off duty.'

He had been sitting opposite her, but now he came and sat beside her, his arm about her shoulder. 'I think of you, day and night,' he said, 'wondering what you might be doing. Our casualties go to one of the hospitals in the Somme area at first, but later they may be sent on further. If a wounded man goes off in an ambulance I imagine him arriving at your hospital, and you tending him back to health… It's almost tempting to get a wound so I manage to see you!'

'What an idea! And you might not be sent to my hospital or my ward. We do receive some casualties from your area, when they're fit to move, but I don't want to hear anything like that suggestion again!'

There was little fighting near Amy's hospital and when men arrived their wounds had been cleaned up. She had heard stories of the clearing stations receiving men with smashed limbs bound to splints by filthy bloodstained bandages.

He put out his cigarette and sipped his drink before leaning towards her and kissing her tenderly. 'I'll pay the bill and we can go back to the hotel,' he whispered.

They walked back and climbed the stairs to their room. The fire was low in the grate and they shed their clothes quickly before scrambling into the bed. Soon they were making up for all the time spent apart.

–

'I begged them to find something special for us to eat tonight,' Edmond said, as they waited to be served the following evening. 'I explained that tomorrow is our anniversary.'

She reached across the table and squeezed his hand. 'Who would have thought last year that we'd be celebrating it here?' she said.

'You look sad.'

'For a moment I was thinking how little time we've spent together.' The waiter bustled across with their dishes: there was duck in some kind of sauce with an appetising smell.

'This looks lovely.' She cut into her meal and enjoyed its rich taste.

Edmond sampled his. 'I think they've laced it with cognac,' he said.

The waiter returned with a bottle of wine for him to try. 'This is good, too,' Edmond said, and the man filled their glasses.

There were few customers but the restaurant was cosy. The wine made her feel mellow and they lingered over the meal before setting off back towards the hotel, her arm through his. Fog was closing in until they could barely find their way back to the hotel.

The following day was Sunday, their actual anniversary. They lingered in the warm bed. 'Remember how you rushed off, the morning after our wedding?' she said, her arm around him.

'That was a terrible wrench, but I knew I'd be in serious trouble for returning late from leave.' His widest smile lit up his face. 'There's no hurry this morning!'

By the time they eventually got dressed the church clock was striking half past ten. 'We'll have most of the day before we need drive back to our posts,' he said.

They went out but it was cold now and misty. 'We must find a different town to visit next time,' he said as they passed buildings still unrepaired from the bombardment.

They dawdled back to the café and ordered omelettes for lunch. They were seated by the window, looking out on the misty street. Amy shivered as she remembered the misty morning after Bertie's memorial.

'My life seems like trying to see ahead through mist and without a signpost.' She told him how that image plagued her. 'Uncle Arthur tries to tell us God has a purpose for us all, but it doesn't seem right since Bertie was killed.'

'So long as we can spend time together I'm happy,' he said.

As the townspeople set out for their evening service, Amy and Edmond began their journey back.

Amy was seldom allowed in the operating theatre with the regular nursing staff, but she had to pass that wing of the building to reach her usual ward. One day, she saw Lavinia outside the theatre, talking to a familiar-looking tall middle-aged man.

Of course: it was Mr Westholme, her father, the highly respected surgeon who worked at their hospital, among others.

Lavinia greeted her as she was walking past.

'Good day,' Mr Westholme said to her vaguely, peering at her from behind his spectacles. 'I know you from somewhere, don't I?'

'This is Amy Fletcher, Father, from Larchbury. I've brought her back to the house once or twice. Actually she's Amy Derwent now, because she's married.'

'Pleased to meet you again,' he said, shaking her hand vigorously. 'Is it your break time? I've finished my operations for the day unusually early. I'm just taking Lavinia to a restaurant for lunch – would you care to join us?'

'I'd love to, if it doesn't make me late back.'

'We're only going to the nearest village – there's a restaurant of sorts. You know how stuffy they are here about how nurses and VADs behave. They won't let Lavinia eat with me in the hospital.'

The early December day was chilly as she followed him to his motor car outside the main entrance. It would have been a smart vehicle, were it not for all the mud spattered on and around its wheels. He let her and Lavinia into the back before climbing into the front and driving towards the gate, then out onto the road. Amy held on to her hat in the breeze. There was little chance to talk as he drove into a small village of stone houses clustered round a church. He led the young women into the modest restaurant. There were no other customers but there was a savoury aroma.

Amy sat down at the table with them, grateful for the change of routine. There did not seem to be a formal menu, but the waiter told Mr Westholme he could bring them onion soup followed by braised pigs' kidneys.

'Aren't you the young lady who kept my daughter out of trouble by not giving her name to the police?' Mr Westholme asked suddenly.

'Oh, yes – it wouldn't have been right for me to betray her. I'm sure she'd have done the same for me if she'd been the one who was found out.'

'I like to think I would have done,' Lavinia said. 'But poor Amy had to go to jail for a week, Father – imagine!' Her eyebrows raised above her dark eyes.

'There was always the risk,' he said. 'You and she must have known that.' He did not sound angry with them. Lavinia had told her once that her parents recognised the merits of their cause. If only her own parents and the Derwents felt the same.

She felt the usual jolt of dismay at the memory of her humiliating week in jail. It still upset her that her one act of rebellion had caused such repercussions, blighting her relations with Edmond's mother and sister.

The soup arrived and proved to be tasty.

'How long have you been married now?' Lavinia asked her between courses.

'Just over a year, though we've hardly spent any time together.'

'It's the same for so many young couples now,' Lavinia's father said, sympathetically. Amy watched his skilled fingers which, she had heard, wielded the scalpel effectively, driving his knife systematically through his pigs' kidneys.

Amy told the others of her good fortune in spending the weekend of her wedding anniversary with Edmond. Since then, she had received more letters and was waiting for him to get leave and arrange a meeting. Probably it would be another rushed rendezvous.

'Where's he stationed?'

'Somewhere near Amiens. He tells me some of the casualties there are being treated under canvas, even now it's winter,' she said.

'Yes, there's a shortage of suitable buildings in the Somme area. The clearing stations need to be near a railway line. High Command are trying to take space in hotels to get the men proper shelter before the weather gets worse.'

'I heard a patient say the offensive is being scaled down now,' Lavinia said.

'So I understand,' her father said. 'There's even a chance that the statesmen might get together to negotiate for peace.'

'Oh, if only they would!' Amy cried.

–

Soon the Front was quiet and the weather very cold and intermittently snowy. They had not managed to meet but Edmond applied for Christmas leave and Amy did too. His unit had not been moved on as planned. Conditions seemed favourable for being granted leave around Christmas or New Year, but everyone wanted to take advantage of the lull and the men could not all be spared at once; neither could the nurses and VADs.

'It's too bad they couldn't have given us the same days off,' Amy complained to Emily when her leave was official.

'Edmond reaches home three days before Christmas and goes back two days afterwards. I don't arrive till Christmas Eve, though I get a whole week.' They were sitting in their chilly hut drinking cocoa after work.

'At least you'll be together for Christmas Day.'

'Yes.' Edmond's family were longing to see him, for he had not managed to get home leave for a whole year, since they were married. She supposed that the whole of his leave would be spent at The Beeches, with them having little time to themselves.

At last she was travelling across the stormy Channel, sitting with some other VADs in the cramped area below deck, next to a steamed up window. She and Edmond had last seen each other on a hasty day's leave in the second week of December.

It was late evening when she reached Larchbury. She alighted from the train into a snow flurry and saw the delightful sight of Edmond rushing down the platform to meet her.

'Darling!' he wrapped her in his arms.

'How long have you been waiting?' She was later than expected because the sea crossing had taken longer than usual.

'I've spent nearly two hours in the waiting room,' he said calmly. He picked up her small suitcase. 'The stationmaster will let me use his telephone to ring Ma and she'll make sure Cook has some soup ready when you arrive.'

When he had made the call, he led her outside to where the chauffeur was waiting in the motor car. Edmond apologised for his lengthy wait. 'I should take a lesson or two in driving the car,' he said.

At The Beeches, Edmond led her into the dining room where she was greeted by all the family. The room was decorated with seasonal foliage as usual.

Peter commiserated with her about her extended journey. He was still working in London at the War Office, renting a small flat nearby but coming home when he could. 'I'm hoping they'll send me to Headquarters in France soon,' he said, 'so I'll at least feel more in touch with what's happening.'

'What about the peace talks?' Amy asked him.

He shrugged. 'They're not making much progress. It's almost impossible to find a deal to satisfy both sides. The stakes are too high.'

Cook brought her some vegetable soup.

'I expect you got my letter,' Amy said to her mother-in-law, who had greeted her formally. 'I do hope you don't mind that I've arranged to go to my parents for Christmas lunch. This year will be so sad for them without Bertie, and I miss him dreadfully too, of course. It's right for me to be with them.' She took a welcome spoonful of the hot broth.

'Very well,' Mrs Derwent said.

'I've arranged to go there too,' Edmond told them. Amy was glad but suspected her mother-in-law had resented the arrangement. She looked the same as she had done in the summer, generally unsmiling, going round with an air of resignation.

'Edmond has to return so soon afterwards,' Mr Derwent said. 'We're holding our dance on Boxing Day this year, so he can be there.'

Cook cleared Amy's plate and brought her a portion of pie with vegetables, all rather dried up. Edmond passed her the cruet.

'I hope you'll forgive me for not attending the dance this year,' Amy said. 'It wouldn't be right while I'm mourning my brother.'

'I believe I should be there, at least for a while,' Edmond said, looking relaxed out of uniform. 'There are a lot of people I haven't seen for over a year.'

'There won't be so many guests this year, thanks to the war,' his father said.

'Food is so expensive now that it's hard to provide the kind of spread we used to serve,' Mrs Derwent complained.

Amy was weary from her journey and ate little of her dessert. She was thankful when she could say goodnight to the family and go upstairs with Edmond.

Soon they were in each other's arms. 'At last we're here, together, in our own room,' he said.

It was the very first time they were spending a night together there.

–

Amy awoke in the thin daylight of Christmas morning. Edmond was already awake, lying with his arm round her, smiling. 'I love it when I wake up and you're beside me,' he told her. 'And I love it even more when I know we'll still be together tomorrow.'

The fire was flickering cheerfully in the grate. Someone must have lit it again that morning, either Edmond or Janet, the maid. She looked around the room. On the table beside the window there was a vase of holly, unmistakably arranged by Beatrice. The carved wooden cabinet stood against the wall.

'Don't you think that cabinet is lovely, the one that Peter brought us from India,' Amy remarked. She had left it empty so that Edmond could decide its use; he was seeing it for the first time this leave.

He got out of bed and crossed the room. 'It's ideal for our records,' Edmond said, opening it to reveal them carefully positioned inside. 'I've arranged them there – what do you think?'

She went across to see. 'Thank you, darling, it's perfect for them.' He had arranged them in composer order, so his and hers mingled together now.

She got up and put on her lavender wool dress, suitable for mourning. After breakfast, she and Edmond walked together into Larchbury to the church, leaving plenty of space for the others in the car. The church was less abundantly decorated than in previous years. As she went up the aisle towards the Derwent pew, she stopped to greet her parents and nod to Florence, standing wanly nearby.

She and Edmond took their seats. The memory of Bertie's memorial service in the church just a few months before made this morning particularly hard to bear. There were other bereaved families there and now, with conscription, the whole congregation must be war-weary. Uncle Arthur led the service, recalling Christ's birth, but there was a good deal of emphasis on prayers for a speedy conclusion to the war.

Afterwards, she said a few words to Uncle Arthur and James, who told them he expected to be sent to France soon in his capacity as medical orderly.

She and Edmond joined her parents and went back to Sebastopol Terrace. As they went in, she could smell the goose cooking. Christmas would never be the same without Bertie, but her parents seemed to gain some comfort from having her and Edmond there. She went into the familiar kitchen and began to help her mother with the vegetables.

–

After lunch, they lingered as Mother played the piano and sang some of the old familiar songs they had enjoyed on previous

199

Christmases, only avoiding the exuberant ones. Occasionally they all fell silent. The armchair nearest the window was the one where Bertie used to sit, and now it was empty. Amy tried to imagine him, somewhere in the hereafter, watching them as though part of their gathering.

'I've got the music for one of those new songs,' Mother said. She began playing '*Roses of Picardy*', and Amy and Edmond joined in.

They had arranged that he would return to The Beeches mid-afternoon, while she called on Florence.

'Shall I send the car for you in an hour or two?' he asked.

'No, I don't mind walking.' The day was cold but it was not actually snowing.

Florence smiled as Amy arrived, but she could not maintain her happy expression for long, and Amy thought she had lost weight. After a few more moments she collected herself and asked about Amy's experiences in the hospital. She was also curious about how she and Edmond contrived to meet.

Mrs Clifford brought them refreshments, but as Florence poured their tea, Amy found her subdued.

'I'll never get over losing Bertie,' she admitted.

'Neither will I,' Amy said, but she at least had Edmond to cheer her.

'It's fortunate I have my vocation,' Florence said. 'And I'm still doing war work, making comforts for the troops, in the school holidays. Even your mother-in-law and Beatrice have joined our group.'

'Beatrice? Doing war work? Is she any use?'

'Perhaps not so much as the others,' Florence said.

Amy struggled to imagine her rolling up her sleeves and preparing packages for the men at the Front.

'In time perhaps you'll find another young man,' she said to Florence presently. 'I'm sure Bertie would want you to be happy.'

'I can't imagine finding anyone else. And they say our generation will be short of marriage partners. Lavinia and I were talking about it, last time she came on leave. She and I are probably destined to remain single.'

'Who knows what the future will bring?' Amy said, realising her own good fortune. She tried never to contemplate the possibility of losing Edmond.

The clock chimed three. 'It'll begin to get dark soon,' Florence said. 'If you're determined to walk back, you'd better leave soon.'

They hugged each other before she left.

–

Edmond had not meant to spend Christmas afternoon talking seriously with his father and brother, but there was so little time before he had to return to France. He knew that the following day they would be absorbed with the dance, and that some of the guests were to arrive earlier in the day.

'I need to be sure Amy will be well cared for if I don't return,' he said to them as they sat smoking in his father's study. They could hear Beatrice playing the piano and singing for her mother in the drawing room across the passage.

'Don't talk like that, Son.'

'I have to, in these times.' He was reluctant to ask favours of his relatives. 'It's not just Amy. Suppose she had a child? Ma and Beatrice have been slow to accept her into the family and I can't face the future with any kind of confidence unless I know that my wife will be secure.' He had never spoken to them so solemnly before.

'I've always respected Amy,' his father said without hesitation, lighting up another cigar. The small room was becoming smoky.

'She's an admirable young woman doing valuable war work,' Peter said. Edmond could see he had engaged his attention.

'Your mother is coming round to accepting her, and Bea will eventually,' his father said. 'I promise you she'll always be part of the family, she and any children.'

'The same goes for me,' Peter assured him.

'Thank you.' His spirit was eased a little.

'I'm proud of your bravery in fighting for your country,' his father said.

—

Next day Vicky arrived mid-morning, looking more grown up than she had when she had been their bridesmaid. Charles rode over on his horse, for he was on leave. How pleased Edmond was to see him. While the women were chatting, the young men went out for a ride. Wanderer shared a stable with horses they had once used for their carriage. They had kept the two young, strong carriage horses to join the teams they used for working on their forestry land. Edmond climbed eagerly into the saddle of the aged chestnut.

The day was overcast and the overnight frost barely showed any sign of melting. He and Charles began exchanging accounts of some of the action they had seen in France. It was so much easier for Edmond to talk of these experiences alone with his friend than in front of his family.

'Do you have cases of shell shock in your battalion?' Charles asked.

'Yes – I've seen it. I try to encourage the men to control their fears.'

'I struggle sometimes when I lead them out into danger,' Charles said. 'I share their fears but have to try to conceal it.'

'Me too.'

'One of our men went to pieces last week,' Charles went on. 'He's awaiting court-martial now.'

Edmond shuddered. If a soldier had refused to advance he could be sentenced to death for cowardice and shot at dawn.

They returned from their ride a little comforted by the opportunity to unburden themselves of their disturbing memories.

—

At luncheon there was a cheerful atmosphere. Beatrice was sitting next to Charles, talking a little superficially of her admiration for the men who went to fight. For many months now she had been starved of young men to entertain her.

'I'm doing war work now,' she was telling Charles proudly. 'I join the others in the village hall to knit gloves for them.'

Edmond found it hard to imagine her helping. He supposed she and Ma might feel obliged to set an example by joining the war effort.

Ma had contrived to produce a fine array of food. Mrs Johnson, who still worked one day a week for the Fletchers, was helping to serve. Amy greeted her and asked after her numerous family. Beatrice stared at her for being so friendly to a domestic.

Anticipation rose as the evening approached, but Edmond was sad to leave Amy to her own devices in her room while he put on evening dress and went to join the party. Were it not for Peter and Charles and a couple of other old school friends who had managed to get leave he would have skipped the evening entertainment to be with Amy.

Compared with previous years, there were a lot of absentees. He circulated to greet the local families. As they moved into the large dining room to eat, a pianist was playing popular tunes for background music.

'She's going to play for the dancing as well,' Beatrice told him as guests began to return to the ballroom. 'They've called up two members of our usual quartet. It's so vexing.'

'I shan't stay for the dancing,' Edmond told her.

'Oh – I wish you'd stay and dance with me,' Vicky said, skipping along beside him in a new white gown.

'Very well; you and I will join in the first dance.'

His parents launched the first waltz and Edmond seized the hand of his pretty cousin to twirl her happily round the room. Charles was soon dancing with Beatrice, seeming captivated with her.

The music came to an end. 'I suppose you must go now,' Vicky said. 'Will you take Amy some supper?'

'Yes, of course. I'm just going to prepare a tray for her.' She followed him back into the other room and helped him select portions of the tastiest dishes.

'What about some wine?' she asked.

He approached Chambers and secured a bottle which was half full and a pair of glasses.

'Thanks for helping me choose, Vicky. Now off you go, back to the ball.'

He was glad he had introduced her to a decent young officer friend who could be relied upon to give her a dance or two.

He hurried upstairs to their room. Amy got up to greet him from where she had been sitting in a chair beside the flickering fire.

'Darling! Is the ball going well? It's sweet of you to come and join me.'

He encouraged her to eat and drink. They could hear the piano music from downstairs.

'If only you didn't have to return tomorrow.'

He put his arm around her: how precious she was to him. 'Listen, Amy, if I get killed in France...'

'No! Don't talk of such a thing!' Her blue eyes were large and pleading.

'I have to. It happens. I don't know why our generation is so unfortunate but we have to face the possibility. Listen, I wouldn't want you to spend your life mourning. I'd want you to find another young man and be happy.'

'I simply can't imagine being with anyone but you.'

'Well, in case it ever comes about, remember that's what I want for you.'

She held him, resting her head against his shoulder. 'One day all this will be over,' she told him firmly. 'We'll have our own little house and we'll be together, day after day.'

Chapter Seventeen

The day after the dance Amy went to the station with Edmond's family to see him off on the first stage of his journey back to France. She tried to hide her anxiety for him, and they talked of arranging a meeting as soon as possible. The train arrived and they enjoyed a final lingering embrace before she had to let him board.

She walked back to The Beeches with Peter, allowing his parents and Beatrice to travel in the car. 'At least you spent Christmas with him,' Peter said.

She realised she had been trudging along the chilly streets silently, wrapped in her own thoughts. 'Yes,' she said, 'I suppose I'm fortunate. And we'll get the chance to meet in France.'

The loss of Bertie still weighed heavily, partly from the absence of his merry presence, but also because it reminded her of the fragility of life in these days when the fabric of normality was lacking. Even Edmond, usually so cheerful and optimistic, was recognising the dangers he faced and urging her to find some future for herself in the event of his death.

Amy passed a few more days at The Beeches. Edmond's family, her own parents and Florence all seemed regularly to sink into dejection. Peter was smoking and drinking more than usual, but encouraged her in her attempts at forced cheerfulness. At least she knew her nursing skills would be put to worthwhile use in France.

Before the new year, she was back at the hospital near Arras. There were few casualties because the Front had gone quiet. Now the wards were half empty, she noticed the fancy plasterwork on the coving, a relic of grander days.

There was frost on the ground every morning and sometimes it did not melt all day. By the second week there were heavy snowstorms. The nurses wore extra woollies beneath their uniforms and went to bed early in the evenings to keep warm.

'They're billeting Edmond and some of the others in houses in the nearest town,' she told Emily when she got a letter from him. 'You can imagine how cold it must be in the trenches.' But at least they were not fighting.

Then she received another letter. *I can only manage a day's leave at the end of the month,* Edmond had written. It would be another rushed rendezvous.

One day, as she ventured outside the hospital at lunchtime she saw a motorbike being ridden through the gate, though it was not Edmond's. She gasped at the sight of a figure in a skirt riding the bike. The bike came to a halt nearby and a tall woman alighted, rearranging her skirt which had been folded up round her legs.

'Lavinia!' she gasped.

Her friend smiled. 'What do you think?' she asked.

'Isn't it dangerous, riding through snow and ice?'

'It's a little milder today, though I needed to be careful. It's just wonderful to have the freedom to go out when I'm off duty.' She took a packet of cigarettes from her pocket and offered one to Amy, who declined. More women were smoking now, but the habit did not appeal to her. Lavinia lit a cigarette and drew on it.

A senior nurse who was passing stared in their direction.

'Has Matron said anything?'

'Not much. I suspect if any other VAD had started riding a motorbike they'd have been in trouble, but my father is influential here, and I'm hoping it will help other women do the same.'

Amy followed her as she wheeled her vehicle over to the area where ambulances and a few cars were lined up.

'I'm determined that now we're part of the war effort we suffer fewer restrictions,' Lavinia said, drawing on her cigarette again. 'It's all part of our struggle. So many women are helping now. Our former parlour maid works in a munitions factory.' She grinned at Amy. 'You should get a motorbike!'

For a moment she considered the idea, but she could not afford it, even if she found the courage to ride one. Should she think of getting a bicycle, at least, in the summer?

'We must go out for a meal in the village when it gets warmer,' Lavinia said.

Next day, it began snowing again and two days later another letter came from Edmond. He was reluctantly calling off their meeting. With the weather so poor he dared not travel, for a sudden storm might leave him stranded.

One cloudy lunchtime when Amy and Emily went off duty, a small group of convalescent Germans were waiting outside for transport. She had heard they were to be transferred to a prisoner of war camp. A British lieutenant and handful of soldiers were standing guard.

As the women approached, a German with a roguish expression, despite an arm in a sling, bent to the ground and scooped up a ball of snow, rolling it against his leg with his good hand and compressing the snow. Then he flung it at one of the guards. It splattered against his coat. There was a moment of silence. Amy watched nervously as the lieutenant and the victim pointed their rifles towards the insubordinate prisoner.

Then the other British soldiers began to chuckle. The target of the prank seemed to relax as he brushed off the snow. Two British soldiers were gathering snow now and preparing solid snowballs which were soon flying through the air and finding their German targets.

Amy exchanged amused glances with Emily. They remembered nursing some of the Germans. One of them was largely fit, though his leg wound had left him with a limp. He was eagerly scooping up snow to hurl at the British. Other Germans, leaning on crutches, were too handicapped to act, but one with a bandage over one side of his head was able to stoop and gather enough snow for an effective missile. Three convalescent British soldiers now arrived on the scene and began to pelt the prisoners. Snowballs burst on their coats and laughter rang through the chilly air.

The few Germans well enough to join in were outnumbered now, but they did their best to continue the onslaught. Amy joined in the mirth, wondering when someone senior would arrive, determined to stop the game.

Then an ancient army bus drove in. The escort party brushed themselves down, stood up straight and pointed their rifles in the direction of the prisoners. The bus came to a halt and the driver got out and held open the door.

'On board! Quickly!' snapped one of the guards.

'*Schnell!*' shouted one of the others.

The first of the Germans climbed into the bus while the lieutenant crossed his name off a list.

'Goodbye, Fritz!' shouted one of the British convalescents.

'Farewell, Tommy!' came the reply as the less mobile Germans were helped on to the bus. Then the escorts climbed aboard, the door was slammed shut and the bus set off carefully down the snowy drive and out into the road.

'I'd never have believed it!' said Emily.

There remained only the tyre tracks in the snow and a few melting remnants of the missiles. Amy was aware that any day now the artillery would begin again and there was no prospect of a truce. All she same, she knew Edmond would enjoy her account of what had taken place, and so would some of her family. How Bertie would have loved the incident, she realised, with a pang of grief.

–

War seemed to be suspended while the very cold weather lasted. When the snow thawed, Edmond sometimes managed to ride over on his motorbike for a few hours or a whole day and night. He was amused by her account of the battle of the snowballs. 'If only that could persuade those in command that we all want peace,' she told him.

He shook his head. 'We need a decisive win,' he said. 'Somehow we've got to make it all seem worthwhile.'

She could not come to terms with the prospect of the resumption of hostilities.

'I'm due three days' leave,' he told her one day in March, 'maybe at the beginning of next month. Where shall we go? We could visit Paris, if you like, or we could go somewhere quieter.'

The sophisticated city that everyone talked of: she had dreamt of visiting it. 'Is it a long way to Paris?'

'It'll probably take us most of the day to get there.'

'Perhaps we should go somewhere nearer where we can relax together, instead of rushing wildly round a busy city.'

'There's a town north of here called Béthune which hasn't seen any fighting. It sounds a lovely place to go.'

The sun was shining when they set out that April day, the day after Good Friday. They passed a column of soldiers on the road heading north. Edmond drove into a village to buy provisions and they stopped beside the road, where there was an attractive view of fields and a stream, to eat their picnic of bread and tasty local cheese. In shady places there were still traces of snow, but primroses and violets were growing on the bank and the birds were singing merrily.

'I've been thinking of getting a sidecar for the bike,' Edmond told her. 'You could travel in it. You'd be more comfortable and not get so dusty.'

She remembered seeing bikes with sidecars, poky little attachments. 'They look awfully claustrophobic,' she said. 'I think I'd prefer to go on riding on the pillion.'

Once they had passed the turning for Arras, there were army vehicles on the road, heading south. Edmond stopped for a moment where the road was a little wider to allow a large wagon to pass.

He was quiet, thoughtful. Will there be fresh action on the Front soon? she wondered.

They reached Béthune by mid-afternoon and Edmond booked them into a small hotel he had been recommended. Amy changed into her suit.

They set out to see the old medieval square with its famous belfry. She gazed up at the beautiful Flemish houses with their steep gables.

211

'It's lovely to see a town which hasn't sustained any damage,' Edmond said.

'I never expected French towns to look like this,' she told him. 'Beatrice showed me some pictures of Nice.' She had gone there with her mother one spring, before the war. 'There were palm trees and mimosa, and she said the villas were painted in pastel colours.'

'The south of France is very different,' he told her. 'The climate there is much warmer. The buildings here are more suited to severe winters.'

'You must think I'm awfully silly, knowing so little about France,' she said.

'You just haven't had the chance to go abroad before, that's all.'

As they walked back, three soldiers were going into a bar. There was the sound of laughter from the popular place near their hotel. Back in their room, a fire had been lit, for the evenings were still frosty. 'What a lovely room,' she said, admiring the tablecloth and curtains made of Flemish lace.

There was a small restaurant attached to the hotel where they took their evening meal. 'We have mussels if you would like some,' the waiter said. 'We are near enough to the coast here to get fresh ones delivered most days.' He spoke with a strange local accent.

'That would be good,' Edmond said. 'Would you like some, Amy?'

She enjoyed the meal. 'I had a letter from my cousin James the other day,' she told him. 'He's in France now, as a medical orderly, near Bapaume, I think. And he told me he saw your brother Peter on the ship coming out.'

'Oh, yes – he's been sent to work at General Headquarters at Montreuil. He was glad to reach France and feel nearer the action. Ma wasn't happy, but at least he's not actually fighting.'

Soon they went up to their room and he helped her unpin her hair, stroking the blonde tresses.

'We'll be together tomorrow,' he murmured tenderly as she began to undress. 'And the day after tomorrow too.'

In the night, Amy awoke once to the sound of raucous voices from the street, in the direction of the bar. She tried not to resent the young men enjoying their leave. By now you could tell the eager-faced new conscripts from the battle-weary veterans from earlier in the war. Beside her lay Edmond, his flesh soft and warm as she relaxed against him. He stirred for a moment and his arm came round her. Soon she drifted off to sleep again.

Next morning, they awoke to delicate tuneful chimes from the bell tower. 'It's the carillon,' Edmond told her. 'It's normal for Flemish towns to have a belfry and each plays a different tune.'

Soon they were eating breakfast in the restaurant. Seated beside the window she looked out at the street, where smartly dressed people were heading towards a nearby church.

'It's Easter Sunday!' she remembered. 'Edmond, let's go and join the service.'

'It's a Catholic church, and the service will be in French, or Latin probably.'

'It's still Easter! It can't be all that different from the service Uncle Arthur will be celebrating in Larchbury.'

They went out and hurried to the church. They were late and slipped quietly into the back. The service was in Latin, but its joyful message was clear and one of the hymns had a familiar tune. A few other soldiers could be seen in the congregation.

Afterwards, they went back to the large square and enjoyed an aperitif outside a bar. 'We should go up the belfry,' Edmond said. 'There are over a hundred steps, I've heard, but there's supposed to be an outstanding view.'

After lunch they went there and clambered breathlessly to the top, where the breeze was fresh. They gazed out across the flat landscape, quiet and pastoral, towards the south and west. Then they looked east, where traffic and military camps could be seen towards the Front. Now she began to grasp the extent of it, following its line towards Belgium in the north, and south as far as they could see towards Arras. And beyond their field of vision it stretched on towards the Somme, then further east across France.

Edmond led her to the north side. 'You're supposed to be able to see as far as the Belgian border here,' he said. 'It's clear enough today, I should think. Over that way you can probably see nearly to Wipers.'

Wipers, she knew, was what they called Ypres, a Belgian town where there had been fighting early in the war. She gazed across towards canals and windmills.

She dawdled back to the hotel with him, wishing their break could last much longer. As they sat down for their evening meal they heard the bells of the carillon sounding once more.

–

Next morning they planned to enjoy a leisurely breakfast and a last walk around the town. They had barely reached the dining room when they noticed the unwelcome sound of artillery somewhere in the distance.

She looked across the table at Edmond's stricken face. 'Let's not allow it to spoil our time together,' she said.

He went to the door and stepped outside to listen. 'It's coming from the south,' he told her, 'some way away.' He sat down again. 'It might be round Arras. There was traffic heading there on Saturday.' Absentmindedly, he chewed a mouthful of bread.

Why did it have to start up again now? she thought. The staff of the hotel were talking in the local patois, with an air of concern. The middle-aged waiter brought them coffee. 'My son is at Verdun,' he told them.

'Have you heard anything about a fresh offensive?' Amy asked Edmond, when the waiter had left. She knew they must not discuss troop movements in front of civilians, even pleasant, seemingly friendly ones.

'Only rumours. I didn't hear when or where. They haven't stopped our post or cancelled my leave, so I don't imagine we'll be involved in the near future.' He considered for a moment. 'The road might be clogged again. We'd better not leave it too late to start back.'

They packed their few items of luggage, the carefree holiday coming to a premature end. Outside in the street, soldiers with kitbags were leaving the various hotels and setting off in the direction of the railway station.

Edmond and Amy began their journey back. As before, there were army vehicles heading south. There was a brief pause in the sound of the bombardment, then it resumed. It seemed to be coming from a little to the east of the road ahead, so Edmond was probably right in thinking that it was from the Arras area.

'Let's stop for lunch before we get any nearer,' he said, turning off for a village to the west. They found a small inn where they were served omelettes. The elderly waiter enquired if they had any recent news but Edmond shook his head.

'My unit might be sent to the Arras area if they need reinforcements,' Edmond told her when they were alone. 'At least I'd be stationed nearer you. The High Command try to keep their plans secret from the enemy, so they might stop our post before we're moved.'

'So I won't even know where you are!'

'Try not to worry, darling. I'll keep in touch as best I can.' He was thoughtful for a moment. 'Some men use a coded message to their family if they think there's a chance of action. They'll try to send it out in good time, before the post is stopped.'

'How do you mean, a coded message?'

'Something cryptic that will get past the censor.'

'We need a coded message. I want to know if you're being moved near the action.'

He thought for a while and then smiled. 'I'll send you news of my Aunt Ada,' he told her.

'Have you got an Aunt Ada?'

'No, but the censor doesn't know that.'

They set off again on the bike, the noise of the guns growing louder as they approached the turning for Arras. Where the road was in poor condition it had become churned up. Edmond rode carefully round ruts and potholes.

Once past Arras, they found a column of soldiers were marching towards them from the south. Then as they neared her hospital, an army ambulance overtook them. Perhaps there were casualties bound for her hospital, Amy thought.

When they arrived she got off the bike and stood with her arms round Edmond, not wanting to let him continue on his way.

'If my unit gets sent to the section of the Front near here it might be easier to meet up,' he said.

'But you're liable to be fighting.' The familiar dread was returning.

'I survived the battles on the Somme, didn't I?' She could sense his desperate attempt to remain optimistic. 'Wish me luck, darling,' he said.

'Keep safe. I love you so much.'

'Goodbye, dearest. Till the next time.'

Chapter Eighteen

France, Spring to Summer 1917

Amy's hospital was soon receiving casualties from Arras. The fresh mild days of spring were blighted by the sound and vibrations of artillery and a steady stream of ambulances arriving from the nearest railway station with wounded men. The wards were busy again, and now they were quite near the Front Line. She saw men brought in fighting for breath and with streaming eyes.

'They've been gassed,' a senior nurse told her. She had not seen such cases before.

One day when she had just gone off duty, another ambulance was driving up to the main entrance and her attention was caught by a figure stepping out of the back. For a moment she gasped, briefly taking him for Bertie. But the man was an orderly and of course it could not possibly be Bertie.

'James!' she cried. He was a grown man now, and resembled her brother more than ever.

He turned round and waved delightedly, before turning his attention once more to his task of helping transport the injured into the hospital. She waited on a nearby bench, hoping for a chance to talk.

At last they had passed on all their charges. An orderly attached to the hospital was bringing them mugs of tea.

'Amy,' cried James at last, joining her and folding her into his arms. 'How are you?'

Sister Reed appeared at that moment. 'Nurse Derwent!'

'Sister, allow me to present my cousin, James Fletcher. He's recently begun work as an orderly.'

'Hm – good day, Orderly Fletcher.' She went on her way.

'How's Edmond?' He looked more serious, as young men almost always did when they arrived at the Front.

'I got a letter yesterday – he's still over near Amiens, but there's talk they'll be moved to this area shortly. Are you settling well into the job?'

'I'm glad I'm doing something worthwhile. One of the chaps we've brought in needs operating on straight away.'

'We've got Mr Westholme here, so he'll be in good hands.'

'Then there are a couple of SIs,' he told her. He was picking up the terms; SI for seriously ill and DI for dangerously ill. 'We don't think the other casualties are so bad. They might just need stabilising before being sent further from the line for treatment.'

The following day she received a letter from Edmond in which he told her *Aunt Ada is coming to stay with my family*. So he was being moved on, probably heading for the fresh outbreak of fighting. There seemed to be a leaden weight inside her, preventing her from enjoying the spring sunshine.

The day afterwards she started the morning on the ward, mainly helping to apply fresh dressings. Then she was allowed to help in the operating theatre, as new casualties had arrived and there was a shortage of fully trained nurses available. She began handing instruments to Mr Westholme as they were required. With an effort she managed to control her shock at the sight of the raw wounds. It was thrilling when the surgeon's skilful work succeeded in stopping the bleeding and closing up the wounds.

The following day she went back to her normal duties. Emily joined her as she prepared drinks to take to the wounded. 'There's a column of men marching past the hospital in the direction of Arras,' she said. She told Amy the battalion: it was Edmond's.

She could not be spared for the next hour. When she rushed to the gate, the road was quiet once more.

Did he march right past, she wondered. He would be leading his men, eager to maintain discipline, so he would not have had the opportunity to stop or leave a message for her. She could feel the sharp edges of her nails digging into the flesh of her hands as she clenched her fists. She took a few deep breaths before going back to get her lunch. She remained engulfed in fear, scarcely able to eat, while the artillery was noisy to the east.

–

There had been a few days with no post, but eventually she heard from Edmond that he was in a reserve trench behind Arras. *We marched past your hospital*, he wrote. *How I wished I could have stopped to see you, but of course that was not allowed.*

He wrote regularly every day or two, though he seldom managed more than a few lines. There was little he was allowed to reveal about the offensive, she supposed, but he often reminded her of their brief happy stay in Béthune.

I worry that you might be gassed, she wrote to him in one of her letters.

He soon replied: *The enemy seldom use gas. The wind blows mainly from the west, so it would simply blow gas back into their own trenches.*

Soon it was clear he and his men were at the Front Line again. *You mustn't worry,* he wrote, *we've advanced and are occupying trenches we've won from the Huns. Isn't that wonderful news?*

If only they could drive the Germans into a full retreat.

–

By May, there was less talk of an advance. Casualties were arriving at their hospital in convoys of ambulances. They were not supposed to reveal any details of the offensive, but those who were beginning to recover would compare experiences, and it sounded as though there was a struggle to hold on to the land they had gained.

Besides her worries about Edmond and the demands of her work, Amy was not feeling her usual healthy self. In the close confines of the hut she shared with Emily, it was hard to conceal any ailments.

'Are you feeling better?' her friend asked her.

'Yes – I'm fine now.'

'You were sick yesterday morning as well, weren't you?'

'Yes.'

'Do you think you could be expecting a baby?'

Amy had been wondering about that. 'I suppose I might be. Don't tell anyone. It's too early to be sure.'

If they got a doctor to examine her, and she was indeed expecting, they would probably send her back to England straight away. She needed to stay as long as possible, in the hope that Edmond would get leave again and she would be able to see him.

She did not mention the possibility in her letters to Edmond, for she might be mistaken, but at night, lying in her bed, trying to ignore the sound of the artillery, she let the idea fill her imagination. How wonderful it would be to give Edmond a son or daughter! His family would probably wonder how he would support them all once he returned to being a student, but she knew they need only live modestly together to be happy. In many ways she would have preferred to wait till peacetime to start a family, but who knew how far ahead that might be?

The Front's a little quieter now, he wrote a few days later. *I'm hoping there'll be a chance of leave.*

Then one morning they were woken by a massive, ear-splitting explosion which shook the ground and seemed to reverberate.

'That didn't sound as though it was from Arras,' Emily said.

'No – it seemed further to the north.'

Later they heard the men talking about it on their ward. 'There was a rumour about trying to take the Messines ridge,' one of them said.

'Where's Messines?' she asked.

'Over towards Wipers. There's a ridge held by the Huns.'

Soon it was official that fighting had broken out there in an attempt to capture the ridge. *At least it's some way from Edmond's position*, she thought. His letters told her that their section of the Front was quieter now and he was hoping to be granted twenty-four hours' leave.

–

One hot day in June she came wearily off duty, made for her dim little hut and slumped onto her bed, pulling off her cap.

'Are you all right?' Emily asked her. Normally she would sit outside for a while but today she had accompanied Amy back, concerned about her.

'Yes – the heat's getting to me, though.' She was seldom sick now but occasionally she felt faint and she became exhausted more easily from her duties.

She reached for their jug of water and poured them each a glass. When she had drunk most of hers she took off her cuffs, pushed up her sleeves, dipped her hand into the remaining water and splashed it on to her arms and face, feeling a little refreshed.

'Shouldn't you get examined by a doctor?' Emily asked, taking off her cap.

'I'll be fine. There's so much to do here – I'd hate to be sent home.' There were still many casualties remaining in the hospital from the Arras offensive.

'You should be taking more rest. They advise expectant mothers to give up work, especially if you're on your feet a lot, like here. Mind you, my mother was always rushing round looking after the others in the family while she was expecting.'

'I'll go on a little longer, providing I feel all right. To be honest, I'm hoping to see Edmond if he manages to get leave. It's so frustrating, not knowing when I'll see him again. You know, after we got married we didn't see each other for nearly a year.'

'Have you told him you might be expecting?'

'No – I wanted to be certain first. I hope to tell him soon, though. If he gets leave I'll tell him then.'

She had not even told Lavinia of her condition. *If it's a boy I want to call him Albert,* she thought. *But maybe Edmond's parents won't like that. Maybe Edmond himself will prefer a different name. Well, then, he should have Albert for his second name.*

–

The summer days drifted past, with vague news of fighting from Messines and then a gradual build-up of men around Ypres. Amy was thankful to Emily for sometimes relieving her of the heavier duties on the ward.

'Are you all right, Nurse Derwent?' Sister Reed asked her one day. 'You're looking a bit peaky.'

She had noticed she was getting shadows below her eyes. 'I'm fine,' she said, 'though I prefer it when the weather's not so hot.'

Sister Reed did not press her any further but she felt guilty about the deception.

By the beginning of July, Edmond was still writing of the possibility of leave. Amy noticed the first signs of her body thickening and wondered how long it would be before one of the sisters realised her condition.

'Have you still not told your husband?' Emily asked her as she strained to do up her skirt.

'No – I keep hoping he'll get leave,' she said. 'I can't put it off much longer, though – I might need to put it in a letter. Once I've told him, I can write and tell my parents. I worry about Mother, since my brother died. I think she'll be thrilled to hear she's going to be a grandma.'

'It'll give her something to look forward to.'

One day she received a letter from Edmond in which he mentioned that *Aunt Ada is looking for a new maid*. He's going to be moved on, she thought. He won't be nearby and maybe he'll be fighting again. He never got granted his leave.

Then there was no mail for a few days. Once James arrived with his ambulance, bringing men from the nearest railway station who had been sent on from a hospital nearer Messines. 'They say there'll be more fighting round the Ypres salient,' he told her. It was a bulge in the Front Line.

Mr Westholme came occasionally to operate. He told Lavinia that units were marching north towards Ypres.

Finally a letter came from Edmond to tell her they had been moved north. There was no mention of Aunt Ada, so presumably there was no major advance imminent.

Then the post stopped again. On the last day of July there came the sound of a heavy bombardment to the north. *It's starting,* she thought, *and he hasn't had the chance to come on leave. I don't want to go home and be further away from him, but it's only a matter of time before I get sent back.*

Chapter Nineteen

Near Ypres, Belgium, August 1917

In spite of what Edmond had told Amy, there were occasional days when the Germans were able to send chlorine gas westwards across the Front Line into British trenches. The men dreaded the creeping green clouds of gas. Up till now it had not reached as far as Edmond's unit's reserve trenches, but he had seen gassed men from nearer the Front Line struggling for breath as they were evacuated. One evening, he and his men emerged from their trench ready to patrol the area. They saw a unit retreating along the nearest stretch of road wearing grotesque masks to avoid succumbing to the gas.

After Edmond's injury on the Somme he had returned to the same unit, so he and Frank were still comrades. They had shared a dugout near Arras, and now one near Ypres, heavily bolstered with sandbags. 'They say those masks are bloody uncomfortable to wear for any length of time,' Frank said. They too had been issued with gas masks and had tried them on, but as yet they had not needed to wear them for protection.

As they watched, a group of cavalry came cantering along the road. The officers were wearing masks and surreally, even the horses had been fitted out with protective covers for their heads.

Edmond and Frank exchanged glances. Such sights made him wonder if life would ever approach normality again.

There was the artillery too, of course. The men in their trenches complained, with a kind of resigned humour, about the 'whizz bangs' coming over. Most days they saw men being evacuated on stretchers from the Front Line, victims of debris from some random shell that had exploded nearby. As they were carried away, they would be crying out for their mothers.

Sometimes, in the privacy of their dugout, Edmond and Frank would question whether High Command knew what they were about.

'Three years ago I'd just finished my first year at Cambridge,' Edmond told his comrade. 'Apart from my studies, all I thought of were parties and punting and merry evenings with my friends.' He poured them both a glass of whisky.

'I was just leaving school,' said Frank, knocking back the drink. 'I went to Henley in the summer, and attended some balls, and enjoyed a holiday in Italy too.'

'I'd been to Europe the year before.'

'There seemed no reason why we shouldn't go on living like that.' Would those carefree days ever return?

One evening, when it was misty, Edmond remembered what Amy had told him about her recurrent image of a misty view, lacking a signpost to show the way ahead. The idea was beginning to haunt him too.

There was the prospect that their own unit would soon be sent forward to fight.

Aunt Ada is growing very restless in the hot weather, he wrote to Amy, and towards the end of the letter, *Remember what I told you once; that if I should die you are not to forget me, but you must make a new life for yourself. That's what I want for you. I believe I would*

*be watching over you, determined for you to be happy and spread your
joy to others.*

She wrote to him almost every day and he treasured her
messages of love. It was tantalising to think that he had spent
part of the summer within twenty miles of her hospital, without
having had any chance of seeing her. The Germans were
bombarding the road parallel to the Front, and on their journey
past Amy's hospital his unit had passed some shattered wagons
and a dead horse. The road was becoming more dangerous,
which was one reason he had not pressed for leave.

Sometimes he dreamed of a contented life with Amy after
the war, perhaps with a child or two, but then some advance or
other would begin along the Front and his plans would recede
further into the distance. At night he would try to imagine her
beside him and the illusion helped him fall to sleep.

–

As expected, they were moved up to the Front Line. Then
came a morning when he had to lead his men over the top
towards the enemy. As they climbed the ladders out of the
trench, a gentle mist lay across the fields either side of the barbed
wire. Then the sunshine broke through, somehow dispelling
his nightmares. Why, there was a lark singing and there were
even poppies blooming in No Man's Land. For one moment
his mind dwelt on the timeless beauty of the summer day. Then
the big guns began to boom again, as he knew they must, but
he kept running towards the German line, rifle in hand. A shell
whistled past, making him stumble for a moment, then he ran
on, conscious of Frank and the men close behind. Then an
immense force caught him in the chest and blew him over onto
his back. Almost at once he was engulfed in pain and struggling
to breathe. He lay, gasping, on his back. He had not even heard

a shell approaching. His chest was nothing but a mass of agony. He hovered on the brink of consciousness, vaguely hearing a call for a stretcher.

Someone who sounded like Frank leant over him. 'Hang on, Derwent! Help's coming!'

He began to shiver but someone placed a tunic over him. What was happening about the advance? Were Frank and his men placing their own lives at risk by attending to him? He closed his eyes against the bright sun, still fighting to draw each breath, feeling something sharp cutting into him each time. He felt cold and faint.

'Take a swig of this – it'll do you good.' It was Frank again. Some of the whisky trickled down his face but he managed to take a small gulp. There was a warm sensation as it went down his throat.

'We're here, Sir, we're going to get you to the casualty clearing station!' He could just make out the matter-of-fact voice of someone medical. 'No, don't give the officer a cigarette! We're going to make you comfortable, Sir… Not too much morphia: we need him to go on making the effort to breathe.'

There was a sharp pain in his arm: they must have given him an injection.

'Gently, now.' He was manhandled on to a stretcher, groaning at the pain of the movement. Then he felt himself being humped across the uneven ground, but gradually the pain eased a little. He was shuddering now with each breath. 'Amy!' he cried as he began to wonder if he could go on. Had his luck finally run out? Was this how it was going to end?

I have to get better for her sake, he thought, as the terrible transit continued. Only the sudden dimness persuaded him that he had made it to the ambulance. The journey along the rough roads was nightmarish. Spots appeared in front of his eyes, as though he might lose consciousness.

'Steady, Sir, keep on breathing. We'll be at the hospital soon.'

'I want Amy's photo,' he told his escort. 'It's in my pocket… the left hand pocket.'

Someone was fumbling around, feeling for it. *Is it still there? What if it's in pieces from the shell?*

'Here you are, Sir. Pretty young woman.'

He took her picture gratefully in his hand and tried to focus on it. One edge of it was torn and bloodstained, but her image was unspoilt. 'Amy!' he said.

Will I see Amy at the hospital? he thought. *No, she's miles away, I'm up near Wipers.*

The ambulance came to a halt and light flooded in as the door opened. 'Straight up to the operating theatre,' said an authoritative voice.

–

He was still engulfed in pain but it was different from before. Breathing was a constant struggle but there was less of a feeling that something sharp was digging into his lung. There were fresh pains around the area, as though they had needed to cut him open and stitch parts of him. Elsewhere in his chest he was just stiff and achy. He thought he could taste blood in his mouth.

'How are you feeling, Sir?'

He could barely find the words. 'It's so hard – to breathe.'

'Just keep on, shallow breaths will do.'

'Can I have some water?'

A nurse held a cup and he raised his head enough for him to take small sips.

He could barely find the energy to look round. He had a glimpse of dressings across his chest before someone pulled up a blanket.

'Keep him warm, nurse, he's in shock,' someone was saying. 'And stay beside him. If he seems to stop breathing, wake him up. Call me again if his condition worsens.'

He was vaguely aware of the nurse sitting there. It was quiet now and the light was dim. All kinds of images flooded into his brain; memories of other men badly injured or crying out from the barbed wire in No Man's Land. He recalled the men and the horses masked against gas, and a dying casualty in his ward after he was injured on the Somme. There were other images too. There were his men, advancing bravely towards the salient; he should be with them, he knew, as he struggled to catch up. Then he imagined riding through the grounds at home on Wanderer, heading for the forest. Then he recalled Amy, beautiful in her wedding dress, being cross-examined in court.

The nurse gave him a little water. It was growing light. He felt exhausted still, simply from the effort of breathing.

Will I recover? He wondered. *And if I do, will I be any use to anyone now? What will Amy think when she sees me in this state?*

Chapter Twenty

Near Arras, and Ypres, August 1917

It's high time I told him, Amy was thinking. *He's liable to be involved in the fighting round Ypres. He needs to know there's someone else to stay alive for now.*

She began to plan what she might put in a letter. *Aunt Ada tells me there will be an addition to the family* might convey the news.

That morning she was sent for by Matron. As she headed for her office, she saw Lavinia hovering nearby. Inside, she found Mr Westholme standing, looking solemn, beside Matron, who was seated at her desk.

Amy froze, suddenly alarmed, and looked from one to the other.

'Your husband's been injured, Amy,' he told her. 'I'm afraid it's severe.'

She felt herself swaying and reached for the chair opposite Matron's desk.

'Sit down, nurse,' Matron told her, less stern than usual.

'It's his lungs,' Mr Westholme told her. 'We're hoping for the best but he's not in good shape.'

'Where is he? I need to go to him!' she cried.

He told her which hospital it was, in Ypres. 'Matron, I'd like to suggest Mrs Derwent comes back with me to the hospital, with your permission,' he said. Relatives were sometimes sent for, even from England, in grave cases. 'It could help the patient to rally.'

'Please let me go!' she begged Matron. *I have to see him,* she thought. *He doesn't even know about the baby.*

'When was he injured? Has he had an operation?' she asked Lavinia's father frantically.

'I operated on him yesterday. His right lung was badly wounded and the left one slightly injured. I could only do a preliminary operation to stitch up the wounds, but he needs more surgery. I need his breathing to begin to improve before I can do that. I left another surgeon in charge as I had to come to this hospital to help a patient with complications from his operation last week.'

Once she had assisted him at an operation, and now her mind was invaded by the memory of that patient's ghastly raw wounds. But Mr Westholme had calmly stitched, staunching the bleeding and setting the young man on the road to recovery.

'Very well, Nurse Derwent, you may have leave to go to him,' Matron said. 'I'll give you twenty-four hours.'

'Thank you so much.'

'I'll arrange transport for Mrs Derwent's return,' Mr Westholme said. 'Amy, go and fetch a few overnight things but don't be long, as I need to get back to Ypres.'

She got out of the chair as though in a dream. *He must recover,* she thought, tears coming to her eyes. *I couldn't bear to lose him.*

Outside Matron's room, Lavinia caught her in her arms. 'Come on, Amy, let's get your things ready.' Lavinia took her by the hand and led her to her hut, where they filled a small bag with necessities.

'Have you got a scarf?' Lavinia asked. 'You'll probably be glad of it in the car to hold your hat on.'

'I need some writing paper and envelopes,' she realised suddenly. 'I have to write to Edmond's parents, and Peter at Headquarters.'

Scarcely aware of her surroundings, she let Lavinia lead her back to her father's motor car in front of the hospital. Mr Westholme was waiting to drive off.

'If there's any trouble finding transport back I might offer to fetch you on my bike,' Lavinia told her. She folded Amy in her arms again. 'Seeing you will be exactly what Edmond needs,' she said.

What if he's dying? she thought. *What if I'm too late?*

Mr Westholme started the car.

'How bad are his injuries?' she pressed him as he slowed to go through the gate. 'What chance does he have?'

He turned and looked at her, as though trying to decide how much to tell her.

'Look, I'm a VAD. I've seen men come in with dreadful injuries. You can tell me what's happened to him.'

'The damage to the left lung was less severe but it was within two or three inches of his heart,' he told her. 'It just missed killing him outright. He was on the operating table for over an hour while we stitched up a blood vessel which needed attention, took out a large piece of shrapnel and dealt with the worst wounds to the right lung.'

'Oh, heavens.' She felt faint, thinking of the extent of his injuries.

He paused before turning out onto the road. 'He's been in good health up to now, I imagine.'

'Yes.'

'Then he may have enough strength to make a decent recovery.'

She had known all along he might be badly injured one day; she had dreaded it. 'Please tell me he'll pull through.'

'I can't make any promises, but I'll do what I can.'

He turned on to the road and the noise of the car's engine made it almost impossible for them to talk. The wind rushed past her head, flipping the ends of her scarf around.

How can I bear it, now the worst has happened? she thought. *But he's still here. So long as he survives we can make a life together. If he's handicapped, I'll nurse him. We'll manage just so long as he's with me.*

They headed north towards the distant sound of the artillery. The road was busy with traffic again and they were held up waiting to pass some slow-moving carts.

'I'm expecting Edmond's child,' Amy confided. 'He doesn't even know yet.' She had not told Lavinia. Only Emily had guessed so far.

'You're pregnant?' He looked at her. 'How many months along are you?'

'About four.'

'As much as that, and still working?'

'I last saw Edmond at Easter. We hoped he'd get some leave this summer, and I meant to tell him then. I didn't tell them at the hospital because I didn't want to be sent home.'

He looked towards her, his eyes alert behind his glasses. 'Listen, Amy, you can't take chances like this. You need a check up to see that everything is all right with your pregnancy, and you must go back to England as soon as you've had the chance to see Edmond. If you don't tell Matron, I will.'

'I suppose I should do that.'

The delay was making her screw her hands with desperation. Was Edmond making progress? At last they were moving fast again.

'Hold on tight, Amy,' he told her. 'I need to get back to Ypres quickly. There are bound to be fresh casualties to see. Sorry about the bumpy road.'

He got up speed and surged ahead now the road had less traffic. They passed a sign to Béthune and continued northwards. The noise of battle was closer now and the day was growing hot again. As they drove across a canal she remembered the time she and Edmond had looked across the countryside towards Belgium from Béthune belfry. *We're still quite a way from Ypres*, she thought desperately.

After a while, there was a sign marking the border. After a few more miles, they began passing trees that had been reduced to stumps in some earlier battle. She stared about her at craters and houses reduced to piles of rubble. They were reaching the outskirts of Ypres.

'This town has been fought over fiercely,' he told her as they waited at a road junction. 'The Germans seized it in 1914, then the British drove them out to the east. They fought over it again in 1915.'

She looked around at the scene of devastation.

'It's been under bombardment several times.'

Desolation was creeping into her soul; it was worse than at Arras. They were in Belgium now, where Madame Rousseau and the other refugees had come from. 'Is it much further to the hospital?' she asked.

—

At last, they drew up outside a substantial building. Casualties were being brought in from ambulances. Amy's own hospital had seldom been so busy. Once inside the main entrance, Mr Westholme attracted the attention of a sister. 'This is Mrs Derwent. How is Lieutenant Derwent this morning?'

'He's hanging on.'

'I'll look in on him when I've dealt with any critical admissions,' he told them.

The sister looked at Amy's VAD uniform with approval. 'Your husband is a valued officer,' she said. 'We've had enquiries about his progress.' She led Amy along a stuffy corridor towards the wards. This place looked like a normal hospital, rather than some other building hastily pressed into use.

They went into a ward that was more frantic with activity than any she had ever seen at her own hospital. There was the sickening smell of blood from fresh wounds. Medical staff were rushing from bed to bed and some casualties were still lying on stretchers on the floor awaiting a place.

'Lieutenant Derwent is in a small room at the end,' the sister said. Amy knew that a few smaller rooms were usually kept for critically ill patients. There was a hollow feeling in her stomach as she was forced to acknowledge that he fell into this category. How much was he suffering?

'His breathing is a little better today,' the sister went on.

Amy looked at the woman directly. 'So what shape is he in?' she demanded.

The sister seemed to form the opinion that as a VAD nurse she could be given more details. 'They got the shrapnel out and the broken fragments of ribs.'

They went in and there he was, propped up with pillows. Amy was shocked at his pallor and the hurt and distress clear in his eyes, but he was still her darling Edmond.

He stared at her as though she were an apparition. 'Is it really you?'

She rushed across, seized his hand and kissed his cheek. 'I came as quickly as I could. Mr Westholme brought me in his car. How do you feel? It must be very painful.'

'It hurts so much… when I breathe… but it's not so bad… as when they brought me in.'

There were dark shadows under his eyes. He must have lost a good deal of blood to be so pale.

'What day is it?' he asked.

'Friday. It was yesterday they brought you in.'

'What time is it?'

'Just after two.'

'It's hard to tell.' He groped for her hand and squeezed it. 'It's so wonderful to see you. Did you have a comfortable journey?'

'It was fairly easy in the car. They've only given me twenty-four hours' leave, though.'

'I don't know how— if— I'll get better… if I'll ever be fit again.'

'Nothing matters so long as you recover. You mean everything to me.'

She leant across him and with her free hand she felt his forehead. He was a little hot, but not seriously feverish. She passed him the glass of water by his bed and helped him take a few gulps.

'Edmond, there's something I've been meaning to tell you,' she said. 'You're going to be a father! Isn't that marvellous? Now there are two of us you need to get well for!'

'A father? You're expecting a baby?' His blue eyes searched her face.

'Yes! Those nights at Béthune – it must have happened then.'

His face relaxed into a contented smile. 'That's such wonderful news.' Then he frowned. 'Only, when I thought it might one day happen… I never imagined I'd be an invalid… Do you think I'll ever be capable of work, after this?' He stopped and for a minute, he gasped for breath.

'We've always just wanted to be together. We'll find a way to manage.'

'Are you keeping well, darling?'

'I get tired sometimes, that's all.'

'When will you be having the baby?'

'Round about the new year, I think.'

'Ever since Béthune you've been expecting… That's quite a long time, isn't it?'

'At first I wasn't sure, then I thought I'd tell you when you had leave – only you didn't get any. And I kept quiet at the hospital because I didn't want to be sent back home. But Mr Westholme knows about it now so they'll send me to England very soon.'

'Our own child…' He was smiling again. He leant back on to the pillow and began to doze.

With those injuries my poor darling must be exhausted, she thought. She pulled down his blanket far enough to see the dressings extending over much of his chest, professionally applied, though the wound had seeped slightly. She pulled up the blanket again. His breathing was strained and not quite regular but she could hardly expect more.

A nurse looked in and came across to check Edmond's pulse.

'Do you know if anyone's written to notify his parents?' Amy asked her. 'Or his brother, who's with High Command?'

'I'm not sure if Sister or one of the others contacted them this morning,' she said. 'As his wife you're next of kin, and we knew Mr Westholme was going to tell you. We may not have had addresses for his other relatives.'

Amy took her writing paper from her bag and balanced it on her knee. Soon, there were brief letters for his parents and Peter, enough to tell them he had been injured and was making progress.

I can't tell them he'll definitely recover, she thought, a chill passing down her spine. *I can't be certain he'll pull through.*

The sister came in. 'Why don't you take a break while he's sleeping?' she said. 'I'll look in every few minutes. Go and get a drink. Did you have any lunch?'

'No – we were in a hurry to get here.'

'They'll give you something to eat in the dining room.' She told Amy where to find it. *The baby – he or she – needs me to eat regular meals,* she realised, and she tore herself away from Edmond's side.

In the large ward they had got most of the casualties into beds now, she found, as she slipped through between the busy staff.

She went and made sure her letters would go in the post. She found the dining room, realising how thirsty and ravenous she was, though she was scarcely aware what she was eating.

–

She could not keep away for long. When she returned, Edmond was stirring and she sat with her arm round him, chatting.

'Your photograph is still with me,' he told her, pointing to it on the bedside table. It was slightly torn at one edge, she noticed. 'It was in my pocket when I was hit… and I was afraid it might have been damaged… but it's almost untouched by fragments from the shell.' He paused for breath. 'I made them put it on my left hand side… so I can reach it easily. I kept picking it up to look at this morning. I wanted to see you so much.'

Mr Westholme arrived with a nurse. He checked Edmond's pulse while the nurse took his temperature. 'You've made some progress,' he told him. 'Let's take a look at the wound. Would you wait outside, Amy?'

'I'm a VAD. I'm used to seeing wounds.'

He looked dubious. 'At least stay sitting down,' he said.

He pulled back the blanket while the nurse removed layers of bandage until there was only a large pad above the right lung. Amy winced at the dark violet bruising and lines of stitches already visible.

He released the edge of the pad at the opposite side to where she was sitting. 'There's inflammation, of course, but no sign of infection,' he observed. 'We won't disturb the wound tonight. We'll change the dressing tomorrow.'

Amy took Edmond's hand again. 'Darling, how dreadfully painful that must be!'

'I can't sleep for long without waking up.'

'We give him a little morphia, of course.'

She knew it could be dangerous to administer too much.

The nurse was bandaging him again. 'I'll bring you a light supper soon,' she said.

'Now then, Amy,' Mr Westholme said, 'there's a hostel for the nurses and I've arranged for you to have a room there tonight. From the hospital you just turn left, walk along for a couple of hundred yards, and go down the first turning on that side. It's not far, but make sure you go while it's still daylight. If you wait by the main entrance you'll probably find another nurse heading that way.'

'Thank you for arranging it – but I'd like to stay here with Edmond. I've only got till tomorrow morning.'

'In your condition I insist you get some rest,' he said. 'Stay a little longer, then go to the hostel.'

'Very well.' The journey had been less comfortable than she had told Edmond and she felt tired.

'I've got to perform an urgent operation shortly. I'll send you a message when I've arranged some transport back for you.

Lavinia had some idea of collecting you on her bike but that's out of the question in your condition.'

After he had left, a nurse brought some tea and a bowl of mashed up food. Edmond struggled to try to sit up better and they helped prop him up with the pillows.

The nurse had a spoon to help him feed.

'I can give him his meal,' Amy said. The nurse seemed relieved to get back to her other duties while Amy patiently spooned food into Edmond's mouth, though he could not manage to eat much, and helped him take the tea.

Afterwards she wiped his mouth, then cleaned his face and combed his thick dark hair.

'Thank you, darling. You're so gentle.'

She was used to performing these tasks for sick and injured patients but it seemed now that it had all been preparation for this time when he needed her care.

She sat with her arm about him. 'If only I didn't need to go back tomorrow,' she said, as the room became less bright. 'I've written to your parents, and to Peter. I expect he'll manage to visit you.'

I must write to James as well, she thought, trying to remember where he was based. *Does he sometimes work at this hospital? He'll find time to visit.*

'You look exhausted, darling,' Edmond said. 'You should go… and find your room. You must take care of yourself. Think of our baby.'

'Yes.' She got up and kissed him. 'I hope you sleep better tonight, my darling.'

She went to the door, and turned and waved before leaving.

Will I get time for a quick visit tomorrow morning? she wondered as she passed through the ward outside, still noisy though the light was growing dim. As she made her way down the corridor she could not hold back the tears.

Chapter Twenty-One

Ypres, August 1917

Amy set off alone from the hospital, for there was no sign of another nurse coming off duty. For early evening it was darker than she expected. It was still sultry, as though a storm might be brewing. She took off her cloak and crammed it into her bag. Along the dim street there were shattered houses between the surviving stone ones, and rubble overflowing on to the narrow pavement. On the other side of the road there was a side street from which came sounds of merriment, probably from a bar.

She walked along, deep in thought. Seeing Edmond had been a relief at first, but the extent of his wounds had horrified her. He might not even survive – the thought was unbearable. If he did, he faced an arduous path to recovery. Enfeebled casualties were also prone to all the infections around.

Loud voices came from the right and two officers, the worse for drink, lurched out of the side street.

'Hello, there, Nurse!' cried one of them. Where had she seen that lofty figure before? Now she was nearer the side street there was light from the nearby bar and she recognised Wilfrid Fairlawn. She hurried on but he crossed the road and continued towards her. His friend sniggered and went off in the opposite direction.

'Amy Fletcher!' he exclaimed. 'Is it you?' He caught hold of her arm.

'Amy Derwent,' she snapped. 'Leave me alone – I just want to get to the hostel – my husband's been wounded…'

Nothing else figured in her mind but that.

He caught hold of her other arm. 'Come and spend the evening with me,' he said, leering at her. 'We can have a lot of fun!'

How could this be happening? 'Please take your hands off me!' she cried.

She tried unsuccessfully to struggle free, horrified at his strength as his hands pressed into her flesh. 'Just let me go!' she cried. Surely he would not force himself on her?

His hot beery lips found hers. Incredulous, she tried to wriggle free. Distracted with worry about Edmond, her mind could not seem to grasp what was going on.

Her effort to escape was ineffectual. He held on to one of her arms while his free hand began to range over her breasts and hips as she recoiled with dismay. He was handling her like some kind of trophy he could use as he chose.

Fighting off exhaustion, she dropped her bag and wrenched herself free of his grip. She ran ahead towards the turning on the left where she should find the nurses' hostel, her heart thumping.

The road was darker here and the paving uneven, impeding her progress. The turning for the hostel could not be much further now. It was growing darker and the street was deserted, apart from her and her pursuer.

She thought she could hear Wilfrid's heavy footsteps coming after her. Prickles of alarm ran up her arms at the thought of him catching her again. She turned her head for a moment and saw him close behind her. *He's drunk,* she thought, for even in the dim light she noticed his erratic steps. She turned back, almost stumbling, and ran desperately on towards her destination. Panting with exhaustion, she heard his footsteps closing on her, and screamed as he seized her once more. no one seemed to be within earshot. She trembled as his hands began to grope her again.

'I've got you, you little tease!' he sneered. 'I'll have you, whether you like it or not.'

I won't let it happen, she thought, taking a deep breath and then using all her remaining strength to try to pull away. His hands were busy, trying to cover her mouth as she screamed again, and still hold on to her. Almost free, she struggled to escape his long arms. With a sudden twist she wriggled out of his grasp, striving to keep her balance. As she ran towards the hostel, trying to get up speed on the uneven paving, she suddenly lost her footing. Instinctively, she held out her hands to try to control her fall, but she slipped and slid on the loose rubble in the street and landed heavily on her left ankle. The sudden pain made her cry out, then almost lose consciousness for a moment.

Alarm forced her to rouse herself and look in Wilfrid's direction again. He was approaching rapidly. In a minute he would seize her again – she was at his mercy now.

'Go away!' she screamed. 'Go and find a brothel. There's bound to be one.' She tried to pull herself to her feet but her left foot would not take her weight and another wave of pain engulfed her.

There were headlights suddenly as an army vehicle of some kind approached along the road. She waved her arm. 'Help me!' she cried, but the vehicle drove on. Tears were flooding into her eyes.

Wilfrid took another step towards her, then she saw him falter and stop in his tracks. Perhaps he was wondering if he had been seen. He hesitated for a moment, then began lurching towards her again.

'No!' she screamed, desperate for someone to hear her. He stopped again uncertainly, looking around. From somewhere in the distance came the sound of another vehicle. He paused, as though becoming aware suddenly that here was an injured nurse who might hold him responsible for her accident. He turned round and hurried away.

Relief mingled with pain and fright. She lay panting in the ravaged street, then made another futile attempt to get up. If only some kindly passer-by would come to her aid. She began to drift in and out of consciousness as minutes passed.

As if it's not enough that Edmond's gravely wounded, she reflected in one of her more lucid moments, *now I'm injured too. And what about the baby?* A fall could jolt the unborn child and cause a miscarriage. She could not feel any disturbing symptom but the idea of losing their child was unbearable. *Why wasn't I more careful?* she asked herself. *Why didn't I wait for another nurse to accompany me? There's been no sign of anyone coming off duty: I should have checked what time the shifts end.*

It can't be too much further to the hostel, she thought. *Can I crawl nearer? I might be more likely to attract attention.* She tried to shuffle along the street, but the pain was excruciating and she was afraid she might pass out.

There was a rumble that did not sound like artillery, followed by a flash of lightning. Now there was going to be a storm and her cloak was back along the street inside her bag where she had dropped it.

Then she heard the murmur of voices, soft, female voices. Two figures had come round the corner and were approaching.

'Help!' she cried, 'Oh, please help me!'

Two nuns were leaning over her. What was that language they were speaking? Flemish, she supposed. She pointed to her ankle. One of them bent down to examine it as best she could in the dim light, and Amy cried out. She suspected it was broken, not just sprained.

They made reassuring noises, then one of them ran in the direction of the hospital. The other one sat beside her on the rubble, holding her hand. Amy could not see her clearly but she had a vague impression of a broad face with a serene expression. Her words were incomprehensible but soothing.

There was more thunder and another flash of lightning. The nun's clothes looked rather like her own nursing uniform, but with solid wooden sabots on her feet. Raindrops began to fall; they were refreshing, but soon they might come down harder.

Then there were the lights of another vehicle. An ambulance was approaching from the direction of the hospital. It stopped beside them and at last, kindly orderlies were lifting her onto a stretcher. She murmured her thanks to the nun as they closed the door. She was shivering, and wished she could wash out her mouth to be rid of the taste of Wilfrid's kiss.

If only the baby is safe, she thought as she found herself back in the hospital. Soon a nurse was helping her remove her stocking and examining her ankle.

'Send for a doctor,' the nurse told a junior. 'Mr Westholme might still be here.' Meanwhile, she tucked a damp bandage loosely round Amy's ankle to numb the pain and reduce the swelling.

'Now, let's take a look at your hand,' she said.

Amy had scarcely noticed the cuts and grazes on her hand where she had thrust it out to break her fall. The nurse wiped it gently with antiseptic.

'There's blood on your other stocking,' the nurse said, removing it to reveal more superficial damage. She sponged the cuts and applied a bandage. 'You've got a tear in your skirt as well,' she said.

Amy was scarcely bothered by these problems. 'What about my baby?' she asked. 'Will it be all right?'

'What, you're expecting a child? Why are you still working?'

Amy could form no coherent sentence. As if the Germans had not done their best to kill the man she loved, Wilfrid Fairlawn had attacked her, and her baby could be threatened from her resultant fall.

'Try not to worry, dear. We'll get you a doctor as soon as we can.' At last they brought her a glass of water.

They took her to a small ward for nurses and found her a nightdress as her belongings still lay somewhere in the dark street. She lay back on the bed in the dimly lit room, pain plaguing her even as she was distracted with dismay at what had happened and frightened about the threats to those she loved.

–

She could not tell how long it was before Mr Westholme arrived. He looked even more tired than she felt as he examined her foot. She gathered he had spent the early part of the evening operating.

'I'm afraid it's definitely broken,' he told her. 'I'll schedule you for surgery tomorrow as we need to set the bones carefully before we plaster your ankle.' The sister accompanying him took notes. 'Of course, if there are a lot of new casualties you'll have to wait for a gap in the urgent operations.'

'Yes, I understand.' Everything was horribly amiss: she felt as though she was unravelling. 'Mr Westholme, I'm worried about the baby, because of the fall.'

His forehead wrinkled. 'Have you had any abdominal pains, or bleeding?'

'No.'

'Probably everything's all right, but it's high time you were checked over. Sister, please act as chaperone while I examine this patient closely.'

He felt around gently. 'You're about four months pregnant, as you thought. Everything seems fine. You should have your baby around new year.' He beamed at her.

'Thank you.'

'I'm afraid I won't be doing your operation tomorrow. They've sent for me at another hospital to help an airman who's crash landed.'

After they left, fatigue allowed her to sleep for a while, until the pain of her ankle woke her. Her mind was engulfed once more in anxiety about Edmond.

–

'Your operation has been put back to later this morning,' Sister told her next day.

'They know I'm pregnant, don't they? I mustn't have any kind of treatment that would harm the baby.'

'Yes, Nurse.' Her look seemed reproachful, as though it was completely unacceptable for a VAD to expect a child or to need a bed and treatment for herself when they were so overstretched dealing with wounded soldiers.

'Please, can you find out for me how Lieutenant Derwent is this morning?'

'I'll enquire for you.'

In due course, the sister she had seen the day before looked in to say Edmond was holding his own. 'It did him no end of good seeing you yesterday,' she said.

'I can't see him this morning. I'm waiting to be taken to theatre. Don't tell him I'm injured: I don't want him upset... Do you happen to know if James Fletcher ever comes here as an orderly? He's my cousin.'

'Why, yes, he's based here now. I've seen him this morning. I'll tell him you're here.'

Soon they came to take her to the operating theatre. Going along the corridor on a stretcher, she saw new casualties arriving and supposed she was lucky they had managed to fit in her operation.

Edmond probably thinks I've left by now, she thought. *I told him I only had twenty-four hours' leave.*

–

She lay uncomfortably in bed, her lower leg and ankle now in plaster but still aching. Another nurse occupied a bed in her ward, recovering from one of the infections that went round. The afternoon dragged on, though it was fresher now after the storm. *I need to see Edmond again,* she thought, *but I can't just get up and walk to his ward. Can I persuade a nurse to wheel me there in an invalid chair? But they all look so busy.*

The sister in charge of her case looked in. 'So long as your recovery continues well, we'll send you back to your own hospital tomorrow,' she said. 'We have to move out a lot of patients but we'll fit you in an ambulance with some others.'

'Can't I stay here a little longer?' She was anxious to see Edmond somehow.

'Nurse, this is a major army hospital and you're not a serious case.'

251

Shortly afterwards the door opened and there stood James, smiling encouragingly. 'Whatever happened, Amy?' He handed her a sweet-smelling bunch of pink carnations.

'Thank you – they're lovely.' She reached the short distance to lay them on her bedside table. 'I'll ask a nurse to put them in water... I fell over, that's all. I wish I wasn't causing all this trouble. I'm so glad you've come to see me.' She was unwilling to tell anyone the circumstances of her accident. Relating what had happened would make her relive her ordeal, bringing back the feeling of his hands roving over her, and his hot breath on her face.

'It's my meal break. Is it true you're having a baby?'

'Yes. I must write to tell my parents now it's official.'

'That's wonderful news!'

'I should be going home soon. Did you know Edmond's in here? He's got shocking injuries.'

The news had not reached him. She told James about his wounds and saw dismay on his face. '...Listen, I need to see him again,' she said. It was tantalising to think of him lying in a ward nearby with her unable to reach him. 'Can you get an invalid chair and take me there?'

'I'll have to ask Sister if you're fit to be moved.'

Presently Sister came to help her dress, though her bare toes still poked out of the plaster cast. Then James was back with an invalid chair and helped her gently into it.

'Edmond might ask you about the fighting,' she told James. 'Please try not to say anything alarming.'

'I'll do my best.'

He wheeled her along the corridors and through the large ward, where some of the patients stared at them. Then they went into Edmond's room.

He looked up and smiled to see them. 'You're still here, darling! But what's happened to your leg?'

'I slipped over on some rubble in the street,' she said. She had explained to James that she was going to make light of her injury to Edmond, for he had enough to concern him with his own wounds. 'My ankle's sprained, but there's a slight crack so they've plastered it.' When she was better, she might confess that the injury had been worse than a sprain but she shrank from ever telling him exactly what had happened on that street.

James wheeled her close beside Edmond and she felt his pulse and checked that his forehead was still cool. His breathing seemed slightly more regular now.

'You're getting better! I can tell.' The improvement was barely perceptible, just enough to raise her spirits a little. But he must still be in dreadful pain. 'They've checked on the baby and everything is fine.'

He squeezed her hand. 'That's wonderful. But you need to take care of yourself, darling. No more accidents!' Up to now he had barely acknowledged her cousin. 'Hello, James, how are you getting on?'

Edmond asked for news from the salient and James gave him an optimistic account of progress along the Front. *Edmond's probably aware of the casualties pouring in, though,* she thought. *He'll hear all the noise from the ward.*

She leant back and tried to relax as they talked. Her ankle still throbbed with pain and she could not take morphia because of her child. She wriggled the toes of her left foot. She had a slight sensation of bones grinding together and wondered if they had made a good job of setting it.

–

Next morning, Mr Westholme looked in briefly. 'You can have your plaster off in a few weeks,' he told her. 'You'll be back in England by then.'

'Have you seen my husband this morning?'

'Yes. I'm sure your visit has helped him. I scarcely dared hope he would make such good progress. As soon as he's stabilised, I'll operate again. I'll spend longer and get his lung into as good shape as possible.'

'Thank you so much.' How fortunate they were that Edmond had him as a surgeon.

James managed to take her on another swift visit to Edmond's ward. The black circles remained beneath his eyes and she suspected the pain still interfered with his sleep.

'I have to go back to my hospital now,' she told him. 'I promise I'll write every day. You write back, if it's not too uncomfortable. Just a line will do.'

'I managed to write when my wrist was injured on the Somme, didn't I? James, will you be able to get down to Amy's hospital to see how she's recovering?'

'I'll see if I can.'

She embraced Edmond and kissed his brave face.

James came to the ambulance with her. Two injured soldiers were already there, waiting to travel. They were fairly quiet, probably dosed with medication to relieve pain.

'I'm relying on you,' she told James. 'Write to me regularly and tell me how Edmond's progressing.'

'I promise I'll be in touch.'

Then they closed the door and drove off.

Chapter Twenty-Two

France and Larchbury, August 1917

Sister Reed's pale blue eyes looked at her critically from behind her glasses. 'So you're back! And not in a fit state to work.'

Amy was in the small sick bay for nurses, sitting in a chair with her plastered foot on a stool. They had allowed her to leave bed for the afternoon.

'Sorry, Sister.'

'And expecting a child, I hear. You were unwise to continue working – though I can't deny you made yourself useful.'

'How much longer will I be here?'

'A week, maybe ten days. Till you're well over the operation.'

'My plaster will need to stay on for longer than that, won't it?'

'Yes. You'll have to have it removed when you're back home.'

Emily came to see her in her time off duty, and brought her a bunch of cornflowers. Amy asked her for some notepaper – her own having been lost with her other belongings in the dark street in Ypres – and a needle and some cotton. Emily soon brought them and she wrote to her parents, giving them the latest news of Edmond's injury, and the joyful tidings about the baby. She told them she expected to be sent home soon. Details of the state of her ankle could wait for then.

Then she sat mending the torn skirt of her uniform dress. The minor cuts and scrapes on her hand and right leg were healing well. If only her memories of that evening were easy to erase.

The following day there was a brief letter from Edmond, assuring her his pain was easing a little. He was getting out of bed occasionally but he admitted to still feeling desperately weak.

There was also a letter from Peter, to say that he had visited Edmond and that the sister had told him he was improving. A note from James said much the same.

When the mail from Britain arrived, she was delighted to find a letter from Mother – receiving so much mail in one day relieved the boredom of being confined to sick bay. Mother was thrilled about the baby, though she sounded a little reproachful that Amy had not told her earlier.

The following day dragged past. In the evening, Lavinia looked in on her. Amy noticed she was wearing a red efficiency stripe on her sleeve, which meant she had completed a year's service in a military hospital, reaching a good standard.

'I've had a day's leave and I've been over to Ypres to see Edmond,' she told Amy. 'He's making progress. That wound must be agony, but Sister told me it's healing. Father is planning to operate again soon to tidy up his lung.'

Some areas hit by shell fragments might be beyond repair, Amy thought, sitting up in bed. *I know that, even if Lavinia doesn't want to alarm me.* 'Poor darling, he's very brave. I can hardly bear the idea of him undergoing another operation.'

'You know they have to do it. He might still have debris in there.'

'Yes, I understand.' She noticed Lavinia's hair was messy. 'So you went on your motorbike – did you really get to Ypres and back in one day?' she asked with admiration.

'I set out at first light.'

'You must be exhausted.'

'How's your leg now?'

'Not very comfortable.' She was impatient to be mobile again. 'Listen, Lavinia, I need your advice on something.' For the first time she revealed exactly what had happened that night in Ypres.

'So Wilfrid Fairlawn tried to seduce you? It's all his fault you're injured!' Her eyes widened.

'I don't know what to do, whether I should report him or not. Remember what they told us at the beginning of the war, about Hun soldiers raping Belgian women? I can't bear to think of an officer in our army trying to do the same and getting away with it.'

'You're right – you should report him. It won't be easy, though, if you haven't got a witness to what happened.' She drew up a chair and sat down.

'Some kind of army vehicle passed us, but it didn't slow down or stop. I don't imagine the driver saw anything.' She sighed. 'Wilfrid's father's very influential and might pull rank if he's in trouble.'

'He might.' Lavinia took off her cloak, for the room was still warm.

'You warned me once that Wilfrid had a bad reputation.'

'He's known, unofficially at least, for being a pest to nurses,' her friend said, a serious expression in her dark eyes. 'I haven't heard of anyone who's reported him – they seem to find the prospect embarrassing, as though they'll somehow get the blame for inviting his attentions.' She sighed. 'All too often

257

the authorities are reluctant to challenge a man's behaviour, especially if he's someone prominent. I'm afraid it's just another area in which women need the right to be heard and respected. The thing is, if Wilfrid thinks he can go unpunished he'll keep on preying on women.'

'I believe I should make a stand,' Amy resolved.

'You're doing the right thing. I'll bring you pen and paper. You can write down what happened as a formal complaint and I'll send it to Headquarters.'

Lavinia was soon back and Amy propped herself up in bed, writing on a pad of notepaper. She concentrated on recalling the details of her encounter that night. Committing to paper what had happened in the dim Ypres street was an ordeal. She struggled to keep her tears from falling on the paper as she wrote.

'I was already desperate that day, with finding Edmond so badly injured,' she told her friend. 'Having to fight off Wilfrid was ghastly, and when I fell down I was afraid the baby might be hurt.'

Lavinia put an arm round her. Sometimes she seemed a driven, purposeful woman full of political zeal, but she cared for her friends. 'Poor Amy! You've had such a lot to bear. It's plucky of you to confront Captain Fairlawn with what he's done.'

When at last she left with the letter, Amy felt relieved.

–

A few days later, James wrote to say that Edmond had had his second operation. He was in severe pain again but being brave. She was grateful that her cousin looked in on him regularly. The following day, she got a letter from Edmond himself, insisting that he was not nearly as ill as he had been after he was first injured: his breathing was not so badly impaired. She was still worried and frustrated that she could not visit him herself.

Soon James wrote again. *I can tell Edmond is improving,* he told her. *He's in pain but determined not to complain.*

A further letter from Edmond boasting of his recovery cheered her.

Then there was a letter from Florence, concerned about Edmond. *I keep thinking of the trials you are going through,* she wrote. *Please God he makes a good recovery. I know your love will support him.*

Amy persuaded Sister Reed she was well enough to visit her old ward. Emily accompanied her as she limped along with the aid of crutches. She settled in a chair next to a convalescent patient with an injured arm. She helped him eat his meal and wrote a letter to his family for him. She chatted to him and to the patient on the other side. When they asked about her ankle injury she gave a vague account of falling over in the Ypres street.

That afternoon she was called to Matron's office and set off there on her crutches. She found she had a visitor: it was Peter.

Her heart churned. 'Edmond?' she cried.

'He's progressing,' he told her quickly. 'It's very slow but on the whole they're pleased. They're talking of moving him into a normal ward.'

This was an encouraging sign. Had he come here to tell her this, she wondered.

'I need to speak to you about another matter,' he told her. 'There's a spare office we can use. It's to do with an allegation you've made about an officer.'

'Oh.' She allowed Peter to help her to the nearby poky office. He was smart as ever, his uniform neat and shoes shiny. Another officer, a little portly, was waiting outside and followed them in. She sat down at a desk facing Peter and the other officer, who he introduced as Captain Lambert.

'Good afternoon, Nurse Derwent,' the newcomer said. He had sandy hair.

'Strictly it's my job to investigate your allegation,' Peter told her, 'but the fact that you're my sister-in-law complicates matters. The accused might say the case won't be handled fairly, so I'm delegating it to Captain Lambert.'

'Yes, I understand,' she said. She had been barely aware of what Peter did at Headquarters. How strange it was that he had been handed her allegation to deal with. Would he take her word for what happened? She had met him occasionally as a child, and since he had returned from India she had only spent limited time with him when they were both on leave. He had shown his respect for her medical skill that time she had tended his arm after his accident. She had grown to like him, for he was a decent man, almost as light-hearted as Edmond had been when she first knew him, and friendly towards her.

'This is a serious matter, Amy,' Peter said, unsmiling now. 'I'm shocked that one of our officers should behave like this. It must have been dreadful for you.'

'It was very distressing.' She shuddered, trying to describe her feelings about what happened. 'It was demoralising. I feel I can't begin to put it behind me until I make Captain Fairlawn face some consequence for his actions.'

'I'm sorry to make you go over what happened again,' Peter said. He sent for some tea. The sturdy young man beside him gave her a smile which looked sympathetic.

An orderly brought them mugs of strong tea. 'Now, Amy, just take your time,' Peter told her. They went through her account of what had taken place, going over important details, with Captain Lambert taking notes. It was stuffy in the office and a bluebottle was buzzing round.

'I'm disgusted with the way Fairlawn behaved,' Peter said eventually, frowning. 'You're quite right to bring the complaint but I'm afraid I can't guarantee the Army will take action about it.' He clenched his fists.

'That's my impression, too,' Captain Lambert said.

'You mean Captain Fairlawn's too important to the war effort?' she said.

'He has got a good war record,' Peter told her. 'He's been mentioned in despatches and so on. The authorities will be reluctant to take action.'

'And his father's a colonel.'

'That too. The colonel's still very influential, though he's getting older and hasn't been much involved in decisions lately.' He got up and paced the small office. 'How frustrating it'll be if he gets away with it.' He sat down thoughtfully.

'There's the question of evidence,' Captain Lambert said, looking back over her account. 'You haven't got a witness to what happened. I'll make enquiries as there was a vehicle going past, but the driver may not have noticed anything.'

'I'm afraid that's true.'

'Fairlawn might say you misunderstood his intentions or even led him on,' Peter explained gently.

She gasped. 'The very idea!'

He looked at her encouragingly, his eyes so like Edmond's. 'I know you'd never do such a thing, but he might try to suggest it.'

She fiddled with a strand of hair. 'There are so many reasons why they won't take the matter seriously,' she complained. The scales seemed weighted against women in this kind of situation.

'I promise I'll do my best for you,' Captain Lambert said. He shook hands with Amy and left to get a meal.

Peter accompanied Amy back towards sick bay. The late afternoon was still hot.

'I'm afraid there are other factors too,' he told her.

'There's more?'

He stooped towards her. 'Amy, I was in India at the time, but you've told me about that business at the cricket pavilion. You were convicted of criminal damage.'

She caught her breath. 'It seems like years ago that I did that!' How much longer would that event from when she was young and silly go on haunting her? She stopped, just outside sick bay, leaning on her crutches.

'Colonel Fairlawn was instrumental in bringing the case,' he said. 'His son will know about it and is bound to mention that you went to jail and imply that you're of poor character.'

'Oh, goodness.'

'They might even suggest, since the Colonel wanted you prosecuted, that this allegation is some kind of attempt at revenge.'

'It's not like that at all!' she cried.

'No, of course not, but it's only fair to warn you what they might say.'

She blinked back a tear, dismayed at what he had told her. 'Do you want me to drop the allegation?'

He looked at her steadily. 'It's up to you. I just wanted to warn you of all the implications.'

She looked down at her plaster cast. 'It's thanks to him that I'm injured,' she said. 'If I drop the complaint he's free to assault some other girl. No, sorry, Peter, I'm going to pursue my complaint, whatever happens.'

'I thought you might say that. I'm behind you really.' He bent and kissed her cheek, then his expression changed to a cheeky grin. 'It's as well for Wilfrid Fairlawn that duelling is illegal now, or I might have to challenge him.' He sounded only half joking.

She smiled in spite of the seriousness of the situation.

'I haven't told Edmond what happened,' she said. 'He thinks I just fell over. Please don't tell him, though if my complaint is upheld I suppose he might have to know. I'd just prefer not to worry him while he's so ill, unless absolutely necessary.'

'I understand, Amy. I'm sure he'd approve of the stand you're taking, though. I promise I'll back up Robert Lambert in pursuing your case. I'm confident he'll do his best for you.'

'Thank you for being so supportive,' she said. 'How are you getting on at Headquarters?' She had the feeling that her allegation would not make life easier for his department.

'My work's worthwhile,' he said, 'though I sometimes feel guilty for not being on active duty like Edmond.'

A nurse was returning to sick bay from an errand. 'Nurse Derwent has been giving me information on an important matter,' Peter told her. 'She's quite tired now. Could you bring her a drink of water and then make sure she gets some rest?'

'Yes, of course, Sir.'

He waved and went off, with his usual purposeful stride.

The nurse helped her into bed, pulling back the blanket. It was stifling in the ward. Amy drank the water gratefully and sank down beneath the sheet. As she was left on her own, she was able at last to congratulate herself for taking action against Wilfrid's monstrous behaviour. She leant back and succumbed to her drowsiness.

–

James visited her two days later and told her that Edmond was in a normal ward now, a small one for officers. 'He wants to know how you are.' He held her arm and helped her to a shady bench at the edge of the lawn in front of the hospital.

'I'm well over the operation,' she said. 'I think they've just been waiting for a suitable convoy to send me home. I'm leaving tomorrow. You'll go on keeping an eye on Edmond, won't you?'

'Count on me. He's family.' He smiled encouragingly. 'If he goes on making good progress they'll send him back to Blighty, too. He won't be fit enough to take any further part in the war.'

How thankful she was for that! 'He's made quite enough contribution already,' she said.

'Listen, I need to ask you a favour,' James said. He brought a small notebook out of his pocket. 'It's my jottings,' he explained. 'I'm trying to record some of what I see. In years to come, people will find it hard to believe all that has happened in this war.'

'You're keeping a diary!'

'We're not supposed to. I'm keeping it secret.' His grey eyes, so like Bertie's, looked serious.

'They're afraid of information falling into enemy hands,' Amy said, for she had heard the matter discussed. 'It's the men on the Front Line who are most vulnerable to capture.'

'It's not just that. Some of the horrors are whitewashed out of the official accounts.' He lowered his voice as one of the sisters walked past. 'There are places where I question the decisions of some of the officers and the High Command.'

Now she understood. 'You're doing the right thing,' she told him.

'I'm afraid of my notes being discovered,' he told her. 'I'd be in big trouble, of course, but also my account would be confiscated and destroyed. I'd like to begin a new book and get this one somewhere safe. It's asking a lot, but could you take it back to Blighty for me? They're not likely to search you.'

She knew she must do what he suggested. 'Don't worry – I'll smuggle it back somehow,' she said, smiling at the prospect of outwitting the authorities.

'Once you get it back to Larchbury, give it to Father to look after,' he said.

'Yes – I'll do that.'

He embraced her. 'I knew I could rely on you,' he said.

–

I wish I could be with you as you recover, Amy wrote to Edmond, *but they are sending me home. It's easier to accept because it's best for the baby.*

Emily came to see her before she left and brought her a tiny white bonnet and mittens she had knitted.

'How wonderful! Our very first baby clothes,' she said.

They embraced and promised to write. Amy would miss her cheerful companionship.

Next day they sent an ambulance, for her and some other casualties who were being sent back to Blighty.

Now that her condition was public knowledge, she was not trying so hard to pull her stomach in.

'Ho, ho, we can see why you're going home, nurse!' the soldiers teased her, though her leg was an additional factor.

Beneath her uniform, Amy wore a muslin slip. She had used a handkerchief to make a pocket in it to allow her to conceal James' notebook.

This time she travelled in one of the ambulance trains, the only patient in a compartment reserved for nurses. The journey was tedious, but now she realised how she had missed seeing her family. They reached the Channel and then boarded the ship. Hospital ships sailed at night now, as that was generally safer.

Her increasing bulk made it less likely James' book would be discovered. She tried to look unconcerned as she passed officers and customs officials, her secret package out of sight.

I suppose this is the end of my army service, she thought. *My leg should get better, but Edmond will probably still need nursing when he gets home and then there'll be the baby.*

They reached the British coast early the next morning. In London, the medical staff helped her off the train. Mr Derwent was there as she limped along the platform with her crutches. He bent and kissed her. She was growing attached to her kindly father-in-law. He took hold of her small case, which an orderly had been carrying.

'What's the latest you've heard from Edmond?' his face seemed more lined than before. It must have been tough for him waiting at home for news.

He relaxed a little as she told him about Edmond's move to the main ward.

'And you're to have a baby? That's simply capital!' He was smiling now, his eyes twinkling.

When she told him that the child was due in the new year it was his turn to question why she had stayed so long in France.

'There was always the chance Edmond might get leave and I'd be able to see him,' she said.

Outside he had the car, but there was no sign of the chauffeur. 'He was called up,' Mr Derwent told her. He settled her as comfortably as possible and started the car.

'Remember when our gardener George joined up and his younger brother Henry took his place?' he asked her.

'Yes – George was injured at the Somme, wasn't he?' His comrades had been killed, she could not help remembering.

'Henry's been called up now and the youngest brother Joe is working for us. He has even less idea what he's doing than Henry.'

It was nearly lunchtime when they drove through London. Businessmen and a few men in uniform wandered the streets but the atmosphere was subdued.

'I'm having to take on more tasks myself, with such a shortage of staff,' he went on. 'And of course the forestry business occupies much of my time still. It's flourishing, thanks partly to the war.'

'It must be tiring for you.' It was far easier to talk to Edmund's father than to his mother or Beatrice.

'Sometimes I prefer it like that. I'm so exhausted at night I don't stay awake for long worrying about Edmond.'

'Yes, that's what I've found,' she said, 'though the anxiety often makes me wake early.'

He spent a few moments concentrating on the traffic. 'I think after the war there'll be fewer servants,' he told her presently. 'In some ways it seems old-fashioned, being so dependent on staff. Chambers is getting on now, so I'm reducing his duties, and when he's too old to work I think we'll try managing without a butler.'

At last they reached The Beeches. Amy greeted Mrs Derwent and Beatrice and gave them the latest news of Edmond.

Beatrice looked with distaste at her bare toes emerging from the plaster. Amy had told them all that she had fallen in a rubble-strewn street in Ypres, sparing them a full account of how her accident had come about. Beatrice still showed little sympathy. *She really has no idea what conditions are like out there,*

Amy thought. She could not help resenting her sister-in-law's lack of interest in the trials of those caught up in the war effort, while she tried to pursue her usual pampered life.

The family all accompanied her to the dining room as Cook set some cold ham and salad in front of her and Mr Derwent. They were still able to obtain good quality meat, she realised, better than anything she had eaten recently in France. For a few moments she allowed herself to enjoy the tasty pickles and the cucumber and radishes in the salad. Even the restaurants she had occasionally visited in France had mostly been quite frugal. She had almost forgotten what it was like to sit at a table set with white linen and a vase of roses. It seemed incongruous after the privations of life near the Front.

'And you're having Edmond's baby – at last there's some good news,' Mrs Derwent said. Her eyes lit up and she looked genuinely pleased.

'We've been so worried about Edmond,' Beatrice said. 'Peter wrote that he was fortunate to survive.' Now, at last, she looked more strained, showing some comprehension of her brother's misfortune.

'When he writes to me he often mentions getting a letter from home. He loves hearing from you all,' Amy told them.

'I'll go on making the effort,' Beatrice said, 'though not much is happening round here to tell him about. We held the fête on Saturday, and managed to raise funds for the war. However much longer will we have to wait for victory?'

There was a telephone call. It was Amy's father, calling from Florence's family's telephone to see if she was back. She got up and limped into the hallway to take the call.

'Darling, are you all right? How's your leg now?'

'Not too bad. Oh, Father, it's so lovely to hear your voice! Will you and Mother be able to come and see me tomorrow?'

He would not yet be back at school for autumn term. 'I can't walk round to your house easily at the moment.'

'Yes, I'm longing to see you and so is your mother. She's thrilled about the baby. We just want to make sure you're well cared for, dear.'

They asked after Edmond and she told him the latest news of his gradual recovery.

When the call was over Amy excused herself from her in-laws as soon as possible, telling them truthfully that she was very tired.

In a way it's good to be home, she thought, *with the opportunity to see Mother and Father again, but being separated from Edmond again is heart-breaking. Please God they send him home soon.*

Chapter Twenty-Three

Larchbury and London, August to September 1917

Amy was delighted to see Mother and Father again. She asked Cook to bring tea and cake. It was so difficult to carry anything herself with her ankle in plaster. They settled outside on the veranda, where it was not too hot, on one side of the house, facing west. From the southern end you could see the view down towards Larchbury.

They were concerned about her ankle. 'But at least now you can relax till your baby arrives,' Mother had said. 'I'm going to make you something suitable to wear.'

'Thanks, Mother. The dressmaker is coming to see me tomorrow, but I'll need two or three garments.'

'How's Edmond?' Her father was anxious for the latest news. 'Will he be recovered enough to be sent back to England soon?'

'I think so. He tells me he's making good progress, and James says so too when he writes. He's still weak, though.' How she longed to see him!

Mrs Derwent appeared briefly to greet her parents.

'Mother tells me there's a working party on Monday, to provide comforts for the troops,' Amy told her.

'It's held in the village hall. Beatrice and I usually go.'

'Does Mr Derwent drive you there?' There had never been the kind of intimacy that would allow her to call her in-laws Mother or Father.

'Yes.'

'Then I should like to join you,' she said eagerly. 'I feel so useless, just sitting here.'

Not long afterwards, her parents set off home and Janet cleared away the tea things. Then almost immediately Florence arrived, wearing a large straw hat to keep the sun at bay. Amy asked for some more tea and cake.

'It was lovely getting your letters,' Amy said, glad to see her friend again. Florence looked well, her light brown hair arranged in large glossy coils on either side of her head, but she still seemed subdued. *Will she ever get over losing Bertie*, Amy wondered, remembering her liveliness in the past.

'It sounds as though you're busy at the school,' Amy said. 'Father told me you're one of the most competent among the junior teachers.'

'I do my best. Sometimes I feel restless and wish I was doing war work, like you and Lavinia.' She looked at Amy's injured leg. 'How much longer will you need to wear the plaster cast?'

'About another three weeks. I'll be so relieved when I can get around properly.' When she wriggled her foot she was still not certain the surgeon had set it well.

'Now at least you're away from the war,' Florence said.

'Yes,' she said half-heartedly, wondering how her patients in France were progressing.

–

'I was hoping that cake would last us a couple more days,' Mrs Derwent told Amy sternly from her armchair when Florence had left. 'There's a shortage of flour and sugar, you know.'

'I'm happy to go without, to make up for it,' she said. 'I need meat and vegetables, because of the baby, but cake isn't so important.'

How she wished she could spend most of each day with her mother or Florence. She appealed to Mrs Derwent. 'I can't walk far, so I'd like my family to feel welcome here,' she tried to explain.

There was a glimmer of understanding in the older woman's eyes. 'I'll do my best to be hospitable.'

'As the wife of a serving officer I receive an allowance. I should be giving you most of it towards my keep.'

'Nonsense! That would be completely inappropriate!' Mrs Derwent told her. It seemed no course of action was acceptable.

There was still plenty of food on the table at dinner, but the servings were not as lavish as they had once been.

'Why aren't there ever any summer vegetables except peas?' complained Beatrice.

Later, in her room, Amy could not resist glancing at James' diary. She justified it to herself on the grounds that she was entitled to look since she had taken the risk to smuggle it home! His accounts of the terrible injuries he had witnessed did not much surprise her, but he also recorded some comments from the wounded men. Some were keen to unburden themselves of their conviction that bad decisions had been made by their superior officers, who had sometimes sent them into battle with insufficient support. Amy had heard a few remarks like that herself and admired James for recording the men's views. He had written passages intermittently over a few months. She read several pages, disturbed by some entries. She was tired, so she returned the book to its hiding place under her mattress. She must pass it on to Uncle Arthur as soon as she could.

The next day Mrs Johnson was due to help at The Beeches. Her round face took on a cheerful grin as she welcomed Amy back.

'Could you do something for me?' Amy asked her. 'Can you help me out into the vegetable garden? I want to see what's growing.' She remembered that the previous year there had been a good harvest.

She limped out with Mrs Johnson. The morning was cloudy but sultry as they found young Joe struggling with some weeding. He was a slim, healthy-looking lad of fourteen or so.

'Look at all these runner beans!' she told him, admiring the fine young green vegetables growing beside the last of the red flowers. 'They're ready to eat. Can you pick us some to cook for dinner?'

'Yes, Mrs Derwent.'

Her father had always grown vegetables down the end of his garden, for they were a thrifty way for the family to eat well. She was used to enjoying fresh produce from the garden, each crop picked at the season it was at its best. Since the war had started, Father and his neighbours had redoubled their efforts to grow food. She doubted whether Joe had had much experience of gardening when his brother had been called up and he had suddenly been asked to fill the vacancy. She seemed to remember that the boys' family lived in a poky terraced house with very little garden of their own.

'Go on picking some beans each day, please,' she told him. 'They're nicest before they get too large.' She looked round the rest of the garden. 'Make sure you pick some more apples before they fall off and spoil.'

That evening Beatrice remarked on the delicious beans, and Amy was gratified when Cook remarked on her success with the gardener.

—

At last it was Sunday and she could see Uncle Arthur. She went with the others in the motor car to church. Several friends and neighbours greeted her and enquired about her leg. She tried to concentrate on the hymns and prayers and forget the notebook concealed beneath handkerchiefs in her bag. After the service, the Derwents lingered briefly to exchange gossip.

'Please excuse me for a moment,' Amy said. 'I need to speak to Uncle as I have a message from James.'

Her uncle broke off his conversation with a parishioner to greet her. 'Might I speak to you in private?' she asked. 'It's important.'

There were a few curious looks as he led her into the vestry. She explained about James' notebook and handed it over, rather relieved to be rid of it. 'He says he's revealing some of the details you don't find in newspapers,' she warned him.

'How like James,' he said with a wry grin. 'Of course I'll keep it for him.' He stuffed it into a pocket. 'I'll conceal it in a drawer with some old sermons. His comments might attract a stormy reception. Now isn't the time to question the actions of the superior officers but after the war they should be held to account. I'm proud of James for making a stand.'

'Me too.'

—

Next day, she joined Mrs Derwent and Beatrice as they set out for the village hall in smart summer dresses and flowery hats.

She herself was wearing her old straw hat with a partly buttoned skirt and the loose blouse she was obliged to wear now.

Everyone looked up when she came in. She was glad to see Florence there, and Aunt Sophie, who was struggling to adjust the curtains so that enough light came in to illuminate their work without dazzling them. The women were taking seats round trestle tables laden with balls of wool, knitting needles and half-completed garments. Soon her mother arrived.

'How are things now in France?' asked Margaret Leadbetter, the schoolmaster's wife.

Amy had received a brief letter from Emily and gathered that casualties were still pouring into the hospitals. Occasionally she wished she was still able to play her part there. What was she to say to Margaret? She knew little about progress in France or Belgium that was not in the papers, and what she did know related mainly to suffering in hospitals.

'The men love getting parcels from home,' she told them. 'In a couple of months it'll be getting cold again, so they'll need more gloves and socks and balaclavas.'

Incongruously Mrs Derwent seemed to be leading the group, handing out tasks for the volunteers. Amy supposed her status had allowed her to assume the role of leader.

At times, Aunt Sophie had to intervene politely. 'Might I just point out, Mrs Derwent, that there isn't enough wool in that shade to complete a pair of socks? There'll be enough for gloves, though.'

Beatrice had picked up a sock she had started knitting the week before, and looked at it uncertainly. 'I'll never get used to handling four needles,' she complained. She continued it laboriously while chatting. 'Did I tell you Peter's coming on leave next week?' she told an elegant friend, who Amy thought was the daughter of Mr Brownlee, the auctioneer at the market.

Amy cast on stitches for some gloves. She had sat down next to Florence, whose dainty hands were manipulating her needles at top speed.

'Any more news from Edmond?' Florence asked.

'He's hoping to be sent home before long,' she said, still agonising about the extent of his injuries.

'Amy, could you help me?' asked Beatrice. 'I've finished the ribbing and the straight part, but I can never understand how to turn the heel.' She stared at the pattern in bewilderment.

'I'll do it for you,' Amy said, and took over the work while Beatrice went on chatting.

Florence was looking forward to term starting soon at the school. She worked with the youngest children, while Amy's father was one of the teachers in charge of older ones.

Margaret Leadbetter finished her pair of gloves and gave it to Mrs Derwent to pack in a cardboard box, ready to send.

'Do you ever visit the Belgian refugees?' Amy asked Florence. They were both experienced enough at knitting to keep busy with their needles while they talked.

'Occasionally. They held a party for their national day on the twenty-first of July and I joined them for the celebrations. But they're more dispersed now. Some of the men have enlisted in units and gone back to fight.'

'Give my best wishes to the ones who are still here.'

By the end of the afternoon, she had turned the heel for Beatrice and handed her back the sock, but had had little time to get far with her own gloves. 'I'll take my knitting home,' she said. 'I've plenty of time now to complete it.'

-

Her parents called again on the day Peter was due to arrive. She knew they changed into smarter clothes when they came to visit her at The Beeches.

Mrs Derwent bade them good afternoon again, offering them tea and cake. She had instructed Cook to prepare a larger but more economical one than her usual Dundee cake. They went to sit in the drawing room, as the weather was showery.

'Mrs Derwent, I've brought you one of our garden marrows,' Amy's father said, handing her a basket. 'We've got more than we can eat this year. I dare say you can make use of it?'

'Oh – how very kind. As it happens, we've only a very young gardener now who's barely making any impression on the kitchen garden.'

'Perhaps I can help,' Father said. His face was tanned from working outdoors. 'We haven't got much space but I'm growing what I can while the war is on. How would it be if I had a word with your gardener? It sounds as though he needs some guidance.'

'Would you? We'd all be so grateful.' Beneath the genuine appreciation and polite thanks, Amy detected her mother-in-law's reluctance to be beholden to her parents. 'I suppose I should become better informed about what Joe should be doing each month.'

'I could give you some advice,' he offered. 'I start back at the school on Monday, but I can call here in the late afternoon to help in any way I can.'

An hour later they heard the motor car and saw it approaching up the drive. 'Mr Derwent's been fetching Peter from the station,' Amy told her parents.

They heard excited noises from the hallway, and then Mr Derwent and Beatrice brought Peter through to greet them.

'It's so wonderful to have you back,' Beatrice cried.

He greeted them warmly, especially Amy. 'I saw Edmond two days ago,' he told her. 'He's weak, but much better than when he was first wounded. I believe they'll send him back to Blighty in a few weeks.'

—

'Have you got any friends who are on leave?' Beatrice asked Peter next morning at the breakfast table. 'You could invite them to visit you here. It would be such fun to have some young men around again.'

'Their families will want to spend as much time as possible with them while they're over here.'

Chambers came in with the mail. Amy had a long letter from Edmond, who mentioned some of his comrades in the hospital. She was cheered by the thought that he must be much fitter if he was able to move around chatting to them. The family looked up eagerly from their bacon and eggs as she passed on some of his news.

She was sitting out on the veranda reading his letter again when Peter came out and sat down in the wicker chair next to hers. 'Is everything well with your friends in India?' she asked him. 'I suppose your mail goes to France now.'

'Yes, they won't forward it here as I've only got a week's leave.' He smiled. 'I've heard quite recently from the young lady I care about in India. I'm happy to say we correspond regularly, though of course the mail takes weeks to arrive.'

'I'm glad for you.' After the war he would go back there, she supposed.

His smile faded. 'I expect you're wondering what happened to your complaint about Wilfrid Fairlawn,' he said.

'Yes.' She was still anxious to hear that her attacker would be punished, and was glad they had a private moment to discuss it.

Peter took out his cigarette case, offered her a cigarette, which she declined, lit his own and started smoking it. 'Robert Lambert did his best for you,' he said. 'He tried to find out if anyone saw what happened that night. He traced the army vehicle which drove down the street but no one remembered seeing anything.'

She wondered if some of the men were unwilling to report someone as prominent as Captain Fairlawn.

'Robert took the case forward,' Peter said grimly, 'but they didn't want to pursue it without better evidence.'

For a moment she was dizzy with dismay. The man was still free to molest nurses – why were they incapable of bringing him to justice? 'Do you think they heard about me being in jail?' she asked miserably.

'I don't know – possibly. Anyway, just before I came on leave I urged them to consider your complaint again.' He spread his hands, impotently. 'They'll go through the allegation afresh, but I'm not optimistic.'

'I was afraid they wouldn't do anything,' she said, 'but I had to make a stand.' A tear rolled down her face at their refusal to believe her.

'Fairlawn has a good record of leading his men,' Peter said. 'They're anxious not to disrupt his military career.' He fixed his candid blue eyes on hers. 'I'm trying to persuade them that appalling conduct off the battlefield shouldn't be overlooked.'

'Thank you for supporting me.' She shrugged as she made an effort to accept the situation. She would hate Peter to jeopardise his own career by making himself unpopular.

'Whatever the outcome, I'm determined the allegation must be left on his record,' he said.

'What's it like out there now?' she asked. 'When I look in the newspapers it sounds as though there's no let-up in the fighting.'

He stubbed out the cigarette in the ashtray on the glass-topped wicker table. His expression grew still bleaker. 'No, I'm afraid they're still pouring more troops into the salient.'

–

'I don't know why they've given me a hospital appointment in London,' Amy said as the date approached to have her plaster cast removed. 'Why can't they deal with it at a local hospital?'

'It might be as well, dear,' her mother said. 'They've got the leading hospitals in London.'

The appointment was for St Luke's, the hospital in west London where she had once worked. She had occasionally exchanged letters with Katherine, her friend there, and now she wrote to her in the hope that they might have the chance to meet.

Peter had returned to France now. 'If only I didn't have to ask Mr Derwent to drive me to London,' Amy said. 'He's kind to me but I don't want to keep inconveniencing him.'

Recently, he had driven her to Sebastopol Terrace to be with her parents and uncle and aunt as they remembered Bertie on the anniversary of his death. Florence had been there to mourn him too.

'Suppose we went with you to London on the train?' Mother suggested now. 'We could take you from there to the hospital in a cab. It's a while since we've been on a trip, and we could call on Louisa while you keep your appointment at the hospital. She lives not far away.' Her aunt had moved house after becoming widowed and now lived in west London.

'Do you think Father would be able to get the day off?'

'I think Mr Leadbetter will cover for him if it's just for one day.'

'Then that would be lovely.'

On the morning of her appointment, Mr Derwent drove her to the station for an early train, before the one on which most businessmen travelled. Her parents, smartly dressed for their outing, were waiting at the station and helped her into a carriage.

'I shouldn't need any help when we come back!' she told them as the train steamed off.

When they reached Wealdham, the carriage door opened and a familiar figure in a dark blue dress got inside.

'Mrs Rousseau! How are you?' Amy said, pleased to see the Belgian lady again. Father raised his hat as she introduced her parents. He offered to put Mrs Rousseau's basket in the luggage rack but she explained she was getting out at the next station.

'Florence has been telling me most of the refugees have dispersed now,' Amy said.

'We'll always be grateful for the way we were welcomed here, of course.' Her accent was less obvious now. 'We make ourselves busy here but most of us are longing for war to end so we can go home – please God, the fighting can't go on much longer. Florence tells me you have visited Belgium.'

'I only went there once, to Ypres, when my husband was in hospital there.' She was unwilling to talk of that time.

'Ah! Yes, I heard he was badly injured. Is he recovering now?'

Amy reassured her.

'Yolande and I are from Liège, the other side of Brussels, so you will not have seen our home town. So much of our country is in the hands of the Boches… As for Ypres, I understand it has sustained a good deal of damage.'

'I'm afraid so,' Amy said, with restraint.

Her father was interested. 'Didn't you have a battle at Liège at the start of the war?' he asked Madame Rousseau.

'We had big fortifications along the Meuse, where we fought back against the Boches. I often wonder about my relatives. My father was too old to fight, of course, but he lives in a house with a view of the railway. I sometimes imagine him watching movements of troops and supplies along the line and trying to find some way of sending a message to your army.'

The train was slowing down as it approached the next station.

'I get out here,' Madame Rousseau said, rising to her feet and picking up her basket. 'I've started to give lessons in lacemaking, in Wealdham, and once a week here. Local women have shown quite a lot of interest.'

'Lacemaking! How lovely,' Amy said. 'I saw some beautiful examples in the hotel we stayed at once in Béthune.'

The train pulled into the station and they said goodbye.

'How I should like to take lessons in lacemaking,' Amy said. 'Perhaps I could go on the train to one of her lessons.'

'You might, if your ankle is completely better,' Mother said.

'I didn't want to tell Mrs Rousseau about Ypres,' Amy said. 'It's suffered from repeated bombardments. I hope the rest of her country isn't smashed up so badly.'

The London terminus was crowded as usual with troops. Her parents looked strained. The young men in uniform would always remind them of Bertie.

'A cab to the hospital will be expensive,' Amy said. 'Let's take an omnibus. You'll only need to help me on and off.' She hoped they need not go up the winding staircase to the top.

Once on the bright red bus, she found a seat easily. The cheerful woman clippie with light brown hair who sold them tickets somehow looked familiar to Amy. As they crawled along the streets, teeming with carts and motor vehicles, she wondered where she had seen the woman before.

'Look at those damaged houses!' Father was shocked at the gaping façades.

'They must have been hit in a Zeppelin raid,' Amy said. The destruction in Ypres had been much more widespread.

At last, they reached the nearest stop to her hospital.

She pulled herself to her feet and limped towards the platform, using her crutches. As she passed the clippie, they stared at each other.

'Polly!' she cried.

'Blimey, it is you. What you done to your leg?'

Amy gave her a brief account while the bus was halted. It could not start again until Polly rang the bell.

'Have you been doing this job for long?' Amy asked.

'Over a year now. They need women to do it. It's a lot better than what I did before.'

'Good luck,' Amy said, pleased for her.

'And you. And the kid.'

Father helped her off the bus.

'Who was that?' Mother asked.

She waited until there were few passers-by.

'Someone I met in prison.'

Mother gave her one of the dubious glances she bestowed when she compared Amy's recent life with her own sedate days in her early twenties.

At least she didn't ask what her crime was, Amy thought, relieved.

They went into the main entrance of the busy hospital and down a tiled corridor towards the fracture clinic.

'How soon do you think you'll be ready to go home?' Father asked her.

'I don't know. But Katherine's asked for some hours off, so she'll meet me here and take me to the dining room.' That was what they called the small, unwelcoming room where nurses could get lunch. 'I can wait there till you come back for me. Give Aunt Louisa my love.'

A woman at the desk told her where to wait for her appointment. Father left her a newspaper and she began to read a report about fighting round the village near Ypres called Passchendaele.

'Mrs Derwent?' She got up and walked with her crutches to the consulting room where they would remove her plaster.

At last it's nearly over, she thought. *Just let it have healed properly.*

The medical staff soon cut her plaster off and she examined her leg and ankle. They had swollen within the plaster cast as expected, but she could tell the shape was not quite right. The orthopaedic surgeon looked a little concerned.

'Put your foot to the ground,' he told her, while a nurse held her arm.

She did as he said. It felt strange. Even allowing for it having been in plaster for weeks, the ankle seemed distorted.

'Now take off your shoe and walk towards me.'

She removed the shoe from her good right foot and began to walk, still relying on the nurse for support. She could not put her left foot flat on the floor and there was a slight sensation of one bone grinding against another.

'I don't think they've set it right,' she said, unwilling to acknowledge the problem. She had seen cases like it before.

The doctor felt around where the fracture had been. 'I think it's less than perfect,' he admitted. 'I gather you had it done when you were serving in Flanders?'

'Yes.'

'See how you get on. If it's still bad in a few months, when you've had your baby, you might consider having it reset.'

'Thank you, Doctor,' she said, sniffing hard in an attempt not to cry.

'Can you walk with just the one crutch?'

She attempted to do so. It was not elegant but she could walk a little way.

She went behind a screen to put a stocking on her left leg. She put on her right shoe, then crammed her left foot into the other one, which she had brought in a bag. They were her loosest shoes and she needed the right one tightly laced. The left one would barely do up at all. She went awkwardly from the consulting room to the corridor where she saw the plump figure of Katherine waiting for her.

'Well done!' said the doctor, who had followed her out. The nurse handed her the second crutch. 'That shoe's very tight,' the doctor said. 'Take it off as soon as you reach home.'

Katherine embraced her and helped her to the nearest chair. 'It's wonderful to see you again! Are you keeping well in your pregnancy?'

'Yes, everything's fine.' Doctor Stanhope back in Larchbury had checked her progress. He was elderly but had been brought out of retirement when younger doctors were sent to Flanders.

'Your walking doesn't look too good,' Katherine said. 'Did they mess up setting your ankle?'

'I think so. It wasn't done under ideal conditions.'

285

'I'm so sorry. Would you like to go to the dining room for lunch? I can't promise it'll be especially tasty.'

Amy limped along the corridor, her erratic progress confirming her view that her operation had failed. Katherine gave her an arm.

Soon they were sitting eating a watery stew. 'Anyway, how are you?' Amy asked her friend.

'Fine.' Katherine told her a little of her life at the hospital. It sounded as though she had developed from an anxious novice into an efficient member of the nursing staff.

'What about your young man?'

'He's suspended his university course and joined up,' Katherine said, fiddling with her dark hair. 'He's finished his officer training and he's in Flanders now, the Belgian part.'

'I supposed he's in the Ypres area,' Amy said.

'Yes. I worry about him so. I've put my name down for service abroad if I get the chance.'

Amy had mentioned Edmond's injuries in one of her letters to Katherine, and she found herself making light of them and exaggerating his progress now Katherine had a sweetheart at the Front.

'Do you think you'll have your leg reset?' Katherine asked presently. 'You could wait till after you've had your baby.'

'They'd need to operate again – I know that much,' Amy said, shuddering.

'Yes. You'd need to be brave. But they've got those modern X-ray machines now so they can get a picture of the bones in your leg before they operate.'

'That's true.' She had not had her leg X-rayed in the Ypres hospital, or even in the mobile X-ray unit driven around by the scientist called Madame Curie. 'If this war ever ends I might have my ankle reset then. I don't want to be on the operating list again when wounded are streaming in and there's a shortage of surgeons.'

While they were waiting for her parents to arrive, she practised walking up and down with one crutch. She began to adapt to the feel of her joint and to develop an ungainly but steady way of progressing.

'You're doing better,' Katherine encouraged her.

She sat down to recover from her exertions. Her friend brought her up to date with the gossip from the hospital where she had once worked. Katherine mentioned that she might visit her aunt and uncle who lived some ten miles from Larchbury. 'Perhaps you can come to see me at The Beeches,' Amy said. 'It's not far. Do try to come.'

When her parents arrived she embraced Katherine again, passed Father one of her crutches and set off towards the door with the other.

'Your leg doesn't look much better than before,' Mother cried.

'It is. And I'll get more used to it in a day or two,' she said, trying to sound confident.

Chapter Twenty-Four

Larchbury and Lymington, October 1917

When she reached Larchbury there was fresh news: she was thrilled to hear that Edmond was returning to Blighty at last.

Two days later he was brought back by train to a London hospital. Mr Derwent drove Amy there the following day to visit him, and Mrs Derwent and Beatrice accompanied them, anxious to see him.

'Are you sure you should be travelling again?' her mother-in-law had asked Amy. Her poor walking was hampered by her increasing size. She had put on a loose coat which partly concealed her condition.

'I'll be fine,' she replied. 'The baby's not due for another three months.' She had longed for this day: she simply could not wait any longer to see Edmond.

'He's out of danger now, or they wouldn't have let him travel back,' she told the others, 'but he's probably still weak.'

The hospital was not the one where Amy had worked. Once more she was among bustling nurses and the smell of antiseptic, but the atmosphere was less frantic than at the Front. The sister was stern and only allowed two visitors at a time, so Amy went into the ward with Mrs Derwent. It was a small ward for officers, with only three beds, and there Edmond was, in the middle bed, sitting up. He caught sight of her and his weary expression was transformed. 'Darling!' he cried.

She almost stumbled in her rush to be beside him. She stooped awkwardly to kiss him. 'How are you feeling now?' she asked. His complexion was a better colour, no longer pale, and not flushed with fever either. If only she could take off his pyjama top and examine his chest to see how it was healing.

'Much better. Hello, Ma, how are you?'

She was staring at him, probably alarmed by his hollow cheeks and the circles below his eyes which suggested he was still not sleeping well. 'Edmond, dear…' She was at a loss for words. 'How you must have suffered!' she managed, as Amy found her a chair.

A young nurse brought another chair and Amy sat down, feeling sorry for her mother-in-law. 'He's improved greatly since he was first wounded,' she told her.

'I've had visitors to cheer me up,' he told them. While he had been in Ypres there had been others besides Peter and James. 'Frank Bentley, who's been with me through the war, came more than once. Charles Shenwood arrived one day last week,' he told them. 'It was good to see him again. He found out from Beatrice that I was injured and being treated in a hospital in Ypres.'

'From Beatrice?' his mother asked.

'She's been writing to him regularly, apparently. He says he longs for her letters.'

His mother stared ahead, smiling for a moment, clearly enjoying the idea of a match between the pair, then appeared concerned again when she looked back to Edmond.

Before long, he was telling them about the choppy crossing he had endured, and asking for news of Larchbury. His mother became more collected, reassured by his normal conversation.

The only other patient in the ward was asleep and barely stirred as they talked. Probably he was dosed heavily to suppress pain.

Next, Edmond wanted assurance that Amy was keeping well and she was able to tell him that everything was fine with the baby.

'What about your ankle?' he asked, having noticed how she was walking.

'It didn't mend quite right,' she told him.

'You told me it was just sprained!'

She had to admit that one of the bones had been broken. 'I didn't want to worry you when you were so ill,' she said.

He seized her hand and looked at her seriously. 'Promise you won't keep things from me like that. I'm your husband.'

'I can get around better without the cast,' she said. 'I can walk to my parents' house, or to call on Florence.' These visits were more of a struggle than she chose to admit.

He became more relaxed. 'What about my moustache?' he asked her suddenly. 'Should I shave it off, do you think?'

'It's your decision,' she told him, secretly wishing he would get rid of it. 'I love you either way.'

Soon it was time for them to leave the ward so that his father and sister could see him. Amy and her mother-in-law sat down on chairs outside.

Mrs Derwent took a little bottle out of her bag and the pungent aroma of smelling salts wafted along the corridor.

'Will he ever be well again?' she asked Amy.

The sister was leaving the ward and Amy asked her if they might see a doctor to discuss Edmond's prognosis.

Eventually they were joined by a serious-looking man in a white coat. 'Lieutenant Derwent's wound is healing,' he told them, 'but with his lung capacity reduced it's unlikely he'll ever completely regain his former good health. He'll be lacking in stamina, but otherwise may manage to lead a fairly normal life.'

A tear coursed down Mrs Derwent's face, leaving a slight trail through the powder. Amy took her hand.

'We're arranging for him to be transferred to a sanatorium,' the doctor went on. 'It'll be in a healthy area, well away from any city, and quite possibly by the sea. He can sit outside, at least while the weather remains mild, breathing in fresh air to help his lungs heal.'

When the doctor had left Amy tried to comfort her mother-in-law. 'We must make the best of it,' she said.

–

Next day she was sitting with the others in the drawing room, completing the gloves to send to the troops. 'I need some more tasks to fill my time,' she said, half missing her frantic days on the wards. 'I want to do lacemaking but my leg isn't strong enough for me to travel easily to one of Mrs Rousseau's classes.'

None of the others could advise her.

'I've had one idea,' she told them. 'I can play the piano, but as you know, I never got beyond playing quite easy pieces. I'd like some more lessons.'

Beatrice looked at her, her mouth open.

'I know I'll never reach your level of accomplishment,' Amy told her, 'but I should very much like to improve, now I've got time to practise. Does your teacher still live nearby?'

Realising she was determined, Mr Derwent recommended Beatrice's former teacher.

'It would give me real pleasure to pay for the lessons from my allowance as wife of a serving officer,' Amy said.

'You'll do no such thing!' Mrs Derwent cried. 'We don't want the whole village to think that we can't afford to support you.'

'We're happy to pay for your lessons,' Mr Derwent assured her.

'Thank you.' Amy began to compose a note to the teacher.

'Shouldn't you be concentrating on waiting quietly for your baby to arrive?' her mother-in-law asked her. 'You went on working in France for longer than recommended.'

'But at least she was there when Edmond was injured,' Beatrice said unexpectedly. 'He told me how it cheered him when she managed to visit him.'

'Yes, that's true.' The older woman looked at her more approvingly.

She was grateful for her sister-in-law's support and Mrs Derwent's recognition.

'I assure you I won't over exert myself,' she promised.

She had compared notes with another expectant mother at the most recent working party in the village hall. It was clear her own pregnancy had not been a typical one. For the first two months she had been uncertain of her condition, and then she had been determined to hide it from the senior nursing staff. Then Edmond's wound had almost completely distracted her thoughts, and there had been her fall and her ankle injury too. Now she was becoming more aware of the changes to her body, and she was thrilled to feel her baby moving inside her. She made a point of resting for part of each day.

Soon afterwards, Chambers came in with a letter for her.

'It's from Edmond. They've found him a place in a sanatorium,' she told them. 'It's near the sea – the nearest resort is Lymington. They're transferring him there tomorrow.'

'Capital,' said his father. 'It's on the south coast, which is the mildest. I wouldn't have wanted him to be on the east coast – they get the occasional bombardment there.'

'Where's Lymington?' asked Beatrice.

'Not far from Poole,' her father told her. 'It's a fairly quiet part of the coast.'

'Shame it isn't somewhere lively,' Beatrice said. 'We might have stayed nearby so we could visit him.'

'I was going to suggest Amy does that, if she cares to go there,' Mr Derwent said, his eyes twinkling as he smiled at her. 'Would you like to stay in a hotel for a week and visit him?'

'Oh, I should love to be able to see him!' she cried.

'I'll drive you down there when Edmond has had a couple of days to settle,' he said. 'Meantime I'll contact the sanatorium and see if they can recommend somewhere suitable for you to stay.'

Beatrice was becoming envious now, and before long he was promising her and her mother a weekend in London to see a show.

–

Amy was wrapped up well in the car as Mr Derwent drove down to the coast.

'It's very kind of you to let me take this holiday,' she said. The car was moving slowly down a road behind a herd of cattle, so it was easier than usual to talk.

'Nonsense.' He smiled. 'It'll promote Edmond's recovery, having you nearby.'

'I'm very disappointed my leg isn't better,' she told him. 'Edmond's been through so much, without having me as an invalid as well. One day we'll set up house together, with the baby as well. I'd hoped we could live modestly without a servant, but now it seems I might not be able to manage everything myself.' Generally she still needed a hand free to help her move around.

'I don't want you to worry about your future,' he said gently. 'I'm proud of everything Edmond and you have done in the war.'

The resort where they were headed was some way further, so presently they stopped for lunch at an inn.

'Edmond will be entitled to some kind of pension as a wounded soldier, won't he?' she said, unable to leave the subject alone. She had the feeling that Mrs Derwent and Beatrice saw her as a liability.

'Yes, he certainly will,' he said as a waitress took their order. 'I expect they'll arrange it soon. I'm sure I can give Edmond any extra allowance he needs so the three of you can live decently.'

I must find some way to help support us, she thought. *While the baby is small I could at least take in needlework to earn some money.*

Soon they were heading south west again and she began to smell the fresh sea air. Her father-in-law drove her to a small hotel and waited while she was shown to a charming room.

'Is everything to your liking?' he asked when she came down again.

'Yes, thank you. I even have a view of the sea. Let's go and see Edmond.'

From the hotel they could see the sanatorium, a large building up on the hill. Visitors were welcomed in the afternoons.

'Will you take a meal at the hotel later?' she asked as he drove them up there.

'No, when I've seen Edmond I'll drop you there, then I'll need to set off back to Larchbury. I'll stop for dinner on the way.

While you're here, you're to take a cab when you visit Edmond,' he insisted. He had made sure she had enough money.

'Thank you so much for everything you've done for me, Mr Derwent,' she said.

'You know, it's high time you stopped calling me that. Can't you just call me Pa?'

She was touched. He had supported her when his wife and Beatrice had been cold towards her. She was coming to regard him as a father figure. 'I'd love to,' she said.

'And you must call my wife Ma.'

'Yes – so long as she's happy with that,' she said as they arrived, wondering how her mother-in-law would react.

They went in and asked to see Edmond. An orderly took the small suitcase of clothes for him, then another led them along a corridor and out on to a veranda, Amy keeping up as best she could.

Edmond was sitting there in a wicker chair, breathing in the fresh breeze. He broke into a smile when he saw them, and got to his feet. He stepped forward and kissed her.

'Darling!' she said. It was the first time she had seen him out of bed since he had been wounded. He had a blanket round his shoulders and looked thin, a little wasted even. He had not been able to take any exercise for weeks.

'I look a wreck, don't I?' he said, reading her thoughts all too well.

'You've shaved off your moustache!' she said. 'That's what I noticed. And I do prefer the way you look without it.'

'What's it like here?' his father asked.

'We have big wards, but the other men are good chaps, determined to keep cheerful. They make us keep quiet after eight at night, so we get plenty of sleep.'

Most of the men had been brought out to the veranda, some in invalid chairs. A nurse was in attendance, stopping to speak to a patient from time to time. There was a peaceful atmosphere that had been lacking at the Front Line hospitals.

The nurse began to help a patient walk slowly along the veranda. Amy noticed another one stepping out cautiously, supported by a woman she took to be a relative. *I should be encouraging Edmond to take exercise,* she thought. She was about to propose a walk along the veranda when she saw Pa looking at his watch and remembered he had a long drive home. She embraced and kissed Edmond, promising to return the following afternoon.

How can I help Edmond recover? she asked herself, as Pa drove her back to the hotel.

–

She went to bed soon after her meal that night and spent a relaxing morning sitting in the hotel lounge looking out towards the pale grey sea. She met Mrs Dixon, another guest, who had a son being treated in the sanatorium, and they arranged to share a cab up to the sanatorium for afternoon visits. 'My neighbour's daughter was there once, when she had tuberculosis,' Mrs Dixon said, 'but they've moved the TB patients elsewhere now, so there's no risk of them passing on the infection to the troops.'

Edmond was out on the veranda again that day, in the faint sunshine, but this time he was wearing a jacket, which was looser than it had once been. Some of the men were chatting to one another in an optimistic mood. Edmond happily introduced her to some friends.

'We're not allowed to smoke here,' he told her.

'I should think not! Doctors believe it's bad for your lungs.' Not everyone agreed that smoke could damage the airways. 'Heavy smokers often develop a nasty cough.'

'We've got a gramophone so we can play music in the ward at certain times of day,' he went on.

Mrs Dixon was speaking to her son Archie, who had been brought out on his bed. 'He's come from Wipers too,' Edmond whispered to Amy. 'His lungs are damaged from being gassed. I think he's in worse shape than I am.'

How unfair life had been for her generation of young men, she reflected

'I need to exercise my bad leg,' she said presently. 'I rest it for part of the day, but I need to use it a little as well, to strengthen it. Shall we try to walk along the veranda together and see which of us succeeds better?'

She was using a stick now instead of a crutch. She placed her free hand in his. They set out slowly, enjoying the view towards the Isle of Wight and the Channel, with a minesweeper in the distance. Seagulls wheeled around, uttering their mournful cries.

'Remember the first time we met, as adults, when we were staying at Hove?' he asked her. 'We were competing for a bathing machine, weren't we?'

She burst out laughing. 'I'll never forget that wonderful day.'

Before long he was slowing, short of breath. She waited patiently, noticing the strain on his face, though when he saw her looking he forced a smile. They had nearly reached the end of the veranda. As they set off back he seemed weary, so they dawdled back to his chair. For a moment they embraced, laughing at their indifferent efforts, then he sat down again.

He fingered her fair hair. 'I'm glad you're wearing it loose again,' he said.

'Most married women wear it up,' she said, 'but I decided to leave it loose for a change now I'm not in uniform.'

'What do you find to do in the hotel?' he asked her. 'Is it boring for you?'

'I've brought a book, and my knitting. I've stopped making gloves and socks for the troops so I can concentrate on clothes for our baby.' She loved doing the fine, white, lacy work.

He looked at her admiringly. 'I'm determined to get my health back, to do the best for both of you.'

'I'm convinced you will.' She could feel the baby kicking now. She opened her jacket a little, took his hand and laid it gently on her abdomen, so he could feel it too. His eyes moistened.

'In another few months we'll have our own child!' Excitement seized her when she thought of them becoming a proper family.

'I'm thrilled,' he said, 'though it's not the ideal time to bring a child into the world.'

'I know – I've sometimes thought the same. But mostly it seems like a miracle, bringing forth new life, to help make up for all we've lost.'

She longed to hold her baby in her arms, but Edmond's frailty still frightened her.

Chapter Twenty-Five

Larchbury and Wealdham, Autumn 1917

Soon Amy's brief holiday was over and Mr Derwent, now known as Pa, came to take her back to The Beeches. The weather was beginning to turn cold and windy, but they agreed that Edmond looked fitter, thanks to the outdoor air and exercise.

Back with her in-laws she could only write to him regularly and wait for his replies. He seemed in good spirits.

Pa had encouraged her to call his wife Ma, though her mother-in-law was sometimes slow replying.

Beatrice's former piano teacher came to give Amy her first weekly lesson. She was glad of the opportunity to improve, but aware that she was depriving the others of the use of the drawing room during her lesson. Soon after she had finished, Beatrice took over the piano and played a Chopin étude with her usual flair, as though to emphasize Amy's lack of skill.

Three days later she walked slowly over to Sebastopol Terrace, where Mother greeted her delightedly.

'I hope you're not overdoing the walking,' she said. 'I'll make you a cup of tea.'

'I've brought my piano exercises,' she said. 'Do you mind if I practise here?'

'Of course you may,' Mother said, 'though it's not such a fine piano as the one at The Beeches.'

'I feel embarrassed to practise there,' she admitted. 'Beatrice is so gifted. It doesn't seem fair to disturb them in their drawing room with my amateurish attempts.'

Mother frowned. 'I wish they'd be more encouraging.'

'So do I, but it'll help if they see I'm improving.' The previous day she had managed to practise on the piano while Beatrice and her mother had gone shopping.

The weather was poor now, and after Edmond had spent three weeks at the sanatorium, they went back to bring him home. Amy could scarcely wait to see him again.

'We weren't allowed to stay outside for long after the first week,' he told her. 'It was too cold.'

'At last we can be together all the time!' she said as his father tucked blankets over them in the back of his car.

Edmond smiled, but said, 'This isn't how I imagined it would be.'

As the reunited family took dinner, Ma and Beatrice chattered constantly. When they discussed food shortages or fashions Edmond began to look bored. 'I'm afraid I'm quite out of touch with female company,' he admitted, when they noticed his lack of interest.

When they went to bed Amy watched him undress, horrified at his scars and skin discolouration, and the depression in his chest left from the lost ribs and lung tissue. His breathing was still shallow.

He noticed her expression. 'I like to think I used to be a good-looking young man,' he said.

'You certainly were,' she said, remembering their encounter at the seaside when she had noticed his strong swimming, and how fit he had looked earlier in their marriage. 'And you're recovering your looks a little each day.'

'I'll never be the man I was before I got hit.'

She enclosed him in her arms. 'You're still my Edmond, that's what matters. And we're all so proud of you.'

That night at last he was able to cuddle up to her increasingly bulky body. Soon he was asleep, but she lay awake, still shaken by the extent of his wounds.

Two nights later, she was woken by him calling out in his sleep. 'Keep going, men!' she heard him say, then he screamed and woke up shaking.

She held him in her arms. She had heard men call out in the hospital when the horrors revisited them in the night. 'It's all right, Edmond,' she said. 'You're out of danger now.'

His shaking subsided and he clutched her arm. 'I really am safe now, aren't I? I'm with you, my angel. I used to long for you when I was there in the trenches.'

They both flitted between wakefulness and sleep for the remainder of the night. *It's not entirely over,* she thought. *How could he ever be the same as before?*

By day they would spend some time with his family. Sometimes her parents visited, relieved to see Edmond on the mend. If the day was fine, Amy would take him for a walk round the grounds in the warmest part of the day. Sometimes he winced with pain or she glimpsed an anxious expression on his face, before he noticed her gaze and smiled to please her. Neither of them had much energy, but each short walk was a small victory.

At other times they retreated to their own room, simply content to be together. 'You sit in the easy chair, darling,' he told her. 'I'll perch on the bed.'

301

'It would be lovely to have a little sofa in here,' she said, worried she might sound demanding.

'You're right, we should get one,' he agreed.

Another piece of furniture would make their room a little cluttered, though, she thought.

–

'My brother George is home on leave,' Joe the young gardener told them one afternoon as they went for a short walk in the chilly garden.

'Glad to hear it,' Edmond said. He had last spoken to George over a year earlier, when they had both been in hospital after being injured on the Somme. More recently he remembered hearing that George had been wounded in the leg at Passchendaele, not long after his own injury. Eventually he had been sent back to Blighty.

'He's had a few days with the family now, but he's soon going back to his unit.'

'I must visit him.'

'We live in Wealdham now, with my aunt,' Joe said. 'Mum couldn't afford to go on renting the house after Dad died.'

'Sorry, I'm out of touch,' Edmond said. He had forgotten that the boys' father had fallen ill and died, and could not remember hearing that the family had moved.

'No reason why you should know, Sir, you've been serving in Flanders.'

'I'd like to see George while he's here,' he went on.

'He's got to go back the day after tomorrow, Sir.'

'I must try to get over to Wealdham.' He got the address from Joe.

The wind was bitter again and they began their slow progress back to the house. He felt fitter since the weeks at the coast but still tired easily.

'Joe has a long journey to work now,' Amy said. 'I've noticed him arriving on his bike once or twice but I didn't realise he was cycling from Wealdham.' On his wages, he would not be able to afford to travel by train.

Once inside, Edmond asked his father for a lift to visit George the following day.

'Does it have to be tomorrow? I've promised to take your mother to visit her friend, and Beatrice is invited somewhere too.'

In the end, Pa took them there in the early afternoon after they had spent a relaxing morning. Amy insisted on going with him.

'I'm not happy you'll need to come back on the train,' Pa said as he drove through the countryside, where leaves were blowing off the yellowing trees.

'It's a regular service,' Amy reminded him. Edmond knew she was quite looking forward to an afternoon out.

'When I last saw George he'd just lost both his old school friends, who he'd joined up with,' Edmond said. 'He was at a low ebb but he welcomed the chance to talk.'

'Whereabouts is Bank Street?' Pa asked as they reached Wealdham. 'Which side of the river?'

Edmond gave them the directions from Joe. They found themselves heading for the rundown factory area. Smoke was belching from the chimneys.

'It's not a pleasant district,' Amy faltered.

Edmond had spent enough time mixing with lower ranks in his battalion to realise that he and most of the other officers led very comfortable lives compared with many of the soldiers in the lower ranks.

'How unfortunate that George's family are reduced to living here,' Pa said as he stopped the car. 'Listen, when you come back be sure to get a cab to the station. I don't want you walking through this unhealthy area. When you reach Larchbury, phone the house to see if I'm back from collecting Beatrice from her friend's house. If not, take another cab home.'

He looked reluctant to leave them but Edmond assured him they would be fine.

The afternoon was cold. Just taking the few steps to the dark brick façade of the little house, Edmond had to cough as the smoke assaulted his nostrils. He knocked on the door.

'Lieutenant and Mrs Derwent – do come in!' He recognised George's mother, probably wearing her best Sunday dress. 'Joe told us you were planning to come.'

She took their coats and showed them into a cramped parlour, with a small coal fire. George stood to greet them, grinning broadly. His aunt, huddled in a brightly coloured crocheted shawl, was sitting in one of the easy chairs.

There were photos of George and Henry, his brother who had been called up, and a picture showing another young man, probably his cousin, who was also away fighting.

'Please sit down.' Their hostess indicated the settee. The neat parlour was plainly furnished, and only just large enough for them all. 'I'll get Peggy to make the tea.' She opened the door to the kitchen and spoke to someone Edmond thought must be her daughter.

'I was shocked to hear of your injuries, Sir,' George said. 'Are you making a good recovery now?'

'Don't call me Sir – we're not on parade now. Yes, I'm much better. I won't be fit enough to fight again but I'm still very aware of the struggles you're facing. I feel a fraud, wearing my uniform.' Only one of his two tunics was fit to wear.

'Of course you should wear it! You've been wounded in service!'

Edmond asked after Henry, and gained the impression he was fitting into army life as best he could.

'Are you keeping well, Mrs Derwent?' asked George's mother. 'How soon is the happy event?'

'Round about new year.'

Peggy, a young girl with her hair tied back, came in with a tray and served them all with tea and seedcake. It was plain compared with the cakes Cook baked, but they must have used up some of their precious flour and sugar, determined to welcome him and Amy.

'I believe we should retire to the kitchen to allow George and Lieutenant Derwent to talk in peace,' George's mother addressed her sister.

'I'll join you, if I may,' Amy said. 'I know the men like to talk on their own. I can help you clear the tea things.'

'Certainly not, in your condition! But there's a chair for you in the kitchen, if you'd like to come with us.'

'What was it like out there?' Edmond asked, offering George a cigarette. They both lit up. 'Passchendaele looks ghastly in the photographs I've seen in the papers.'

'I've never seen mud like it. We struggled to get across it, even where there were duckboards. While I was in the hospital I heard the trees had all gone and there are crump holes everywhere.'

Edmond had only witnessed the beginning of the campaign there. They went on talking for a while longer, discussing the fate of other men from the area who had gone to fight. Two men had been lost when their dugout had collapsed on top of them.

Edmond sensed George's relief at recounting his experiences to someone familiar with the trenches. He sighed. 'If this nightmare is ever over, you'll be extremely welcome to be our gardener again.'

'Is Joe any good?'

'He tries. He's still very young.'

'It's hard work, gardening, but now those years with your family in Larchbury seem like paradise.'

Outside it was getting darker, though according to the clock it was little past four: probably grime from the chimneys was obscuring the daylight.

'I'm afraid we need to go home,' Edmond said. 'I tire easily now. Good luck when you're back with your unit.' The poor fellow had to return the very next day. 'We need to get a cab to the station.'

'A cab? I'm afraid you won't find one round here.'

Of course he wouldn't – why hadn't he thought of that? Even Pa hadn't realised.

He and Amy said their farewells, thanking the family for the tea and cake. An expression of panic crossed Amy's face briefly when she realised they would have to walk. As George's mother opened the front door they could barely see across the road.

George seemed to grasp their predicament. 'You two shouldn't have to walk!' he said. 'You'd better start out, but I'll see if I can find anyone with transport to send after you.'

Edmond linked arms with Amy and they set off slowly in the direction of the station, about a mile away. They were both coughing now. As household fires were lit, their smoke was mingling with the fumes from the factories. He could hear the clanking of heavy industry, as well as the sound of goods trains.

They turned off into another street and then hovered, perplexed, as the road forked. The wrong choice now could be disastrous, prolonging their struggles. A large man loomed out of the darkness, almost walking into him.

'Sorry, mate.' The man's glance took in his uniform and Amy's condition. He was able to tell them which way to go.

As they laboured on, Edmond coughed some more and found himself gasping for breath.

Terror showed on Amy's face. 'I'm so sorry, dearest,' she said. 'We simply must keep going.'

They heard the sound of hooves behind them and a horse and cart appeared.

'Lieutenant and Mrs Derwent?' said a lad's voice. 'George said you need a lift to the station. Would you like to sit beside me, Mrs Derwent, while your husband goes in the back?'

'How kind of you – but I'd prefer to sit with him in the back.'

It looked like a costermonger's cart. Once they were inside, they seemed to be sitting on stray stalks from vegetables.

She tied his scarf loosely across his nose and mouth. 'How does that feel? Better or worse?'

He tried both, but either way he strained to breathe. The horse plodded ahead but their journey seemed endless.

Amy was coughing too. 'I think the air's slightly better here,' she said as they approached the station. At last they were there. Edmond climbed out clumsily. Amy tried to give some money to the carter, but he refused to take it.

They went into the station and Amy sat him down in the ticket office while she bought their tickets. Then she led him onto the platform. 'The train's due in five minutes,' she told him. 'Can you breathe any better here?'

He took a couple of deep breaths and then began to cough again. He felt dizzy and weaker than he had done at any time since he first got out of bed after being wounded.

'Let's go in the waiting room,' she said. '… No, I can hear the train coming.'

He struggled to remain upright.

'Here, Sir, lean on me.' A railway worker had noticed his plight. As the train arrived noisily, he helped Edmond into a carriage and onto a seat. Amy joined him. Her eyes were red from the smoky streets. He sat beside her, his chest heaving, scarcely aware of anything except his own desperate efforts to breathe.

–

Amy was appalled to see Edmond in this state. At Larchbury she was thankful when a strong young woman helped the two of them off the train. It was bitterly cold on the platform but the air was fresh. 'Take some deep breaths,' she told Edmond.

He tried, but he looked as though he might collapse at any minute. A porter helped him into the ticket office, and on to a chair. Amy asked to use the station telephone and called The Beeches. She was relieved that Pa was home and ready to set out in the car at once. 'Try not to alarm Ma but get her to phone for Dr Stanhope,' she said. 'The fumes from the factories have got into Edmond's lungs.' She was coughing herself as she rang off.

The staff found another chair so she could sit beside Edmond. His breathing was still laboured. The everyday travellers shot curious glances in their direction.

How could I let this happen? she asked herself. *I knew about those factories. I used to go to work in Wealdham every day and you could smell the fumes from the station if the wind was from that direction.*

Pa arrived sooner than she expected. He was visibly shocked as he helped Edmond into the car, then her. Tears filled her eyes. *Why didn't I prevent him taking this outing?* she thought. *I'm medically trained — I should have known better.*

Pa was equally desperate, blaming himself. 'I should never have let you both visit that area and try to make your way back alone,' he said as he drove off. 'I should have made Beatrice wait for me to collect her, or asked her friend's family to kindly bring her back.'

Edmond was silent with exhaustion. When they got back, Ma and Beatrice were in the hall. 'I'm taking Edmond upstairs and helping him get straight to bed,' Pa said. 'Send up some tea, could you?'

'Good Heavens!' Ma reached for her smelling salts. 'Thank goodness Dr Stanhope should be here soon. Really, after all the progress Edmond's been making… Why did you allow him to go on this foolish visit?'

As Amy followed the others upstairs, Beatrice's eyes were open wide and a tear was running down her face. 'Why didn't you look after him properly?' she demanded.

Edmond looked relieved as he settled in bed. 'I'll be better now I can lie still,' he said faintly as Amy sat on the edge, with her arm round him. Then Ma came up with Dr Stanhope.

'Dear me!' The grey-haired doctor held his stethoscope to Edmond's chest. 'I'd have advised against going to that part of Wealdham if I'd known. It's at its worst in winter when the smoke from house fires mixes with the factory emissions.'

Edmond had another coughing fit. 'Try to bring up the mucus,' the doctor told him. Edmond grew red in the face producing some sputum, which the doctor collected in a cup and examined.

'Your bronchial tubes are infected, Lieutenant. You're developing bronchitis, very unfortunate with your lung in such poor shape. I'll prescribe some medicine to ease your throat and lungs.'

'We've set back his recovery!' Amy cried, inconsolable.

'I'll have the medicine delivered this evening, and I'll call again tomorrow. Keep Mr Edmond in bed for the time being,' he told Ma. He turned his attention to Amy. 'Your eyes are red from the fumes – it wasn't wise going there in your condition. You should have an early night too.'

It was only when Edmond was drifting off to sleep, his breathing a little less strained, that she went down to the kitchen to ask for some broth and light food to be sent up. Ma and Beatrice had followed her to the kitchen and were still looking at her accusingly.

She dragged herself wearily upstairs and sat beside the bed, waiting for the medicine to arrive. If Edmond began to stir she would administer the broth and the medicine.

In some ways, she was impatient to crawl into bed next to him, but she was not sure she would sleep. It was her fault he had relapsed. Was all the recovery from the sanatorium lost now? And would there be any ill effects on her baby? She realised there had not been much movement inside her recently and was relieved when she felt a definite kick. In one disastrous afternoon she had allowed them all to be imperilled once more.

Chapter Twenty-Six

Larchbury, November 1917

The following morning Pa knocked and came into their room, followed by Ma, just as Amy was opening the window.

'What are you thinking of?' demanded Ma. 'Haven't you done him enough damage already, encouraging him to visit that awful rundown area?'

'I've just freshened up the air briefly,' Amy said crossly, closing the window again, exasperated that his mother would not trust her judgement. 'I haven't let it get cold in here.' She was interrupted by a coughing fit. Her own lungs still felt irritated from the hostile atmosphere they had both inhaled. '...Edmond needs some very fresh air to help him recover. I don't suppose he'll be fit to go outside for a few days.'

'Go outside! The very idea!'

'Ma, I've been trained in nursing!'

They were interrupted by the arrival of Dr Stanhope. He listened to Edmond's chest again with his stethoscope and pronounced a slight improvement. Edmond was sitting up in bed and his breathing was a little less forced, though he had frequent coughing fits and was worn out.

The doctor said he should continue taking the medicine and confirmed that he needed fresh air. 'When he's rested a few more days he should take a little exercise, outdoors preferably, if it's warm enough. In the middle of the day, perhaps.'

'There you are,' Edmond said. 'That's what Amy recommended—' he broke off, coughing.

'I'm sorry, Amy.' Ma managed a rare apology. 'I should take account of you being a nurse.'

'If only Edmond could go back to the sanatorium,' Amy said. She supposed places there were much in demand.

'It's less effective in winter because the patients can't stay outside for long.'

She made an effort not to cry. It seemed they had squandered the benefits of his time there.

Beatrice came into the room. 'I've written to Peter to tell him Edmond is ill again,' she said. 'He'll be shocked.'

'I'm sorry I've been so foolish,' Edmond said feebly. 'Don't any of you blame Amy.'

—

Pa had sent word to Amy's parents and two days later they came to see them, immediately Father had finished at the school for the day. She welcomed them, thankful they would not be critical. Edmond was eager to get up and join them, though he still looked frail. Ma and Beatrice were installed in the drawing room with a visitor so Edmond proposed they went to the conservatory, which had warmed up during the faint sunshine earlier in the day.

They sat in the wicker chairs, Amy's parents admiring the potted palms, less well tended than before the war when George looked after them.

'Edmond's making some progress now,' Amy said. He was exhausted after the slightest activity but showed signs of improvement from his wretched state when he had returned from Wealdham. 'He's still weak from being wounded and we simply mustn't have any more setbacks.'

Janet came in with a plate of sliced cake and poured them cups of tea.

'And the baby?' Mother asked, touching Amy's arm anxiously.

'Reassuringly active!' she replied. 'Dr Stanhope couldn't find anything amiss.'

'Your uncle Arthur was concerned,' Father said. 'I'm to tell you that if ever you need taking out somewhere you're to telephone him and he'll take you if he's not too busy.'

Edmond began to cough. Afterwards, he had to take several deep breaths.

'How kind of Uncle,' Amy said, when he was more at ease. Her uncle's pony and trap might provide useful transport. 'Perhaps later on, when Edmond's well enough for me to feel happy leaving him for a couple of hours, I might go into Larchbury to buy a few things I'll need when the baby comes.'

'Yes, you must make sure you have everything ready,' her mother said. There were less than two months to wait now.

'I'd love you to come with me and help me choose,' Amy said, to her obvious delight.

After her parents had left, Amy and Edmond joined the family for dinner. It was the first time he had taken a meal with them since his relapse. He did his best, but had less appetite than normal. The rest of the family seemed in poor spirits, as though something was wrong, but no one said anything. *They don't want to risk upsetting Edmond*, she thought. *Has there been another casualty among the families we know well?*

'Aren't you enjoying your food?' Ma asked Edmond. 'We could tell Cook to serve you normal meals if you'd prefer that to the invalid diet.'

Amy had devised a suitable menu for him and was dismayed that once again Ma was questioning her wisdom. *But she has reason to do so,* she told herself miserably. *I let him get into danger and I don't suppose she will ever completely trust me again.*

'Not at all, Ma, this kind of food is all I can manage at the moment,' Edmond said. 'I couldn't tackle three normal-sized courses.'

The meal continued uneasily. Amy could hear the ticking of the clock.

'Has Peter written lately?' Edmond asked.

The others exchanged glances nervously. 'We haven't heard so far this week.' So that was what was bothering them.

'I'm sure his letter is just held up,' Pa said rapidly.

Ma and Beatrice looked concerned. 'He normally writes very regularly,' Beatrice said wretchedly.

'It doesn't mean anything,' Edmond told them, sounding confident. 'Sometimes they stop the mail if the unit is to be moved nearer the action. It's the procedure to avoid making the enemy aware of troop movements.'

'But Peter's at Headquarters!' Ma said.

'He visits fighting units as part of his work,' Edmond said.

This was little comfort for Ma. She mentioned other families who had received letters normally that week.

'Mail goes missing sometimes in wartime,' Edmond said. 'But if a man is killed or missing in action they're very careful to inform the next of kin by telegram. I'm sure there's no need to worry.'

–

By the following week, it was a little warmer in the middle of the day and Edmond felt fit enough to go out into the grounds for a walk. Amy made sure they were both well wrapped up as

314

she accompanied him through the gardens and on to the lawn, where golden leaves were drifting into heaps. 'You'll soon be walking more quickly than I can,' she told him, for apart from her bad ankle, her increasing weight was impeding her.

'I'm still shocked at the conditions in Wealdham,' Edmond said, sufficiently recovered to be aware of matters beyond The Beeches. 'I had no idea till recently that Joe has to cycle to work all that way, or that his family are living in that awful area by the factories.'

'I used to work in Wealdham and I never considered what it might be like to live in the industrial area.' Now she realised that people she knew, hardworking, decent folk, were obliged to live in treeless, unhealthy surroundings. She could not see any way of avoiding the injustice, but it disturbed her almost as much as the issue of votes for women.

'Their house is very small,' Edmond said, enumerating all the family who lived there. 'The uncle goes to work in the factory and there are younger children at school.'

'Their kitchen was very basic when I went in there with them,' Amy said. Apart from the shortage of pans and utensils, she remembered the steamy windows and overpowering smell of cabbage. Very probably they were unwilling to open the window because of the fumes outside.

Edmond was slowing up now and she insisted they started to go back to the house.

'I phoned the War Office this morning,' Pa said at lunchtime.

The others fell quiet. It was now over a week since they had heard from Peter, and normally he would have written twice in that time.

'They couldn't tell me anything. They said he must be away on manoeuvres or training.'

'Why can't he write to us even if they've sent him away from Headquarters?' asked Beatrice.

'Sometimes they're unwilling for men to reveal their movements,' Edmond said.

'They confirmed that there's no news of anything wrong with him,' Pa said, to their relief.

'It's still very remiss of them not to get his letters through,' Ma said.

—

Towards the end of November there was a pleasant sunny day. 'Would you and Amy like to spend some time up the hill by the forestry plantation?' Edmond's father asked them. 'You could go up there on one of the wagons.'

Soon Amy was seated next to the carter, being hauled along by the pair of heavy bay horses, while Edmond sat in the back of the wagon, which was generally used to transport timber. The journey up the rough track was less than comfortable, but Amy was pleased with the outing. She had only gone up there once before, when Edmond had led her along the path outside their land, before they were married.

'We used to come up here on a wagon sometimes when we were children,' Edmond told her, when they had reached the edge of the forest and the carter had helped them down. The wagon continued along a forest track to help collect timber.

Nearby there was a bench to sit on, facing south into the thin sunshine. There was birdsong and the smell of pine from the forest. In the distance they could see The Beeches, with Larchbury beyond. It was easy to pick out the brook and the church.

'It's market day!' Amy said, pointing out a small crowd around the enclosed area where it was held. Peering into the misty distance, they could make out cattle milling around, and a man with a dog guiding a flock of sheep away from the area. If they listened carefully they could hear them bleating.

'It's all so peaceful after Flanders,' Edmond said.

She shared his occasional feeling of guilt that they had escaped the horrors of the Front. Sometimes letters arrived from their friends out there.

'Frank tells me they're still fighting round Passchendaele,' Edmond told her. 'He says the same as George about the rain turning the battlefields into a sea of mud.'

Amy sighed. Lavinia and James had sent letters implying that streams of casualties were still needing help. She suspected that they were toning down the full grimness of the offensive.

'Do you realise it's our second wedding anniversary?' he asked, kissing her.

'So it is! But we've spent so little time together.'

'I'm determined not to live my life as an invalid,' Edmond said. 'I want to be fit enough to go back to university next September. Afterwards I'll find a suitable occupation.'

How perfect that would be, she thought: *if only he became well enough.* He was still going to bed early each evening, exhausted from his recent relapse. He was continuing to have coughing fits and became breathless easily. How frail he still was! Was it presumptuous to plan for the future?

'I can come with you to Cambridge, and the baby of course,' she told him. 'We can find a little house and I can look after you. Won't that be wonderful?'

'Our nursery must be nearly ready by now,' he said. The little room at The Beeches where he and his brother and sister had spent some of their early years had been used more recently as a spare bedroom, but now it had been prepared as a nursery once more, and the old cot taken out of the attic and cleaned.

'My mother's making a lovely patchwork quilt for the cot,' Amy told him. She would be relieved when they had a house of their own, instead of encroaching on more of The Beeches.

They had agreed that if the child was a boy they would call him Albert after her brother. They were finding it harder to decide on a girl's name.

'How about Elizabeth?' she suggested.

'I like that. Any special reason why you thought of it?'

'I was thinking the name is often shortened to Beth, and I thought of Béthune, where we spent that weekend.' She considered. 'Do you think that's a stupid idea? It might remind us of the view of the Front, and the bombardments.'

'I don't think so. The place itself was charming and peaceful.'

They relaxed in the sunshine until they saw the wagon returning to take them back.

'I know I'm fortunate,' Amy said. 'Florence is still devastated at losing Bertie. So many fine young men have been lost that there's a shortage of potential husbands for my friends like her and Lavinia. They might have to go through life without a husband or children.'

'And Beatrice too,' he said as they set off back.

—

The family were sinking into gloom as there was still no word from Peter. They had not confided their worries to anyone outside the immediate family. By the end of November they would normally have been planning the Christmas dance, but now they were paralysed, waiting desperately for reassurance that all was well.

'Do you think he's really all right?' Amy asked Edmond one day when they were taking a short walk in the grounds in the middle of the day. 'I know he sometimes has to travel as part of his work,' she said, remembering his arrival at her hospital to investigate her complaint about Wilfrid Fairlawn, 'but I can't think why he's failed to write or send word somehow.' He must know the effect it was having on the family.

'I can't believe anything is seriously wrong,' Edmond said. 'I feel I'd somehow sense if he was badly injured or killed.'

I didn't know when Bertie was killed, she thought. She had not suspected anything was wrong until the telegram had arrived. She found it hard to remain confident like Edmond. Peter was probably far enough from the Front to escape the dangers from enemy action. Disease was common, but that too spread most easily in the squalid trenches. There were also accidents as men travelled on roads that were narrow and poorly maintained.

As they returned towards the house, she forced herself to prepare for the possibility of dreadful news. Peter had been kind to her and would be a great loss to her personally, but the others would be devastated. Less aware than she and Edmond that he might return to India, his parents would mourn the loss of the heir. They would be left with Edmond, who was valiant and determined to make a success of his life in spite of his injury. She, as the new heir's wife, would still be the disappointing creature with the undistinguished background and criminal record, besides her recent failure to take good care of him. What a burden she was proving to be.

'Try not to worry, darling,' Edmond was telling her now. 'The chief thing that matters is that we're together and soon we'll be parents. It'll be all right, you'll see.'

319

Chapter Twenty-Seven

Larchbury, December 1917

One day at the beginning of December, Uncle Arthur called on Amy with his pony and cart and took her into Larchbury. She and her mother were able to shop for items she would need for the nursery, and the baby when he or she arrived.

'It's been a lovely morning,' she told Mother as she said goodbye. 'I'm pleased with everything we chose for the little one, though best of all I love what people have made – the beautiful quilt you sewed, and the lovely baby clothes that Florence has knitted, and Emily at the hospital.'

As her uncle conveyed her back to The Beeches, she was thrilled at the prospect of motherhood in less than a month.

As Chambers let them in, Beatrice rushed into the hall to greet her, her eyes sparkling. 'We've heard from Peter!' she cried. 'He's all right!' She flung her arms round Amy.

'How wonderful! I'm so pleased.'

Edmond joined them. 'We're all so relieved,' he said, kissing Amy.

She explained the situation to Uncle Arthur, who had been unaware of their worries.

'You hadn't been getting his letters?' he said. 'I'm extremely pleased to hear your good news.'

'Please join us for a drink,' Edmond urged.

'Thank you, but I need to go and visit a parishioner.' He kissed Amy and went on his way.

They joined the family in the drawing room. 'Did Peter say why he didn't write?' Amy asked.

'He was sent on manoeuvres and they didn't want his movements known, like Edmond said,' Pa told them.

'It's totally unreasonable that we should be left worrying like that,' Ma said.

'He's hoping to get Christmas leave,' Beatrice said, looking joyful as Chambers poured them drinks.

She actually embraced me, Amy thought. *It must be the first time she's ever done that. How very much she cares for her brothers.*

–

The atmosphere was much lighter now, and the annual dance was being planned.

Edmond was delighted when Charles Shenwood came home on leave just before Christmas and visited them. He seemed eager to satisfy himself that Edmond's condition was improving. He was also pleased to see Beatrice again, for she had continued to write to him.

After dinner Charles sat with Edmond and his father, discussing the progress of the war. Normally they would have smoked, but Edmond had been advised not to touch tobacco, and the others refrained from doing so while they were with him.

'Is it still dreadful round Passchendaele?' Edmond asked.

'There's not much action at the moment. There's mud as far as you can see. The land's so churned up that a soldier who falls over, laden with a heavy pack, is liable to drown.' Charles took another mouthful of port. 'In a week I'll be back there with the mud and the rats.'

Pa stared and shook his head at his images of the fighting, and Edmond looked stricken at Charles' account of conditions there. He had fought there earlier in the campaign, but had not envisaged how much worse the situation might become for the troops fighting there. 'I've got my old tunic at the bottom of my kitbag,' he told the others. 'It's badly damaged where I was hit by the debris from that shell. The holes are dark red round the edges with caked blood. I wouldn't care to show it to Amy or Ma.'

'What are you keeping it for?' asked Pa.

'Perhaps one day I'll show it to a son or grandson. The war will be over eventually, won't it? If the next generations know what we had to face they might have the sense not to start anything like it ever again.'

'At least the Americans have joined us,' Charles said. 'Maybe we really will have victory before long. And we've got tanks now. They can keep moving through the mud.'

Edmond took another swig from his glass of port and topped up Charles' glass. They fell silent. The others were probably wondering, like him, how much longer the battles would go on.

–

The following day as they sat in the drawing room, Beatrice was trying to persuade Charles to stay longer but he insisted he had to return home for Christmas.

'Can you come back for our ball, two days later?' she pleaded.

'I might, if I'm invited,' he smiled.

'You'll be extremely welcome,' Mrs Derwent told him, 'only, you know, it will be a quiet event: so many young men

322

are away. But we've just heard that Peter's leave is confirmed: he should arrive on Christmas Eve.'

'I'll be delighted to come.'

Charles set off for home that afternoon.

'It's hardly worth holding the ball this year,' Mrs Derwent complained as they sat eating their evening meal. 'It'll be very poorly attended.'

'Nonsense, Ma!' Beatrice said. 'There's so little going on round here now, people will love to come for a few hours of amusement.'

'At least Edmond is back with us and Peter will be too,' his father said, sounding relieved that the family would be together, unlike many others.

'I daresay you'll give the party a miss, as you're so near your time,' Amy's mother-in-law said to her.

She was uncertain. Traditionally, heavily pregnant women withdrew from public gatherings.

'If Amy doesn't come, I won't!' Edmond asserted. 'I want to dance with my wife.'

'I'll wear my best shawl,' Amy promised. It would make her condition less obvious. 'I'd like to accompany Edmond for the beginning of the evening but then I'll need my usual early night.'

-

Peter arrived home on Christmas Eve morning, to be greeted rapturously by the family, though Ma was reproachful about all the worry he had caused. He told them he had been away on manoeuvres. He was smart in his uniform and apparently at ease.

'I don't think he's telling us everything,' Edmond told Amy when they were alone. Peter was liable to find an excuse for leaving the room if any of them began questioning him.

After lunch, the brothers went for a short walk. Peter was concerned that Edmond still tired very quickly. 'Let's sit on the veranda,' he said. The sun had moved round and was shedding its faint rays there.

Edmond sank down into a wicker chair. 'So, what have you really been doing?' he asked his brother.

'Look, if I tell you, you must keep it entirely secret. Don't even tell Pa, or Amy or Charles – no one at all must know.'

He promised.

'I have to travel around for my work. If I'm investigating a disciplinary matter I may need to track down witnesses and take statements. It makes a good cover for… other operations.'

'What kind of operations?'

'Sometimes loyal Belgians on the other side of the Front Line want to give us helpful information, about troop movements, for example. I speak good French and I've been learning Flemish, too.'

'I've heard they send carrier pigeons across with messages,' Edmond said.

'The Germans watch out for them now. We sometimes need someone to sneak across the Front Line. It's not easy, as you can imagine. Even where a river or canal crosses the line, the area is heavily guarded.' He looked around. Young Joe was sweeping up leaves on the opposite side of the garden but no one was in earshot. 'Now our men have built a tunnel underneath No Man's Land – I'm not telling you where.'

'Are you saying you actually crossed the line into occupied Belgium?'

'Yes. Once there, I had to move secretly at night. I spoke to several brave men and women. There's a chap near Liège who watches train traffic for us, to track troop movements.'

Edmond stared at his brother. 'Espionage – that's dreadfully dangerous!'

'I've always felt guilty for not taking a more significant part in the war – I welcomed the chance. But once I was there, I was terrified and longing to complete my mission. Then, when I was due to cross back, they had subsidence in the tunnel – hardly surprising, considering the weather. I had to wait a few days more, till they'd patched it up.'

'Thank God you finally made it back safely.' His brother's movements amounted to one of the most dangerous missions he had ever heard about.

'Let's go back indoors before someone comes looking for us,' said Peter. They joined the others in the drawing room and tried to chat normally.

Later that night, when Edmond was alone with Amy, she was curious.

'Did Peter tell you anything more about why he didn't write?' she asked.

'It was just as he said, they were on manoeuvres which went on longer than expected.' He hated not telling her everything, but he had given his word to Peter.

–

On the day of the ball, Charles arrived for luncheon and Beatrice was unusually animated. Vicky had also come, and after lunch she sat with Edmond and Amy. At first she had been shocked at his coughing and occasional breathlessness, but she relaxed once Amy had assured her he was showing good signs of recovery.

Later Amy caught sight of Beatrice and Charles, talking together in the conservatory.

Most of the people who attended in the evening were middle-aged, or single women. Amy's parents had come, though she suspected they would not stay till the end. Charles was handsome in evening dress and Beatrice gorgeous in a dress of peacock blue.

Amy was pleased that Florence came this year. She was delighted to find that Edmond's breathing had improved since his setback at Wealdham. Her light brown hair was rather plainly arranged at the nape of her neck, but she had a new gown in cream-coloured satin.

'Mother made it for me,' she told Amy. 'I told her to keep the style plain.'

Would she ever recover her spirits and resemble the lively young woman she had been before Bertie's death, Amy wondered.

The pianist began playing jaunty airs and to begin with there was a kind of forced jollity. As Chambers took drinks round, the guests began to relax, determined to forget the situation across the Channel for a few hours.

Amy circulated with Edmond as he greeted the guests. The local families were glad to see him well enough after his ordeal to attend the gathering.

'You're out of it all now,' Mr Leadbetter, the headmaster, congratulated him.

'I can't rejoice about that, knowing my comrades are still out there,' he replied. Amy knew that his pleasure at seeing Charles was overshadowed by the awareness that his friend was merely experiencing a brief respite before returning to the Front.

Soon they were enjoying the festive meal. Amy's mother complimented Mrs Derwent on the spread she had produced, in spite of the war.

'I've been keeping an eye on the kitchen garden,' Ma said. 'Cook used surplus autumn vegetables to prepare the chutney, and lately Joe's managed to produce some beetroot.'

Ma's becoming more resourceful, Amy thought.

'I shall retire soon after the dancing begins,' she told her in-laws. Already, she felt tired.

'I shall leave when you do,' Edmond said. 'I've been advised to get plenty of rest.'

'Oh, please, don't leave so soon!' Beatrice begged. 'Pa, Edmond wants to leave early! He won't hear our announcement! Please stay, Edmond.'

From the way Charles was hovering beside Beatrice, Amy had a notion what might be coming.

'I'll announce it earlier than we planned,' Mr Derwent told them.

Before long, guests began to go into the ballroom. When they were all there, Mr Derwent asked the pianist to play a few dramatic chords as he had an announcement to make.

The host and hostess stood with Beatrice and Charles. 'I'm delighted to announce that Mr Charles Shenwood and my daughter have just become engaged,' he told everyone, to cheers and clapping. Champagne was brought round for a toast to the happy couple.

Charles held Beatrice in his arms and kissed her. He brought a box from his pocket and produced a beautiful ring with a cluster of diamonds, and she blushed with delight as she placed it on her finger.

'I'm sorry it's a bit loose, darling,' he told her. 'It was my grandmother's, and she didn't have such dainty fingers.'

'It's so lovely – we can get it fitted better, can't we?' she said.

Everyone was watching. 'What an attractive couple they make,' said Florence.

'It's wonderful to hear some good news,' Amy's father said.

Edmond took Amy by the hand and thrust his way through the guests. 'Congratulations!' he told Charles, seizing him by the arm. 'I'm overjoyed to welcome you into the family.'

'I'm a lucky man, finding such a beautiful young woman for my bride,' he said. Vicky joined them, followed by Peter, to add their congratulations.

'We'll get married next time Charles has leave,' Beatrice said, her eyes shining.

'Have you met Charles' family yet?' Amy asked her.

'I was introduced to them at a party once,' she replied. 'They're charming people.'

'I only asked Beatrice this afternoon,' Charles told them, 'but I'd mentioned my intentions to my family, and come prepared with the ring.'

'I'll never get used to these sudden wartime engagements!' Ma said, though she was clearly delighted with the news.

The pianist started playing a waltz and Edmond's parents began to dance. The newly engaged couple soon joined them. *How well they both dance,* Amy thought, *moving almost as one, and Beatrice looking especially refined. She's chosen an excellent husband. Beatrice and I have never had much in common, but with her ladylike accomplishments she will make an admirable wife for a well-off man.*

'Good old Bea, I needn't have worried about her remaining single,' Edmond said. He took Amy into his arms. 'Come on, we can at least have one dance together.' He held her firmly.

'Are you sure you can manage a dance?' Amy's mother looked at her, concerned.

'Lean on me if you're not entirely steady on your feet,' Edmond said. She was determined to do no such thing, mindful of his impaired fitness. Her increased size made it harder for him to hold her close and her injured leg hampered her progress, but they travelled round the room as best they could. At first she was anxious she might look ungainly, but soon the thrill of joining in the dance with him drove out other thoughts. When the music ended, they continued holding each other close, content with their achievement.

'I really should go to bed now,' she told him. She said goodbye to her parents and Florence, and went upstairs with Edmond. As they reached their bedroom they could still hear the music from below, but soon they were drifting off to sleep in each other's arms.

–

Next morning on her way down to breakfast, Amy passed Charles, in his uniform. He was gathering together his luggage, for he had to go to London that morning on the first stage of his journey back to Flanders. Peter would be leaving the following day.

Beatrice was at the table finishing a cup of tea. 'You managed to have one dance,' she remarked to Amy. 'You can't waltz very well now, can you?'

Amy knew she would never be as graceful as Beatrice, and hoped she had not made an exhibition of herself in her present situation. She suspected her sister-in-law would have been less scornful if one of the others had been there. 'No,' she said, 'I can't dance well at the moment, because I'm soon to have a child.' *If I sounded reproachful I don't care,* she thought: *I've had quite enough criticism from her.*

'Suppose the baby had chosen last night to arrive!' Beatrice said, fixing her green eyes on Amy. She looked genuinely concerned. Was she anxious Amy should not do anything else embarrassing in public, or did she actually care for her, after all?

'I'd have had time to withdraw to my room,' Amy told her. Perhaps, after all, she had been taking a chance, with her baby around full term now, but the prospect of dancing with Edmond had been irresistible.

He joined them, and by the time he had finished his meal, Charles was ready to set off for the station. Amy wished him well, trying not to think of the perils he might face. Edmond and Beatrice went in the car to see Charles on to the train.

When they returned, Beatrice was subdued and Edmond looked strained. However Beatrice was beginning to recover by lunchtime and soon after was huddled with her mother planning a stylish wedding.

—

As the family ate dinner on the last evening of the year, Chambers poured them some of the best wine from the cellar, though Amy would only take a few sips. It was understood that she and Edmond would not stay up till midnight.

Mr Derwent rose to his feet. 'Let's drink to 1918!' he proposed.

'I hope it's an improvement on this year,' his wife said.

'But it's bound to be! I'm marrying Charles!' Beatrice said.

'Of course you are, darling,' her father said, 'and Edmond and Amy will have their baby.'

'May Edmond grow fitter!' Mrs Derwent said, as they toasted the future.

'I'm making progress every day,' he insisted.

Amy had to agree. *Back in August things were desperate,* she thought. *Edmond was mortally ill, I was in danger of being assaulted and even the baby was threatened when I fell over in the street. Then we had that dreadful setback in the autumn. But we've come a long way since then.*

'We're together, and that's what matters,' she said. All she needed now was for their baby to arrive safely.

She still worried what lay ahead for Florence and Lavinia, but so long as she was with Edmond, she was content for herself.

As they completed their meal, Amy found her back was aching. She rose to leave the table and felt the kind of sharp pain she had been led to expect. 'I think the baby might be coming,' she told them.

'Come up to our room at once!' said Edmond, taking her arm.

When the burst of pain subsided, Amy was overcome with excitement. She sat down on their bed and he sat beside her, his arm around her. Subdued light came from the lamp and the fire.

'Now we're about to be parents, we should take more care, avoid doing anything impulsive,' she said.

Edmond grinned. 'Must we? Let's stay as we are!' he told her.

He telephoned Mrs Phelps, the local midwife, and sent for Doctor Stanhope too, as a precaution.

'He's dealing with an emergency in Wealdham,' he told Amy. 'I managed to speak to him on the hospital phone and he promised to come as soon as he could.'

Soon Mrs Phelps arrived, hurrying breathlessly into the room. 'How are you doing, Mrs Derwent?'

She examined Amy briefly. 'You've a while to go yet,' she told them. 'I'll come back later.' She had just delivered a baby in Larchbury, it turned out, and was concerned about the mother, who had lost a lot of blood. 'I must see how she's progressing, but I'll come back in an hour or so,' she said. She reminded them of the preparations they needed to make.

'You're young, healthy and full term,' she told Amy. 'It should be an easy birth.' She went off to return to Larchbury on her bicycle.

When the pains were closer together, Amy took to her bed. 'You'd better wait outside now,' she told Edmond. 'Mrs Phelps will be back soon.'

Suddenly she felt uneasy and wished she had asked her mother to come.

'Must I go?' Edmond said.

'Yes,' she said unwillingly. She knew he would have stayed with her, given any encouragement.

'I'll be waiting next door, in the nursery.'

Now she was alone. The glow from the fire flickered on the ceiling of their room. Between contractions, she concentrated on the prospect of giving Edmond his child. The minutes passed as she waited for Mrs Phelps to return. The clock chimed half past nine.

Ma looked into the room and asked if she was all right. Amy told her all was well, then asked her for a glass of water. Once Ma had supplied that, she hovered awkwardly. 'Cook has offered to sit with you until the midwife comes,' she told Amy. 'Would you like that?'

'Yes, please.'

Ma went out and Amy was grateful to see Cook arriving, with her calm smile.

The contractions were still coming, without getting much closer together, and Cook held her hand. Amy was perspiring as she began to tire.

Gently, Cook mopped Amy's brow. 'The baby might take a while longer,' she said.

There's no need to panic, she told herself. *I'm not in any danger. After my accident my leg was agony for days, so I'm not afraid of pain.*

The clock struck ten, then eleven.

'Are you sure everything is progressing properly?' she asked Cook. She had learnt several important medical skills as a VAD nurse, but of course there had been no call for midwifery.

'Your labour is a little slower than some but nothing to worry about. Just lie back and relax.'

Edmond knocked at the door and burst in without waiting for her to answer. 'Mrs Phelps telephoned: she thinks she'll be nearly another hour,' he said.

She noticed concern in his expression. *I must look a sight,* she thought. *Probably my hair is sticking together in clumps.* 'It's all right,' she told him. 'Childbirth is a perfectly normal process. It's taking a while, that's all.' She could not bear to cause him worry.

He fetched her another glass of water and took his turn at holding her hand while another contraction came. He was beginning to look pale and strained as he sensed her discomfort. However hard she tried she could seldom help crying out.

'You'd better leave, Mr Edmond,' Cook told him. 'Wait outside.'

He kissed Amy's damp face and left reluctantly.

She lay there tensely. *Edmond has been through so much,* she thought. *I've had problems to deal with as well, and I simply can't let this defeat me. All I want is to give him a healthy baby.*

333

She was feeling increasingly exhausted. She could not hear any sound at all from outside and wondered if Edmond was still there or in the next room. *When will Mrs Phelps reach me, or Dr Stanhope?* she thought.

Suddenly there was the sound of footsteps on the stairs – more than one person, she thought. The door opened and in rushed Edmond, followed by her mother.

'Oh, thank you for coming!' Amy exclaimed as Mother put her arms round her.

'Edmond came over with his father to fetch me in his car,' Mother told her. 'Now, run along, Edmond, and wait outside. I don't want to risk you fainting if things begin to happen.'

'I'm sure I've seen worse at the Front Line,' Edmond told her, but he did as she asked.

Amy felt a wave of relief. Mother was a reassuring presence: there was no one she would rather have with her at this time. They allowed Cook to take a break and Mother sat by the bed, holding her hand as the contractions came.

Surely they're getting a little more frequent now, she thought.

Soon Mother told her that the birth would not be much longer.

There were fresh footsteps and Mrs Phelps arrived. 'Sorry I was so long,' she said, 'but the other young mother is making better progress now.' She examined Amy. 'I can see baby's head now,' she said. 'You're doing fine.'

By the time Dr Stanhope arrived, a quarter of an hour later, he could see that the birth was imminent.

Soon after one in the morning, her daughter was born. When the midwife called Edmond into the room he embraced Amy, scarcely able to take his eyes off them both.

'Are you all right, darling? I was getting so worried,' he said.

'I'm very tired, but every moment was worth it for this.'

Edmond held his soft, sleepy child for the first time. 'Little Beth,' he said, 'our new year baby.' He looked truly serene.

Amy gazed at the tiny pink bundle, wrapped in a white shawl. Her blue eyes opened briefly and then closed again.

His parents arrived and joined the congratulations. Mrs Derwent embraced her as well as Edmond.

Beatrice arrived, wearing an Indian shawl over her night-dress. 'Oh! What a sweet baby,' she approved. 'She looks like you, Edmond, but her eyes are more like Amy's.' Her smile seemed genuine as she kissed both of them, and little Beth. 'You look tired, Amy. Can I fetch you a drink or anything?'

'Thank you for offering, Beatrice, but I can't think of anything. I believe I have everything I want here!'

'Let me drive you home,' Pa said to Amy's mother. 'It's getting late.'

It was Mother's turn to embrace them all.

At last, Edmond and Amy were left alone with their precious new-born.

'Together we can make our future,' Amy assured Edmond.

He reached out to enclose her and Beth in his embrace. 'We'll manage, as a proper family,' he said. 'I promise you, one day soon we'll have a home of our own.'

A Letter From Rosemary

It's wonderful to see *Until We Meet Again* published. I'm thrilled to have the backing of Hera Books, and that you have chosen my historical romance to read.

Over the last few years we have seen the centenary of World War I and have been reminded of the sacrifices the soldiers made and the horrors they faced. Their families at home also faced anxiety, hardship and sometimes bereavement.

It was a challenge to set a story in this era without making it unbearably grim, but I was inspired by accounts of soldiers enjoying songs and jokes even in the trenches. My hero and heroine needed to be special people. Edmond and Amy are resourceful and brave, and deeply in love; together they are determined to overcome the trials they face.

I hope you enjoyed their story. If you did, I would love to hear your impressions in a review. I welcome readers' feedback, and it helps others to discover my book.

Amy and Edmond will be back before long in the second book in the series, so you can discover what happened next!

If you would like to talk to me directly about *Until We Meet Again*, you can find me on my social media pages:

Twitter: @RoseGoodacre
Facebook: Rosemary Goodacre Author
Linked In: Rosemary Goodacre

Thank you again for choosing my book and for your support. It is lovely to receive your comments, and encourages me to write further stories.

Best wishes
Rosemary

Acknowledgments

I am very grateful to Keshini Naidoo and Lindsey Mooney at Hera Books, for giving me this wonderful opportunity and guiding me through the process of being published.

I have learnt a good deal about the Great War through the moving memoir of Vera Brittain, in *Testament of Youth*. (Virago Press, ISBN 0-86068-035-5.)

I have also referred to *A Nurse at the Front*, based on the First World War diaries of Sister Edith Appleton, edited by Ruth Cowen. (Simon & Schuster, ISBN 978-1-84983-366-0.)

I have learnt how Belgian refugees were welcomed and supported through the Royal Tunbridge Wells Refugee Community.

I have a great respect for the Suffragettes, active in the period before World War I, and the Suffragists, who were less militant. Many of them did valuable war work and helped women to be recognised as deserving the same rights as their menfolk.

I must also mention the Romantic Novelists' Association, a valuable source of helpful advice and encouragement for novice writers.

Sincere thanks to all who helped me in my path to becoming a published writer.